A
Summer
at Sea

Also by Katie Fforde

Living Dangerously
The Rose Revived
Wild Designs
Stately Pursuits
Life Skills
Thyme Out
Artistic Licence
Highland Fling
Paradise Fields
Restoring Grace
Flora's Lot
Practically Perfect
Going Dutch
Wedding Season
Love Letters
A Perfect Proposal
Summer of Love
Recipe for Love
A French Affair
The Perfect Match
A Vintage Wedding

A Summer at Sea

CENTURY

1 3 5 7 9 10 8 6 4 2

Century
20 Vauxhall Bridge Road
London SW1V 2SA

Century is part of the Penguin Random House
group of companies whose addresses can be found at
global.penguinrandomhouse.com.

Penguin
Random House
UK

First published in Great Britain by Century in 2016

www.randomhouse.co.uk

A CIP catalogue record for this book
is available from the British Library.

ISBN 9781780890869

Typeset in Palatino LT Std by Palimpsest Book Production Limited,
Falkirk, Stirlingshire

Printed and bound in Australia by Griffin Press

www.randomhouse.com.au
www.randomhouse.co.nz

Penguin Random House is committed to a sustainable future
for our business, our readers and our planet. This book is made
from Forest Stewardship Council® certified paper.

To Vic 32, Clyde Puffer, built 1942,
and Mandy the Midwife,
I couldn't have written this book,
without either of you.

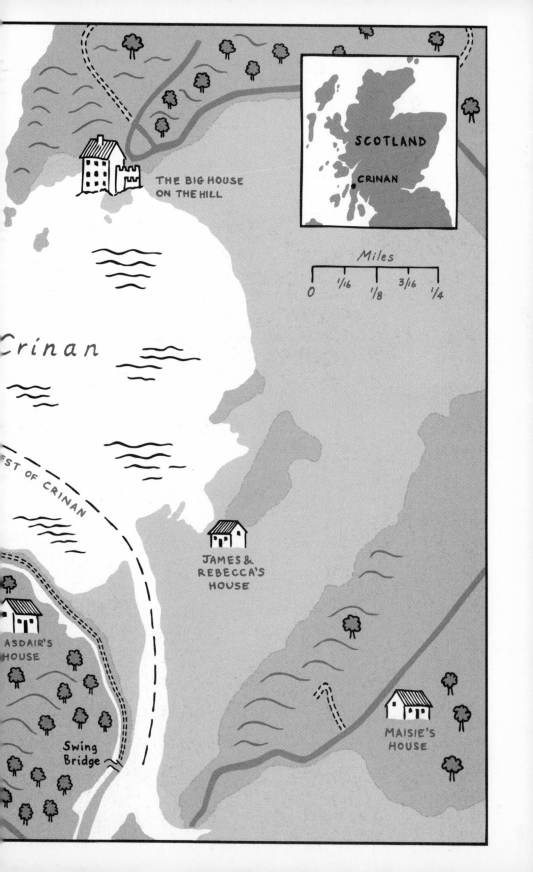

Acknowledgements

Massive thanks to Nick and Rachel Walker, custodians of the puffer, and friends of ours for over forty years. Equally massive thanks to Mandy Robotham who was generous with her time. She really helped me get under the skin of a midwife and I loved it. Extra thanks for assisting my grand-daughter into the world. I will have made mistakes in spite of your best efforts so I do apologise.

Also thanks to Alice and Robert Walker, who also assisted in various ways, Alice for getting married in the wonderful Crinan Hotel and Robert for valuable artwork. Thanks to the Crinan Hotel for picking the most beautiful spot on earth to be and inspiring me to set my book there.

Thank you, too, to the inspiring Jane Griffiths, who told me about Fair Isle Knitting (and who does it amazingly) but who also had such a lovely house, I had to borrow it for my book.

I'm always very grateful to my wonderful agent Bill Hamilton but I am extra grateful this time because he suggested I put the puffer (which he had seen in full steam while he was on his way to Jura) into this book. I decided to make the puffer the star.

Also to the wonderful team at Random House. To my editors Selina Walker, Georgina Hawtrey-Woore and Francesca Pathak – you are amazing, inspiring and reassuring, depending on what I need you to be. To the wonderful sales team, Aslan Byrne, Chris Turner, Ruth Tinham and Emily Bromfield. To Jen Doyle, Vincent Kelleher and Sarah Ridley in Marketing for forcing people to buy my book. And as always thank you to the wonderful Charlotte Bush and Rose Tremlett, never forgetting Richenda Todd, who stands in for missing bits of my brain so often.

Prologue

Emily and Susanna, midwife and mother-to-be, were quiet and settled in the candlelit room. Everything was going to plan; so far it was a textbook birth. Emily was confident that nothing would go wrong and, as always, she felt a frisson of excitement. She would never get bored with assisting new life into the world.

Although her posture was relaxed as she waited for the labour to progress, every sense was alert. She heard a key being turned in the front door and arrived in the hallway at the same time as a man. She realised it must be Susanna's husband, Ed, an army officer, who had been training overseas with his regiment. Emily was startled: neither she nor Susanna had been expecting him back so soon.

'You must be Ed,' she said. 'How wonderful that you managed to get here in time. Susanna said you wouldn't be able to make it.' He looked tired – he must have been travelling for hours. He was also visibly upset. He had probably spent his entire journey home fretting over the knowledge that his wife had chosen to have a very different sort of birth from the one he thought she should have.

'Where's Susanna?' he said curtly. 'I must see her!'

Emily knew she had to keep him away from his wife while he was so obviously tense as this could easily transmit itself to Susanna. She stood in front of the door of the room in which Susanna was in labour. It wasn't usual for her to bar the door from a soon-to-be new father but this was different. She needed him to calm down first. His irate presence could upset everything.

'Of course,' said Emily, smiling, and in her most soothing tones, frantically thinking of a way to keep him away from Susannah. Then she hit on it. 'But I must ask you to wash your hands first. And maybe have a cup of tea? After your journey? You must be shattered.' He would never know that as a partner, he wouldn't be asked to do anything intimate and hand-washing could be soothing.

He was not to be placated. 'Look, Susanna knew I wanted her to have our baby in hospital, so for you and her to conspire behind my back . . . I can only imagine what my father would say!'

Emily knew about her client's father-in-law. A consultant obstetrician, he was retired, very old-school, and violently opposed to anything remotely 'natural' in childbirth. Anything that didn't involve women lying on their backs in hospital, with every medical intervention going, was unacceptable. His daughter-in-law, Susanna, had quite other ideas, and had been almost pleased when she discovered her soldier husband was

2

unlikely to get home for the birth. Ed, on the other hand, had been fully indoctrinated with his father's views.

'Really, I promise you there's been no conspiracy. And nothing will happen for a while yet. You've got plenty of time to freshen up and have some tea.' She smiled again. 'I'll go and see how Susanna's getting on.'

But it appeared that Ed had no intention of freshening up or calming down. 'You can't stop me!' he said. 'It's my duty to protect my wife.'

Quite what he wanted to protect his wife from was unclear but he was very insistent. He was about to push Emily aside but stopped himself just in time.

'No,' she repeated. 'You can't go in until you're—' She stopped, wondering what she could say that would stop him blundering in like a male elephant. 'Just have something to eat and drink and then come in.'

She went back into the living room, hoping she hadn't sounded too much like somebody's nanny. One look at Susanna, though, and she realised things were not as they had been. She looked utterly miserable.

'It's not going to happen now, is it? He'll make me go to hospital?'

Emily opened her mouth to protest, but Ed had followed her into the room.

'Susanna!' he said. 'What the bloody hell has got into you?' He looked at the birthing pool, currently only half full, and kicked it. 'For God's sake! What's this all about? What sort of crazy idea did you get into your head this time? I thought we'd agreed on a traditional birth!'

Emily knew about this too. Susanna had told her everything at their first visit.

3

'We didn't agree, you decided. But this is what I wanted,' said Susanna bravely. 'Flora was going to be here with me but she's got a sick bug. You knew how I felt. I just wanted to have my baby here, at home, with Emily and Flora.'

'Well, without Flora that plan's out of the window,' said Ed, sounding relieved. 'We'll get you into hospital ASAP and everything will be all right.'

'But Susanna wants a home birth,' said Emily. She knew she wasn't going to win this argument – not now – but she had to fight it.

'I'm not prepared for Susanna or our baby to take any sort of risk. She needs full medical supervision, and that what she's going to get.' He turned to Susanna. 'Let's get you into the car.'

Before Emily could protest further, there was a banging at the door.

'That'll be the GP,' said Ed. 'I'll let him in.'

'The GP?' said Emily. 'Why has he come?'

'When I discovered on my way here what was going on, I got on to our GP. Just in case I didn't make it in time.'

Emily realised that Susanna, not unreasonably, had texted her husband to tell him the baby was on the way, but it had had desperate consequences. Because she knew who Susanna's GP was: Derek Gardner, new to the area, who'd already established himself as a highly conventional practitioner when it came to childbirth.

And indeed a few minutes later, Derek Gardner came in, Ed fast on his tail. He looked at Emily, eyebrows raised. 'I might have known it would be you!' His eye was caught by the knitting Emily had been engaged on before this beautifully planned birth had been interrupted. 'So! The rumours are true! How can you concentrate on a woman in labour when you knit!'

It was a rhetorical question so Emily didn't bother to answer. However, she could have easily explained how her knitting actually helped her look after her birthing mothers better. When her hands were occupied (and she only ever knitted very simple things in those circumstances) her ears were more alert and she could tell in a second if anything had changed and the mother needed to be checked. But Derek Gardner would never understand these subtleties, even if she spent hours explaining it.

'Come along, sweetie,' said Ed to his wife, rather more gently now. 'Let's get you to hospital where you can get the pain relief you need.'

As Susanna's contractions had now stopped Emily wondered why Ed thought she needed pain relief, but she realised the battle was lost.

Susanna looked up at Emily. 'I'm so, so sorry. I thought we could do this.'

Ed had taken hold of his wife's arm now and was hauling her to her feet. 'I'll find your coat.'

'She'll also need her overnight bag,' said Emily. 'Do you want me to fetch it?'

For a second her eyes met Ed's and animosity crackled between them. Then his eyes fell away. 'If you would.'

When Ed and Susanna left, the GP stayed on. It wasn't long before Emily found out why.

'You've got to stop this, you know,' Derek said. 'You know the risks of having a baby at home are higher for first-time mothers.'

'Really? I'd have thought you of all people would know that statistics show that actually home births are extremely safe.'

'What would you do if there's a problem? Whisper some spells and hope for the best?'

Emily bit down on her anger. The pleasant room where Susannah had planned to have her child may have looked as unlike a delivery suite as possible, but in Emily's boxes and bags, hidden behind the chairs and sofas, was every piece of equipment needed to ensure a safe and happy outcome.

'Have I ever lost a baby?' Emily asked him, rigid with the effort of keeping quiet after the upsetting and un-necessary interruption of what should have been a lovely birth.

'There was an investigation—'

'Yes – and if you'd read it thoroughly you would know that no one could have predicted that breech birth. The baby turned at the very last minute and was and is perfectly fine.'

Derek Gardner sighed. 'Look, Emily—'

Emily, usually the most informal of people, stiffened at the use of her Christian name. 'Ms Bailey,' she said.

Derek had the grace to look embarrassed. 'It's only a matter of time before something goes dreadfully wrong.' He paused. 'Quite frankly I'm concerned for you – and for the whole maternity unit. You've upset a very influ-ential person there. Sir Roger may be retired but he's on every board and committee. He could make your life very hard indeed.'

Emily almost smiled. 'My life is already quite hard, thank you.'

She wasn't going to tell this man that she'd been with a mother until that morning, having supported her for over twelve hours. She'd barely had time to shower and stuff a sandwich in her mouth before Susanna had called. If Susanna's friend, Flora, who was going to be her birthing partner, hadn't been unable to be with her, she'd have grabbed a couple of hours' sleep before coming. But she'd promised Susanna she wouldn't have to be on her own in labour, so here she was.

Derek shrugged, and Emily could see suddenly that he too was tired and under pressure. 'All I'm asking you to do is to think carefully about the way you practise,' he said. 'Or even about coming back into the hospital and doing it properly. We're desperately short of midwives there, you know.'

Emily's moment of sympathy vanished and her anger felt like solidified lava in her stomach. But she knew that unless she was very careful she would say or do something completely irrevocable. 'I happen to think we *do* do it properly! We practise in an utterly professional manner. I think that every day I go to work, and every time I deliver a baby safely.'

'I'm only trying to be helpful,' Derek said. 'You know better than I do that the maternity unit is under threat, and getting a reputation for being uncooperative and inflexible will only make things worse. I'm telling you this for your own good, and for the good of the unit.'

7

The fact that Derek was right about the unit being under threat didn't help. Emily's anger boiled over. 'How dare you? What right have you—' She kicked the rubber birthing pool so hard that quite a lot of water slopped over the side, soaking Derek's legs in the process. He jumped backwards, swearing, and Emily clapped her hand over her mouth. There was a moment's fraught silence, then she said, through gritted teeth: 'I'm going to take some leave, and then I may well take a sabbatical. Now please go. I have a lot of tidying up to do.'

'Emily . . . Ms Bailey, I'm trying to help you.'

Emily took a deep breath. 'I wouldn't accept your help if I was blind and needed guidance across a six-lane highway. Now please go away!'

Emily did some of the breathing exercises she taught expectant mothers and then cleared up the water, put out the candles and gathered all her kit, including her knitting, before considering her options. She had gone too far with Derek Gardner, she knew that. She was in danger of blowing everything, both for herself and the unit. She would never have exploded like that had she not been so tired. No, not just tired: exhausted. It was not simply that she had had no sleep the night before; she had not had a break for far too long. She had lots of leave owing and, as she'd said to Derek, she could take a sabbatical. She didn't have any mums due for the next couple of weeks – plenty of time for them to get to know one of the other midwives. She needn't think she was abandoning anybody.

Quite where she'd go or what she'd do was a minor detail she'd work out later.

A couple of days later, she was on her computer at home looking at travel sites wondering why none of the glorious sunlit beaches really appealed when her phone went. It was her best friend from university, whom she had not seen for far too many years.

'Rebecca! How lovely to hear from you!' As there was no answering scream she paused. 'Are you OK?'

'Actually, Em, I'm in a spot of bother. But before I ask the biggest favour ever in my life, tell me how you are?'

Emily kept to essentials, eager to know what Rebecca wanted of her. '. . . so basically, I'm a bit fed up and looking online for somewhere to go for a break,' she finished. 'So what's this favour?'

'Oh, Em! There is a God! I need someone to do some cooking on our puffer – you know, the steamboat James and I run as a hotel? And you're the only person I can think of who I trust and won't drive me mad.' She paused. 'Maybe I should explain. I'm pregnant.'

Emily took this in. 'How pregnant?'

'About six months. I thought I'd be all right to carry on until the end of the season. But I've become very short-tempered recently and James has put his foot down.'

Emily bit her lip to stop herself chuckling a little. 'Oh, love!'

'I just haven't the energy to explain my jokes. Or my kitchen rules to a stranger,' went on Rebecca. 'We had

9

that wonderful summer in the wholefood café, do you remember? We worked so well together and you'd be so perfect . . .'

'But, Becca!' Emily tried not to sound judgemental. 'You knew you were pregnant, so why didn't you hire someone earlier?'

'As I said, I didn't think I'd need anyone. I do have people who can do the odd week, but not nearly three months. I breezed through both of my other pregnancies but I'm so tired this time.'

'You would be, you're six months pregnant. When's your due date?'

'End of September. And I am organised, really I am; I just hadn't planned on feeling so tired and sick.'

Emily sighed. 'Third babies are often different.'

'So, will you come? You said you're really fed up and looking for somewhere to go on holiday? Not that it's a holiday, precisely . . .'

When she and Rebecca disconnected an hour later, Emily had made her decision. All she needed to do now was to go and see Sally.

Sally and Emily, who had been colleagues for two years, didn't often get a chance to talk about things properly. Mostly they were doing quick handovers and discussing either the pregnant mothers due to give birth or the classes they ran for them. But Sally had said to come over straightaway when Emily had called, and Emily was grateful for this opportunity.

'The thing is,' she said after a while, 'I need to take some leave. Rebecca is my best friend, and she's pregnant. I got the impression it wasn't entirely planned. Anyway, she can't cook for their puffer—'

'Which is? Some kind of train?'

Emily laughed. 'It's a boat, an old cargo vessel. It used to carry cargoes all round the Highlands and Islands in the old days. Now it's a sort of floating hotel. People go on it for holidays.'

'And you'd be the cook?'

Emily nodded.

'Can you cook?'

Emily threw a pistachio shell at her friend. 'You know I can. And it's the perfect time for me. I'm so fed up with being bullied by the system, and being told that home births are dangerous. I need a break.'

'So you're leaving us with all the fallout – all the stuff that makes our jobs even more difficult than they already are?'

Emily looked stricken. 'I'm sorry – so sorry! It's just that I'm so tired—'

'Oh, be quiet. And don't worry' – Sally picked up the bottle and shared out the last drops between both glasses – 'we'll survive. I hope.'

'You will. I know the unit has no funding but we do such good work.'

'And you want to go and cook on an old boat instead of doing this good work with me?'

'Yes! But I'll be back. I just need a change of scene.' She got up and hugged her friend. 'I have such a good feeling about this. I know I'll come back energised and strong, and then I promise I'll fight the system for all of us!'

11

Chapter One

Emily regarded her rucksack, currently sitting on top of a vessel that looked like an overgrown bath toy. It had a large funnel and high wheelhouse – which must have its view obscured by the funnel, she realised – and a high bow that went down to the water in a straight line. A mast rose near the bow, painted yellow, with wire rigging coming from it. The rest of the boat was smartly painted in red and black and, had she not been travelling for about six hours, would have made Emily smile. She'd forgotten that Scotland was quite so far away from the South-West of England.

'I shouldn't have come,' she muttered. 'I shouldn't be about to take a summer job – something I might have done when I was a student. I'm thirty-five, with professional qualifications. It's ridiculous!'

But then she looked around her and saw the July sunshine sparkling on the sea, the islands set off against a blue sky, the mountains, and, nearer, a very pretty harbour – Crinan – edged by brightly painted houses and what looked to be a nice hotel. She remembered the scenery – first from the bus and then the car journey – and thought she might well be in the most beautiful spot in the world. It wasn't raining, and it seemed that currently there were no midges. All good enough reasons to join her rucksack, which had been flung on to the boat by the dark and almost entirely silent man who'd picked her up from Lochgilphead bus station. She'd made this mad decision, she'd better follow through.

She stepped aboard the puffer, described to her by Rebecca as almost a family member. In fact it was an old cargo vessel, one of a fleet built during the Second World War, designed to deliver everything that the Highlands and Islands might need, from farm equipment to groceries, livestock to whisky. Many years ago it had been converted to carry passengers. It was powered by steam and, according to Rebecca, had a lot of character. Emily's job was to cook for the passengers now Rebecca, who owned it with her husband, James, and ran it as a thriving business, was no longer able to, being so pregnant.

Emily had rented out her house, arranged to take all the leave due to her, to be followed by a sabbatical for when her leave ran out. This done, she got the plane and two buses and now was here.

'Hello!' she called. 'Anyone at home?' As a midwife she was used to letting herself into houses where there was a lot else going on but this was different. All was silent.

She stayed on deck for a few moments longer, drinking in the view and letting the stress of the journey fade away, before deciding to go below. There must be someone here.

Rebecca had warned her she would be shopping and James was organising a coal delivery, but had definitely said there'd be at least one crew member on board to greet her.

She found a flight of wooden steps leading down to what would have been the hold but was now the first level of accommodation and descended. 'Anyone in?'

Still no answer, so she looked about her, deciding to make herself at home if there was no else to do it.

There was a long, polished mahogany table, which, going by the brochure Rebecca had sent her, was where everyone ate together, passengers and crew. Now it had a large bowl of fruit on it and a pile of unread newspapers. On one side there was a built-in wooden seat with comfy-looking cushions and, on the other, a bench. Looking at the length of these bits of furniture told Emily she'd be cooking for a lot of people. It had been a long time since she'd worked in a café, producing vegetarian lasagne for twenty, and she hoped she hadn't lost the skills.

The rest of the saloon (described as such in the brochure) consisted of built-in sofas arranged around a huge wood-burning stove. Although it was a warm summer day, it was smouldering gently, giving off a pleasant, aromatic smell as well as warmth. There were paintings on the walls (bulkheads – she mentally corrected herself) and plenty of woven woollen throws and cushion covers, all with a definitely Scottish feel, which added homely style and comfort. There were steps that obviously led down to the guest cabins below and all in all it gave the impression of being a sociable and cosy space.

Although tempted to make herself comfortable beside the wood-burner with a colour supplement, Emily felt she ought to explore the galley, which would be her place of work. After all, if the worst happened and the maternity unit at home was closed, or she had offended too many important people, it might have to be her job next year as well. Goodness knows what she'd do in the winter, when the puffer didn't operate.

On the way to the galley, she allowed herself to be distracted by a painting. As most of them were, it was of the puffer, but in a different setting to the gentle, distant islands and hills where it now lay. In the picture the mountains were nearer, majestic, almost over-powering. The puffer was gallantly under way, steam streaming from its funnel, obviously fighting against a stiff breeze. Emily was just struggling to read the title of the piece, which was in tiny writing underneath, hoping it would give a clue to the location, when there was a loud rustling noise. She jumped. 'Hello?'

There was no reply, just more rustling.

Oh my God, thought Emily, rats! I'm alone on an old boat and there are rats! She had a fear of rats people described as irrational. She didn't think it was irrational at all; they were vile, disease-ridden creatures who urinated as they ran. Rebecca had never said anything about rats. She'd have to spend the night on a rat-infested ship. Well, she couldn't. She'd have to decamp to the hotel.

Movement caught her eye, sending another stab of panic through her. It was in the galley and although she really didn't want to actually see the rat, she found her gaze drawn to the sound. There was a plastic carrier bag in the sink and it was heaving.

She screamed. Not loudly, but loud enough to make someone laugh. A girl appeared from where the galley turned a corner. She was younger than Emily, and very pretty, with a cloud of dark curls and a curvaceous figure, revealed by jeans and a tight sweater. This girl had obviously been keeping out of sight, waiting for Emily to be alarmed by whatever was making the noise.

'They're prawns,' the girl said scathingly. 'Langoustines. We bought them this morning. Don't say the new cook Rebecca brought in is frightened of shellfish?'

Emily, who was good at people, realised this girl was not happy to see her and wondered why. Had she thought she could do the job and resented Rebecca for bringing in a stranger? She feared she was going to have work hard to get on with her. Well, she'd just have to do it.

'Hi, I'm Emily. No, I'm usually fine with shellfish but mostly they're not still alive when I deal with them.'

'Only the freshest is good enough for us.' The girl spoke possessively, obviously proud of the puffer's high standards of produce.

'And what's your name?'

'Billie,' she said.

Emily nodded. 'I've come to help Rebecca out, as she's quite near to term.'

Billie frowned slightly, and Emily realised she'd used a rather medical expression but she didn't patronise Billie by explaining. She'd work it out.

'Rebecca didn't need to get anyone else in. I could

17

have managed. I've got loads of energy – I'm not pregnant! Or she could have got someone else to be galley slave.'

Emily winced inwardly at the expression but suspected it was what they called the cook's assistant on the puffer. She didn't need to worry about it being politically correct or not. 'Well, maybe we can work together? Sort of a job-share? So both do both jobs?'

This seemed to soften the expression of resentment on Billie's face. 'That might work. Only of course you won't know how to help out on deck like I do.'

'Is that part of the galley slave's job?'

'There is a deck hand. Drew. But when we're doing a difficult manoeuvre, or coming alongside or something, it's useful to have extra people with fenders.'

Emily smiled inside. Billie was using technical terms that Emily didn't quite understand, but like Billie, she would work it out without having it explained. 'Will I have to learn how to do that?'

'Oh yes.' Billie's expression doubted her ability.

'Would you mind showing me round? As Rebecca and James aren't here.'

'OK.' She wasn't enthusiastic but she'd do it. 'So, this is the galley, obviously.' Billie waved a casual hand. 'It's small but there's a bit of extra space at the back. Quite useful. Two of us can work at the same time. You have to be tidy.'

Emily was a very tidy worker in the kitchen. Rebecca knew this from when they'd worked together. It was one of the reasons Rebecca had wanted her and not someone she didn't know. They'd made a great team.

'I'll show you where we sleep,' said Billie. 'Bring your bag. Have you got any more luggage?'

'No.'

'Cool. There's no room for more than the basics.'

Emily followed Billie up on deck and across to a metal hood that Billie pulled back as if she was opening a tin of sardines.

Underneath was what looked like a dark tunnel but then Emily noticed rungs. There was a vertical ladder downwards.

'You go down backwards, always,' said Billie. 'I'll take your bag.'

With the ease of practice, Billie got hold of Emily's rucksack and swung herself down on to the ladder and disappeared. Emily took a breath and then, trying to remember Billie's technique, somehow got herself on to the ladder and down it.

'Oh God,' she said, before she could stop herself. 'Rebecca didn't sleep here, did she?'

There were two built-in single bunks with lockers underneath. A bank of netting over what was obviously Billie's bunk held toiletries, a bottle of water, magazines, a book. Right at the end of both bunks was a space big enough for a rucksack as long as it wasn't big or full.

'Of course not. She's in the owner's cabin. Although that must be a squash now she's the size of a whale.'

Rebecca was almost seven months pregnant so this might not have been much of an exaggeration but as Emily hadn't seen her yet, she didn't comment. 'So I'm in your space now?' she said instead. 'I am sorry. I can see now why you weren't thrilled to see me.' The cabin was small for one; for two, the space would be – was – very restricted.

Billie shrugged, acknowledging what Emily said was true. 'Just hope you don't need to get up in the night for a pee.'

'Er – where are the bathrooms?'

'In the hold. There are three. Oh, and one under the wheelhouse but the boys use that usually. Bit pongy.'

'I can see I'm going to love this job,' said Emily seriously. Now she could see why Rebecca had asked her if she still liked camping when they were going through the details together. But actually, she didn't let things like cramped conditions and far-away facilities bother her. If she could get Billie to unbend a bit more, it would all be fine.

'Emily!' roared a familiar female voice. 'Did you get here all right? Alasdair promised he'd picked you up OK.'

Emily set off up the ladder, bursting with joy at the thought of seeing her old friend. 'Becca!'

Both women floundered towards each other clumsily, Emily because she'd tripped over something and Rebecca because she was pregnant. They hugged tightly.

'Oh! It's so lovely to see you!' they both said at once.

'You haven't changed a bit!' said Rebecca, standing back to look at Emily. 'Although you've got highlights now. Your hair was always so dark.'

'When I started going prematurely blonde I decided not to fight it and have a few more streaks put in.'

'Otherwise, you're just the same. Haven't grown or anything.'

Emily laughed. 'The same can't be said for you,

although apart from being the size of a house, you're still the same Becca I was a student with.'

'I am huge, aren't I?'

Emily nodded. 'Are you sure that baby's got a few more weeks in there?' Emily hugged her friend again; any doubts she might have had about coming dispersed.

'Fairly sure!' They both laughed from the joy of being together after so many years.

'So, have you shown her round, Billie?' Rebecca asked as Billie appeared.

'A bit.'

'Well, let's have a cup of tea or something then I'll give you the complete tour.'

'If the tour could start at the loos, I'd be grateful,' said Emily.

A little while later, Emily and Rebecca were sitting in the saloon with mugs of tea and a plate of home-made biscuits. Emily had a notebook and pencil at the ready. Billie had gone off somewhere, to Rebecca's evident relief. Emily suspected her friend wanted to tell her things about Billie she couldn't say in front of her.

'You're sure you don't want lunch?' said Rebecca, picking up a biscuit and taking a bite.

'I had sandwiches on the bus. And at the airport waiting for the bus.'

'That's OK then. Now, let's run through what you need to do. The passengers are arriving at about five. Tea and cakes will be served. Then, dinner at about eight? There's an honesty bar but James will give them the welcome speech and the first drink to get them in the mood. I've made you two massive lasagnes – enough for twenty—'

'Oh!' Emily felt a stab of nostalgia in among scribbling notes and 'first-day' anxiety. 'Do you remember those ones we used to make at the café? Sold like hot cakes!'

'I use the same recipe for the vegetarian one. We ask people to tell us if they're veggie but sometimes they forget so I always do options on the first night. There are a load of baguettes for garlic bread . . . James'll cook the prawns for the starter – they're his speciality although he doesn't usually cook so don't get used to it . . .'

Rebecca continued talking about how everything worked until Emily had three pages of notes.

'So, tell me about Billie,' said Emily, putting down her pencil. 'Why didn't she get my job? It would have been easier to find an assistant, wouldn't it, and let her be the cook?'

Rebecca exhaled. 'Well, apart from me really wanting you to come . . .'

'I could have been a galley slave.'

'Billie is great in many ways. She's brilliant on deck. She can steer and even humps bags of coal, given half a chance. But she's not so great in the kitchen. She's sloppy and although she makes great cakes and biscuits she can't make bread. Can you make bread?'

Emily shrugged. 'I watch *Bake Off*; I can follow a recipe.'

Rebecca frowned slightly. 'Oh. Oh well, I expect you'll pick it up. Or I could make it at home and bring it in.'

Emily shook her head. 'No, I'll learn to make it. I've looked at the schedule. It'd be a poor show if you have to drive all over the Highlands and Islands to bring us bread in your condition.'

'And will you be able to cope with Billie? She's tricky! And I'm so sorry you have to share such a tiny space. I didn't mention it on the phone because I thought you wouldn't come and I so wanted you to.'

Emily did her best to hug her friend but was mostly prevented by her bump. 'It's fine. I can manage and, most importantly, I can get through the night without needing a wee.'

'Which is more than I can do,' said Rebecca gloomily. 'No sooner does the baby finally stop kicking and keeping me awake so I can drop off than my bloody bladder wakes me.'

'At least now you can catch up during the day and get some proper rest. Archie and Henry are old enough to understand if you need to fall asleep on the sofa while they watch that thing about dragons.' Emily caught up on children's TV while doing home visits. It was handy.

'Actually, the thought of curling up in front of the TV with my boys is absolute bliss. Not having to worry about the childcare rota is also bliss.'

'And you won't have to worry about me and Billie because we're going to job-share, so I won't be telling her what to do, just making tactful suggestions.'

Again, Rebecca frowned. 'Well, good luck with that.'

They finished going through everything that was expected of Emily and Rebecca gave her a thorough tour of the galley. The langoustines still heaved and rustled in the sink in a worrying way but Emily was used to them now.

'If ever a fishing boat offers to sell you anything wonderful, abandon the menu plans and buy the fish. The petty cash should have enough in it for that but if it doesn't, tell James and he'll sort it.' Rebecca leant against the counter, taking up the entire gangway. 'I love that spontaneity. It wouldn't work for some cooks but although I like having a plan, and I like knowing there are five dishes I could make without having to go shopping, I really prefer it if something lovely comes flapping on to my worktop, demanding something a bit special.'

'I went on a fish course once, with an old boyfriend, so that excites me too.' Emily realised that Rebecca didn't only need her cooking to be left in safe hands, she wanted the ethos to be passed on too. 'This is going to be great. Perfect for me. I'll be so busy I won't have time to brood about what's going on at the maternity unit. I'll have to think about food all the time! And how lovely is that!'

'Lovely,' agreed Rebecca, much less enthusiastically. 'Now bring me up to date on your love life. Have you left behind a broken-hearted lover?'

Emily giggled. 'No! I may have left someone who would like to see himself in that role but he wasn't doing very well.'

'So you don't have a love-life currently?'

'No.'

'That's good. I'd hate to think of you pining while you're up here working.' She paused. 'What did you think of Alasdair?'

'Who?'

'The man who picked you up from the bus station.'

'Oh! Well, he hardly opened his mouth for the entire

24

trip from the bus station. I assumed he was the local taxi but he wouldn't accept any money so—'

'Did you fancy him?' Rebecca asked before Emily could finish her sentence.

Emily put this down to hormones. Rebecca would never usually have said this about someone Emily had barely met. 'No! I just want to know why he gave me a lift if he's an elective mute. It must have been torture for him. In fact I could tell it was.'

'Don't take it personally.' Rebecca paused, obviously thinking how best to put what she wanted to say. 'He's James's brother. I told him you'd be tired and probably wouldn't want to chat.'

'Really?' Emily was astounded. 'When have you ever known me not want to chat?'

'Well, you'd had a long journey and you know how tiresome it is having to tell people what you do and things.'

'Why on earth should I mind telling people what I do? I'm proud of it.'

'I thought you might have felt a bit awkward, in the circumstances,' Rebecca explained.

Emily wasn't quite convinced by this but as she didn't greatly care, she just said, 'No, I'm cool about it. I didn't do anything wrong, after all.'

'No, well, back to business, I've made a cake for tea today.' Rebecca seemed eager to get off the subject of why Emily had suddenly dropped her career and come up to Scotland. 'The passengers will be here at about five, so they get tea before James's welcome drink at seven. Then, as I said, dinner at eight. That's in case anyone has difficulty getting here on the first night. We have it at about seven usually.'

'That's fine. And you've cooked that already so I just do garlic bread and make a salad?'

Rebecca nodded. 'There's one guest I must tell you about. She comes every year with her son. He disappears into the engine room for the duration, being a steam buff. She sits and knits and helps with the washing up.'

'So passengers help with washing up? Don't they come away to avoid household chores?'

Rebecca shook her head. 'No, this is different from most holidays. People come because they want to get involved. There's no obligation, of course, but they enjoy it. It's different from doing it at home. And Maisie, who I just mentioned, she loves coming. I worry about her getting about as she's no spring chicken, but there's always someone to chat to, and it's time with her son. At mealtimes, anyway.'

'I look forward to meeting her. I love old people. There's always so much behind the wrinkles and dodgy hairstyles.'

'I'm so glad you said that! Billie gets a bit impatient. She says we should have an age limit. In some ways she's right, getting people on and off is a struggle some-times, and I do worry about the steepness of the steps going down to the accommodation, but in other ways, this is a perfect holiday for them. And Maisie loves it, so, as long as she can come, I'm happy to have her.'

At last Rebecca managed to tear herself away, almost content that she'd left her beloved puffer galley in safe hands. Emily familiarised herself further on her own, locating utensils that were her personal essentials, glad that Billie still hadn't come back from wherever she'd gone.

When she did come back, Emily handed her a mug of tea with 'Chief Cook' printed on it. 'So, how are we going to divvy up the chores? I'll do tea so I can practise getting to know the clients—'

'Pazzies. We call them pazzies – short for passengers.'

Emily nodded. 'Cool. And we'll do dinner together? I need to jump in at the deep end, I think.' She smiled. 'Not literally, obviously. I'm not that great a swimmer.'

Billie didn't smile at this feeble attempt at a joke. Emily bit her lip. If her companion in the galley was going to be so taciturn it was going to make for a far from jolly time.

Before she could dwell on this further she heard boots on the steps and looked up to see James, whom she nearly didn't recognise now he had no beard, and a younger man coming down.

She came out of the galley at the same time as Rebecca appeared from the sleeping quarters to do the introductions.

'James! You remember Emily, don't you?'

'Of course! How could I forget? The prettiest of our bridesmaids.' He embraced Emily warmly.

'I was the only bridesmaid, James,' she said, hugging him back. He'd grown a little bit fatter since his wedding but he still had huge charm. It was easy to see why he was so successful at a business involving people.

'But still pretty,' he said. 'I remember your lovely smile. Now, let me introduce the first mate, Drew.'

A young man in jeans and a sweatshirt with 'Puffer Crew' on it stepped forward. 'Hi, pleased to meet you. I'm usually referred to as the deck hand but I'll take the promotion.'

Another man, a bit older, wearing a boiler suit and a big smile, appeared and put out his hand. 'And I'm Bob, chief engineer, often known as McPhail, after the Para Handy stories.'

'Hi, Drew. Here's your coffee, black, two sugars,' said Billie. 'It's how he likes it,' she added to Emily, proprietorially, as if only she would get it right.

'It's instant coffee and I'm very happy to make it myself,' said Drew with a grin that made him very attractive.

Emily intercepted Billie looking at him and diagnosed a bit of a crush. 'That's good to hear.'

'Well, welcome, Emily! It's lovely of you to agree to have a Highland summer with us,' said James. 'Now, is there time for a cuppa before our guests arrive?'

As tea was made and 'crew cake' produced, Emily suddenly remembered that Alasdair, her silent taxi driver, was James's brother. They were very different. James's accent was English and a bit posh and he had an easy, friendly charm. Alasdair was silent, but had had a slightly Scottish burr in the very few words they had exchanged. She had thought that Alasdair was good-looking, in a brooding sort of way, although she wouldn't have dreamt of saying so to Rebecca. It would only have given her ideas. Still, Emily realised she had more important things to think about now than the difference between the two brothers.

Chapter Two

Before long, Emily began to feel at home in the galley and, because Rebecca had done so much preparation for the evening meal, she found time to make a batch of cheese straws and a tea-bread for the following day. Rebecca had told her to take advantage of any free time to bake, as chatting to the passengers was as much part of the job as the cooking.

Billie wasn't around but that was fine, Emily preferred finding things by opening cupboards and drawers and shutting them again rather than being told where to look with an expression that was almost a sneer. She was going to have to work on her new colleague, and get Billie to stop seeing her as a threat.

She also found time to make herself familiar with the cabins down below, so by the time various 'Hellos!' floated down from on deck to tell her people were arriving, she felt ready to meet the guests.

Emily positioned herself at the bottom of the steps to the saloon, a welcoming smile ready to be produced at any moment.

'I'm sorry, we're always the first to get here.' A faintly Scottish voice belonging to a fairly elderly woman indicated that Rebecca's favourite passenger had arrived. Rebecca had given detailed instructions about how Maisie was to be treated which could have been summed up by saying, 'Look after her as if she was your own, much-loved, granny.'

Emily met her halfway up the steps in case she had difficulty getting down them, but although she was elderly, she seemed fairly spry and obviously well used to these particular steps. Emily was relieved.

'Hello, I'm Emily,' she said.

'And I'm Maisie,' she said when she got to the bottom. 'Rebecca told me about you. She telephoned when she realised she wouldn't be able to be here. Silly girl! She needn't have worried. I said we'd get along just fine.'

'And we will!' said Emily. 'Rebecca told me about you too and that you knit. I'm a bit of a knitter myself.'

'Well, that's good, dear.' She allowed herself to be supported as far as the banquette by the wood-burner. 'Robert's got my bags. He'll be down in a moment – he's just catching up with James on all that's been going on with the puffer since we were last here, so if it's all right with you, I'll just make myself comfortable by the fire. I do like a fire, even in summer.'

'So do I. Now, can I bring you a cup of tea? A bit of something to eat?' She wasn't sure if Maisie would be up to tea-bread, thickly spread with butter, or might prefer a plain biscuit. Emily suddenly yawned.

'You're tired? Rebecca mentioned you'd have been travelling all day,' said Maisie.

'You always have to get up before dawn to catch a plane these days,' said Emily. 'But I'll gladly make you a cup of tea.'

'You don't mind me; I'll be just fine. I'll wait until everyone has it. I've got my knitting and Robert will help me down to my room later.'

As she did seem very at home sitting there, Emily returned to the galley to warm the enormous teapot and put mugs on a tray.

The other passengers arrived in dribs and drabs, most of them very glad of tea after their journeys to the puffer's base in Crinan. Eventually, they were all there, and they assembled in the saloon to listen to James, thoughts of tea abandoned; there was a whisky bottle to be opened.

James, having introduced everyone and given a short welcoming talk, added, 'And our special entertainment for tomorrow after lunch is bunkering. As I speak there's a load of coal being delivered to the wharf we're heading to. So anyone who wants to help load it will be given a boiler suit, a shovel and a beer at lunchtime. Anyone else should stay well clear as the coal dust gets everywhere. And now – ring the bell – I declare the bar open.

'This drink is on us,' he went on. 'But after that you have to pay for your own. There's an honesty bar. Each cabin has its own card and you just write on it what you drink. Now Billie is coming round with sherry or drams, depending on what you want. Soft drinks are available.'

As Billie circulated with a tray of drinks, Emily passed round her cheese straws.

'Oh, these are my favourite!' said Drew. He took several and ate them enthusiastically. Then he caught Billie's eye.

'You want a beer?' Billie said. 'I'll get you one and put it in your column. We're allowed to drink,' she explained to Emily, 'as long as we write it down and pay for it at the end of the week.'

'We do get it for cost price,' said Drew. 'It's cool.'

He looked at Emily directly and she saw interest. She was a bit older than him and she wondered if he was at that age when older women were especially attractive. Emily realised that if Drew even looked at her Billie would never stop resenting her, and working together would never be easy. She gave Drew the kind of smile that made it clear she wasn't interested. At least, she hoped it did.

As she moved among the passengers with her plate she inspected the group of people she would be cooking for during the coming week. Rebecca had told her how fond you became of them and how sad you were to see them go. But when another lot came, you became just as fond of them.

'I think it's because you're looking after them,' Rebecca had explained. 'It sort of makes you love them. Like guinea pigs. You know? When you have to look after someone's pet when they go away. Just by feeding it, you become fond of it.'

Emily wasn't sure if people were all that much like guinea pigs but Rebecca was pregnant and so was permitted flights of fancy. There was nothing about any of her passengers she felt might make them difficult to look after and Rebecca had said this very rarely happened.

'Coming on the puffer is a very different sort of holiday. Most people know that and aren't expecting a five-star cruise.' Then she had frowned. 'They do get a five-star service – ten-star really – but not like on cruise ships.'

After a few more drinks were consumed it was time for dinner. Billie rang the ship's bell and, after much discussion and changing of minds, everyone sat down. Emily was in the kitchen, keen to make everything go smoothly. She was supposed to join everyone at the table but convinced Rebecca – who'd popped back to see how she was getting on and check that the puffer hadn't sunk the moment she turned her back on it – that she'd rather tidy up, and wash up as the plates came back.

James cooked the langoustines and Emily produced two huge bows of aioli. Bowls for the bits were placed in among the plates and napkins. It was all rather messy but everyone loved it. Emily put out bowls of hot water with slices of lemon for people to wash their fingers in. Billie sneered, obviously feeling finger bowls were a step too far.

Although it all went like clockwork, with no ghastly hiatuses caused by things failing to brown at the right time, or awkwardness caused by someone being allergic to garlic, Emily did find she was exhausted by the end of the meal. Rebecca had gone home and the men were all on deck, having either more coffee, malt whisky or even a cigarette. Some of the passengers had gone for a stroll in the light summer evening. If Emily hadn't felt as if she'd been hit by a heavy object she'd have been doing this too. It was all so beautiful. But she felt too tired to put one foot in front of another.

'I'm shattered!' she said to Billie, wringing out her dishcloth and tossing it into the freshly cleaned sink.

'I don't know why,' said Billie, tipping coffee dregs where Emily had just wiped. 'You didn't even cook the meal.'

Emily didn't mention her early start to get to the airport in time, or how tiring learning a new job always was, or anything like that. There was no point. Instead she said, 'Us old things don't have the stamina of you young ones. If you don't mind, I'm going to turn in now. And I think Drew said he wanted another cup of coffee. Do you think he can make it himself?'

'I'll do it,' said Billie.

Silently chiding the girl for being so eager to please a man, who, if not hers yet, was the object of her attention, Emily negotiated her way up the steps, across the deck and down the ladder to her sleeping quarters. The narrowness of the bunk and the strangeness of it all would cause her no problems that night.

Emily awoke, fairly sure she was in the same position as she had been when she fell asleep. She felt wide-awake and excited at the prospect of the day. She was determined to enjoy her summer in the Highlands and that meant making the most of every moment. So, although her phone told her it was barely five o'clock, she decided to get up.

She managed to get her clothes on without disturbing

34

Billie, and climbed up the ladder. She looked around from the top of the ladder and saw that the rest of the world was still asleep. She would have a quick shower and then go and explore. Breakfast wasn't until eight so she had plenty of time.

Moving carefully over the dew-covered deck, Emily slid back the hatch to the saloon and found her way down to the shower. She ignored the galley; she would be at work there shortly, but this time was her own.

Ten minutes later she was back on deck again, desperate to get out into the beauty of the morning.

The sun was concealed behind a fine mist promising a beautiful summer day, but for Emily the sense of expectation was even more wonderful. She took a moment to relish the sight of the harbour, full of boats of all sizes, but dominated by the puffer. A few small white houses flanked the hotel, which must have the best views in the world, and a thread of mist trailed across the masts of the boat like a chiffon scarf. Close to, fine cobwebs were covered with tiny drops of dew, like fairy decorations, occasionally catching the sunlight and flashing like diamonds. It was breathtaking.

Emily stepped ashore and set off, looking for a way upward. She wanted to get to the top of the hill so she could appreciate the view of the islands even more. She saw the road leading uphill and followed it swiftly, her feet light as she almost ran until at last she found a viewpoint from which she could see the world.

Panting slightly after her climb, she took in the view again. It was a different from here. The view was clearer: calm sea; the islands, both near and far off; mist here and there like splashes of milk in water. A curlew called. It was so beautiful she almost wanted to cry.

It had been a risk coming, she knew that. She could go back home and find her job had changed radically, that the midwife-led unit where she was based had been closed down and that all births had to take place in the general hospital, twelve miles away. It was a worry. The potential closure of the unit was something that had been hanging over their heads for a while now. GPs like Derek Gardner didn't help, telling the world that what they did was unsafe. But she felt certain that coming here had been the right decision. A complete break, away from everything, would send her back to her beloved unit refreshed, re-energised and positive. If she had to fight to save it (again) she would do it with new vigour and determination.

Her opposite number in the unit, Sally, had said the same when she and Emily had a farewell lunch together in their favourite pub. 'If you can manage without the money, it'll be brilliant for you. You work so hard and never seem to take any leave.'

'And you know I'm only planning to stay for a couple of months?'

'Try and stay longer and I'll send a search party.'

Emily smiled fondly. 'And although it isn't great pay, I get full board. I only need money for wool, really. Knitting is my only vice.' She considered the truth of this. 'And the odd glass of wine.'

'Will you get some money from renting out your cottage?' asked Sally, obviously wanting to satisfy herself that Emily would be all right.

36

'Most of it will go on the mortgage, of course, but there is a bit of change.'

'Well, we expect some wonderful sweaters and things when you get back. Something other than the scarves and blanket squares you knit when you're working.'

Emily laughed. 'I promise you something you'll love. I might be able to get some really special wool. It'll be nice to have time to actually follow a pattern, rather than just zoning out and listen to my labouring mums.'

'A cardigan would be wonderful. And I'll pay you for the wool, of course. But only after you've knitted it!' said Sally. 'Your new job sounds really full on. There may not be time to knit!'

'Well, if there is, I'll do something for you. I owe it to you for being so nice about me jumping ship.' She grinned. 'Or maybe I'll just buy you a lovely kilt, with all those flattering pleats round your hips . . .'

Sally, who described herself as 'a bit plump', pushed her affectionately. 'You dare!' And then, possibly to repay Emily for the reference to her hips, she said, 'And when you get back, we'll sort you out with a father for your unborn child.'

'Sally! I know you think only women who've had babies should be midwives, but I'm perfectly happy without one. And I don't want a man, either. I relish my freedom. I wouldn't have been able to just take off like this if I had a man or a child, would I?'

Sally had to acknowledge this was true. 'But you can't leave it too much longer, you know that.'

'I know! But the urge to have a baby of my own hasn't hit me yet. I'm quite happy delivering other people's.'

'You'll live to regret it if you don't have a baby.'

'You're obsessed, you know that?'

Sally had laughed. 'Oh go and play with your puffer and come back with your head set on straight.'

The conversation came back to her as she gazed. Sally would never think Emily's head was on straight until she was in a committed relationship and pregnant. But Emily was happy single. And while there might come a time when she was prepared to have a baby and bring it up on her own, that time was not yet.

Emily was just about to go back down and start on breakfast when her eye was caught by something on the hill opposite. It was the silhouette of a man and a dog walking along. A little behind, skipping for all she was worth, was a small girl. Emily smiled. How lovely, she thought, a man taking his dog out early, presumably before work, his daughter going along for quality Dad-time. Just for a second, she found herself wistful. Maybe there was a woman in a nice little house, stirring porridge, sorting washing, burning toast, waiting for her family to come home for breakfast.

The thought reminded Emily that she was hungry, and she had porridge for at least six to make. She'd better go and do it.

She was taken aback to find a surprising number of passengers in the saloon. It wasn't even seven o'clock yet. A bit early! Billie was in the galley making tea and coffee.

'Oh, you're here,' she said, stony-faced. 'You're on

duty all the time, you know. You can't just skip off when you want to.'

'Morning! How are you? Yes, I slept fine actually, thanks for asking.'

Not even the glimmer of a smile.

'You can take tea to Maisie, in her room,' said Billie, apparently feeling this was a just punishment. 'Rebecca always does it. I don't think she should. No one else gets tea in their rooms.'

'I don't mind. I'll do it.'

Emily knocked softly on the door of Maisie's cabin. If Maisie was peacefully sleeping she wouldn't wake her. She might usually be an early riser but Emily felt that if for some reason you'd had a disturbed night, and had only dropped off again at six, you really wouldn't want to be woken at seven.

When she received no answer, she opened the door. Emily did have some sympathy with Billie's reluctance to deliver tea; you didn't want to be the one to discover that someone had died in the night. But gentle snores emerged from Maisie's sleeping form so Emily left the tea on the little shelf next to the bunk and resolved to check on her again later.

Upstairs people were sitting round with their mugs and James was coaxing the wood-burner back into life. It wasn't as though it was cold but having it alight gave the puffer a beating heart until eventually they got steam up and could start the engine and set off.

'Morning, Emily,' said James. 'How was your first night aboard?'

'I really couldn't say, I was asleep for most of it.'

He laughed. 'Good. Bunk not too hard or anything?'

Emily chuckled back. 'Would you be able to do anything about it if I said yes?'

'No, but it's only polite to ask.'

Emily smiled. 'I don't think you have to be polite to crew members, James.'

'On the contrary, it's essential to be polite to crew members.'

He was laughing but Emily knew he meant it. Good manners were essential, at all times. She realised there was something a little bit old-fashioned about James and it was probably part of what made him so good at his job.

'Now, you know the score for breakfast? Put everything out, including the porridge, and let people help themselves. But if anyone wants a cooked breakfast, you do it to order.'

'Fine. Rebecca told me. I just hope no one asks for haggis for their "Scottish Nuance".'

'They hardly ever do. Porridge is the Scottish Nuance; in fact, people even call it that. '"I'll have cream on my Nuance today."'

'Really!' Emily was enchanted. 'I love that!' She glanced at her watch. 'I'd better start the bread. Unlike Rebecca I can't do it without a recipe.'

When Maisie hadn't appeared by eight thirty, Emily left Billie in charge of the bacon and eggs and took her more tea. To her relief, Maisie stirred when she came in.

'My dear girl! That is so kind of you. I see there's another mug there I never knew about.'

'You were fast asleep and I didn't like to wake you in case you'd had a bad night.'

'Well, I did have a slightly bad night as it happens. But I'm fine now and I'll be up shortly. Thank you so much for this tea. It's really very welcome.'

Emily hadn't worked as a nurse for many years but something about the old lady told her all was not quite well with her. She didn't say anything because Maisie hadn't mentioned it but she made a mental note to check on her from time to time.

When the clearing up was at last over (it seemed to take forever in spite of the enthusiastic and welcome help of passengers) Emily peered through the clingfilm that covered her bread dough. She was surprised and pleased to see that it had risen beautifully. After knocking it back she put it in the tins to rise again. Then she thought about lunch, slightly wishing her galley slave was there to consult. But Billie's heart, and currently her physical presence, was with Drew so Emily was on her own.

Rebecca had said, when in doubt, make soup, but it said quiche on the menu plan. It might be a bit early to start making pastry, but whatever she cooked she'd need onions. She plucked a couple from the string hanging up and began peeling.

Noises from on deck alerted her that the puffer's departure was imminent. She ran up the steps so she could watch. She would keep well out of the way but knew that soon she should be able to hold a fender, coil a rope and maybe (fingers crossed this would never happen) catch or throw a line to or from the shore. Billie

41

was clearly very adept. She was up at the bow now, preparing to catch the line from Drew, who, having tossed it to her, stepped neatly back on board.

Emily wondered if Billie would have preferred to be a deck hand to a galley slave, had the position been available.

Eventually the dockside seemed to slide away from the puffer and there was a loud blowing on the steam whistle. For a moment it made Emily feel she was in a children's television programme, with everyone laughing and waving, James visible in the wheelhouse, calling out of the window to Bob, the engineer, all in the calm and gentlemanly manner that made him so good at what he did. At last the slightly comical craft pulled away from the harbour and set off for the Islands.

Lunch was nearly ready when Maisie appeared.

'Hello,' said Emily, wiping her hands and going out of the galley to greet her. 'How are you feeling now? What can I get you?' As she said this she made sure Maisie got across the floor safely and then found a cushion to go in the small of her back.

'I have felt better, I will admit. But I'll be just fine shortly. I wouldn't like my son to be worrying about me, so please don't say anything.'

As her son hadn't been surprised when his mother hadn't appeared for breakfast Emily didn't think he'd be worried, especially as she was going to be there for lunch.

'Can I get you a cup of tea or something? Piece of toast? It's quiche for lunch. I could give you a bit early, if you fancied it.'

'A cup of tea and some toast would be just the ticket. With some of Rebecca's home-made marmalade.'

'I'll bring it right over.'

'And then I'd love a wee glass of sherry.'

Emily laughed and went to get the tea. There couldn't be too much wrong if Maisie was asking for sherry.

'Going by what I can hear from on deck, we'll be mooring up soon,' she said when she came back with a mug of tea.

'Oh yes,' said Maisie knowledgeably, 'on this route the first morning is only a short hop. The coal is always delivered here. Something to do with the wharf, and where the lorry can reach.'

'I'll know where to come if I want to ask a question but don't want to look stupid,' said Emily.

'Asking questions never makes you look stupid, my dear, but if everyone else is busy and you need to know something, I may well be able to help.'

Soon after lunch, which was served next to a large pile of coal, the passengers divided themselves up. There were those who retired to their cabins for naps (blaming this on being unaccustomed to drinking at lunchtime) and those who donned the boiler suits provided and helped with the bunkering. Billie explained that this meant getting the coal on board and that they should make sure the portholes and windows were closed or coal dust would get over everything. As James had told her the same thing some time previously, Emily wasn't all that grateful for this information.

The passengers' enthusiasm for hard physical labour, given that they were officially on holiday, was amazing, but Emily understood that a change was as good as a rest and if you spent most of your days behind a desk, or in front of daytime television, shovelling coal in the company of others could well seem a pleasant way to spend your time.

Emily stayed in the kitchen, clearing up and making and delivering tea or cans of beer to thirsty shovellers. She also peeled potatoes ready for the evening. Billie had promised to make fish pie. Emily made a batch of scones for later, all the while keeping an eye on Maisie. The minute the scones were in the oven she came out of the galley and went to sit beside her.

Maisie had brought her knitting bag up with her and she'd taken something out but since Emily had been watching, she hadn't actually extracted the needles from the ball of wool.

'So, do tell me, what are you knitting?' said Emily.

'Actually, nothing. To be honest, I find the arthritis in my hands makes it too difficult for me to knit any more, but I keep thinking it'll get easier.'

'Oh, that's a shame. Have you got medication for the arthritis?'

'Yes. But I still can't manipulate the needles like I used to. I wouldn't mind so much but I've promised to make this slipover – you know? A sleeveless jumper? It's for my youngest grandson and I've made one for all the others. He'll be twenty-one in September. It should be plenty of time except . . .' She sighed.

'Let me look?' Emily asked and Maisie handed over the knitting.

'Oh, this is beautiful!' she exclaimed. 'Fair Isle! I

44

haven't done that for ages. But I love it!' Emily inspected the intricate pattern carefully. The background was fawn and the pattern was dark blue, a wonderfully warm red, and yellow.

'I've done the front and, as you see, started the back, but I haven't got very far.'

'It's gorgeous!'

'My mother taught me to do it, but I could never get the hang of the pad. You know? On the hip? To support the needles?'

'I've seen pictures,' said Emily, still examining the knitting. 'I knit a lot in my work – I mean my real job, not cooking here, obviously – but I have to stick to plain stuff.'

'What is your work, Emily?'

'Oh, I'm a midwife!' She laughed. 'I know you probably wouldn't think that knitting was part of that but I do it while the mother is in labour and doesn't need help. It keeps me occupied and seeing me do it reassures the mother. She knows if I'm doing that everything must be going well.' She didn't add that she'd got into trouble for doing it.

'You're a midwife? How interesting! And have you children of your own?'

Emily laughed again. She was often asked this. 'No. There is no truth in the rumour that you have to have had them to deliver babies.'

'No, but you must be approaching your thirties now. You need to be thinking about it if you want children.'

'I'm thirty-five, you flatterer, you, and I don't want children, I don't think. But I'd love to help you with your knitting.'

Maisie was not as grateful as Emily felt she should be. She seemed to doubt her abilities. 'Hmm. That's a nice idea, but would you be able to follow the pattern?'

'Well, I think I could!' Emily tried to hide her indignation. 'I'd practise – do a few squares – but I'm fairly confident.' Emily wasn't used to having her knitting skills questioned. But Maisie didn't know her, so it was fair enough.

'I tell you what,' said Maisie, making a great compromise, 'I'll let you have my pattern. If you can knit a square, and get the pattern right, you can help me with my knitting.'

'I haven't any suitable needles with me,' Emily said, a little more humble now.

'I'll let you have mine. And here's the pattern.' Maisie burrowed in her knitting bag for a few seconds and then looked up. 'You know, dear, I might have to go back to bed. I really don't feel very well.'

Chapter Three

Emily put a hand on Maisie's arm. 'Don't move just for the moment.' She moved a cushion. 'Here. Put your feet up on the banquette. I'll get Robert.'

Emily went on deck, not quite knowing where to look for Maisie's son. She saw James in the wheelhouse and called up. He leant out of the open window. 'Can I help?'

'Probably. I'm looking for Robert. Maisie's not too good.'

James frowned at this news. 'He's in the engine room. He's one of our keenest stokers. Give him a shout.'

Robert came up rubbing his hands on a rag so dirty it threatened to put on more dirt than it could take off.

'It's your mother,' Emily said. 'I'm a bit worried about her.' Then she went on to explain.

'We're going to tie up very soon,' said James, who, hanging out of the wheelhouse window, was listening to the conversation. 'You go and see her, Robert, and then we'll think about what we should do.'

As Emily followed Robert along the side-deck she remembered something Rebecca had once said about

James: he sometimes worried but he never panicked. It was a good characteristic for one's boss to have.

Maisie was determined she was not going home. 'No, dear. If I go home, you'll have to take me and you deserve your holiday. Besides, if I took a turn for the worse who would look after me? Who would even know? I'd have to get the neighbours to look in on me.'

'But, Mother—'

'No, really,' Maisie insisted. 'I'm better off here. Emily will keep an eye on me. She's a midwife.'

Robert laughed. 'What is or isn't wrong with you, Mother dear, I don't think you'll need a midwife to cure it!'

Emily laughed. 'I think Maisie means I'm in a caring profession and I was a nurse for a short time before I did my training.'

'I don't think we should give everyone extra work,' said Robert. 'It's all hard enough for them without adding nursing duties.'

'That's very true, Robert,' said his mother. 'But what's the alternative?'

'I don't mind looking after Maisie,' said Emily. 'So far she's been no trouble.'

'Tell you what,' said James. 'We'll get a doctor to call in. If he thinks you need to go home, or to hospital, or whatever, you can go.'

'I wouldn't like to bother a doctor with my trivial aches and pains.'

'No bother. He's my brother. He'll come if I ask him.'

Maisie was still not happy with this idea. 'But we've moved. We're probably miles away from where he lives.'

James laughed. 'We haven't moved that far and my brother has patients all over the area.'

'That would be really kind,' said Robert quickly, before his mother could think of another reason why she shouldn't get medical attention.

Emily went back to the galley, wondering how many brothers James had. Could the man who'd driven her from Lochgilphead in almost total silence possibly be a GP? If so, she doubted his bedside manner would be up to much. She'd had better conversations with her neighbour's dog.

She was peeling hardboiled eggs for the fisherman's pie when she saw the doctor arrive. He came down the steps, murmuring to James, and she realised it *was* the one who'd driven her to the boat. He was still broodingly handsome but looked more relaxed now. Maybe he was one of those people who were happier when working, not knowing quite how to carry on in more social situations. They disappeared into the accommodation where Maisie had been persuaded to rest until the doctor had seen her.

Billie, who, as cook for the night, should have been dealing with the fish, was still absent. Emily considered going to find her but felt that might look like nagging; and Billie was probably helping Drew do something she would claim was more important than cooking. Emily decided to carry on without her. She rescued the haddock from the oven and poured off the milk. She was looking for capers when James came to the galley.

'Alasdair would like a quick word if that's all right. On deck? Maisie's coming back up now. She feels "just fine" apparently. And where's Billie? Shouldn't she be here?'

'She's probably busy doing something else,' said Emily. 'But like Maisie, I'm just fine.'

She went up on deck and saw Alasdair looking across the water. He turned as he heard her approach. 'Hello, I'm the doctor.'

Was there a suspicion of a twinkle in those very dark, heavy-browed eyes? Emily couldn't be sure and didn't take the chance and smile in response. You couldn't take back a smile once it was offered. 'I know. We've met. Only you didn't say you were a doctor.'

'No reason I should have mentioned it, but I am one and now I'd like a quick word with you about Maisie.'

'I've only just met her,' said Emily before he could say any more. 'So I couldn't really tell you much about her condition.'

'I know that. But could you keep an eye on her? Here? On the puffer? As well as everything else you have to do?'

Emily considered. 'I was a nurse once – I told Maisie about it – but it was years and years ago.'

'She doesn't need nursing, she just needs an eye on her. She has low blood sugar and I've given her some medication but you'll need to check she's taken it. Tell me immediately if she doesn't start to get better soon, or if she gets worse. Do what you've done already, basically.'

Emily didn't know what to say. 'I'm really fond of Maisie, we get on well, but supposing she got worse while I was doing something else?'

'Her son is here. He'll have the responsibility. And if she went home – which she really doesn't want to do – she'd be on her own. Here, she'll have company and wouldn't be depending on neighbours.'

'Well then, of course.'

'But would you have time? You're new to the job and I know how hard the cooks work on board. The puffer has a fine reputation for food it has to keep up.' He was smiling now, and there was a hint of challenge in his manner.

'Put like that, I'm sure I could manage. I'm not cooking all on my own, after all.' Having been a bit reluctant to take on the responsibility of an elderly lady, now she felt affronted when Alasdair suggested she might not be able to do it.

'I gather from James that you're not getting the help you should be getting.'

Emily nodded. 'Not at the moment, no, but I'm working on that. I'll have Billie eating out of my hand by the end of the week.' She smiled ruefully, aware she'd set herself a big challenge. 'I'm better with people like Maisie.'

He acknowledged this with a nod of his dark head and the same almost-smile Emily now recognised. 'She told me she's letting you help with her knitting. I reckon she doesn't do that very often.' He was clearly surprised and possibly a little bit impressed.

Emily let herself relax a little. This man may be a GP but he wasn't local to her or her work. Nothing he could do or say could affect her livelihood. She could probably just treat him like any other man. 'I have to do a test piece first, though, and I may not be good enough. It's a shame if she can't do it herself any more.'

Alasdair nodded. 'I gather from her son that it's been a struggle for a while, which is a real loss for her. If you could help a bit it would mean a lot. Do a lot for her health, too.'

Emily allowed herself to smile now. This man understood the connection between happiness and health – he couldn't be all bad. 'I'd be delighted to.' Then she looked questioningly at him. 'So tell me, why didn't you say anything – hardly a word – when you drove me from Lochgilphead? I thought I was sharing a car with an elective mute.'

'I'd had very strict instructions from Rebecca. And you should never go against the whims of a pregnant woman.'

'What? She told you that you weren't to speak to me? Why on earth would she do that?'

'She told me you hated GPs and I wasn't to upset you by telling you I was one.'

Emily blushed slightly. It was a rather extreme description of her feelings but it was based on what she herself had told Rebecca. 'I don't hate all GPs. Anyway, you could have talked about the scenery or something.'

'But you might have asked me what I did for a living and then I'd have been sunk.'

'As you were giving me a lift I would have kept my feelings to myself.'

'Well, that's good to hear. Any particular reason why you hate doctors in general practice?'

Emily didn't want to go into it all now. 'I said I don't

hate all of them and there is a good reason why I hate some of them but now's not the time. I must get back to the kitchen.'

'Galley,' he corrected.

'Galley,' she repeated and went back down below.

Emily was a bit thrown by this encounter. And a bit annoyed with Rebecca. She had obviously meant well, not wanting Emily to have to make polite conversation with a man who may have very different views from her own about how babies should be born. But now it was a bigger thing than it should have been, really. Emily was used to fighting her corner, after all. She was capable of having a conversation with a GP without going off into a rant – provided the GP wasn't insisting that all births should take place in hospital, with every medical intervention currently invented. But Rebecca was pregnant and Emily would make allowances.

Emily was not entirely surprised when Rebecca appeared. She'd gathered now that the puffer's route did not always cover huge stretches and could quite easily be caught up with by car, although sometimes a ferry would be part of the journey.

'I'm just seeing how things are going,' Rebecca said defensively. 'I know Billie's not always a great help. Where is she now, for instance?'

'I don't know, but, Becca, I'm fine on my own. It's easier really.' In fact, Drew had come in wondering if Emily needed a hand and Billie had instantly found an excuse to take him somewhere else. But there was no need to tell Rebecca that.

Rebecca seemed to sense something of the sort

anyway. 'I'll have a word with her. It's not good enough. Oh, and I'm staying for dinner, by the way. Checking up on your cooking,' she added, 'obviously. Alasdair will stay too. His Kate is with my two, who are being looked after by my neighbour, who is also their child-minder a lot of the time.'

Emily peeked in the oven, to see if her mashed potatoes were browning on the pie. What Rebecca had just said seemed very complicated and nothing to do with her.

'He's a single parent,' Rebecca went on, assuming Emily was interested.

'Really? How difficult for him. And maybe sad?'

'Fairly sad. He's a widower.'

This was genuinely sad. 'Oh, I'm sorry. Presumably you're telling me so I don't ask questions about his wife?'

'Mm. Yes, that's right.' Rebecca's expression was bland. Emily was not fooled.

'But actually you're telling me to make sure I know he's single?'

'No!' said Rebecca indignantly. 'Of course not! Why would I do that?'

'I really don't know, Becca. Because you must know that I am absolutely not interested. Now, if you're staying for supper you can help set the table. And is there some more white wine, somewhere?'

'You know me, I'd never match make.' She ignored the disbelieving snort that followed this statement and went on, 'But I think it's easier if people know all they need to know about others.'

'Only if they need to know, surely? I'm really hoping that Maisie will be fine till the end of the week now, and that no other passengers will need medical assistance while I'm here.'

'Well, I do too, but Alasdair quite often pops in to see the puffer – and James, of course. They are brothers, after all.'

Emily's attention was caught now. 'Yes, but they're very different, aren't they? James has no Scottish in his accent but Alasdair does have a faint burr.'

'I know. I think Alasdair cultivated it a bit. It makes him more accessible to his patients. They were both brought up bilingual – you know: RP at home and the local accent when at school and out and about.'

'That would explain it. Now, I'd better get going on the starter.'

'No!' said Rebecca. 'You go and see how Maisie is – she could have dinner in her cabin if she wants to – I'll find Billie. She can do the starter!'

The long table was fairly tightly packed. Rebecca insisted on Emily sitting down to eat although she'd have preferred to keep an eye on her pudding. Once she realised she couldn't stay in the kitchen, she squashed in next to Maisie.

Maisie smiled at her. 'There are disadvantages to living in Scotland, I'm sure, but I do love the long summer evenings.'

'So what are the disadvantages?' Emily asked, more to make conversation than because she wanted to know.

James overheard. 'Midges. Undoubtedly it's the midges. But if you slather yourself in a certain beauty product, it helps.'

'You mean the midges drown in the beauty product?' said Bob, the engineer.

'What is the beauty product?' asked Emily. 'And why won't you just tell me what it is?'

'Because other anti-midge products are available,' said James. 'And we supply the stuff to everyone, so just help yourself.'

'So,' said Maisie, 'with the midges sorted, there are no disadvantages to living in Scotland.'

Emily laughed. Maisie seemed on good form. No nursing or 'keeping an eye' was likely to be necessary.

At the end of the meal Emily was chased out of the kitchen by James and the passengers. Billie was presiding over the sink, and everyone else got the table cleared and the dishes wiped. James brought Emily a single malt whisky to enjoy while she got some fresh air and Rebecca came to join her, sipping ginger tea.

'Well, I think your cooking passes muster,' she said.

'Billie was in charge of the fish pie,' said Emily, who had set her glass down and was examining the pattern Maisie had given her.

'But she didn't do much of it, did she? Honestly, she was desperate to be head cook but how could I rely on her to actually do what's required? If I'd taken on a student as galley slave, the passengers might not have got meals at all!'

'We were students when we last cooked together and we were brilliant!' She studied the pattern once more and then began casting on.

'Students were different in those days,' said Rebecca gloomily.

'Oh come on! Some are great! And Billie will be fine.' Emily felt she could deal with Billie better on her own, without Rebecca wading in, but didn't say it. She understood that Rebecca was having separation anxiety about leaving her galley in the hands of others.

'I dare say. You're demon with those knitting needles, are you? You didn't knit when I last knew you.'

'I love it. It's soothing, creative, and works as a sort of meditation. I also find it useful at work.'

'What, knitting little garments for babies about to be born?'

'Don't mock! There is a pattern for a little hat that takes about as long as a first baby takes to come into the world.'

'What, nine months? That sounds the sort of knitting I might manage.'

Emily shook her head. 'No! A first labour! I've never actually made it because when I'm in charge I only knit very plain things so I can listen to my labouring mother. But I'd do it for someone else, like a shot.'

'So what are you doing now?' asked Rebecca, sipping her tea.

'This is a test piece for Maisie. If it passes muster I'm going to finish her grandson's slipover for her.'

'That would be really kind. Do you want another malt?'

Emily shook her head. 'No, I need to be able to concentrate. Although that was delicious, I can't drink and do complicated knitting. This is a test!'

'I'm glad you and Maisie get on. I love feisty old ladies, but Billie finds them difficult.'

'She's young and only has eyes for Drew at the minute.' Emily counted stitches and then started knitting.

Rebecca sighed. 'And he's really not interested in her.'

'Unrequited love, eh? Who'd have it?' Emily's fingers flew as she did a section of ribbing. It would be much slower when she started on the pattern.

'Not you, obviously,' said Rebecca. 'But I think it's better to have experienced real love, even if it doesn't come to anything, than to just go through life without knowing that excitement.'

'Isn't it time you got back to your bairns?' said Emily, not wanting to get into this conversation. She was aware that she and Rebecca had a bit of catching up to do – not every element of Emily's life had been relayed to her by phone, text or email – but she didn't want to do it now.

Rebecca looked at her watch. 'Actually, you're right. I better had.'

Alasdair obviously thought the same thing because he joined them and handed Emily a glass. 'James said you need another one and, Rebecca, we must both go now.'

'Yeah, we must. Although God knows it's hard to get the kids into bed when it's so light.'

Rebecca went below to collect her things but Alasdair waited with Emily. 'So how's your first day been?'

'Busy. And I've just told Rebecca I don't want any more whisky. I've started on this bit of knitting for Maisie and I want to get it right.'

'Well, finish it and then have a drink. It's from Jura, which you can see if you just look over there.'

'The one with two mountains?'

He nodded. 'Technically known as the Paps.'

Emily regarded them for a few seconds. 'I can see why now. I bet a man called them the Paps. They see breasts in everything, so I'm told.'

Chapter Four

A couple of days later, Emily showed Maisie her sample square of Fair Isle knitting. Maisie had just put her glasses on and Emily was a bit anxious about not making the grade. The rest of the passengers were making themselves ready for a hike over the heather with James. Emily had filled enough rolls and made enough sandwiches to mean the puffer had no bread left except the frozen loaf which was now defrosting and the potential of the dough proving under its cling film.

'Well now, dear, let's have a look at this,' said Maisie. She picked up the square and peered at it and then at the front of the jersey that she herself had knitted.

'I'm not going to be able to replicate your tension exactly,' said Emily. 'I'm not that skilled.'

Someone came into the saloon. Emily saw that it was a worried-looking Alasdair and he had a small girl with him. She had bright red hair in a ponytail and seemed to be about nine years old.

'Hello, Maisie, Emily. This is my daughter Kate,' he said.

'Hello, Kate,' said Emily, and then added, 'Alasdair.'

'Um, we have a bit of a problem,' Alasdair explained. 'I was going to leave Kate here while I visit a patient on a farm a little way away but I gather James is leading an expedition and Kate doesn't want to go.' He paused. 'I could take her to the farm, of course, but she'd have to wait in the car and it might be for a while.'

'Well, if she doesn't mind joining in with the knitting . . .' began Maisie.

'Or the bread making,' added Emily, 'she's welcome to stay with us. Although I don't know if she'll want to.' Emily smiled, feeling sorry for the little girl, who had been put into a difficult position.

'I used to help Auntie Becca with the bread sometimes,' said Kate, not looking too unhappy with her options.

'In which case you're probably better at it than I am,' said Emily.

'I can't knit, though,' Kate added.

'We'll teach you, if you like,' said Maisie.

'Would you like that, sweetie?' asked Alasdair, looking slightly less worried.

'It's better than sitting in the car waiting for you,' she said.

Alasdair almost smiled. 'Thank you so much. I was going to leave her with Rebecca but her boys are both off somewhere and she was planning to rest.'

'I'm fed up with boys anyway,' said Kate. 'Why are they always so noisy?'

'Girls can be noisy too,' said Alasdair.

'Different sort of noisy,' said Emily. 'So, Kate, shall we do a bit of knitting while my bread proves and then get down and dirty with the dough? Sorry,' she added as three pairs of eyes regarded her with suspicion. 'Too many cookery shows on TV, I expect. It's affected my language.'

'Will you be all right with Emily and Maisie then?' Alasdair asked his daughter.

'I'll be just fine, Daddy,' she replied, patiently offering her father the reassurance he needed.

He kissed the top of his daughter's head and then was gone.

'Now then, Kate,' said Maisie, 'you come and sit by me here. I've just been looking at some knitting Emily did. Do you think it's as good as mine?'

Kate took her time deciding. 'I can't tell the difference, really.'

'Oh, thanks, Kate!' said Emily. 'That is an amazing compliment.'

'I must admit I can see a little difference myself,' said Maisie, almost reluctantly. 'But they're perfectly alike enough given they're not going to be seen side by side.'

'I'm flattered! Now, shall I pop to my cabin and get some bigger needles and some thicker wool for Kate? Otherwise it takes a long time to get a result,' she explained to the little girl.

'I'll take a peek at the bread while you do that,' said Kate.

Emily met Billie in the cabin. She was stuffing things into a rucksack. 'Hello,' said Emily. 'Planning to run away from home?'

'No! I'm just going on this walk, with Drew – and everybody. Is that such a big deal?'

'No,' said Emily, aware she had to tackle Billie's attitude before it became too entrenched. 'But do you think, when you come back, you could be a bit more co-operative? We should be able to work together, we're both sensible and intelligent women.' Emily didn't quite believe this but hoped she might encourage Billie's good nature by saying it.

Billie stopped.

'The thing is, Billie, if you don't help me a bit more James will fire you. If you put up with working with me you can stay and still see Drew, quite a lot. If you don't pull your weight you won't see him until the end of the season. And he might not think that highly of you if you get yourself sacked.'

'OK,' said Billie, not quite managing not to sound sulky.

'Thank you. I'd really appreciate that. I know I can learn a lot from you and I'd like the opportunity.'

Emily watched Billie climb the ladder out of their cabin aware she had given the younger woman something to think about.

'OK, Kate. Have you got a teddy or something you'd like to knit a scarf for?' asked Emily, getting ready to cast on some stitches. 'Or would you just like to learn to knit but not worry about knitting anything particular?'

'I do have a teddy.'

'And would he appreciate a red scarf? Or I've got these other colours.' Emily pulled her different balls of wool out for Kate to see.

'Or you could have a stripy scarf,' suggested Maisie. 'I've got these colours but it's thinner wool. More appropriate for a smaller creature – say a teddy.'

'But chunky is fun and it's quicker,' said Emily.

'Oh, do him a chunky one first,' suggested Maisie, 'and then, when you're a bit better at it, do another one on smaller needles.'

'Cool! Yes, let's have a chunky stripy scarf and then if I'm good at it, I'll do another one.' Kate was keen.

'Red to start?' said Emily, but very shortly she handed back the needles to Maisie. 'OK, I reckon you're more used to teaching knitting than I am.'

Kate was quick to pick it up and by the time Emily's dough was ready to knock back the knitters had gone on to the first change of colour.

'Well done!' said Emily. 'You're getting on brilliantly.' Glancing at Maisie, she saw she was getting tired. 'Are you up for some baking now?'

'Oh yes! I fancy making focaccia.'

'Kate!' said Emily. 'When I was your age I hadn't even heard of focaccia. What's wrong with fairy cakes? Or at least bread rolls.'

'Boring,' said Kate. 'Women always want me to make fairy cakes.'

Emily wondered what this meant, exactly. Who were these women? 'Oh, OK, no fairy cakes, but I do have to make bread rolls so we'll do that as well as focaccia. Have we got a recipe, I wonder? Otherwise we're sunk.'

Emily spread a cloth under the table to prevent the floor becoming covered with flour. She gave Kate the task of weighing out the ingredients, measuring the yeast and water. The little girl seemed advanced for her age in the matter of cooking, possibly because she lived alone with her father. Or possibly it was because of the mysterious 'women'.

While Kate was levelling off spoons and watching the scales so the exact amounts were reached, Emily prepared the evening meal. She had found and defrosted some venison the night before and was now trimming pieces of venison and cutting up vegetables for a casserole. She hoped it would be stew weather when everyone came back from their walk but in the Highlands, you couldn't really tell. It was sunny now, but it could easily be raining by suppertime.

Maisie had retired to her cabin for a rest but Emily found that Kate was useful and good company. She handled knives fairly safely and Emily felt reasonably confident that she could put Kate in charge of the carrots without blood being shed.

Kate knew more about focaccia baking than Emily did. 'I watched it on telly. You have to add all the water.'

'OK,' said Emily. 'You're the expert here.'

Kate frowned. 'I am only nine, you know.'

'I know, but I haven't watched focaccia on telly like you have, and just because you're only nine, it doesn't mean I know more than you do about everything.'

Kate seemed to find this opinion rather startling.

When the stew was simmering and the focaccia dough was rising and they'd cleared up as best they could, there was a lull in the proceedings.

'So what would you like to do now?' Emily asked Kate.

'I don't know,' said the little girl. 'What can I do? Have you got games on your phone?'

'A few, but really, I think we should do something a bit more interesting than that.' Emily had a think. 'I could show you my room but I expect you've been there lots of times. You probably know the puffer better than I do.'

'I haven't been to your cabin often,' said Kate, 'because mostly I'm with Auntie Becca and her boys.'

'OK,' said Emily. 'As Billie's not here, we can go and look at where I sleep.'

'It's not very big,' said Kate once they'd negotiated the ladder. 'My room at home isn't huge but it's bigger than this and there's only one of me.'

'When I'm at home,' said Emily, 'I have a whole cottage to live in and I manage to fill all the space. But this is OK for now. I like the puffer.'

'Do you like my daddy?' asked Kate.

Emily didn't know how to respond to this. It was a bit loaded. 'Well,' she said. 'I hardly know him but I'm sure he's very nice.'

'So you don't want to marry him, then?' Kate was fiddling with Emily's make-up bag now.

Emily stopped herself saying that marrying Kate's daddy was the last thing on earth she wanted to do – it would sound rude. 'I've only met him a couple of times. We've hardly even spoken.'

Admittedly it wasn't only Alasdair's fault, having been sworn to silence by Rebecca, but Emily did still blame him for this. There was such a thing as being too strong and too silent in Emily's book.

Kate unscrewed the mascara – something Emily hadn't bothered with for a while – and pulled out the wand. 'It's just usually when ladies are nice to me it's because they want to marry Dad.'

'Really? Are you sure?' Emily was horrified.

'Oh yes,' said Kate. She seemed to take it in her stride. 'Auntie Becca says it's because he's so eligible but I'm not sure what that means.'

'Didn't Becca explain?'

'Not really. She was a bit cross when I told her what they say. But not with me.'

'I'm not surprised! Anyway, "eligible" means he's got a good job – people think being a doctor is a good job – and so he probably has a nice house. And he hasn't got a wife already.'

'My mum died.' Kate was now applying the mascara, using Emily's tiny mirror.

'I know, sweetheart. That's very sad.'

'It's all right. I don't remember her or anything, but I would like a mother.'

'Then you'd have to put up with some woman marrying your dad,' said Emily bluntly, not pulling her punches.

'I know. And I think Dad and I are OK on our own.'

'I'm sure you are.' Emily tried to imagine a woman moving into the home that Alasdair and Kate had forged out of the tragedy of his wife's death. It wouldn't be easy and probably shouldn't be attempted. Kate would hate having to share her father after all this time.

For some reason Emily suddenly remembered the trio of man, child and dog she had seen on the skyline that first morning, when she'd got up before dawn to explore. 'Have you got a dog?' she asked.

'Oh yes. He's with Aunt Becca. He's an Irish setter called Rupert.'

'And do you live near Crinan?'

'Yes. We have a house on the hill overlooking the harbour.'

'I think I saw you! You were walking with the dog and it was really early.'

Kate inspected her reflection and added more black. 'We do that in summer. Dad says it's bonding time. I say it's taking Rupert for a walk.'

Emily laughed. 'What will your dad say if you're wearing make-up when he picks you up?'

'Dunno. I've never worn it before.'

'I think you should take it off. Here, use this really nice stuff. It smells lovely!'

As Emily watched Kate slather herself with make-up remover and use nearly half a roll of loo paper to wipe it off she felt a bit deceitful. She'd let Kate put make-up on and now was making her take it off so her father wouldn't know. 'But we'll tell him you put it on, or he'll think I'm a bad influence on you.'

Kate regarded her, head on one side. 'Are you going to tell me what that is?'

'A bad influence is someone who encourages you to do bad things.'

'Is putting on make-up bad?'

'It is when you're nine years old,' said Emily.

'You're not wearing any and you're an adult.'

'I know. I don't wear make-up except for special occasions, when I'm going out. Not when I'm working. Talking of which, I should go and see how the bread's doing. Come on!'

As Kate threw Emily's make-up back in the bag, she said, 'You are sure you don't want to marry Dad?'

'Perfectly sure. I'm sure he's a wonderful man and lots of women would want to marry him but I just want to stay single, living on my own, pleasing myself.'

This seemed to satisfy Kate, who zipped up the bag and put it back in the net that hung above Emily's bunk, holding her possessions. 'So you don't want to have babies, then?'

Questions about babies could go off in any direction and Emily didn't want to risk this one going towards where they came from. She decided to head the question off at the pass. 'Just at the moment I'm more worried about the bread!'

As Emily followed Kate up the ladder and across to the saloon she hoped she had set Kate's mind at rest about wanting to marry her father. But as the two of them went into the galley to inspect the bread, Kate said, 'I'd quite like a baby sister. It's all boys round me.'

'Perhaps Becca's baby will be a girl and then you'll have a little cousin to play with. Now I think it's time this lot went in the oven.'

Alasdair arrived to collect his daughter before the shore party got back from their walk. Kate was sitting on the banquette with Maisie, getting on with her knitting. What with Maisie doing a bit and Emily doing a bit, the scarf was nearly finished.

'I see you've been busy,' he said, kissing his daughter's head.

'Yes. I've learnt to knit and we made bread and played with Emily's make-up. But she made me take it off because she thought you'd be cross.'

'I didn't quite say that, did I?' said Emily, feeling a bit caught out.

'Not exactly,' said Kate. 'But I knew what you meant.'

Kate, Emily decided, was very grown-up for her age. And very perceptive. Any woman her father fell in love with and really wanted to marry would have a very hard time. On the other hand, she would protect her dad from anyone who just saw him as 'eligible.'

All traces of flour on the floor and mess in the galley had been removed by the time Billie and the others came back. Something in Billie's attitude had changed.

'Hi,' she said. 'We picked wild raspberries. You can eat them yourself or put them in a pudding.' She put the plastic bag on the worktop. 'I'll go and change and take over dinner if you like.'

Emily didn't hesitate. She undid her apron and thanked Billie; then she went up on deck to look at her surroundings.

James joined her, leaning over the bow, looking at the hills. 'Here.' He handed her a tube. 'You might need this. Now we're stationary, the midges will gather.

'Oh, thanks,' said Emily, smearing on the cream. 'They've been OK so far.'

'They're not so bad when we're at sea but the instant we moor up, they pounce.' He didn't speak for a few seconds, looking at the scenery. 'Fabulous view, isn't it?'

'So far, they've all been fabulous views,' said Emily. 'Although for me they've been glimpsed out of the galley window. Or is it a porthole?'

'I tend think of portholes being round, windows being

anything with corners. But you must get out of the galley more. I had a word with Billie.'

'I wondered if you had. She sent me off out of the kitchen so she can finish dinner.'

'Good. You've been really busy, looking after my niece and Maisie.' James turned away from the view to look at Emily. 'It was really very kind of you and beyond the call of duty.'

'They looked after each other. We taught Kate to knit and had a great time. And I know Becca wouldn't have asked just anyone to do it but I am her friend and she knew I wouldn't mind.'

'She asked me to talk to Billie. Becca has lost a layer of tact since she's been pregnant and realised if she said anything to Billie she might say too much.'

'And we wouldn't want Billie walking out,' said Emily, with a shudder. 'I had a bit of a word with her myself.'

'Well, she seems to have got the message now. She's actually a really good deck hand and I'll employ her next year like a shot.' James smiled. 'She might not be so keen if we don't have Drew.'

Emily smiled back – young love was rather sweet. 'And she's good in the kitchen, too. So I'm glad she seems to be on the same team as the rest of us now.'

'Becca felt she was a bit untidy,' said James.

'Becca has very high standards. I do too, for myself, but not so much for others.'

'So you taught Kate to knit? That's clever!'

'Maisie did most of it. She's taught all her grandchildren to knit.'

'It's good for Kate to have some female company,'

James went on. 'But she can be a bit prickly if she feels any woman has designs on my brother.'

Emily laughed. 'Maybe that's why we got on so well! I made it quite clear that I do not have designs on your brother. Nice as he is,' she added quickly.

'So you're a confirmed spinster, then?'

Emily made a face. 'Spinster refers to spinning, and I'm a confirmed knitter.'

'A knitster?'

'Mm. Good – I like that.'

'So why haven't you been snapped up, as my mother would say? If you don't mind me asking.'

'I don't mind. It's really to do with my work. Very irregular hours. My last boyfriend got a bit fed up with me never being there in the night and having to sleep during the day. I could see his point. We parted as friends.' She glanced at her watch. 'I've got time to either go for a short walk or look at emails before I get the table set for dinner.'

'Go for a walk. Captain's orders. You need the fresh air. But before you go, I wanted to thank you for leaving everything to help us out. Becca was so grateful and relieved.'

'I was thrilled to come. I needed to get away and this is really "away".' She gestured to the view. 'I haven't been here long but I really love it.'

'And it's not too much like hard work? And difficult sharing such a tiny space with Billie?'

'It's absolutely fine! And if you don't mind, I'll have that walk now.'

*   *   *

Refreshed from her walk, Emily went back into the galley just as Billie was about to mash potatoes. 'Shall I do that? Or would you like me to get the table set?'

'Maisie offered to do that,' said Billie, 'so mash the spuds if you like. Or see to your emails. Your phone beeped.'

'I'll just see what it is and then help you.'

There was an email from Sally, the midwife she worked with.

Hi, love, hope you're having a great time up there with the midges. All v. well here. Local GPs are giving us more support now. It's this thing about home births being safer than hospital births. Even had a mum come to us who's signed on with your GP mate Derek Gardner. Who'd have thought it?

She emailed back. *I expect Derek feels it's all safer now I'm not there any more!* She added a bit more about what she'd been up to and signed off.

But she found herself a bit ambivalent about the email. How come things were going better for local midwives in her home town now she was no longer there? And Derek Gardner referring patients when they'd had that awful row?

She heard herself giving an audible 'Hmph'.

Chapter Five

Life settled into a routine that seemed to suit everybody. In between cooking and copying out the faded pattern Maisie had given her, Emily familiarised herself with the puffer.

When she'd first arrived she'd found the vertical iron ladders a bit of a challenge. But soon she found herself swinging up to the wheelhouse and down to her cabin as if she'd been doing it for years. She got to know the engine room a bit too. Bob, the engineer, got her stoking, showing her how to throw the coal into exactly the right spot. Although she was ready to retire to her galley quite soon, she did now understand why the passengers paid good money to spend a week in a boiler suit, shovelling coal. Their companions got the beautiful scenery, the sea birds and, sometimes, the seals. They just got sweaty and covered with coal dust and loved it. She also learned what 'ashing out' was when she saw it happen. Hot and sweaty engineers, some paid, most not, hauled huge buckets of hot ash from underneath the boiler. This activity was accompanied by lots of shouting and calling out for lime juice. Billie showed her that this was delivered in pint mugs, and everyone involved needed at least two mugs of it.

The wheelhouse was different. It was quiet there, and calm. There was quite often someone ensconced with James, chatting to him, learning to steer, or just looking out of the window.

Emily loved being up there. The view was a bit like watching a film. While there wasn't much plot, the backdrop was ever changing and the chances of seeing a seal, or a something, kept up the interest. She began to understand the fascination of being at sea.

Emily's own duties were a bit more taxing. Copying out Maisie's pattern took time and concentration. It was very much folded and repaired and the ink was fading. She felt she had to have a clear copy before Maisie went home, or she'd have no one to ask when she couldn't work out what she was supposed to do next.

She got Maisie to look at it when she had finished.

'Och, my dear, I can't read the pattern!' she said, amused at Emily's optimism. 'Haven't been able to for years. It's all in my head!'

Emily felt a bit let down. She'd been relying on Maisie to check her transcript for errors.

'It's just an insurance policy,' Maisie explained. 'If I forgot what I was doing I could ask someone to check I'd got it right.'

Emily laughed. 'Maisie! The chances of you coming across someone who could read and understand a Fair Isle pattern are tiny!'

'But I met you, didn't I? And you're going to manage just fine.'

There was no arguing with that. Emily put away her pattern and went to fetch Maisie a glass of sherry.

Saying goodbye to Maisie was a real wrench. Emily had got so fond of the old lady in the fortnight she'd been on the puffer. She'd got on well with all the passengers and was sorry to see them go but Maisie was special. They'd spent a lot of time together and although she seemed perfectly well, there was a fragility about her that Emily found a bit poignant.

'I'm going to really miss you, Maisie!' said Emily after breakfast on the day Maisie and her son were leaving.

'Not nearly as much as I'm going to miss you!' said Maisie. 'It's grand to have company – and not just because you looked after me so well. I'll miss us knitting together.'

While Emily had been getting her head round the Fair Isle, Maisie had been knitting clothes for Kate's teddy, her painful hands better able to knit small items than adult versions. She and Emily had agreed he should have a jumper to match his scarf.

'Do you not have friends who knit?'

Maisie nodded. 'But they live far away and we don't see each other often. When we do, it's at a party, so we're blethering, not knitting.'

Emily felt this was a shame but as there wasn't anything she could do about it she didn't comment further.

'And you,' Maisie went on. 'You must give up this feminist nonsense about being single. Get yourself a good man and have a baby. You'll always regret it if you don't.'

'Well, if a good man comes along, I'll set about getting him, but until then, I'm happy on my own.'

'Don't leave it much longer. You're no spring chicken!'

'Maisie!' said Emily, who didn't know how to react to this. Then she laughed.

Later, when she helped Maisie off the puffer and they shared a hug, she found herself weeping a little bit. She and the rest of the crew waved Robert and Maisie off in their taxi home and then she cleared her throat. 'Come on,' she said, 'beds to change. There'll be another lot coming tonight. We must be ready.'

The puffer schedules were not all the same. Depending on where they were going and where they needed to pick up their passengers, the cruises were different lengths. They were preparing for a five-day cruise now so when they'd done the beds, Emily and Billie were going to take a taxi to the nearest town and do the shopping. Although Rebecca had offered to do this (resting was all well and good but she was getting bored) they had insisted that they do this one themselves 'because we mustn't get too dependent on you', Emily had said.

Emily had made a list, planning out the meals: starters, main courses, puddings; lunches; and breakfast ingredients. Billie took hold of it and looked at it critically.

'Don't let's buy anything we can't freeze. We might meet some fishermen.'

'Good plan. We'll get some venison for a casserole though. I like to have some things already made in the freezer. It's a security blanket.'

Billie laughed. 'Not room for much in the puffer's freezer.'

'Better than nothing,' said Emily. 'I remember Rebecca telling me they didn't have a freezer when they first started, or any help for the cook, so it was just her, making every meal from scratch, on her own, all the time.'

'Shall we get some pizza bases for lunch?' Billie suggested.

Emily considered for a moment and then shook her head. 'No, bought pizza bases would be wrong. We'll make our own.'

'They'd give you a sense of security, being there in the freezer,' Billie said with a sideways smile.

'No, we have a reputation to keep up. We'll either make our own pizza bases or have something else.'

Billie shrugged. 'If I were in charge I'd buy the pizzas and put some extra cheese on them and put that out.'

'That's possibly why you're not in charge, Billie,' said Emily solemnly.

Billie shrugged. 'You'll regret it!'

But as they left the shop, clutching several bags of food, Emily felt glad that Billie and she had come to a point where they could tease each other.

After breakfast the following day, when the new lot of passengers still felt like strangers and hadn't yet properly bedded into puffer life, Emily regretted her high-mindedness. An easy lunch would have been a boon and although she started making pastry she wasn't sure that the couple of large quiches she planned to make would actually be ready by lunchtime. Two passengers hadn't been happy with their accommodation, although to their great credit, they had been quite happy to swap over. This was a good solution but it entailed quite a lot of linen changing and recleaning, so Emily was behind schedule. Still, things were easy-going on the puffer and probably no one would mind.

She was rolling out pastry when Billie came into the galley, full of excitement.

'Never mind about the quiche! There's a fishing boat. Come and look!'

Emily tore off her apron and followed Billie up on deck. There was a fishing boat a little way away and the puffer's engine was slowing down.

'Lunch is on its way!' James called to Emily from the wheelhouse window. 'That fishing boat just got in touch on the radio to see if we'd like any langoustines.'

Emily instantly remembered when she'd first arrived and had been scared by the noise in the sink, only to discover it was full of live shellfish.

'Will you cook them?' she called up, hoping his duties as captain would allow a spell in the galley.

'Sure! Drew can take over. You'll do the aioli?'

'No probs.'

She didn't go back down below until the fishing boat and the puffer had come alongside each other and a huge bag of something rustly was handed across. Drew, who was in charge of the handover, offered a note in exchange. There was a lot of thanks and banter as the bin-liner full of shellfish as fresh as you'd ever get it was brought aboard and both vessels speeded up and went on their way.

'One of the joys of the job,' James said a little later, when he joined Emily in the galley. He was carrying the heaving bag. 'We'll find somewhere to anchor and then I'll be down to cook them. We just need a bucketful of aioli, bread and butter, bit of salad and we're done. It should be warm enough to eat on deck, don't you think? Then people can throw their shells overboard. Save us having a smelly rubbish bag.'

He made it all sound so simple, Emily thought, separating eggs.

And somehow it was. The passengers all carried their full plates up on deck and found a comfy place to sit. The wind dropped and the sun shone hotly on the eaters who were tossing prawn shells over the side with abandon.

'We could be in France or somewhere,' said Emily to James, who happened to be sitting next to her.

'But I'd rather be here,' he said.

Emily realised she'd rather be where she was too.

At the end of the week, Rebecca appeared on the puffer with Kate in tow just after the last passengers had disembarked. Late pregnancy seemed to have given her an unexpected burst of energy.

'Hi! Kate and I wanted a "nearly the end of the holidays" treat. My boys are being sporty with my lovely neighbour who's got boys the same age, Alasdair is working and so we're kidnapping Emily for the day.'

'Oh! Is that all right with you, Billie?' Although she hadn't been aware of wanting to get away now the chance to go beyond what she could see from the puffer was irresistible.

Billie nodded. 'Yeah. No one expected until tomorrow afternoon and we've stripped the beds. You go off and enjoy yourself.'

Emily realised Billie probably appreciated the chance for a bit of privacy. Her going off for the day meant Billie and Drew could spend time together, even if part of that time was spent working.

'OK.' Emily turned to Rebecca. 'Where are we going?'

'It depends. Have you finished that pullover for Maisie yet? I know you haven't had long to do it.'

'I have done it, as a matter of fact. Much to my surprise. I had a good long go the other day when everyone went for a walk and Billie made dinner. I'm rather pleased with the way it turned out.'

'Oh, that's brilliant! Well, I think we should go and deliver it to her.'

'Do you know where she lives?'

'Of course,' said Rebecca smugly. 'Come on then, get yourself ready and we'll be off!'

'This is so much fun,' said Emily. 'Not that I wasn't having a good time on the puffer but it's lovely to see a bit more of Scotland.'

'It is nice to get away,' Rebecca agreed. 'When we first started the business – before we had the boys – we used to go week to week with no time off in between. But after that first year we realised we'd never be able to keep going. We took on a galley slave and I trained up some friends to take over the cooking sometimes. I do miss it when I'm not there, but it's hard work.'

'It is, but I love it. Billie's being really great now, which makes such a difference.'

'Now.' Rebecca pulled off the road. 'If you look over there' – she pointed out of the window – 'you can see the ancient Kingdom of Dalriada, which was the most important of the seventeen ancient kingdoms of Scotland. The view hasn't changed since the year 999 when the last crowning of a king of Scotland happened before the crowning ceremonies were moved to Scone.'

'That sounds like a guide book.'

Rebecca nodded. 'I memorised it so I could tell the passengers.'

'Actually,' said Kate from the back, 'there are two kingdoms of Dalriada. The other one is in Ireland.'

There was silence from the front. 'You should get out more,' said Rebecca. 'You spend too much time with your dad.'

Emily turned round to see how Kate had taken this rather harsh criticism and saw that she was smiling with a mixture of smugness and mischief. This was obviously not the first time Rebecca had implied her young niece was a bit old for her age.

'I like history,' she said.

'Actually,' said Emily, 'I do too. But only the bits I'm interested in.'

'We don't do much history at school,' said Kate. 'Dad tells me stuff if he remembers.'

'He's a doctor,' said Emily. 'He'll have a lot of things on his mind.'

'He says that,' said Kate, obviously not entirely convinced.

'He is busy, love,' said Rebecca, starting up the car again. 'It's not easy being a single parent.'

'People always say that,' said Kate. 'But I don't see why. I'm very good.'

'I should imagine your dad loves being a single parent,' said Emily. 'Just you and him with no one else to complicate life.'

Rebecca started to say something and then stopped.

'That's what I think,' said Kate, having thought it through. 'But people keep wanting to change things.'

'It's just the same for me, Kate,' said Emily. 'I keep telling everyone I'm perfectly happy being a single independent woman but no one ever believes me. They think I must be wanting a husband really, if only I'd admit it to myself.'

Rebecca harrumphed, aware that she was one of those people. 'Well, I will just say, whatever else I've achieved in my life, nothing has been as satisfying and meaningful as my children. Now, let's move on. Maisie's waiting for us.'

For some reason Emily had expected Maisie to live in a conventional Scottish house, grey stone, white windows and a stag's head door-knocker. It was made of stone but otherwise it couldn't have been more different.

'Is this Maisie's house?'

Rebecca laughed. 'Yes. It's lovely, isn't it? It's a converted cow byre.'

The doorway was traditional, a stone porch with a tiled roof. But next to it was glass and wood. Where previously there would have been grey stone walls, small windows and low eaves, now there was a huge pillar of pale timber and next to it a wall of glass. French doors in the middle were surrounded by climbing roses. It was a wonderful combination of tradition and new design.

Before Emily could ask more questions about the building, Maisie opened the door, obviously delighted to see her visitors.

'Come away in.'

Enchanted, Emily went in. The room was big, with high ceilings; one end of it was a kitchen which turned into a comfy sitting room with a large wood-burner in the middle. At the other end, the entire wall was taken up with a cabinet full of small models.

Kate, less concerned with the pleasantries, ran over to it in delight.

Rebecca was taken up by greeting Maisie and Emily took the opportunity to look about her. There were windows down to the floor on both sides. Out of one side she saw a wild hill, above which wheeled a pair of buzzards. Through the other window could be seen a Mediterranean walled garden. It was so unexpected, somehow.

'Kate, dear,' Maisie said, 'if you're good I'll unlock the cabinet but don't tell any little boys they do open. You may take some things out and play with them and then put them back – a bit differently if you like but tidily.'

'What an amazing house!' said Emily a little later when the adults were sitting round the stove drinking tea and eating home-made shortbread. 'I love it!'

'It is nice,' said Maisie, sounding less than enthusiastic. 'But since my husband died I have felt a bit . . .'

'Not lonely, surely?' said Rebecca. 'You've got people all around you. Up at the farmhouse? And the barn?'

Maisie put down her cup. 'I have plenty of good neighbours but I do sometimes miss having a good old chat with someone I've got something in common with.' She looked at Emily and patted her hand, indicating she considered her one of those. 'Have you got something to show me?'

Emily, who had the pullover-back in her bag, shifted uneasily. She'd been so keen to do it, but now the time had come for her to present her work she felt as if she was going into an exam. 'Well, I've done it but I'm not sure you're going to like it.'

'Let me look!'

Maisie picked up her reading glasses and put them on, making Emily feel even more uneasy. She pulled the knitting out of her bag and handed it over.

Maisie inspected it. 'Kate, dear,' she said a moment later, 'can you bring me that little box by the door? The one with the drawer in it.'

Kate, who seemed to be having the time of her life in a very quiet way, quickly brought the box. Maisie opened it and produced the front of the sweater. She compared the two in silence. Emily wasn't near enough to see whether or not they were similar enough.

'That's grand,' said Maisie eventually. 'I only wish my dear friend could sew it up for me. I'm no good at that part these days.'

'Oh,' said Rebecca, full of compassion, 'has she – er . . .'

'Died? No indeed, but she lives too far away for me to see her. One of the downsides of this very beautiful

85

house is living so far away from my knitting pals. We're all so ancient we none of us drive.'

Emily frowned. 'That's sad.'

'What about public transport?' said Rebecca.

'Far too complicated and I'm too slow for buses. Now, more tea, anyone? Kate? Another of those strange drinks in a box?'

'Better not have another one, Kate,' said Rebecca. 'I don't want your dad telling me you wouldn't go to bed because you'd had too much sugar. I'm sure you could have a glass of water if you wanted.'

'She could indeed,' said Maisie. 'Emily, dear, would you care to make another pot of tea? If you just pull the kettle over on to the hot plate, it'll boil very quickly.'

'So you think the knitting is OK?' said Emily.

'It's fine,' said Maisie and Emily realised this was high praise. 'You've done quite well.'

Emily felt very happy. She'd worked hard and done a good job.

'Maybe I could sew it up?' suggested Rebecca.

'Have you done it before?' asked Emily, curious. 'I didn't think you were all that handy with your needle.'

Rebecca laughed. 'That's a polite way of putting it.'

'I'd like my friend Rhona to do it. She did the last one. And of course, Donald is my youngest grandson. There won't be any more knitting from me. At least not complicated knitting.'

'We could post it to Rhona,' said Rebecca.

'Or,' said Emily, who had been thinking, 'we could hire a bus and collect all your knitting friends and get you together.'

'That's a good idea!' said Rebecca. 'I could arrange that easily. We know a lovely man with a vintage bus for hire. He usually uses it for weddings but there's no reason why he couldn't drive round the place and pick you up.'

'I love bus rides,' said Kate, who had been sitting at the table playing with the model flowerbeds and flowers which Maisie had got out for her.

'You could come too,' said Maisie. 'And now you've reminded me you're there, I've got some clothes for your teddy. Do you remember? You knitted him a scarf. Well, I had some wool and knitted a jumper and a vest. Rebecca dear – in that knitting bag?'

Kate inspected the items. 'I'd really like him to have a jumper like Emily has knitted for your grandson.'

Maisie laughed. 'You'll have to talk to Emily about that.'

Kate turned her gaze on Emily, large-eyed and obviously not expecting a positive response.

'Oh, well,' said Emily. 'I suppose if I've done one I could do another. The needles would need to be a bit finer, I think.'

'Look in the bag,' said Maisie.

'I do like the thought of a tiny Fair Isle sweater,' said Rebecca.

'Your baby is getting a blanket,' said Emily. 'At least from me.'

'A Fair isle blanket?' said Rebecca, head on one side, eyes bright.

Emily was quick to disillusion her. 'Do you want this blanket for when it's a baby? Or a cushion cover for when it's at university?'

'Oh, OK,' said Rebecca, disappointed.

'Fair Isle wool would be too scratchy for a baby anyway,' said Emily.

'Would you really knit my teddy a sweater like this one?' Kate pointed to the pullover, looking unprepossessing in its unsewn-up form. 'He won't mind it being scratchy.'

'I'll give it a go. If Maisie can spare me some wool. Goodness knows when I could get to a shop to buy any.'

'For wool you have to go over to the press,' said Maisie.

'A press is Scots for cupboard,' said Rebecca.

'Go and have a rummage and see what you can find. It's not much use to me now,' said Maisie.

While Emily and Kate looked in the drawer dedicated to wool, Rebecca said, 'So, if we arranged a bus, you could get in touch with your friends?'

'Oh yes, we telephone each other all the time. Some of them email.' She said this with an air of pride.

'Golly. You should try that, Maisie,' said Emily. 'You'd find it really useful.'

'Do you think so, dear?'

'Yes. If I were staying up here I'd teach you but I'm sure someone else could.' Emily picked up another ball of wool. 'I think these are nice colours. What do you think, Kate?'

Kate shrugged, suddenly a bit sulky.

'Emily won't go away until she's done your teddy's sweater, love,' said Rebecca, interpreting Kate's change of mood.

'Of course!' said Emily. 'And it won't be for ages yet,

anyway. So . . .' She turned to Maisie, to give Kate a chance to recover her equilibrium. 'Where would you and your gang like to go on your bus?'

'Well,' said Maisie, 'there's the old chapel. We used to meet there in the old days. Have jumble sales, things like that.'

'Give me the address,' said Rebecca. 'I'll look it up and see if they could have you.'

'They'd have us,' said Maisie. 'We've been making them a banner. The kirk is due for a big anniversary this year.'

'Well, that would be fun!' said Emily. 'I can just imagine you all sitting round together knitting and nattering. We have clubs who do that, down south.'

Maisie's expression was scathing. 'We've been doing that for years. Only not recently.'

'We'll organise it,' said Rebecca. 'I need a project.'

'You do!' Emily agreed. 'Otherwise she'll be on to me,' she said to Maisie. 'She seems to think I can't be happy without a man and a baby.'

'Well, she's not wrong,' said Maisie.

'And it's so weird being a midwife and not wanting a baby of her own,' said Rebecca.

'Don't you like babies?' said Kate, adding her twopenn'orth.

'Honestly! Just because I don't want a baby of my own just now doesn't mean I eat them! I mean! It's not a crime, is it?'

But the three people watching her seemed to imply that it was.

Rebecca opened her mouth to speak but before she

could deliver another lecture there was a knock on the door and then it opened.

'Daddy!' said Kate, surprised. 'I wasn't expecting you. Have you come to pick me up?'

Chapter Six

'Well done, Alasdair!' said Rebecca. 'You got here!'

Emily felt a bit confused. Why hadn't Rebecca said anything about Alasdair coming?

'How good to see you,' said Maisie. 'Could we have more tea?'

Emily got to her feet automatically. Maisie was one of those people who managed to get people to do things for them and feel pleased about it.

'So what have you been doing, Daddy?' asked Kate.

Alasdair sat back in the armchair and helped himself to the shortbread that Emily offered with the tea. 'Well, I was at the hospital looking after a lady who'd had a baby.' He looked up at Emily, who was still holding the plate. 'Thank you.'

Emily felt herself blush. She wasn't sure if Alasdair knew she was a midwife.

'Was she all right?' said Rebecca.

'She was fine. Just a few stitches. First baby. Nothing to worry about. Now she can't wait to get home.'

'So why was she in hospital?' asked Emily before she

remembered she'd be better off staying silent. 'Did she choose to have her baby there?'

Alasdair frowned slightly. 'It was a first baby.'

'Emily is a midwife,' said Rebecca, flushing. 'And she's more into home births.'

Emily flushed now. 'I just don't think hospital is necessarily the best place to have a baby, when you think of the infections and things.' She decided to shut up while she was ahead. A heated argument between her and Alasdair about childbirth in front of an elderly lady, a pregnant woman and his daughter was not a good idea, from anyone's point of view.

Rebecca was less inhibited. 'I wanted a home birth but James talked me out of it.'

'Kate!' said Emily. 'Can you show me those garden things you were playing with? We ought to think about putting them back.'

'We have to go now, really, sweetheart,' said Alasdair.

'That's OK,' said Emily. 'It won't take me a moment to get things straight.'

'I want to put them back, with Emily!' protested Kate. 'I like playing with her, she's fun!'

Alasdair sent Emily the anguished look of a dad who didn't want to start an argument in public. He glanced at his watch. 'Really, darling—'

'I can do it, Kate,' said Emily. Kate looked as if she was going to cry. 'Maybe Maisie would let us play with the gardens another time?'

Kate stuck out her lower lip. 'Really? You're not just saying that in the way that grown-ups do?'

Emily swallowed. She wasn't in a position to commit

Maisie or anyone else. 'Maybe next time I have a day off, we could do something together? Even if we didn't have the gardens, we'd still have fun!'

Kate smiled. 'Cool! Will you ask her over, Daddy?'

Another anguished look from Alasdair.

'Of course I'm not sure when – or if – I'll get another day off,' said Emily.

'Of course you'll have another day off!' said Rebecca.

'And if we – Kate and I – asked you to . . .' Alasdair hesitated, searching for the word.

'Play,' Kate supplied.

'You'd come?' He glanced at his daughter, indicating it would be for Kate she'd be invited.

'Of course!' said Emily, also making it clear.

'That's OK then,' said Kate. 'Are we going then, Dad?'

'Well,' said Rebecca, when Kate and Alasdair had left and she and Emily had put the 'floral gardens' back in the cabinet. 'We must be off too. I've got to get my cook back to the puffer.'

'Well, it has been delightful to see you,' said Maisie. 'I do have visitors, plenty of them, but none as compatible. There's nothing like a wee girl to make you feel cheery.'

'Yes, indeed,' said Emily. 'I see so many tiny babies I sometimes forget how much fun they are when they grow up.'

'You see!' said Rebecca, pouncing on this admission. 'You do want children after all.'

'I don't!'

'Don't leave it too late,' said Maisie. 'All this choice about whether or not to have babies isn't necessarily a good thing in my opinion.'

'I quite agree,' said Rebecca.

'Well, I agree too, so we can part as friends,' said Emily. 'Now come along, boss. We need to go.'

Of course the parting took a while and was a little poignant, Emily felt. There was nothing wrong with Maisie – she was in good health now and in fair spirits – but she was fairly elderly and nothing was certain in life. She was very glad she'd finished the sweater so quickly and that it was all right.

She and Rebecca drove along in a friendly silence. Emily was looking out of the window, drinking in the scenery, when Rebecca said, 'So, would you deliver my baby for me? Ms Midwife?'

Emily shot her a look. 'No, I can't. Apart from every-thing else it would be against protocol for me to, and I'm on a sabbatical.' She looked at her friend more closely. 'Don't you like your midwife?'

'I do! She's fine but she's not you and she is very keen for me to go to hospital to have this baby. As is James.'

'Any medical reason?'

'Not that I know of. Of course I am a bit elderly – in their eyes – but basically they just think it's safer.'

'Recent studies have said that's not actually the case. Have you questioned them about it? No reason why you couldn't have a home birth in my opinion.'

'I think it's the distance from the hospital if anything goes wrong,' said Rebecca.

'Ah well, there you go then. And Alasdair would obviously be most upset with you if you had a home birth.'

Rebecca didn't answer for a few moments. 'I think

he would,' she said, possibly wishing she could say otherwise.

They'd gone a few more miles before Emily said, 'So no point in any more matchmaking then.'

'I wasn't!' said Rebecca. 'At least, not really. Well, only a bit,' she finished. 'But I do think you should give him another chance.'

Emily exhaled. 'Listen: I'm sure he's a perfectly nice guy, but even if we fancied each other like mad we'd never get over our philosophical differences. And we don't fancy each other like mad.'

Rebecca looked straight ahead. 'You don't know that.'

'Yes I do,' said Emily. 'At least I know I don't fancy him!' Actually, she had decided this wasn't completely true but if she gave Rebecca even a sniff of an idea that she might think he had a certain something about him she'd never hear the end of it.

'He may fancy you,' said Rebecca, still not even glancing at Emily.

'Even if we both did, Kate wouldn't hear of it. Correct me if I'm wrong but I imagine she's seen off several potential partners for her dad.'

Rebecca sighed. 'You're not wrong.'

'There you go. Now, are you going to have supper on the puffer?'

'I'd better get back to my boys. I've got to start thinking about everything they need for the new term.'

'So why does Scotland have different school holidays from England?'

'It's the potato picking. Traditionally they all had a

potato holiday in October so they could work gathering in the potatoes. James's dad remembers doing it.'

'Oh, OK. So when am I going to see these big boys of yours then?'

'There's a bit of a gap in the schedule coming up. I'll see what I can arrange. We might manage a sleepover or something.'

'I must say, although I am used to it now, and – what with working so hard and all the fresh air – I do go to sleep immediately, a night in a bigger bed would be a bit of a treat.'

'I'll arrange that. You deserve it. I'd have been so stuck if you hadn't come up.'

'Well, it works both ways. I really needed a complete change from everything and this certainly has been that. I've learnt so many new skills!'

'What, cooking you mean?'

'No! I knew how to do that before otherwise you wouldn't have hired me. No, I meant ashing out and Fair Isle knitting.'

Rebecca laughed. She knew perfectly well that no one would have asked Emily to carry buckets of red-hot ash so if she'd done it, it had been voluntary. 'Well, Fair Isle knitting is a skill that will come in very useful, I'm sure.' She was serious for a minute. 'It was really sweet of you to offer to knit Kate a sweater for her Ted. She's very fond of him.'

'He's a sweet teddy. And Kate is a sweet girl. Happy to do that thing for both of them.' She paused. 'You know I told you how useful I find knitting during a long labour? How it helps me listen to the mother? Well, weirdly, it's sort of the same on the puffer. When I'm knitting on the puffer, I'm usually with the passengers. Having something to do makes me feel I'm not just chatting and yet it is important to chat to them because it's part of their holiday, having someone different to talk to.'

'I knew you were the right person for this job!' declared Rebecca. 'You get things like that.'

Emily saw that there was a space in the schedule coming up in the middle of August, when the school holidays ended. But by the time the date arrived, Rebecca hadn't mentioned any sleepovers or trips to see her boys, so when James left to go home soon after breakfast, she concluded that the family were busy and she would just spend her free time catching up on her washing, and possibly giving her roughened hands some emergency treatment.

Billie wasn't going anywhere and neither were the engineers. Emily felt churlish for being disappointed. She'd set her heart on getting away.

Emily and Billie were both in the galley just before eleven. Emily was halfway through handwashing her jumpers (Billie had told her it was the only way to get your hands clean) when there was a call down the hatch and Kate appeared. She ran across the saloon to the galley.

'Hello! We're taking you out for the day, Emily. Auntie Becca said we must and you said you would if you had free time. Have you finished the sweater?'

Her father came down the steps into the saloon. 'Kate's

told you? You're to come out with us for the day? We're going to see the otters – although you don't always see them – then we'll have a picnic and then we'll have a sleepover. I've promised Kate. And you did say . . .'

Emily was suddenly desperate to get off the puffer and go and look for otters. 'I don't know if I can . . .' She looked at Billie. 'Would you feel abandoned if I went out for the day and stayed out all night?'

'Well, obviously, I would call you a dirty stop-out,' said Billie, who had no regard for Kate's young ears. 'But no, you go. And if you're having a picnic you might as well take the last of the crew cake. I'll make another one when you're off enjoying yourself.'

'Are you sure you don't mind?'

'Course not! If you wring them out, I'll even hang your sweaters up for you, and take them in if it looks like rain.'

'You really do want me to go out, don't you?'

'Yup.'

Emily felt a rush of excitement at the thought of getting off the boat and seeing a bit more of Scotland. 'Then come and help me get ready, Kate.'

'Daddy said I wasn't to ask,' said Kate, looking at her father, who'd picked up a discarded newspaper and was reading it, 'but did you finish the jumper?'

'There are a lot of words for sweater, aren't there?' said Emily, wringing out one of hers.

'Is that a yes or a no?' Kate was so serious Emily felt she couldn't keep her in suspense any longer.

'It's a yes,' said Emily. 'Why don't you go and say hello to Drew while I do this and then you can come and help me get my things together? We can try the jumper on Ted.'

Kate was delighted by the little pullover, which Emily had to admit was extremely sweet, and she gave Emily a hug. 'Now he needs a tammy to match.'

'What's a tammy?' asked Emily, hunting for her last pair of clean knickers.

'It's a hat,' said Kate, surprised. 'Didn't you know that?'

'I think it's probably a Scottish hat. I don't know much about Scottish things.'

'I'll teach you – if you make me a tammy for Ted. Now come on. Daddy will be waiting!'

Emily followed more slowly, wondering if she minded being bossed about by quite a small child.

Billie handed Emily a cake tin and some beers, hustling her off the boat as quickly as she could. 'You must be really desperate for some time alone with Drew,' said Emily, laughing.

'Yes. Now push off!'

Alasdair and Kate were waiting for her. Kate was jumping up and down, Alasdair leaning against the side of the car, holding a large red dog on a lead.

'Oh, you've got a dog! I'd forgotten,' said Emily, and instantly remembered seeing the little family silhouetted against the skyline on her first morning. Man, child and dog, all up before dawn.

'This is Rupert,' said Alasdair. 'He belonged to my late wife.'

Now she looked more closely she saw that the dog had white in his muzzle. A sudden vision of the three of them, man, dog and child, huddling together in their grief. She hoped they didn't still need to do that.

Kate chattered away in the back of the car while Emily put sad thoughts out of her mind and enjoyed the scenery. It was so beautiful, and ever changing. Mountains, rivers and lochs, they appeared and disappeared as they drove. Sometimes there was also sea in the distance, sometimes not. Eventually she said, 'So where are we going?'

'To a sea loch. It's a lovely spot. I have friends who live near and we can borrow their boat and row out to an island.' He glanced at her briefly. 'It is really unlikely we'll see an otter though.'

'Well, I thought they were fairly nocturnal anyway,' said Emily. 'Not that I know much about them.'

'Since their numbers have increased you do see them in the day more often, but you'd be lucky.'

Something in his voice made her smile. 'I promise not to cry if I don't see one.'

'I never cry if I don't see one,' said Kate. 'That would be just silly.'

'Now we've established that no one will be crying we can think about the picnic,' said Alasdair. 'It's a bit basic, I'm afraid.'

'What, no Scotch eggs?' said Emily. 'I'd have thought you'd have to have them. Because they're Scotch, obviously.'

'We've got ham sandwiches, and cheese ones,' said Kate. 'I made them, though Daddy cut the bread for me. I am allowed to cut bread when Daddy's there but he says I cut doorsteps and wouldn't let me this time.' She paused. 'How can you cut doorsteps out of bread?'

Emily sympathised. She'd been a literal-minded child herself. 'I think it just means the bread is as thick as a doorstep.'

'Oh.' This seemed to make sense. 'We've got sausages though!'

'I love cold sausages,' said Emily.

'These are cold,' said Alasdair. 'They are also raw. We're planning to cook them over the fire.'

'Surely you can't just light fires anywhere?' she said. 'Not these days.'

'We're fine where we're going. It's the perfect spot for lunch. Besides, the smoke helps keep off the midges,' said Alasdair. 'Nearly there.'

They left the car off the road and Alasdair handed out things to carry. 'Wellies for you,' he said to Emily. 'Put them on.'

A thought struck her. She knew she should ignore the idea but somehow she couldn't. 'They didn't belong to—' she began, sure it was the wrong thing to ask but suddenly squeamish about wearing a dead woman's shoes.

'They're Becca's,' said Alasdair. 'She told me you'd need them.'

'She's very bossy, that woman,' said Emily, undoing her shoes, glad of Becca's forethought.

Rupert seemed to know where he was going and was happily sniffing around. What must it be like, Emily thought, having your wife's dog, but not her? And what was it like for Kate? It wasn't the sort of thing you could ask and she'd already been tactless about the wellingtons.

Kate and Alasdair carried on taking things out of the car. Alasdair handed her a small rucksack, which she put on. Then he gave her a billycan that was stuffed with newspaper.

'Come on!' he said, and the little group followed their leader down the path to the shores of the loch.

'I've found a spraint!' said Kate importantly while Emily was taking in the view, listening to the curlews, waiting for Alasdair to finish fiddling about with the boat and loading it up with picnic paraphernalia. 'That's otter poo!'

Kate was very grown up for her age, Emily thought, but not so grown up she wasn't excited by poo. Which was a good thing.

'Lovely,' said Emily, feigning enthusiasm.

'It's good,' Kate went on urgently. 'It means they're here.'

'I am pleased,' said Emily. 'But although I'd really love to see an otter, its poo isn't quite doing it for me.'

'They reckon it doesn't smell like poo,' said Alasdair. 'It's full of hormones and things, leaving messages for other otters.'

'Clever,' said Emily. 'So what does it smell like?'

'Have a sniff,' he suggested.

'No, you're all right, just tell me. I'll believe you.'

He laughed. 'Some people say it's like jasmine tea.'

'Cool,' said Emily.

'OK,' said Alasdair. 'Emily, if you go and sit in the stern. Kate, you go in the middle and I'll push off.'

'Wouldn't it be better to have Kate in the stern,' said Emily, contemplating getting her leg over the side of the boat.

'No, we need weight down that end to help us get off,' said Alasdair.

'That'll be me in the stern then,' said Emily, and clambered aboard.

Alasdair pushed the boat until it floated freely and then leapt aboard. He was a fine figure of a man, Emily was forced to admit. It was nice to have the opportunity to admire him without Rebecca or anyone misinterpreting her interest.

'Everyone OK?' he asked. 'Let's get going.'

He manoeuvred the boat round so the stern was facing the island and Emily could look at it.

'It's quite far away, actually, isn't it?' she said. 'I didn't realise that before.'

'It's a good stretch,' Alasdair agreed, 'but lovely when you get there. One day, when Kate's a bit bigger, we'll camp there.'

Emily nodded. 'Like *Swallows and Amazons*.'

'Exactly. And maybe there should be a few more people, to make it fun.'

'Emily could come,' said Kate. 'I wouldn't mind.'

Alasdair seemed a bit embarrassed. 'Sometimes Kate—'

'It's fine,' said Emily. 'I can imagine how Kate must feel. You don't need to explain.'

Her reward was a surprisingly lovely smile. He wasn't a very smiley person and so when he did it made a big difference.

No one said much for a while until suddenly Emily caught a bit of movement. It was on the shores of the loch so it was quite far away. 'I think I saw an otter!'

'Grab the binoculars,' said Alasdair.

Kate pulled them out of a bag and then out of their case. She seemed practised at it. She handed them to Emily, who struggled to get them in focus. 'Why don't you look?' she said and handed them to Alasdair.

He rested his oars and took hold of the glasses. 'I think what you saw must have been a little dipper. They do look very like otters when they're swimming.'

'You might see a real one later,' said Kate kindly. 'You just have to keep looking.'

When they reached the island Kate took Emily into the wood to look for firewood. Her father had strict rules, she explained, and he wouldn't like anything that was too green, too big, or remotely damp.

'Surely it's all going to be damp,' Emily objected, feeling she would never find anything suitable and so be despised by her hosts.

'If you take dead branches that are still on the trees, they're the best. And ash is the best sort of wood.'

Emily followed the little girl and found once you got your eye in, you did spot the dead branches. 'This is fun!' she said, having hung on a large branch and got it to break off the tree.

'Daddy may say that's too big,' said Kate. 'But you're not to mind.'

'We'll need some quite big stuff if we're to cook sausages,' said Emily.

'Suppose,' said Kate, but still looked doubtful.

Alasdair had a good big pile of wood already and he was building the fire. He was obviously very experienced at it. He smiled at Emily as she added her wood to the pile. Kate was still on the hunt for the perfect dead branch.

'I hope it's all useable,' she said. 'Kate gave me very strict instructions about what I was to get and what to leave.'

'It looks fine.'

He seemed to be more relaxed now, as if being in the open air, making a fire, had had a calming effect and made him less serious.

'Pull up a rock,' he said, gesturing to the boulders that surrounded the fire. 'We have the fire here because there are ready-made seats. Putting picnic chairs in the boat seems like a step too far.'

'Although if you were camping it might be worth your while. If you were going to spend any time here.'

'Do you like camping?'

'I do and I don't. I hate the thought of a huge camp-site but as long as I feel safe, I love sleeping in a tent, waking up with the dew on the grass, a thread of mist over the water, all that stuff.'

'So, how about if it's rained all night and you can't even think about leaving the tent without your boots on?'

Emily nodded. 'A bit more challenging but as long as you can make a huge greasy breakfast, I'm still up for it.'

He didn't speak immediately. 'It's a shame you're only here until the end of the puffer season. We could come in the October holiday.'

Emily didn't know what to say. The thought that relatively soon she would be leaving all this and going back to her real life felt wrong somehow. What she wanted to do, suddenly, was to go camping with this man and his daughter. She shook her head to bring herself back to reality. 'I thought you felt Kate was a bit young to camp like that just yet.'

'She's a bit young if I'm the only responsible adult, but if there was someone else here, it would probably be fine. But it was just a thought.'

Before she had to think of something nice and neutral to say, Kate came running up. 'Can I take Rupert round the island, Daddy?'

'Got your whistle?'

The little girl nodded her head enthusiastically and gave a little peep on the whistle that was hanging round her neck.

'Off you go then!'

Chapter Seven

The fire was going well and Alasdair had threaded sausages on sticks from which he had peeled the bark. He had arranged stones so the sticks were supported and they were sizzling and spitting away enthusiastically. 'Lunch won't be too much longer now,' he said.

Emily had kicked off Rebecca's wellingtons and had piled up bags and cushions and made a really comfortable place to lie; she was looking at the view, allowing her eyes to close sometimes as relaxation came over her. Rupert had his chin on her bare ankle. It felt very nice.

Kate was building a cairn by the fire, choosing her stones carefully so they wouldn't fall down. When she was satisfied, she sat her teddy on top, still wearing his Fair Isle jumper.

'Won't Ted get a bit hot sitting so close to the fire, wearing his pully?' suggested Emily, drowsily. 'And it's such a lovely day.'

'No. He has a little cold on his chest and I don't want it to get worse.'

Emily looked at Alasdair whose eyebrows had raised. 'She didn't get it from me, I swear,' he said.

Emily laughed. 'Well, feel his forehead from time to time and if he's a bit hot, move him further away from the fire.'

Rupert got up and ambled to the water's edge and took a long drink.

'Would you like a drink, Emily? I've got some beers or there's elderflower? We'll have a brew later, or I could put the billy on now?'

'Have I time for a quick nap? Just ten minutes. I'm a good catnapper. Us midwives have to snatch bits of sleep when we can.'

'Better put some of this on, then.' He found a tube in the rucksack and handed it to her. 'I'm never sure if they really don't like the smell and keep away, or just drown in it. You need to slather it on.'

'James has this and we all use it,' said Emily, applying the lotion. 'It's good stuff.'

He nodded. 'You have your nap, then. I'll tell you when I've made the tea. Kate will butter the rolls to put the sausages in.'

As Emily settled herself and closed her eyes she found herself wondering how come she felt comfortable enough to fall asleep in front of someone she didn't know very well and probably didn't have much in common with. Although they did both like being outdoors, picnics, boats, nature, that would never be enough to sustain a proper friendship.

She was woken a few minutes later by Kate whispering in her ear. 'Look!' she said urgently. 'Otters! Over on the mainland.'

Emily's eyes snapped open and peered, trying to see where Kate was pointing. 'I can't see anything!'

'Here.' Alasdair handed her some binoculars. 'You see that pine tree? Just under there.'

It took Emily a few seconds to get her eye in and then she saw them. It looked like a little family, running along the shore-side.

'Kate, do you want the binoculars?' Emily kept her vision glued to the creatures playing across the water.

'You keep them,' she said. 'I've seen otters lots of times and I'm young, I've got strong eyes.'

'Alasdair?'

'Nope. I can see them again. This may be your only opportunity.'

A second later the little family slipped into the water and disappeared.

Emily lowered the glasses and sighed. 'That was wonderful! I never thought I'd see otters in the wild. Thank you!'

'We didn't actually lay them on specially,' said Alasdair, amused.

'But you brought me to a place where I might see them, and I did. I'm so grateful.'

'Whisht, now! Eat this.'

He handed her a sausage enclosed in a roll. As she took it a drop of melted butter landed on her leg. She took a quick bite.

'That is so delicious!'

'Oh, sorry, did you want ketchup? I have a few sachets somewhere.' Alasdair hunted in the rucksack.

'Not for me, thank you.'

'I want red sauce!' said Kate, coming up. 'Can I put it on myself?'

Alasdair agreed and, after watching Kate and the ketchup, Emily said, 'I think what your daddy meant when he said "yes", was that you could put the red sauce on your sausage yourself, not actually "on yourself".'

It took Kate a second or two to realise that Emily was joking although there was quite a lot of ketchup smeared about her person. Then she laughed. 'You are quite funny!'

Emily shrugged.

'Now what would you like?' said Alasdair. 'We have more sausages, as you can see, although I expect Rupert will eat at least one of them. We have a variety of puddings – shortbread, black bun, and—'

'Tablet!' shouted Kate. 'We have tablet!'

'Um – Kate – can you tell me what that is, please? I don't think we have it in England,' asked Emily.

'It's – well – it's tablet,' said Kate.

'It's a combination of sugar and butter that is probably fatal. It might have condensed milk in it too,' said Alasdair. 'That, like the shortbread and the black bun, were made for me by a patient – one who thinks being a single man, I can't cook and so am therefore likely to starve.'

'Ooh, annoying! Does it make you feel patronised?'

'No, it just makes me feel as if my granny is still alive.'

This was quite endearing. 'So, I know shortbread, black bun can wait, but I still don't quite see what tablet is?'

'It's like a very crisp sort of fudge,' Alasdair explained.

'It is delicious but so sweet you can't really eat much. Unless you're Kate, and she can only have what I give her.'

'It might make me hyperactive,' Kate explained.

'Scary thought.'

Kate nodded. 'And then I won't go to bed.'

'OK, bring on the tablet,' said Emily. 'I like to live dangerously! But I always go to bed.'

The tablet was as delicious as it sounded, and as sweet. 'Wow, that is good!'

'Black bun now?' suggested Alasdair. He offered a very richly fruited cake that seemed to have a pastry base.

Emily was already quite full enough. 'How long are we staying? I'd love to try some black bun later, with a cup of tea.'

'Fair enough. Would you not like tea now? Or something else?'

Emily smiled and nodded. 'I don't often say no to tea,' she said. 'At least, only after the first seven mugs.'

'Seven mugs!' said Kate, impressed.

'I told you I was a midwife,' Emily explained. 'Sometimes babies take a long time to arrive and people make me tea. It's what you do. That and produce boiling water. Although to be fair, not so much these days.'

'And so what do you do while you're waiting?' asked Alasdair.

'I knit,' said Emily, aware she might be getting into dangerous territory, given how some people regarded her habit. 'It's a multi-purpose activity. I get a scarf or some blanket squares out of it, the mother is reassured by seeing me do it – if I'm knitting all must be well – and . . .' She stopped.

'And? We're all ears,' said Alasdair.

Emily hesitated. If she told him the next bit he'd dismiss her as an airy-fairy radical midwife, which in many ways she was, but she didn't want to spoil an almost perfect day by starting an argument. 'You promise not to laugh?'

'OK,' he said.

'But can we laugh if it's funny?' asked Kate.

'It's not funny,' said Emily, although she was smiling – Kate was so entertaining. She took a breath. 'When I'm knitting, looking at my hands, not at the mother, I can hear better. It makes me "all ears", sort of. If there's even the slightest change in the sounds she's making, I'll know, and I'll know if it's time for another look.'

There was the tiniest pause. 'Kate? Would you like to fill the billy from the burn? You know how to do it?'

'Dad! I've been doing it since I was about three.'

'I couldn't just have the tiniest bit of shortbread, could I?' said Emily, absolving him of the need to comment.

It was an exceptionally clear day and although the air temperature wasn't particularly high, the sun was, and Emily lay, feeling the sun on her face, thinking how lucky she was. She had a lovely job, in one of the most beautiful parts of the world, and right now she was enjoying a picnic with a very sweet little girl and her father, who, though a little stuffy, was also very nice.

Her mental description baulked at the word 'nice'. It didn't really cover him. He was kind, his treatment of

112

Maisie proved that, and he was a brilliant and lovely dad – she'd witnessed that all day. But somehow he'd revealed very little of himself. I'll just lie here in the sun for a few more moments, Emily decided, then I'll make an effort and find out what sort of books and films he likes. Maybe music . . .

'You fell asleep, again!' said Kate indignantly. 'The billy's boiling. It's time for tea and black bun.'

'Oh, sorry, sweetheart. I'll do something more exciting than sleep after tea, if you like, if there's time?'

She looked at Alasdair, who'd been reading a book in between tending to the fire and getting the billy going.

'We ought to start heading off at about five. It's only three now so there's plenty of time for fun things before we pack up.'

Emily accepted her mug of tea. Alasdair had taken time to produce it, making sure the water was really boiling before adding loose leaves and boiling it again, three times (to make the tea leaves sink, Kate explained) before tipping it into the mug and adding milk.

'OK, now the black bun. You don't have to eat it if you really don't want to, but the patient concerned knew I was taking you for a picnic and made it specially. She'll want a report.'

'I don't think I've ever seen anything so full of fruit,' said Emily, accepting a piece.

'You can't eat a lot of it, so it's good for picnics or walks. With a bit of that in your pocket and a burn to drink from occasionally, you're all set.'

'Is it OK to drink water direct from the burn?' asked Emily.

'Well, it's good to check it for dead sheep or deer first,' said Alasdair. 'But James and I have been drinking from streams all our lives and have never taken any harm from it.'

'You and James don't sound much alike, do you? Your accents, I mean.' Emily had talked about this with Rebecca but she wanted to hear Alasdair's explanation.

'We both speak posh or more local perfectly well, but when James went to uni it suited him better to be less regional. He worked in London for a bit afterwards so he lost the burr.'

'I think it's a shame,' said Emily. 'I like the accent.'

He hesitated for only a second but it seemed significant. 'I'm glad.'

It was too late to backtrack; she couldn't now say it was only Alasdair's accent she liked. 'I mean,' she blundered on, 'I think it's nice to have the dialect of the place you come from.'

'Where do you come from, Emily? There's nothing in your voice to give a clue.'

'That's my point. I come from the Home Counties and sound as if I come from the Home Counties.' Emily was aware she was being apologetic. 'But I've been living and working in the Cotswolds for a few years now so I always say I come from there. I do in my heart. Home is where the heart is, after all.'

'And does your heart have a home in the South-West?'

Emily frowned. 'Is that a roundabout way of asking me if I'm single?'

He raised an eyebrow briefly. 'I'm not sure, to be honest, but are you?'

'Yes, and I intend to stay that way, at least for the moment.'

'Why is that?'

She glanced at Kate who was a little way away, searching for the perfect stone to take home with her. Knowing she couldn't overhear her, she said, 'Why are you still single when your wife died years ago?'

He didn't answer immediately. 'That's hard to pinpoint.'

'I'll tell you!' said Emily, hoping she didn't sound too urgent. 'It's because it's much easier and less stressful to live on your own, when you can order your life as you please, drink the coffee you like, leave your clothes all over the bathroom floor if you want to, without anyone commenting, or questioning, or criticising.'

'You sound as if you've been in a bad relationship.'

Emily nodded. 'Yes. Haven't you?'

Too late she realised this was a huge assumption and this time the pause was agonisingly long and Emily couldn't think of a way she could break it without sounding like an idiot.

'Yes,' he said. 'Yes I have. And I do see what you mean, perfectly.'

'Everyone has been in a bad relationship, haven't they? Unless they're ten – or like Rebecca and James. They married really young and seem fine.'

'They are the exception, I think,' said Alasdair. 'Relationships don't often work as well as theirs does. I think perhaps it's because they work together in the same business. They're a team: not just a married team, a working one.'

'Mm.' Unwillingly her mind went back to the bad

relationship she'd been referring to. In her early twenties she'd been with a man who cared about her but who was also controlling; he was jealous of her life and her friends and wouldn't join in with either. He had been heartbroken when she broke up with him and she had been devastated by his heartbreak. She had wondered often at the time, and still sometimes since, if it was better to be the one who was left or the one who left, knowing the price of your freedom was someone else's pain and bitterness.

She was just about to ask Alasdair about Kate's mother when Kate appeared, giving her what Emily felt was a testing look. 'Will you come and build a dam with me? It does mean getting your feet wet and the water's awful cold.'

'I'll put my boots back on and then I won't mind cold feet,' said Emily. 'And I loved making dams when I was little. Haven't done it for a while but I'm sure it's like riding a bicycle.'

'Why would making dams be like riding a bicycle?' asked Kate curiously, leading the way to the burn. Although, having secured her dam-building assistant she was prepared to be relaxed about them saying odd things.

'It's an expression,' Emily explained. 'People say you never forget how to ride a bicycle and so anything that you can still do when you haven't done it for ages is the same – like riding a bicycle.' She paused. 'I probably haven't explained that very well.'

'You haven't,' Kate agreed. 'But I think I got it.'

* * *

'I haven't had so much fun in years!' said Emily a little while later, soaking wet and shivering.

She and Kate had created a very lovely miniature loch, set about with suitably miniature boulders and a fore-shore to rival any either had seen. A stream trickled in and out of it and Kate and Emily were very pleased with both it, and themselves. They'd broken bits of larch twigs off a larger fallen branch and created a grove of trees and pressed flat pebbles into a road leading down to it. They kept adding bits and fiddling with it until they deemed it perfect.

Ted, slightly too large for the scale, was seated next to a bonfire on the miniature shore-side which Kate was going to light as soon as she'd wrested the matches from her dad.

Alasdair, who'd been reading and birdwatching while the dam-building went on, came, matches and news-paper in hand.

'Wow, that is amazing!' he said, impressed enough even for the civil engineers who had created the marvel. 'You've got everything in miniature, even a road.'

'Emily's really good at it,' said Kate generously. 'She made the beach all on her own. It's for the otters to run along, she said.'

'Miniature otters,' said Alasdair.

'Fairy otters,' corrected Emily.

'With wings?' suggested Alasdair.

'Yuk! They'd be like insects. No wings,' said Emily.

'But look at you both! You're soaking! Kate, you've got a change of clothes, but what about you, Emily? I'm not saying you'll catch a cold sitting in wet jeans all day but you'll be extremely uncomfortable. Have you got anything else you can put on?'

Emily mentally reviewed the contents of her overnight bag. 'My pyjamas? They'll do. I'll go behind a rock and change.'

'I'll build up the fire and see if we can dry off your jeans a bit.'

'When we've lit Ted's bonfire,' said Kate.

'Oh, don't do that until I'm there to see,' said Emily. 'Maybe do it now. I'll be OK wet for a bit longer.'

Emily got out her camera and looked through the viewfinder. 'He needs a billy,' she said. 'Otherwise he's just sitting by the fire warming his toes. Ah, I know: we had KitKats! KitKat paper will be ideal.'

Luckily the silver paper hadn't been screwed up into too tight a ball and Emily was able to flatten it out and create a perfect little billycan. She used a piece of grass to make a handle.

'OK, this will burn when we light the fire but if we're quick we can take photos before it does. Have you got a camera, Kate?'

'No,' said Alasdair. 'She hasn't.'

'OK, use mine. I'll use my phone,' said Emily. 'I'll set the camera up for you, Kate. Then, when we're all ready, Alasdair will light the fire and we'll click away.'

Kate was beside herself with excitement and took dozens of photos of Ted by the fire as the billy was gradually demolished by the fire.

They all took lots of shots and showed each other the results. 'I declare Alasdair the winner,' said Emily. 'He got the last shot while the billy was still recognisable. Now I must get out of these wet things.

Emily had bought substantial, decent pyjamas before she came to Scotland, knowing she would be sharing the accommodation and a bathroom with others. Thus, although it was a little odd wearing them in front of people she didn't know that well, she didn't mind too much. But since her jersey was also quite wet she was still shivering a bit.

'Here,' said Alasdair, throwing her a jumper. 'Put this on. It's spare. Becca taught me to always take spares. I've got socks, too, if you want them.' He felt around in his rucksack and tossed her a pair.

Emily took the bundle gratefully and went behind a rock to change.

'Wool is the only fabric that still keeps you warm even when wet,' she said on her return, finding a perch next to the fire. 'The same cannot be said for denim.'

'Indeed not,' said Alasdair.

'I don't suppose we'll get these dry before we have to leave,' Emily went on, shaking out her jeans, 'however much you build up the fire. I'll have to spend the rest of the day in my jammies.' She didn't mention she was also wearing damp knickers. He didn't need to know that.

'Well, we'll get them as dry as we can. We can finish them off later.'

He rigged up a washing line with a length of rope he had in the rucksack and soon it was hung with steaming clothes, Kate's and Emily's.

'They say fire and water don't mix,' said Emily,

warming herself by the flames. 'But actually, they mix rather well. I've had so much fun today thanks to them – and you both.' She encouraged Rupert to come a little nearer to her, for extra warmth.

'I think it's oil and water that aren't supposed to mix,' said Alasdair.

'And chalk and cheese?' suggested Emily.

'I think that's different,' said Alasdair.

'Grown-ups talk a lot of nonsense sometimes,' stated Kate, addressing Ted and Rupert, who wagged his tail in agreement.

'You are not wrong, sweetheart,' Emily was forced to agree. 'Now find me a piece of tablet to make my happiness complete.'

They had packed up all their things, which seemed to have multiplied somehow, loaded them into the boat, and been rowed by Alasdair back to the mainland and the car. Loading the things into the car also seemed more time-consuming, especially as most things were now damp. They had driven for about half an hour when Alasdair said, 'Now is the point of no return. We've reached a crossroads. I can take you back to the puffer or you can come back with us and have a sleepover.'

Kate was fast asleep in the back of the car. She wouldn't notice the car going the wrong direction. Emily did wonder if spending the night with Kate and Alasdair would make her too involved with them as a family. But she was already pretty involved with them. 'I promised Kate I'd stay, and having been sleeping in something roughly the same dimensions as a coffin since I've arrived, the thought of spreading myself all over a proper bed is far too tempting to turn down.'

'You haven't found a day of being with me and Kate too much for your good nature? You could cope with another few hours?'

'I think I could.'

Alasdair smiled and set the car in motion again. 'I'm glad. I could have made it all right with Kate but she would have been very disappointed.'

'She's a lovely girl. I've had such fun spending time with her.'

'But not so much fun playing with her dad, though?'

Emily laughed. 'No. He's not nearly so much fun.'

Emily's wet clothes were put in the tumble drier and she was given fresh thick socks and slippers to wear as well as the jumper she already had on. Glancing at herself in the mirror as she went through to the kitchen Emily was glad she wasn't trying to impress Alasdair. She looked a fright, with her hair all over the place and profoundly unflattering clothes.

'Can I help with anything? Kate's watching telly and doesn't seem to need company.'

'Well, I don't need much help but would be glad of company. Glass of wine?'

'Oh, yes please. Are you sure I couldn't peel the spuds? I'm really good at it. I've had loads of practice lately.'

'That's why you shouldn't peel them. You need a break from cooking. Just sit there and drink your wine. I'll put some music on.'

She suspected he wanted the music to avoid having

to make conversation but she was perfectly happy. It was gentle and sometimes a bit haunting with a Celtic feel she found she loved.

'This is nice,' she said. 'Who is it?'

'It's a local band. I play with them sometimes.'

'You play an instrument? And sing?'

'Bit of both. I'm a fiddler. Play a bit of penny whistle if the need arises.'

'Oh, wow! That's – I don't know – not what I expected.'

'From the dour Scottish GP?'

She had to laugh; it was so close to what she'd been thinking. 'That's it.'

'Us Celts, we're like icebergs, there's a lot more under the surface than there is showing.'

Eventually Alasdair declared the meal ready and Kate was dragged away from *How to Train your Dragon*.

'Pheasant casserole – without the bones, Kate – mashed potato and cabbage,' he said, taking two hot plates out of the oven and one cold one for Kate.

'This is delicious!' said Emily, having taken her first bite. Alasdair added wine to her glass. 'Did you make it? Or was it a patient?'

'I made it, but it was a patient who gave me the pheasants. It's been in the freezer a while, it not being pheasant season, but none the worse for that I don't think.'

'It's wonderful. Especially with such buttery mash.'

'My daddy puts a lot of butter in mashed potatoes,' said Kate. 'We like it like that.'

'And so do I!'

Later, after Kate had bathed and gone to bed, Alasdair

came into the sitting room where Emily was going through his DVD collection.

'I know it's a bit rude, but I don't suppose we could watch a film, could we? I've wanted to see *Local Hero* again ever since I've been up here.' It wasn't like they were on a date or anything.

'Good idea! I'll get the fire going. It's got chilly.'

'Probably because it's such a clear night,' said Emily.

'Here, wrap yourself in a blanket till the fire gets going. There's a dribble more wine left in the bottle. Shall I open another one? Or would you prefer whisky?'

'A dribble of wine but don't open another bottle.'

Halfway through the film she said, 'This has been such a lovely day. Thank you.'

'You're welcome,' he said, and pulled her to his side.

She closed her eyes. His closeness felt natural, right – and very, very lovely.

Chapter Eight

Emily had only just got off to sleep. Lying in the sun with her eyes closed during the day had made her less sleepy than usual. She was awoken by Kate rushing into her room. 'They're here! They're here! The Merry Dancers! You must come!'

Emily followed the little girl out of the room at speed, not sure if they needed to evacuate the house.

Kate led her into the sun-room, where the huge picture window gave a view over the bay, with the Paps of Jura in the background. Alasdair was there. Emily calmed down – there was no emergency but something else.

'Hey!' he said softly. 'Come and see. It's the Northern Lights – terribly rare in these parts at this time of year.'

'Have I time to go back and get a jumper?'

'Possibly not. Here, wear this.' He handed her a pullover so soft if felt like fur. She recognised the slight feltiness of much-washed cashmere. She put it on and it smelt of him. It could have been expensive cologne or fabric conditioner but either way, she liked it. 'You do seem to have an endless supply of jumpers,' she commented.

'It's all anyone gives me for presents. Now look!'

They were all standing in a line in the sun-room, gazing at the phenomenon before them. Emily was in the middle, flanked by an open-mouthed Kate and Alasdair with a camera, trying to capture something of what they were experiencing.

They were not the vivid colours Emily had seen in pictures, but far paler, like moving watercolours – mostly water and very little green and sometimes a tinge of pink – long fingers of coloured light playing an invisible instrument reaching to the sky and beyond.

'Why did Kate call them the Merry Dancers?' Emily breathed when it no longer felt sacrilegious to talk.

'It's what they're called in Shetland and Orkney,' Alasdair explained. 'My parents liked the expression so much they passed it down to us.'

'Have you seen them before?'

'Once, as a boy. James and I were woken by our parents to see them. I woke Kate.'

'Would you have woken me?'

He laughed very quietly. 'I would have done if I'd had a chance but Kate was there first.'

'I didn't want Emily to miss them,' said Kate.

'I'm so glad,' said Emily, feeling almost tearful. Then she said, 'Remind me what they are again? Scientifically?'

'It's the solar wind colliding with particles from the earth's atmosphere. I once saw them from a plane, coming back from Miami. That was truly spectacular, but somehow this is more special.'

'Why?'

'Because it's so rare. In Scotland, in the summer.'

'Like true and lasting love,' she said and instantly could have bitten off her tongue.

He sent her an earnest glance. 'Indeed.'

'I really don't know where that came from,' went on Emily quickly, desperate to explain. 'I think I was just overcome by the moment.'

There was a pause. 'That's fine. It's a perfectly normal reaction.'

Emily didn't know if she was relieved by his response or a bit annoyed.

The lights only lasted a few more minutes and Kate gave a shuddering sigh. 'That was magic, Daddy. People say magic doesn't exist but that was magic, wasn't it?'

'It certainly was,' her father agreed. 'But maybe when people say magic doesn't exist they just mean it's very, very rare.'

'I can say I've seen them now, can't I? I've seen the Merry Dancers?'

'You can. But now, you must pop back into bed.'

'Oh!' Kate's disappointment at this suggestion was audible.

'Tell you what,' said Emily. 'When I was little and I didn't think I was going to be able to sleep, my mother used to give me hot chocolate in bed. I always used to be asleep before I finished it. I liked it in the morning too, as it would have gone all thick.'

'That sounds a good idea,' said Alasdair. 'We've got drinking chocolate, I think.'

'I'll make it,' said Emily. 'You have to whisk it with a fork or something, to make it fluffy.'

'We don't usually go in for such high-tech refine-ments,' said Alasdair. 'We just add the milk and stir.'

'You go and get Kate all tucked up ready,' said Emily. 'And I'll bring the hot chocolate.'

Finding her way round other people's kitchens was part of a midwife's stock-in-trade. You might never know when you had to make tea and toast – or whatever – for exhausted parents. Alasdair's, being very tidy and organised, was easy to negotiate. She was soon bringing a mug which was obviously Kate's – given it had a picture of Katie Morag on it – along to where she could hear Alasdair reading a story.

'Here we go,' she said quietly.

'Stay!' said Kate imperiously, patting the bed. 'Stay and hear the story.'

Emily perched and listened as Alasdair's deep voice with the faint Scottish burr she'd admitted to liking told a story about a rabbit, a squirrel and a mole who were lost and then the sky lit up and they found they were very near home; they'd been rescued by the Merry Dancers. Kate sat in bed, sipping hot chocolate, and Alasdair's voice got deeper and quieter. Eventually he took away the mug and set it on the side. Kate was asleep, but he finished the story. The animals had a picnic to celebrate their return home. It was all very sweet and just a little bit sentimental.

They both tiptoed out. 'You've got that down to a fine art,' said Emily. 'I'm very impressed. Most children I know don't go to bed that easily.'

'She doesn't always, I must admit. I think she was putting on a good show to impress you.'

'Me? Why?'

He shrugged. 'She likes you. You're fun. And more importantly you play with her for her own sake, not because you want to get to me.'

Emily opened her mouth to speak and then realised almost anything she'd intended to say would come out wrong. Denying she wanted to get to him would sound almost rude, and now, what with one thing and another, it was no longer entirely true.

'Right,' she said vaguely.

'Are you sleepy?' he said.

'No, not at all. It would take more than fluffy hot chocolate to make me sleep just now.'

'Then let's light the fire and have a dram.'

Alasdair's fire only took a puff of the bellows and another log to get going. Emily sat on the sofa near it, pulling the rug over herself and drawing up her feet under her. Rupert settled himself in front of it with a groan.

Alasdair handed her a glass. 'I hope you like this. It's from Islay.'

Emily breathed in the smoky fragrance. 'Did a patient give it to you?'

'No,' he said indignantly. 'I bought it myself, with my own money.'

'It's delicious.'

'Would you like an oatcake and some cheese to go with it?'

Emily sighed contentedly. 'Yes please.'

The sofa was squashy and, with two of them sitting on it, they were thrown together. Yet somehow this didn't feel awkward, and nor did it feel wrong when Alasdair's arm fell off the back of the sofa on to her shoulder.

'We shared something very special just now,' said Alasdair. 'In fact the whole day was special.'

'It was. I haven't had fun like that for ages. Playing with Kate was so much fun. Even when I was a child I didn't have many friends who liked that sort of thing. And obviously nowadays, it's even harder to find someone to make dams with.'

'She loved it too. She comes across women who give her presents, do weird things with her hair, but not many who play properly.'

Emily considered this. 'I think the advantage for Kate is that she hasn't met me through you, but through her Aunt Becca, and Maisie. You're just an afterthought.'

'Indeed.'

'I got the impression that Kate isn't keen on the idea of you having a partner. Which must be hard for you.'

'What Kate wants is the most important thing for me. It's not a big dilemma.'

'So, if it's not too painful, tell me about Kate's mum?' Emily wasn't sure why she described her like this, and not as Alasdair's wife.

'Oh well, she was very beautiful.'

'Losing her must have been just so tragic. I can't imagine anything worse than having to tell a little girl her mother has died.' She sipped her drink, suddenly feeling a bit tearful.

'It was horrible, of course, but maybe it would have been worse having to tell her that her mother had left her.'

Emily sat up. 'What do you mean?'

'I mean that when my wife left on that day – when she was killed in a car crash – she was on her way to meet her lover. She was leaving us.'

'Oh my God! Alasdair! That's awful!'

'To be fair, I expect she would have come back for Kate – she wouldn't have abandoned her forever.'

'Would you have let her have her?' Emily could only imagine the hurt and anger he would have been feeling.

'I really hope I'd have done what was best for Kate – she's not a possession, after all. But I would have been reluctant to let her grow up with a man who wasn't her father.' He paused. 'And of course they were going to live far away from here so access would have been difficult for both of us.'

'I don't know what to say.'

'Don't say anything. And also, you're the only person who knows this, apart from the man she was running to. I haven't told my brother or parents. They had enough to cope with without that as well.'

'So why did you tell me?'

He shrugged and indicated his whisky glass. 'This, I suppose, and because it won't matter to you. It's been good to be able to tell someone, actually. Everyone thought she was the perfect wife and mother. Actually she was prickly and very difficult to live with.'

'Quite a heavy burden for you all on your own.' Emily frowned into her now empty glass. 'Weren't you tempted to say something when everyone was commiserating with you?'

'Not really. I couldn't risk Kate finding out. I will tell

her eventually, of course, but not until I'm sure she's able to cope. At the moment she sees her mother as a sort of dream – someone who loved her very much and then died. And that much is true.'

'I do understand why you'd never want to have anyone else in the role of mother for her.' She gave a little laugh. 'Although it does mean you'll have to handle the birds and bees conversation on your own, which might be a bit embarrassing.'

'Emily,' he said, gently reproving, 'I'm a GP. I don't get embarrassed by periods.'

'I'm not sure that always follows. I think GPs can get just as embarrassed talking about these things to their daughters, but I'm glad. And you've got Rebecca to take her to buy her first bra and things.'

'I have.' Without asking her he added more whisky to their glasses. 'It's been good to tell you, though.'

'Why in particular?'

'Because you didn't know my wife, Kate's mother. You only see it from my and Kate's point of view.'

'Your family would always be on your side, Alasdair, I know that.'

'I know it too, but they loved Catriona for her own sake. I'd feel unkind marring her image when she died tragically.' He cleared his throat and drew a breath. 'So, your turn. Tell me about your bad relationship? Or was there more than one?'

She laughed gently. 'I'm thirty-five, I have had a few boyfriends, even with my uppity ideas about preferring to be single. There was one fairly recently who couldn't cope with my working hours, but only one serious one.

And I was the one who broke it up. I felt guilty about it for ages.'

'Why guilty? Did you cheat on him?'

'No, no! Nothing like that. I'd become part of his family, who were lovely, but things weren't right between us.'

'In what way?'

Somehow his questions didn't seem intrusive, but interested, and Emily was happy to expand. He'd shared something very private with her, after all. 'He'd become controlling. He liked me to dress a certain way – he wanted me to be more feminine, as he called it – wear make-up and short dresses. And he didn't like some of my friends.'

'Difficult.'

'And we'd stopped doing things together. One day, when we were shopping in Waitrose, which was the highlight of our week, I suddenly started to cry and knew I had to end it.' She sipped her drink. 'He was heartbroken, didn't see what was wrong. It was ages before I had any sort of relationship after that. I kept things very light. It is easier to stay single.'

She shifted her position and found she was leaning into the warmth of Alasdair's side. He pulled her in closer. She sighed and then he lowered his lips to hers.

After a moment of surprise she realised how much she liked the taste of whisky in his mouth, the smell of wood smoke from his sweater and feel of his hands on her body through her pyjamas.

She sensed this had never been his plan, to end up kissing her, and it certainly hadn't been part of hers, but now it was happening she didn't want it to stop. It was warm and sexy and altogether delightful. She found herself lying back on the sofa cushions being kissed with care and sensitivity. She realised she'd forgotten how lovely this could be.

Then he pulled back and sat up. 'This had better stop. It would be bad if Kate caught us like this.'

It took Emily a second to come to. 'Yes, of course.' She struggled upright, brushing her hair away from her face.

'I mean, I don't think she's going to walk in on us but she's already very fond of you. If she suspects we're more than friends she'll be devastated.'

'What? If she thought we were more than friends? She'd be upset?' She'd thought she and Kate had got on really well. Surely she wouldn't reject her as a girlfriend for her beloved dad?

He nodded. 'Yes. As it is – was – how it's got to go back to being – she'll understand when you go home. If she thinks there's more she'll feel abandoned all over again.'

Now it was set out for her she understood perfectly. 'I see.'

He seemed apologetic, obliged to explain more. 'She'll accept that as a friend, you have to go home after the holidays' – he chuckled gently – 'although it probably doesn't seem like a holiday.'

'Well – it does and it doesn't.'

'But if Kate saw us together – like this – she'd think it was forever and it's not even until Christmas.'

Emily ran her fingers through her hair. 'Yes, yes, I

133

absolutely understand and I'd never do anything to hurt Kate.' She cleared her throat. 'And I think this means I'd better go to bed now.' She smiled, she hoped cheerfully. 'See you in the morning!' She tried to sound casual and upbeat but in her heart she felt a sudden bleakness.

She lay in bed thinking about everything. It had been such a magical day – almost literally magical when she thought how extremely rare it was to see the Merry Dancers in the summertime. And lying in Alasdair's arms had been fairly magical too. She'd forgotten how lovely it was to be held, to be touched; while she was convinced the single life was for her, her body seemed to think it would be good to have someone else there sometimes. Just now it would be really lovely not to have stopped but to have brought things to their natural conclusion.

Annoyingly, Emily finally fell asleep when it was nearly time to get up. She realised she was late when tempting cooking smells came in under the door. She jumped up and rushed for a shower before she could be tempted to go back to sleep.

Still in her pyjamas, she went into the kitchen and found Alasdair and Kate in the kitchen making Scotch pancakes directly on the hotplate of the stove.

'Sorry I'm not dressed,' she said, 'but I need my jeans.'

'They're quite dry now,' said Alasdair, 'but of course it would have been better if we'd washed them and then dried them. They seem to have quite a bit of loch-side stuck on to them.'

'That's OK. I'll just pop back and get dressed properly,' said Emily.

'Don't be long! Or we'll eat all the pancakes!' said Kate.

As Emily pulled on her clothes, some of which were indeed a bit crispy and odd-smelling, she reflected that, judging by his relaxed manner towards her, Alasdair seemed to have wiped last night from his mind. She brushed her hair quickly and then went back to the kitchen.

Alasdair handed her a large mug of tea.

'Some people have metal things they pour the mixture into on the stove,' said Kate, who was standing on a chair with a jug of batter in her hand, 'but I like to have different patterns.' She paused. 'Though Auntie Becca has a heart-shaped one I quite like.'

Emily sat at the table, watching father and daughter cook. They had a routine all worked out and she didn't want to interfere with it.

She realised how near she'd come to interfering with it last night. She was fairly sure if she'd persisted Alasdair would have done what they both wanted and that would have been wrong. Neither of them were suited to casual sex, she knew that – her instincts were very certain – and so unless there was commitment between them there couldn't be a physical relationship.

'So have you got to go back to the puffer after breakfast?' asked Kate, who was now very sticky from maple syrup.

'I'm afraid so. I've had such a lovely holiday with you two. It couldn't have been better in any way.' Emily was fairly sticky herself and so got up to rinse her fingers under the tap.

'And we saw the Merry Dancers,' said Kate. 'It feels like a dream!'

'It was very like a dream,' Alasdair agreed, 'but I think we'll find that someone took a picture of them and they'll be up on YouTube soon.'

Kate became reflective. 'I don't think I want to see them on YouTube because then everyone would have seen them. I want it to have been just us.'

'Not even your cousins?' asked Emily, who, having washed her hands, was on to her third cup of tea.

'No. I hope they were asleep and missed them!' said Kate.

'Well, if they did, and don't believe you've seen them, you can tell them to look on YouTube,' said Emily. 'But I think you're right. I'd prefer to think it was just us who saw them. And the otters.'

'Everyone's seen otters,' said Kate.

'Not where I come from,' said Emily.

'So what's it like where you come from?' asked Kate, assuming it must be vastly inferior to somewhere that had otters.

'Nice! Lots of people – me included – love it. It has pretty stone houses, lots of trees, hills, views—'

'Chocolate-boxy?' said Alasdair, trying to sound unbiased but failing.

'Not the bit I live in, not really. It's full of real people doing real jobs and it has a fine industrial heritage.'

'What does chocolate-boxy mean?' asked Kate.

Emily went for this one. 'It's a quite old-fashioned expression.' She gave Alasdair a look. 'In the olden days boxes of chocolates often had pictures of thatched houses with roses round the door on them. But as they haven't done that for years and years, I don't know why people keep using that expression.'

'Sorry,' said Alasdair.

'Will you be sad to leave Scotland when you go back home?' Kate went on.

Emily realised there must have been some conversation about her departure before she got up. Probably a good thing.

'Of course I will. I've loved being here. But I'm not going just yet, Kate. I've got to stay until the end of the puffer's holiday season and then I'll probably hang around until Rebecca has had her baby.'

'So you're not going for a bit yet, then?' asked Kate.

'No. It'll be ages! I really hope we can have another day out together. I enjoyed myself so much.'

'And I did,' said Kate.

'Cool,' said Emily.

'Then we must make sure it happens again,' said Alasdair. 'Although I'm afraid we can't guarantee otters and certainly not the Merry Dancers.'

'Well, I've seen them,' said Emily. 'If I saw them again, it would take something away from this time.'

No one spoke for a few seconds.

'I loved us all seeing them together,' said Kate. 'You, me and Dad.'

'Don't forget Rupert,' said Alasdair, possibly trying to distract her from the familial image she had created.

'Daddy,' said Kate firmly. 'You know perfectly well Rupert was asleep!'

Chapter Nine

Kate and Emily continued to chat all the way back to the puffer. When she saw her aunt on deck, Kate ran towards her. 'Auntie Becca, we saw the Northern Lights! The Merry Dancers! Did you?'

'No!' Rebecca wailed. 'I was asleep. I am so disappointed.'

'I always sleep very deeply when I have time at home,' said James ruefully. 'So we only saw them on the internet.'

'Me and Emily aren't going to look at them on the internet,' said Kate proudly. 'Because we saw them in actual real life.'

'We did,' said Emily. 'You are allowed to hate us.'

'I don't hate you, honey,' said Rebecca, who, having hugged her niece, turned her attention to her friend. 'You didn't happen to look at your phone, did you?'

'Only once. Battery was flat as a pancake. Did you want me?'

'Um, I don't want you but I rather think you need to go home for a week. Nothing ghastly, no need to look so worried, but it's your house.'

'What's happened to my house?' Emily demanded.

'Your tenants had a barbeque and burned down next-door's fence.'

Emily exhaled hard. 'Honestly! Of all the things to happen!'

'I've had next-door and your tenants on the line. You need to sort it out but it shouldn't be hard. I've booked a stand-in chef, Jess – I have a few people happy to do it for a week or so but not for the whole season. And I've booked your flight.'

'Becca!'

'It's fine! I'll drive you to the airport when you've sorted yourself out a bit. That needs to be in an hour . . .'

'I've packed for you,' said Billie. 'No need to thank me. It wasn't hard. I just put all your clean clothes in your rucksack.'

'Oh, well, that gives me time to have a cup of tea, I suppose,' said Emily.

She had emerged from her cabin, having made sure that Billie had indeed packed for her and made some adjustments, when she saw Kate and Alasdair on deck, obviously wanting to leave.

Kate ran up to her. 'You will come back, won't you?' she said earnestly, looking on the verge of tears.

Emily knelt and put her arms round her. 'Of course, sweetie! I'm only going for a week and then I'm coming back until the end of the season and then until after Auntie Becca has had her baby.'

Kate hugged her very hard. 'That's OK then.'

Emily straightened up and saw Alasdair. 'I suppose

I'd better give you a hug, too.' And she did. For a second they just hugged and then there was an awkward kiss, both aiming for the cheek and somehow ending up half kissing each other on the lips.

'Now, you look after each other, you two, and you lot!' Emily's look took in everyone who happened to be on deck: Billie, Drew, James and Bob. 'I'll be back!'

She found herself unexpectedly tearful and stepped ashore quickly before anyone noticed.

'So, what was that between you and Alasdair?' Rebecca asked before the car was properly out of the car park near the jetty.

Emily sighed and decided she might as well tell Rebecca now; she'd only get it out of her eventually and she was obviously dying of curiosity. 'We shared a bit of a kiss after we'd seen the Northern Lights, but that was all.'

'You don't fancy him?'

'He doesn't fancy me. Or rather, I suppose he does, but doesn't see a future in it and so was sensible.'

'You'd have gone on?'

'I would have actually, I have to confess. But he said Kate might have found out about it and as I'm only here for the summer that wasn't fair on her.'

'That sounds like Alasdair. He's very careful about introducing women to Kate. She does take agin them so.'

'She didn't take agin me! We got on brilliantly. I haven't had so much fun since you and I used to get up to mischief all those years ago.'

'Then I see his point. If Kate likes you – and she obviously does—'

'And I like her! Really.'

'And you are only here for the summer, it would be cruel for her to even think you and Alasdair might be an item—'

'I'm not sure she'd put it quite like that, she's only nine.'

'—if you're going to leave her and her daddy, just like her mother did.'

For a second Emily wondered if Rebecca did know about Alasdair's wife being on her way to meet her lover and then decided not. It was difficult, knowing more about someone you didn't know well, really, than members of their family did.

'I do agree. We were probably just carried away with the moment, having seen the Merry Dancers and things.'

'So how did the day go before that?'

'Amazing! They took me to an island we had to row out to and we saw otters. And it was so beautiful. Really lovely. Thank you so much for arranging it all for me.'

'Actually, it was all Alasdair's idea. I thought it was a brilliant notion and knew that you'd promised Kate to spend time with her, but it was his idea to spend all day together and stay the night.' She paused. 'Perhaps he does fancy you.'

'I don't think so or he wouldn't have stopped while we were on the sofa together. It was all about Kate.'

'No,' said Rebecca. 'He fancied you – fancies you – and thought it would be nice to spend a day with you – for Kate too, obviously – but didn't want it to go too far.'

'Very sensible of him.'

Rebecca glanced across to her. 'Do you mean that in a good or a bad way?'

Emily shrugged. 'Good, probably. I think I just feel a bit rejected.'

Rebecca laughed, heartlessly in Emily's opinion. 'Get over it!'

Sally, Emily's midwife colleague, was holding a ridiculously over-decorated sign with 'Emily! Welcome Home' and hearts and flowers all over it. It was somewhat embarrassing. Still, Emily was pleased to see her friend and swung her bag over her shoulder and joined her. 'I'm only back for a week. No need for all this.'

'Yeah, but I told Cally you were staying at ours and she got over-excited. You know what little girls are like. And then I thought it would be fun to embarrass you.'

'Thanks, mate!'

'But really, I have so much news. All of it good! You will never believe it.'

'So tell me then.'

'Wait till we're home. I've got fizz to open.'

'The news is that good?'

'Definitely!'

A little bit later, her thinking power not exactly enhanced by two glasses of Prosecco, Emily said, 'Can you repeat all that slowly?'

'OK, pay attention this time. Since you've been away which is what – a month?'

'About that.'

'These things have changed. Number one, the powers-that-be are a whole lot keener on home and midwife-led maternity units. There have been statistics – everyone seems to love a statistic – saying what we already knew – that they're better and safer.'

'That's good.'

'Two, all the local doctors seem to have jumped on the bandwagon.'

'What? Blimey, that was fast. Even Derek Gardner? I'll believe that when I see it!'

'Well, you will see it. I bumped into him yesterday and mentioned you were coming back for a week and he made me promise to tell you that you've got to go out to dinner with him tomorrow.'

The bubbles that had been so much fun a second ago seemed suddenly to go flat. 'Sally! Why?'

'He wants to apologise for being so awful at that home delivery where the husband came home unexpectedly.'

'I don't have to go out to dinner with him for that! He can just say sorry – or not. I really don't care.'

'Well, he wants to take you out – but that's not the really good news.'

'Really? You surprise me. I thought you were opening bottles of fizz to celebrate me getting a date.'

'Don't be daft. No, the really good news is the Mat. Unit is safe forever!'

'Really?' This was a surprise. 'You mean we're not going to be closed the moment the government want more cuts?'

'No! One of the trustees died. She was mega rich.'

'Oh, I knew about that. Imogen Strickland. She was a midwife. But that was a couple of years ago, surely.'

'Yes, but she left all her money – and there was lots and lots of it – to charity but the bulk of it is going to the unit! To keep us safe! And we can refurb, have all the equipment we need, properly support mothers who want a home birth – all the bells and whistles.'

'I know I've been away from midwifery for a bit but we didn't use bells and whistles in my day.'

Sally gave her a look and handed her a board, a knife and an onion. 'I was going to give you a complete break from cooking as I know you've been doing a lot of it, but for that, you can sit there and chop.' She looked stern. 'Besides, I'm a bit behind with dinner. I need the help.'

Emily smiled and accepted her task. 'Sorry. And this is really good news! In fact, it's amazing. I can't believe it.'

'At last!' said Sally, her hands held up in relief that finally her colleague was reacting appropriately. 'Now you understand the fizz!'

The following morning, with a very slight headache, partly caused by the Prosecco and partly by the prospect of visiting her neighbours, who were not known for taking anything calmly, Emily set off towards her house, via the WI cake stall. She hoped they would recognise this as a goodwill gesture and not an attempt to swindle them out their rights.

'Can you just tell me again what happened?'

Emily was the personification of appeasement, sitting in her neighbours' sitting room drinking tea. The cake she had brought was sitting on a doily, as yet uncut.

'Well, we were sitting in the garden . . .' began Mrs

Mitchell, whom she'd never quite managed to call Elsie although they'd been neighbours for three years now.

'I wasn't,' said Mr Mitchell, whom she did sometimes call Reg. 'I was in the greenhouse, watering the tomatoes.'

'And all of a sudden we were aware of smoke!' Mrs Mitchell had a sense of drama, Emily had to concede. 'We thought it was just the barbeque at first. They had friends over, there was drinking . . .' Her opinion of people who drank was made clear by her expression.

'Of course it was just the barbeque at first, dear, the smoke,' said her husband.

'But then it got worse! The smell! I can't be doing with those hot spicy sauces. If you want a barbeque, what's wrong with a sausage?'

'The fence caught fire,' said Mr Mitchell, keeping to the facts. 'And it's our fence.'

'I called the fire brigade,' said Mrs Mitchell. 'Reg said there was no need, but you can't take chances, can you? And they came straightaway. Lovely, they were, and do you know? Two of them were women?'

'Goodness, they'll be having male midwives next,' said Emily under her breath.

'As I said,' Mrs Mitchell went on. 'They were lovely but really, I don't think women should be firemen, do you, Reg? They should be doing something more feminine. No man wants to marry a woman who wears yellow rubber dungarees, surely.'

Emily considered. Put like that, it did sound a bit niche.

'So, what have you done about getting your fence replaced?'

145

'Your tenants,' said Reg, making Emily feel the respon-sibility of their misdoings sharply, 'your tenants said we should claim on our insurance, but why should we? We'd lose our no-claims bonus.'

'I quite understand. It's not your responsibility at all. I'll claim on my insurance,' said Emily, wishing they'd break out the cake. Only a sugar fix would get her through the rest of the conversation without her wanting to say a rude word.

'But it won't affect our insurance, will it?' asked Mrs Mitchell. 'If it does, it's not fair and we'll go through the small claims court!'

'It won't, really it won't. There's no reason why it should.' Emily realised she was using her special calming voice. Any minute she'd suggest Mrs Mitchell breathed through the contraction, as if Elsie was having a baby and not just making a big fuss. Then she realised it must have been frightening at the time and tried harder to feel conciliatory.

She cleared her throat. 'I am really sorry you've had this horrid incident. It must have been terrifying, but I'm here to assure you that your fence will be replaced by the insurance, and if any plants have been damaged and are for some reason not covered by the insurance, I will pay for them personally.' She got to her feet and walked to the door, abandoning the cake with good grace. 'I'll be in touch very shortly. Goodbye!'

Then she went round to see her tenants.

It was odd seeing her little house and knowing she wasn't currently living in it. Still, the front garden looked nice and tidy and there were a few more pots by the door. She knocked.

'Hello!' said Isobel, the female half of the couple renting. 'I am so sorry about this!'

As Isobel had taken the day off work so she could see Emily and was already apologising, Emily's annoyance over the incident started to diminish.

'Do come in!' Isobel went on. 'I've made a cake.'

Emily went into her home, so familiar and yet different. She looked around the sitting room. The paintings were not hers but looked lovely. The fire surround was dotted about with more plants and candles than she had had. There was a different rug and pretty cushions.

'You've made it look lovely!' she said.

'I really hope you don't mind,' said Isobel, still sounding flustered and guilt-ridden, 'but we gave the walls a coat of paint. We made sure it was the same paint.'

'No, that's fine,' said Emily, glad that the tenants she had been so sure were good really were. Setting fire to next-door's fence was obviously a blip.

'Do you want to come through to the kitchen? Would you like tea or coffee?'

Emily followed her hostess and saw a cake that looked far nicer than the one she had left with the Mitchells on the table.

'Tea will be lovely. As long as we can have cake. I was just next door and I brought one with me – from the WI stall – but they didn't cut it.'

'This is a Mary Berry recipe,' said Isobel, lowering a

large wedge of chocolate heaven on to a plate and putting it in front of Emily. 'What sort of tea do you like?'

'Whatever you're making would be lovely,' said Emily. 'Do you mind if I start?' A moment or two later she decided whatever her tenants had done she forgave them. 'This is so lovely! You might have to write down the recipe for me. My passengers on the puffer would love it.'

When she got up to leave a little later, everything resolved, she felt confident that her house was in good hands. It had transpired that no one had suggested that Reg and Elsie Mitchell should claim on their insurance, it had been a misunderstanding caused by one of them – or maybe both – not wearing their hearing aids. Once she'd sorted out the insurance she'd be done.

Emily had gone into town to see her insurance brokers and, having got through all the form-filling, was wondering if she should walk back to Sally's house or do some window shopping when she heard herself being hailed from across the street.

'Emily!' said a young female voice. 'How are you? Where've you been?'

She looked up and after a few moments recognised Susanna, the mother whose peaceful home birth had been interrupted by a grumpy husband. Then she had been red-faced and tired, with no make-up and her hair in a stringy ponytail. Now she was the picture of a Yummy Mummy and bouncing with health. As Susanna was accompanied by a pushchair, Emily hurried across the road so they could speak.

'No need to ask you how you're getting on!' she said when she reached Susanna. 'You look amazing! Not the wrung-out wreck lots of new mothers look like.'

'I'm very lucky. Clorinda only wakes a couple of times in the night and always goes straight back to sleep. So – what about you? I've been trying to get in touch with you and they said you were off for a while.'

'I'm on a sabbatical,' Emily told her, although as she said it she was aware that the word usually applied to something more peaceful and academic than cooking for passengers on a small steam ship. 'And here's the small person I never got to meet!'

Susanna smiled. 'She's called Clorinda. I'm really hoping that when she goes to school there won't be three other Clorindas in her class but there probably will be.'

'I don't suppose you've time for a coffee?' said Emily. 'I've just had a very boring time filling in forms and I need a treat.'

'Lovely!' said Susanna. 'Any opportunity to talk to an adult and I'm there! And I really want to catch up with you. Shall we go in here?' She indicated a café popular with young mothers because it had plenty of room for pushchairs and would give toddlers a small cup of foamy milk for nothing if the parents were going to be there for a while.

'Brilliant idea. I might have a giant meringue. I'm owed it, the day I've had.'

'Then if you don't mind taking Madam . . .' Susanna unclipped the baby from her pushchair and put her into Emily's arms.

'This is a bit of role reversal,' said Emily, looking at

the pale pink, crumpled little face. 'I'm usually handing little bundles over to exhausted mums, not the other way round. And she's a bit old for me. If a baby isn't red and screaming and covered with vernix, I don't know what to do with them.' As she spoke, the little bundle smiled and Emily melted. 'But oh, isn't she gorgeous?'

'Absolutely, almost all the time,' her mother agreed, folding up the pushchair with a neat kick and flick. 'Let's go upstairs. I can't usually, without a responsible adult.'

Emily laughed, holding Clorinda tightly to her as she followed Susanna up the stairs. 'I'm not sure that's what your husband would call me.'

'Possibly not. He panicked rather, I'm afraid. It comes from having an old-school obstetrician for a father.'

'I realised afterwards that I'd fallen out with the wrong dad! I didn't know about his father until too late.'

'No need to worry, actually.' She paused. 'Are you having some of that meringue?'

'Actually, I'm full of cake. You go ahead though.'

'I'll just get Clorinda settled first. And I've got some gossip.'

'Well?' said Emily when she felt she could. 'Tell all.'

Susanna, who now had her baby apparently stuffed up her floral top, glanced down at her feeding infant. 'Family scandal! Apparently he had an affair with a nurse that went on for years. It's all come out.'

'Oh no! His poor wife.'

Susanna acknowledged this with a shake of her head. 'Yes. Utterly ghastly for her, of course, but she's taking it very well. Actually . . .' She leant in. 'I think it's changed the power structure of their marriage. He was always in the right, knew best, bossed her about rather, but now she's much more assertive.'

'Well, that's something. Of course it is – was – certainly easy for men in powerful positions to have affairs. Even if they weren't being abusive in any way. Many women are attracted to powerful men.'

Susanna nodded. 'I know. But there's been good spin-off for me, too. My husband's been much less dominant and bossy since it's all happened. I think he realises his father's not a god and his selfish behaviour could have broken up his marriage. So he's being really nice. He'll have to go away again soon.'

'You must miss him?' Emily found her thoughts whizzing to Alasdair and Kate and brought them back under control. She was getting sentimental. It was probably due to Susanna and the baby being so gorgeous.

'Yes I will,' she agreed. 'I'm determined to do something constructive while he's away.'

'Do you have time, with Clorinda to look after?'

'Oh yes,' Susannah said confidently. 'I've discovered just how much I can do one-handed.'

Emily laughed. 'So breastfeeding is going well, then?'

'It's going pretty much non-stop, so yes! It's going fine.'

'So, what are you going to do?'

'I want to set up some talks for mothers – during the day so they can bring their babies – something to stop the brain-mush.'

This sounded a good idea. 'OK. So how will you make it work?'

'We'll get a supportive grandmother to keep an eye on the babies who aren't with their mums in one part of the building, and the talk will go on in the other. But there'll be free movement between them both so no one has to worry about their baby.'

'Hmm. You'll have to get speakers who are up for this sort of thing.'

'I know,' said Susanna. 'That's why I thought of you.'

Emily laughed. 'Well, I'm not quite sure when I'm going to be back in town, but when I am, I'll get in touch. I think it's a great idea.'

She walked back to Sally's thoughtfully. A few weeks away and things had changed so much in her home town, but as far as she could tell, all of it for the best. Which was great, really. So why wasn't she more excited about it?

Chapter Ten

Emily's positive feelings about what was going on in her home town diminished somewhat when she realised she had to go out to dinner with Derek Gardner that night.

'It's only one evening,' she said to Sally as she checked her appearance. 'I suppose I can spare that.'

'Mm. And that dress does look nice on you,' said her friend. 'I might have to give it to you.'

'Oh! Really? Doesn't it look good on you?' Emily was pleased with how well the dress suited her.

'Not as good as it does on you,' said Sally. 'On me it clings in the wrong places.'

'In clings a bit on me, too.'

'Yes, but in a good way. And you should never trust a thin cook.'

Emily made a face at her and looked at her watch. 'We'd better go, I suppose. Are you sure you don't mind giving me a lift? I could easily walk, or take a taxi.'

'Take a taxi back. And I don't mind driving you. I've a little lull at the moment. You know how it is with mothers – they all seem to have their babies at the same time. And Pete is here for the kids.'

'Let's go.'

Derek Gardner did look good in a suit, Emily had to admit. Although the restaurant didn't really warrant such dressing, he might have known that dark, formal lines improved him hugely. He got up as Emily approached the table.

'Ms Bailey – or may I call you Emily?' he said, kissing her cheek. 'This is so kind of you. I owe you such a big apology I wasn't sure I'd be able to get you to even hear it.'

Emily didn't really want to spend the evening hearing him grovel but supposed she'd better let him get it all off his chest. 'Of course call me Emily and of course I'll listen.' She sat down opposite him.

'Well, let's get you a drink first. They do marvellous cocktails here. Or champagne? Anything else?'

'Let's have a look at the cocktail menu,' she said, picking it up. She knew the sensible thing to have would be a glass of wine of some kind, or even a soft drink, but somehow she felt she deserved something more frivolous – and stronger. 'I'll have a whisky sour,' she said.

As she regarded Derek, really quite handsome in his suit, she thought about the last time she'd had whisky. She'd been with a man who was more likely to wear a kilt than a suit, and at the time had been wearing jeans and a cashmere sweater that had little bits of wood stuck to it, from when he'd made up the fire.

'What does that taste like?' asked Derek, having ordered it and a sparkling water for himself.

'Sort of like a hot toddy,' said Emily. 'Only cold. Whisky, lemon and sugar. It's delicious.'

'I'm not drinking at the moment,' said Derek. 'I think it had got a bit out of hand. I thought I'd give it a rest for a bit.' He smiled, a bit sheepish. 'I think it's made me nicer.'

At that moment their drinks arrived and, after an awkward toast, Emily took a sip. 'You know what? I think it works the other way with me. I think I'm nicer after I've had a bit of alcohol.'

Derek laughed. 'In which case, I'll get my apology over, in case you change your mind and it turns you into Medusa.'

Emily smiled encouragingly. This was going to be embarrassing, no matter what, and she wanted it out of the way. Then she could eat her dinner, chat politely, and then get a taxi and get back.

'I was completely out of order when I barged into that delivery, just because I was asked by the father. The thing is, William Redbridge – you know? The father's father? – was a sort of mentor of mine when I was training. Mind you, I gather now that he isn't quite the role model I thought he was.'

Emily nodded. 'We all make mistakes.'

Derek nodded. 'I'm not planning on making any more of them. I was always so prejudiced against natural births I never properly researched them. I have now. I'm ashamed I never made the time to do so before.'

This was genuinely impressive. 'Good for you.'

He nodded. 'I would never recommend home births in very remote areas, miles from medical help if it's needed, but round here, I see no reason why it shouldn't be offered as an option all the time.' He smiled, a little sheepishly. 'I guess you could say I've had a Damascene moment.'

Although delighted that Derek had turned around his ideas, Emily couldn't help being a little argumentative. 'Of course, not all mothers want a home birth. They want the calm, supportive environment of our wonderful maternity unit. Which I gather has inherited a lot of money.'

Derek nodded. 'It has. Enough to ensure its future. Mothers will come from miles around to give birth there, when it's had it's total refurb and a bit more equipment installed.'

'Mothers already came from miles around to give birth there. It's not all about the equipment.' Emily took a sip of her drink, hoping it would stop her being so spiky.

'I know,' said Derek, leaning forward. 'It's because of the amazing team.'

Not even in her present mood could Emily think of anything to argue about in this statement. 'Well, thank you.'

'But the team is going to get bigger and we need a team leader.' He looked at her meaningfully.

'You mean? Do you mean . . .? Derek, what exactly do you mean?'

'On behalf of the hospital board, I'm asking you to head up the team. Of course there will have to be a process: you'd have to apply, but if you did you'd get it. And we all want you.'

Emily's head swam a little and she knew it wasn't the cocktail. 'Can you run all that by me again?'

He obliged. Then he added, 'This is a wonderful job opportunity for you, Emily. And it would be wonderful for the unit, too. You could have all the equipment you needed, and more staff, too.'

'But what about Sally? We're a team, equals – and there are others who'd be just as good . . .'

'Currently you're the only one without family commitments. You're a little bit younger and a little bit better qualified. It's you we want. Our first choice.'

Emily knew she should be absolutely delighted. A promotion, heading up the team at a wonderful refurbished maternity unit. No more scrambling to get one of the few birthing pools; there'd be enough for all of them. Extra staff; maybe somewhere nice to have classes. It was probably just the shock. She'd be thrilled when she got her head round it a bit.

'I have commitments – I couldn't start for a while. I need a bit of time.'

'Of course, but I will need to know. If you turn this down – and I really hope you don't – we'll have to advertise soon.'

'So, how long can I have?'

'The end of September at the absolute latest. Oh, and Emily . . .'

'Yes?'

'Please keep this to yourself. At the moment it's all highly confidential.'

'Oh, OK.' Emily had been thinking it would all be all right if she could talk it through with Sally, make sure she wouldn't mind her friend suddenly becoming her boss. But now that wasn't possible. She was on her own with this.

'Now, I think we should eat. What do you fancy? The salmon is very good here.'

She ordered the salmon. Her head was so full of this job offer, she really couldn't concentrate on anything else.

A few days later, Rebecca was waiting for her at the airport.

'Becca!' said Emily, hugging her. 'Really! I could have got the bus. You shouldn't be driving long distances.'

'It's not that far and I'm not taking you back to the puffer.'

'Oh! What happened?' As Rebecca looked mischievous and happy Emily realised it wasn't a disaster, whatever it was.

'Maisie and her cronies are having a wee celebration and they want you there. They've made a special banner to celebrate Maisie's kirk's hundredth birthday.'

'I thought you looked smart in your Jojo Maman Bébé outfit! But how kind of them to want me there. And what brilliant timing. I could so easily have missed it.'

'Actually they planned to have it when you could come. It's all quite last-minute. We won't be there in time for the dedication in the kirk, but just right for the bun-fight afterwards.'

'And that's all right with the stand-in cook – Jess, was it? She doesn't mind staying on a bit longer?

'Oh yes. She's perfectly happy cooking for another day.'

'That's so flattering! But why? Why me?'

'It's me as well. We gave them the idea of getting together and they finally sewed up the banner they'd been making but somehow never finished. Anyway, it'll be a good spread,' Rebecca finished.

'There speaks a pregnant woman.'

'We thought it would be good to swing you straight back into Highland life.'

Emily couldn't help wondering if she'd ever been part of Highland life. Since her short time at home her time in the Highlands had seemed like a dream. A lovely and even faintly erotic one, but a dream nevertheless.

The dream-like feeling wasn't diminished as the scenery became more and more rural and beautiful. And while she looked out of the window she allowed herself to think about Alasdair. He was bound to be at Maisie's party, surely?

'So,' said Rebecca. 'How did you get on, down south?'

'Oh! Very well, actually. I confirmed that my tenants really are nice people who are looking after my house brilliantly and the fire was just a horrible accident, that my neighbours just got frightened and anxious about it all, but the best news is about the unit. It's inherited enough money to make its future secure.'

'And? There's an "and", isn't there?'

Emily nodded. 'Yes. I've been offered an amazing job. I can't talk to anyone about it down there, but it should be OK to talk to you.' She went on to relate the details.

'Goodness me, Emily!'

'I know. I should be thrilled but somehow I just feel daunted.'

Rebecca shot her a quick look. 'So why did this Derek offer you the job? You must be up to it. Unless he had an ulterior motive.'

'Like what?'

'He fancies you.'

Emily found herself blushing. Now she thought about it, there had been signs that he found her attractive during their dinner together. She'd been too distracted at the time to really notice. 'Well, I don't fancy him. Chemistry: it's either there or it isn't.'

'So what about Alasdair? Is there chemistry between you?'

Although Emily had told Rebecca about what had gone on after seeing the Northern Lights she realised there was a bit more to her question than her casual enquiry implied. 'Well, yes, I can't deny it, but nothing can ever come of it, so don't go getting ideas.'

Hearing her own words Emily realised how true they were and it made her a bit sad. Still, she reasoned with herself, there was nothing wrong with a little crush, even if it would come to nothing.

'I'm not really dressed for a do,' said Emily, changing the subject. 'I'd have worn a dress if I'd known.'

'I've brought you a dress,' said Rebecca. 'You can change in the Ladies.'

Although a quick scan of the car park showed no sign of Alasdair's car, Emily remained hopeful that he might be there. So far he'd only ever seen her in jeans or pyjamas and while it was only a crush that couldn't go anywhere, she did want him to see her looking a bit more dressed up. 'I borrowed one of Sally's dresses while

I was home and it went down a storm. She made me keep it. It's scrunched up at the bottom of my rucksack otherwise I'd drag it out.'

'This one is on the back seat, sort of ironed, given that I'm hopeless at it. I thought about bringing some linen trousers – rather like the ones you have on – but I'm a bit taller so I thought a dress was safer. It's quite short on me so should be knee-length and kirk-appropriate on you. Off you go!'

Rebecca pointed to a door that obviously led to a toilet block added on to the much older building of the hall that was next to the church. 'You're lucky. You can get into the Ladies without being seen by anybody. You change and I'll meet you out here. We'll go in together.'

'Ooh, you have scrubbed up well!' said Rebecca. 'Make-up and everything!'

'I thought I might as well. I won't be wearing it for the next month or so.'

Rebecca laughed. 'Let's go in. They're waiting.'

'Just before we do, will Alasdair be coming?'

Rebecca shook her head. 'No, I don't think so. No reason why he should really.' She sent her friend a querying glance. 'That wasn't why you put on make-up, was it? In the hope that you'd see him?'

Emily blushed. 'No! He's not the sort of man who'd be impressed by make-up.' This last part was true, but Emily knew men often didn't realise you were wearing make-up. They just thought you looked a bit better than usual.

They were greeted like celebrities. 'You're the young

161

woman who finished Maisie's pullover for her,' said the woman who was watching out for their appearance. She was in her mid-sixties, Emily guessed, and had merry eyes, a tanned skin and short, curly grey hair. She was wearing a multi-hued scarf that looked hand-dyed. 'I'm Isla. We've all heard about how she couldn't finish it and were so pleased for her.'

'I was happy to be able to do it – not only for Maisie's sake but because I hadn't done Fair Isle before and wasn't sure I could. Quite tricky, isn't it?' Emily allowed a cup of tea to be put into her hand.

'Have you knitted anything else in Fair Isle since?'

'Only a pullover for a teddy. Where is Maisie?'

'Over there,' said Isla. 'She's longing to see you. Her grandson is here too. You may be expected to marry him, even though he's probably a bit young for you.'

'My, don't you look smart?' said Maisie as soon as she saw Emily. 'You have got legs, then? You don't always wear trousers?'

'Mostly I wear trousers,' Emily admitted. 'When I'm working, that is. But this is a celebration and Rebecca brought me a dress to put on.'

'It's so kind of you to come when you're just off the plane. I find travelling quite tiring.'

'I'm fine! Delighted to see you and be here for your special celebration.'

Maisie patted her hand. 'Now, let me introduce you to a certain young man.'

As the young man was wearing a fairly familiar Fair Isle pullover it wasn't hard to guess it was Maisie's grandson. He seemed to be in his early twenties and very shy. Emily put out her hand. 'You're Donald? How very nice to meet you. I'm so relieved to see the pullover fits. It was my first attempt at Fair Isle.'

Donald blushed deeply. He was very tall and thin, with thick dark hair and eyebrows. In a few years, Emily decided, he would be very good-looking indeed. Right now he was too Bambiesque, all long limbs and lack of coordination. 'It's a grand pullover. Thank you so much for knitting it for my grandmother.'

'I only did the back. Turn round.' Donald obliged.

'It's perfect!' said Maisie. 'I wasn't sure you'd be able to do it but I'm sure not many people could tell I didn't do that myself.'

'I think she's proved herself just fine,' said Isla. 'She can be an honorary member of our knitting guild.'

Emily laughed, embarrassed. 'Oh, I don't know about that. I'm only in Scotland for the summer.'

'The summer might be long enough,' said Maisie. 'Now, let me introduce you to the rest of the gang.'

Emily thoroughly enjoyed herself. She met everyone there and as a friend of Maisie's was treated instantly as a friend of them all. Emily had always enjoyed the company of elderly ladies, especially when they were relaxed and full of stories. After all, she reasoned, you didn't get to be their age without gathering a bit of wit and wisdom on the way.

She was full of sandwiches, shortbread and sausage rolls, weak from having laughed so much, when Rebecca came and said it was time they were off.

'Before you go . . .' a younger woman came up to her. 'I'd just like to introduce myself. I'm Heather Morrison, the health visitor for the area. I'd like to say how wonderful you've been with all these old biddies.' She used the term with great affection or Emily would have been offended on their behalf. 'If ever you need a job as a health visitor, just let me know!'

For the second time Emily was disconcerted by someone assuming she was a permanent resident. 'I'm a midwife actually, but I'm only here temporarily. I'm working as a cook for Rebecca here.'

'Hmm.' The health visitor regarded Rebecca's well-developed bump. 'I'd have thought you'd be more use as a midwife!'

They all laughed. 'I'll be going home to my own maternity unit soon,' Emily explained. 'I'm not delivering Rebecca's baby, no matter how much she begs. I'm on a sabbatical and not licensed to practise up here.'

'Well, from our point of view that's a shame,' said the health visitor. 'There'd be plenty of opportunities to work up here for someone like you.'

It took Emily and Rebecca some time to make their farewells but just as they were near the end, Emily was aware of the door opening. Alasdair stood on the threshold outlined in sunshine. Emily's heart did an involuntary skip. She batted it down as she watched him enter the room.

'Hello!' he said to various of the women who were obviously his patients. 'I thought I ought not to miss out on what promised to be the party of the season.'

Emily wondered if she and Rebecca should take this opportunity to leave. They'd said their goodbyes and the ladies were distracted by Alasdair's arrival. She glanced at Rebecca but she was smiling at her brother-in-law and didn't seem desperate to go. If Jess was doing the evening meal on the puffer, there was no great urgency.

Emily wandered away from the group to go and look at the picture of the banner that was now in pride of place in the church. There hadn't been time to look at it earlier, she'd been far too busy socialising.

It was a lovely thing. Small panels representing different historical happenings, either of national importance or of significance to the community, were represented in embroidery, appliqué or in some cases Fair Isle. It made Emily smile. She could see from the photograph, which was a work of art in itself, that while the overall impression was of something quite naïve, the individual squares were very beautifully done.

'Hello,' said Alasdair from behind her shoulder.

'Hello! Rebecca said you weren't invited – or she gave that impression anyway.'

'The local GP doesn't need a special invitation,' he said. 'He can just turn up if he's got time.'

'Well, that's nice. There's lots of food left over.'

'I didn't come for the buffet, splendid as it is.'

'So why did you come then?'

'I thought I'd better just make sure you'd come back from wherever you went.'

'I went home. And I'm only here for the summer. I've said that a couple of times this afternoon.'

'I know. But I wanted to make sure you were here for the whole summer, and not just a bit of it.'

Emily felt her mouth go dry and butterflies start

Highland dancing in her stomach. 'I promised I'd be here and so I am.'

Before he could reply, Rebecca came up. 'Come on, Em, I must get you back. And my boys will need feeding. I've got them a wee food parcel.' She held up a bulging carrier bag. 'As usual, they cooked for a regiment of working men, not a bunch of old ladies who don't have much appetite. I do like that!'

'I'll be seeing you then,' said Alasdair.

'You will,' said Rebecca. 'We're related.'

'And Emily,' he said. 'I'll be seeing her, too.'

Emily found herself smiling inanely, not sure how to respond.

As she got in the car she wondered if it was really wise, seeing him while she was up here. It couldn't go anywhere. It would be impossible to keep the relationship going when she was home. He wouldn't move south; she couldn't move to Scotland: her work – her career – was based in the Cotswolds. And now she had that amazing job offer to consider – her chance to make a real difference to pregnant women, not only in her immediate area but for miles around.

A holiday romance would be all very well, but only if everyone knew it was just for the summer.

Chapter Eleven

Emily woke up feeling sad. It took her seconds to work out why. It was the second week of September and the last day of the last trip. Soon she would be leaving Scotland and going home.

She lay there and wondered why she felt sad at the prospect of going to her beloved home town, seeing her friends, possibly starting an exciting new job (she still hadn't quite made up her mind about it) and moving back into the little cottage she loved. It didn't make much sense, really.

She rationalised it as she scrambled into her clothes. She was leaving Rebecca and James, she was leaving Scotland – a place she had come to love – and, of course, she was leaving Alasdair.

There was no reason to be sad about the first two: neither Scotland nor Rebecca and James were going anywhere; she could come back as often as she liked. And Alasdair had only ever been a holiday thing. Really, she was being ridiculous.

She allowed herself a brief glance at the hills, colour-washed with purple now the heather was properly out, before heading for the galley.

The puffer was quite a way away from her home base and tomorrow a mini-bus would pick up the passengers after breakfast. Then the crew would take the puffer back to Crinan on their own: James had described this passengerless cruise as a sort of holiday. Of course the puffer had to be steered, the boiler stoked and meals cooked, but it was quite different from when there were passengers, however lovely and helpful those passengers might be.

'I'll get the kettle on,' she said brightly to Billie. 'We'll have a cup of tea.'

'I'll make it,' said Billie agreeably. 'I know you like a walk first thing. You go. I'll be fine.'

Emily hesitated for a second and then hopped off the boat and set off.

Once off the wharf she followed a rough track that led her to a footpath and on to the heather. She stopped to examine a single flower and marvelled that something that was individually so small could have such a dramatic scenic effect. She sighed and carried on.

Emily would hardly admit it to herself, let alone anyone else, but the reason she so valued her walks, apart from the exercise, was they gave her an opportunity to think about Alasdair.

In spite of what he'd said when they had seen each other at Maisie's party, she hadn't seen him since. Emily missed him and Kate terribly. She didn't really understand why. They didn't have a relationship and she'd always known it could only ever have been just a summer thing, so why was she still feeling like a teenager with her first crush? And why couldn't she just throw it off and put him out of her mind? She had so much else to think about! Should she take this job, which would be exciting and terrifying but also a chance to really make a difference? Surely she shouldn't even need to think about it! Of course she should take it. Only someone without an ounce of ambition would turn it down.

And although she did think about it, Alasdair and Kate kept intruding into her sensible plans about how to get the team to feel OK about her being promoted and what equipment she should buy first.

Over the past weeks she had longed to ask James why Alasdair hadn't called in on the puffer recently but feared he might pass on her casual enquiry to Rebecca, who would make a lot of it. Rebecca would either then worry that Emily was going to get her heart broken or try and throw her and Alasdair together in a well-meaning attempt to hook them up.

She had heard from Kate though. James, who went home when he could to make sure Rebecca was well and not overdoing it, came back one day with a picture for Emily. Kate had drawn a bonfire, with hills behind and a teddy bear sitting next to it. The teddy was wearing what, with a bit of imagination, could be recognised as a Fair Isle pullover. The teddy had a speech bubble saying, 'Where's my tammy!'

Emily had accepted the challenge, got in touch with Maisie for some pointers as to how to make a tam-o'-shanter for a teddy and got to work. The passengers had been very amused to learn what she was knitting on such small needles with such a complicated pattern.

'You know why it's called a tam-o'-shanter, don't you?' one male passenger said to Emily as she was knitting, half an eye on the galley where her soup should be coming to the boil any minute.

She smiled brightly, certain she was about to find out. This particular passenger had a great deal of knowledge and felt it was his bounden duty to make sure everyone in his vicinity had the opportunity to hear it.

'So why is it called that?' Emily did quite want to know but she – and everyone else present that week – was a bit fed up with the Walking Encyclopaedia, as she and Billie privately dubbed him.

'It's after a character in a poem by Robert Burns,' he said, possibly hoping she'd ask who he was.

Emily didn't oblige him. 'Oh, well, we'd love you to recite it one day but just now I must see to my soup.' She put down her knitting and got to her feet.

'It's quite long,' said the passenger. 'So maybe you won't have time to hear it.'

'Probably not,' said Emily, whisking into the galley. 'But I'm really pleased to know about Tam o' Shanter.' This last bit was true so she gave him an especially warm smile.

In honour of the last day, Emily and Billie decided to do a special dinner – 'dinner adieux' as James said it should be called. As there was no need to think about the following week, all their best ingredients were got out and examined.

They'd been lucky with passing fishing boats. One had provided some hand-dived scallops (one of their crew members was a keen scuba diver), some pollock and some mackerel. As they had some smoked salmon that needed using and some smoked haddock in a vacuum pack for emergencies, they decided on fish pie for the main course. In a fit of extravagance Emily suggested using the three last threads of saffron in the sauce to make it extra special-looking.

'Nigella does it,' she explains. 'Her fish pie is lovely and looks really wonderful too.'

Billie nodded agreement. 'We need to make it a bit different as we have fish pie quite often!'

They discussed turning the scallops into coquilles Saint-Jacques and then realised that would be more or less the same as fish pie and got out some chorizo that had been in the back of the fridge for a while. They would make a soup – a velouté as the recipe called it – and put scallops and chorizo into it. The scallops needed padding out a bit anyway.

For pudding they decided to make a multi-layered cake, with cream, frozen raspberries and a couple of layers of very thin meringue for extra crunch. Billie wanted to put spun sugar on the top but they decided to see how they got on before going to those lengths.

Just before they were ready to serve, James came into the galley to get a drink of water. 'Soup smells good,' he said.

'It's not soup!' said Emily and Billie in unison. 'It's velouté!'

The dinner was declared superb by everyone. Emily

and Billie were delighted with how well it had gone. The scallops were plump and tender, the velouté (which everyone referred to as soup) creamy and the fish pie declared by all to be a pie to end all pies. And the pièce de résistance, complete with spun sugar, was photographed by all.

After coffee, made and served by James, Bob the engineer and Drew, there were very many toasts and speeches. Special awards were given by James to all his crew members, each one with a hyperbolic citation that made everyone laugh and Emily blush, unaccustomed as she was to such fulsome praise. The citations were accompanied by giant chocolate coins in gold foil that each had a small cartoon drawn on it as well as the person's name.

One of the passengers had written an 'Ode to the Puffer', which he read aloud to many cheers and calls for more.

'You can't help noticing how people's bar bills go up on the last night,' said Billie. 'I reckon we've sold an entire bottle of Famous Grouse and a case of beer.'

'Yes,' said Emily, 'and if you consider how generous James has been with his personal, captain's whisky, it's amazing they want to buy any at all!'

'They have been a particularly relaxed and boozy lot this week,' said Billie. 'Perfect for the last week.'

'I suppose we should start clearing,' said Emily, trying to summon the energy to move.

'Certainly not!' said the poet. 'You're not lifting a finger, either of you. Go and sit down!'

But instead of sitting down, Emily went to the stern

for a last look at this particular view. She found Bob leaning on the rail, a can of beer in his hand.

'It's beautiful, isn't it?' he said and together they took in the calm water, the distant islands with their peaks and hills and the pattern of the clouds to the west.

'Really lovely. I'm going to miss all this so much,' said Emily.

'So you'll go back home to real life after this?' Bob asked.

'Mm. I have to. It's where my work is. What about you?'

'I'm a college lecturer in my real life. I enjoy it, but I enjoy it more because I have this' – he made a wide gesture – 'in the summer.'

'That's the best of both worlds, really.'

'Really, it is.' They watched a group of ducks, silhouetted against the sky, fly along and then land with a lot of wing-flapping, causing a small bow-wave. 'So,' Bob went on. 'Would you stay here, if you could?'

Emily felt her sigh was so deep and so heartfelt that it actually caused ripples on the water. 'It would depend on finding work. I'm a midwife – can't remember if I told you that – and delivering babies is what I do.'

'Nothing else makes you happy?'

There was something about the setting and Bob's calm presence that made Emily question the things she'd thought were certain. 'There are other things. I really like old people. I find them interesting and funny and while they don't bring hope with them, in the way a little wrapped-up bundle all red and crumpled does, they have so much to teach us.' She laughed. 'I don't just mean Maisie teaching me to knit Fair Isle. But I'm trained as a midwife and I'm good at it.' She paused. 'Besides, I've been offered an amazing new job. It's not just more money and responsibility but the opportunity to really change midwifery in my area for the better. I have to go back to that.'

'You don't sound convinced.'

She sighed again. 'I know. I'm not convinced but I ought to be. It's a head-over-heart thing and I've always been ruled by my head. I have to be this time too.'

'I think you'd do it brilliantly. You're obviously the sort of person who could find work anywhere and make a go of it,' Bob said. 'Look at how you fitted on to the puffer so quickly. I've been chief engineer for years and a lot of people can't cope with the cooking. It's why Rebecca has so many she can call on in an emergency, in case it's too much for the regular cook. But you fitted in straightaway.'

Emily was delighted. 'Well, I suppose I'm used to unsocial hours – i.e. long ones – and I did want a break from midwifery and to help Rebecca out. And I did have some days off,' she added. Although she was trying hard to forget about him, she couldn't stop her mind going back to that wonderful night, seeing the Northern Lights with Alasdair and Kate and what happened afterwards.

'Did it unsettle you? Going back for a week?'

She shook her head. 'Yes – no – I'm not sure.'

'I think I have to take your first answer, Miss Emily!'

They both laughed.

Bob played with his empty beer can as if this would help him to understand something. 'It's a funny thing,' he said. 'It's the same every year. I look forward to the end of the season because I'm a bit tired and want to go home – but come the last couple of weeks I get sad and sentimental at the prospect. And now it's the last night and I wish there was another month of the season left.'

Emily nodded. 'I really don't want to go home – at least I don't now, this minute. It's all so beautiful. But the prospects at home are really great.'

'I do believe you. You don't have to say anything more, I am convinced!'

'Maybe if I say it often enough I will be too.'

'Come on. Let's go back in and have a drink.' He crushed his empty can in his bear-like hand and gently took her elbow.

Emily was even feeling fond of the Walking Encyclopaedia by half past nine the following morning, when she could see the taxi waiting to take him away. She allowed him to hug her quite effusively.

'Well,' said James, when the last passenger had gone. 'I really wish those delightful people come back again next year.'

'What, even old Geoffrey?' said Billie. 'Forever chewing your ear off with facts you don't give a stuff about?'

'Even him,' said James.

'Easier for you though,' suggested Bob. 'People have to climb up a vertical ladder to chew your ear off. The galley crew are much more vulnerable to being bored to death.'

'He did tell me why a tam-o'-shanter is called that,' said Emily, generous now her informant had left.

'Have you finished it? Let's see,' said James.

Emily retrieved her knitting from its special corner behind the lifeboat collection box. 'Here you are.'

'Oh, that is sweet!' said James. 'I want one!'

'Stick to your other hats,' said Emily. 'You have a vast collection. I only knit teddy-sized tammies.'

'Oh, OK,' said James. 'Now, we need to start getting ready to go back. It's not an emergency but there are gales forecast.'

'When for?' asked Drew.

'It said "soon" which means within twelve hours,' said James. 'We've got plenty of time really, but I don't want to hang around.'

'You mean because you can't always rely on the forecast being accurate?' said Bob.

'Not so much that, but Rebecca is having twinges.'

'Oh,' said Emily. 'Third babies. They can never quite decide whether they're coming or not. But you can't take the chance.'

James nodded. 'And although I could get back by taxi or ring for a lift I don't want to leave the puffer here, running up mooring fees, if I don't have to. And she'll be harder to bring back home when you lot have all pushed off.'

'I wanted to do my washing, get myself sorted,' said Billie.

'Sorry. I don't want to hang around. Time for a cup of coffee first, though.'

'So how long will it take us to get back to base?' asked Emily, thinking about Rebecca and her baby.

'Well, if the weather holds off we should be back this afternoon.'

Something in James's usually relaxed tones alerted Emily. 'But you think it might not hold off?'

'There's a chance that it won't. We'll have to strip down the galley, the bar, anywhere else where everything's not nailed down or there'll be breakages.'

Emily raised her eyebrows. So far they'd had wonderful weather and she'd somehow forgotten that this could change.

'Don't look so worried, young Emily,' said Bob. 'The puffer is famous for its rocking-horse motion. It'll be like a ride in a theme park.'

'Mm,' said Emily. 'I'm not much of a one for roller coasters.'

'But everyone loves a rocking horse, surely?' said Bob.

'Suppose,' said Emily, and went into the galley to make the captain his coffee.

Rather to her surprise, considering they were in a hurry to leave, James followed her into the galley. 'So what do you think these pains are that Rebecca's having?'

Emily shrugged. 'I can't possibly tell you from here, I'm afraid. But third babies – they stop and start. The baby might not come until next week. The twinges might mean nothing or they might mean we'd better get a move on.' She smiled. 'You won't want to miss being there, James.'

Bob, who'd joined them, carrying a load of breakfast dishes, shuddered. 'You may have to lay the keel but you don't have to be in at the launching,' he said.

'Bob!' said Emily indignantly. 'You are talking to a radical midwife – well, fairly radical – and we positively encourage fathers to be present at the births of their babies!'

'Well done for getting what he was talking about,' said James. 'It was a bit obscure.'

'Well,' said Billie, with a tray of cups and plates. 'I know how babies are made but I've never heard it called "laying the keel" before.'

'You learn something every day,' said James. 'Now, quick caffeine hit, a bit of chart-bashing, and we'll be off!'

James and Drew were at the table, looking at the chart. Although James knew the area well, he said he wanted to make sure Drew knew what the plan was if the weather got really bad suddenly and they had to make a run for shore.

Emily and Billie were packing loose mugs, bottles of oil, condiments, jugs – anything not already firmly attached to something – into boxes when there was a 'Hello! Anyone aboard!'

It was Alasdair. He clattered down into the saloon. Emily caught her breath to see him. He seemed different. His hair was a bit longer and it was possible he was flirting with designer stubble – or hadn't shaved for a couple of days.

'Hey! Bro!' said James, obviously pleased. 'Very nice to see you! You got my message? And more importantly, you could get away!'

'Yup. I've taken very little time off these last few weeks – it's been really hectic – so I've got time to be around if you guys need me.' His gaze swept the room and caught Emily, on her knees, mugs in both hands. Just for a second they exchanged glances and Emily sent a message which said, 'Please don't say

178

anything that would make people wonder if anything is going on.'

There could have been just the tiniest shadow of a nod, possibly a tinge of regret that he hadn't managed to see her when he'd said he would. 'I've also got strict instructions, from Kate, on behalf of Ted, to collect his tammy, which I gather is on its way.' His hand went to his back pocket and he produced a much-folded piece of paper. 'Here's a picture of him wearing it. In expectation, you understand. Rebecca told him it was ready.'

Emily unfolded the paper. 'Did he draw this himself? If so, he's very good.'

'Kate helped him,' said Alasdair. 'Ted's hand–eye coordination isn't his best thing.'

Emily laughed. 'I imagine that's being cuddled and demanding knitted garments.'

'You've got him!' Everyone laughed. 'So,' Alasdair went on, 'what's the forecast exactly?'

'First thing it was gales within twelve hours, which would give us plenty of time but – well, you know . . .'

'You mean, you don't quite trust the timing of the forecast?'

James nodded. 'Call it Imminent Fatherhood Nerves or whatever, but I don't, quite.'

Alasdair inclined his head. 'The weather forecast was bad, too. They're warning people of possible structural damage.'

'Thank goodness I spent all last winter getting the house really watertight,' said James. 'Now, let's get a move on. No time to waste.'

'Shall we make soup and sandwiches?' suggested

Emily. 'If people get hungry and maybe – er – other people are a bit seasick and not able to cook, it would be good if people could grab stuff while we're on the go.'

'Do you suffer from travel sickness?' said Alasdair.

'A bit,' said Emily. She meant a lot.

'I've got some tablets I grabbed before I set off,' he said. 'They do make you drowsy but they really help.'

Emily took the packet dubiously. 'I don't want to knock myself out when I should be useful,' she said.

'If you and Billie prepare food there won't be much else you can do,' said James. 'So do that, and then take a pill and retire to your bunk. We'll wake you up when we get there.' He gave her a very reassuring smile.

'That sounds like cheating,' she said.

'Not at all. We've got plenty of people to help,' James assured her.

'I never feel seasick,' said Billie. 'So you go ahead. Knock yourself out!'

Chapter Twelve

Emily realised she was enjoying herself. They were setting off on an adventure and Alasdair was there. She may or may not need to resort to tablets, but if sickness threatened, she could retire until the bad weather passed.

Emily and Billie decided to use up the rest of the flour and bake some rolls. They had enough time and they didn't have a lot of bread.

'The boys eat loads when they're in a sea like this,' said Billie. 'Once these rolls are done we can make up a stash of filled ones to take down to the engine room or up to the wheelhouse. It'll make our lives so much easier.'

Emily nodded, aware that they were both thinking about feeding their men. It wasn't exactly a feminist view but given they couldn't do much else to help their little ship along, they might as well provide fuel for those that could.

When they'd done all they could they went up on deck. It was hard to imagine that soon the weather, so fine and sunny now, would send them a storm. With luck they would reach their home port before the weather struck.

Billie soon disappeared into the engine room, so she could be with Drew. It would be a bit crowded down there, Emily thought, but Billie would find somewhere to perch without getting in the way.

Emily looked at the passing scenery, wondering if she should go below and get her knitting out. She'd been an important part of the team and now, suddenly, she had no role.

'Hey, you!' James called from the wheelhouse. 'None of that slacking on deck! Come up and talk to us up here before we bore each other senseless.'

She was pleased to be asked – it was like being invited into the inner sanctum, where the cool people hung out. Of course she'd been up in the wheelhouse dozens of times but this invitation felt special. And she knew perfectly well that Alasdair and James always had plenty to talk about.

'Shall I bring some coffee with me?' she asked, looking up into James's face as he leant out of the window to talk to her.

'That would be nice,' he said. 'And if there's any crew cake left, we'd love a wodge of that.'

'There's plenty,' said Emily. 'We've only just made one. It should be cool enough to cut by now.'

It was very matey up there, squashed into the wheel-house, eating cake and sipping coffee, chatting and laughing with James and Alasdair.

'I can't believe it's going to be windy later,' she said, leaning, accidentally on purpose, next to Alasdair. She knew it was childish but she couldn't help herself. Something about the trip was making her revert to adolescence. Maybe it was because the relationship – if you could call it that (which you couldn't, really) – was due to end so soon.

'The wind is getting up already,' said James. 'And look at the barometer – sunk like a stone. Bad weather for sure and soonish.'

'Hey!' said Alasdair suddenly. 'Over there. Is that a cluster of freak waves or . . .'

James unhooked the binoculars and looked. 'No, not freak waves.' He handed the binoculars to Emily.

It took a few moments to adjust them and then she said, 'Oh! Dolphins! How wonderful! Here' – she handed the binoculars back – 'you look.'

'No, you have them,' said Alasdair. 'We can see them almost any time.'

'Scotland is showing you all her best sights,' said James. 'The Northern Lights, otters, and now dolphins.'

'Yes,' said Alasdair. 'Anyone would think Scotland wanted you to stay.'

Emily kept her gaze on the dolphins, leaping through the waves. A few moments later they were gone.

A bit later Billie and Emily, having baked the rolls, filled them and took them around. Billie headed to the engine room with hers, some beers hanging from her belt, while Emily took her plastic box back up to the wheelhouse.

'Here's a sight for sore eyes,' said Alasdair.

Emily hoped he wasn't just looking at the plastic box. 'The rolls are still warm,' she said. 'They should be good.'

'Delicious!' said James with his mouth full. 'Not sure why. Perhaps it's knowing we're on our way home that makes them taste so good.'

'No, it's because they're just out of the oven and made by me!' said Emily, pretending to be offended at his suggestion. 'But seriously, you must be desperate to see Becca.'

James nodded and took another bite. 'I am. It's been hard being apart just lately, although of course we speak on the phone all the time.'

'So how are the twinges?'

'Gone away for now. But she's madly baking so when she sends the boys off when we're in hospital, having the baby, they can go fully loaded with cake.'

'It's when she starts cleaning out the coal shed you need to get really worried,' said Emily with a laugh.

'Oh, she's done that already.'

Emily stopped laughing. This was a bit worrying. She caught Alasdair's eye. 'Oh well, third babies . . .'

'Was there soup?' asked James, who hadn't picked up that Emily was just a little concerned. The last of her mums who had cleared out the coal shed went into labour very soon afterwards. But as it wasn't a remotely scientific signal, she didn't mention it.

'There was – there still is. I'll get you some.'

When she got back with the soup, Alasdair said, 'It is getting a bit rough. Would you like a seasick tablet?'

Emily shook her head. 'I'm fine. I'm going to try and do without if I can,' she said. 'This is my last trip on the puffer. I don't want to spend it asleep, really.'

'Oh, don't say it's your last trip,' said James. 'Surely you'll come up and visit us next year?'

'I'd like to,' said Emily, 'but you know what life is like. It's hard to carve out time off sometimes.' She suddenly felt tearful at the thought and then wondered if perhaps she wasn't as fine as she'd said she was.

'Well, let me know if you change your mind,' said James, sipping his soup.

Having fed those engaged in actually getting the puffer along, Emily and Billie sat in the saloon chatting and sipping beer. Emily found the bubbles and the bitterness soothing.

Billie had picked up a magazine left by one of the passengers and Emily had cast on stitches to make Ted a Fair Isle scarf. She knitted a few rows and then thought she'd be better not looking down.

She found herself swallowing and feeling rather hot and decided she needed to get out.

'Just going out for some fresh air!' she said and left the saloon quickly.

The fresh air did the trick. The cold sweat that had suddenly covered her went and she felt OK. She leant on the rail for a while and then went down to get her coat. The wind had got up and it was a bit chilly. She ran back out, wobbling a bit, possibly because of the increased movement.

Emily became aware that she was feeling worse. Now was the time to give in, she thought, to take a pill and collapse on her bunk. She'd do that in a minute. But just for now she wanted to go on holding tight to where she was. It took her a few minutes to realise she couldn't move. Moving would make something very bad happen – she wasn't exactly sure what. She had to stand there and cling on to the rail and watch the sea rise and fall in front of her. She was cold but she was sweating. She wanted to die.

'You not feeling too clever?'

It was Alasdair. She turned to him but couldn't speak. She swallowed a few times instead.

'Let's get you down below with some tablets.'

'Can't go down ladder,' she said, as briefly as possible.

'You mean to the forward-cabin? That you share with Billie?'

She nodded. She was shaking now – it could have been from cold or from sickness.

'Stay there. We'll organise a passenger cabin for you.'

There was no question of her moving, so Emily stayed. She couldn't decide if she wanted to be sick or just throw herself over into the waves. But although the rail wasn't particularly high she knew she couldn't climb over it even if she really wanted to.

She closed her eyes. She felt extremely drowsy and mentally almost smiled. She'd refused pills so she wouldn't be drowsy and now she was drowsy and sick. What a bad decision that had turned out to be!

Alasdair's arm was strong and he half lifted her as she walked along to the hatch. They both looked at the steps for a minute and then he picked her up in a fireman's lift and got her down them. Fortunately the process was so quick she didn't have time to vomit down his back. There was time for the thought that she might to go through her mind but, thankfully, he put her down the moment they arrived in the saloon.

He put her into a twin cabin, on the bottom bunk.

'Easier for you to get in and out than a double and the nearest to the bathroom,' he explained.

There was a glass of water in the special holder that meant it couldn't spill and – mortifyingly – there was a plastic bowl.

He pulled back the duvet. 'Get in. I'm going to get you a hot-water bottle in case you're chilled.'

As she was now shivering convulsively, her teeth going nineteen to the dozen, she thought she probably was chilled.

'Thank you,' she whispered and almost fell into the bunk.

At some time over the next couple of hours she staggered to the bathroom and was sick. Afterwards she felt a great deal better and when she was back in her bunk she slept.

She was awoken by Alasdair. He had a mug in his hands. 'If you're up to it, you might like this.'

'What is it?'

'Marmite in hot water. Love it or hate it!'

'I'll give it a go.'

'I'll leave you to it.'

After the hot drink, Emily did feel much better and decided to get up. Apart from anything else, she wanted to see where they were. How much of life had passed her by while she'd been asleep?

The ship's clock told her it was mid-afternoon. The day still had plenty left in it. It would have been good if they'd been nearer their destination because Emily still felt a bit wobbly but as she had wanted to feel conscious for this trip she was glad. She put on all the available coats and scarves, some of which she owned, then she went up to the bow to watch the waves.

She felt a tap on her shoulder. It was James. 'Why don't you keep Alasdair company? He's in charge up there while I get some rest. Not sure how long it's going to take us to get back. We're not making a huge amount of headway against this weather.'

'Oh, OK.'

If James had told her to go and do this it was like an order. She had to. She didn't need to feel as if she was inflicting her company on a reluctant Alasdair.

'Hey! Company,' said Alasdair as she opened the door to the wheelhouse and went in. 'That's nice.'

'James sent me. I'm here officially. Presumably so I can get you tea or coffee or whatever you may want.'

'Or you could just chat. Perch yourself on that stool.' He glanced at her. 'Are you better?'

'Lots better, but actually, it's nice being up here. Maybe it's like driving. You know how you don't feel carsick if you drive when you can be about to die of it when you're the passenger?'

'I don't get carsick but I can see it would work.'

They watched the horizon in silence for a while, neither of them feeling the need to say anything. Emily's thoughts were all about the moment of parting. She knew she'd be desperately sad to leave this beautiful area she had fallen so deeply in love with. Then she wondered if she'd fallen in love with a man or a land-scape and were either loves lasting? Did she just have a bit of a crush on Argyllshire?

The waves crashed over the bow and every now and

then a particularly large one hit the wheelhouse windows, blinding them. Emily glanced at Alasdair. He seemed perfectly calm, not worried by the waves that seemed to get bigger and bigger, tossing the valiant little vessel around as if it were a toy.

'The weather is quite bad,' she said, trying to quell her fears with understatement. 'Do you think we should get James?'

'Not at all,' he said, sounding very Scottish. 'It may feel as if we're a cork in a car wash but we're safe as houses, just not making any progress. Or very little.'

She decided to believe him. 'Oh, OK.'

Emily forced herself to think about something other than the waves that swelled and broke, sometimes tilting them one way and sometimes the other.

'I wonder how Becca is,' she said aloud, replacing one anxiety with another. 'Those twinges could mean nothing, or they could be the real thing.'

'James is quite concerned, I think. He wants to be there.'

'He doesn't seem twitchy or anything,' said Emily, surprised but quite pleased to learn he was so keen to support his wife. She never quite got the argument that there was no point in men watching their wives suffer. So many of the mothers she took care of wanted their closest ally with them at such a difficult time.

She wondered if Alasdair had been there when Kate had been born but decided not to ask. It wasn't her business.

'He doesn't show his feelings much, but as his brother, I can tell. If he hadn't really wanted to be there for Becca he'd have left the puffer for another day. He wouldn't normally have set out with that forecast.'

'It would have been easier for him just to go back by car, wouldn't it?'

'Yes. But he wouldn't want to abandon the puffer if he didn't have to. And it might be here for weeks. He's going to have his hands full once the baby is born.'

'Tricky decision.'

'The trouble is, the weather is coming up faster than forecast. Of course it's only a guide, but we should have been further along before it got rough. We're making slow progress.'

'He's lucky he's got you to take the wheel for a bit.'

'Oh, Drew could have done that, but with me here as well, it means he can get his head down for a good couple of hours without worrying.'

Emily laughed softly. 'If the baby really is on the way, he'll need to be fit and well to support Becca through it all. And afterwards.'

'He's a very hands-on dad.'

Emily looked at him. Alasdair was holding the ship's wheel with both hands, looking ahead, but something about the way he said this made her wonder.

'No one's a more hands-on dad than you are,' she said.

'Not now, no, but when Kate was tiny her mother wanted to do it all.'

'Oh. Did you feel a bit pushed out?'

'Mm. I was all for changing nappies and giving bottles – Catriona wasn't up for breastfeeding in case it spoilt her figure – but Kate was her little doll to play with.

She wasn't much of a one for sharing.' Then he laughed ruefully. 'Except herself – she did share that.'

'You seem to have recovered OK.'

He smiled. 'I think I have. And Kate's a great girl, so that's all right.'

Emily decided not to say anything, but she'd seen other women who wanted to be the expert and only let their partners lay hands on the baby when they were exhausted and crying and so was the baby. Not a good introduction to fatherhood.

'So, tell me about your band? Do you get together often?'

'Not often enough. Time, you know, the enemy of creativity and fun.'

Emily laughed. 'I've heard that excuse before. In fact, I've made it myself. Lots of times.' She hesitated. 'Are there any rules about not singing when in charge of a puffer?'

'By no means. Singing in the wheelhouse is positively encouraged.'

'So crack on then. Give us a tune.'

It was Alasdair's turn to laugh now. 'OK, what do you know?'

'It's not what I know, it's you! You're the designated singer.'

'Oh no. I'm not doing it alone. Either you join in or we both stay silent. Listening to the wind whistling through the rigging and the waves breaking over us.'

For a few seconds they did just that and, in Emily's case, noticing that the wind was getting stronger and the famous 'rocking-horse motion' was getting more pronounced. She didn't really feel sick but she realised that distraction would be a good thing.

'Oh,' she said. 'That's hoisted me with my own petard! I'm not sure I can sing.'

'Everyone can sing. Just open your throat. We'll start with something easy. "Speed, Bonny Boat". Very appropriate.'

Alasdair began and a beautiful baritone emerged. It was a reassuringly loud noise and Emily felt encouraged. She joined in enthusiastically. When she'd said she wasn't sure she could sing she'd been lying. What she'd meant was, she wasn't sure she could sing in company. But with Alasdair's wonderful voice, confident and loud, she really enjoyed herself.

Inevitably Alasdair's repertoire of rousing, cheerful songs ran out and the mood became less cheerful. He began to sing something in Gaelic, which of course she couldn't understand, but it had a beautiful melody that made her want to cry. She cleared her throat, reluctant to embarrass herself in front of Alasdair yet again but she still felt tearful. She was very grateful when James appeared in the wheelhouse and joined in the last line with Alasdair but in English, 'Sad am I, without thee.'

Before she could speculate too much about why Alasdair should have chosen the song, James said, 'Goodness me, you're getting gloomy up here! It'll be "Never weather-beaten sail", next and we'll all cut our throats.'

'Well, think of something better then,' said Alasdair, laughing, apparently not affected by the words as Emily had been.

'I can do better than that. I've brought the book of

words.' He handed Emily a copy of *The Scottish Students'*
Song-Book. 'Find us something nice – "Hearts of Oak",
maybe. But stay away from "Wrap me up in my tarpaulin
jacket". That always has me in floods.'

'Let's have a look at the book,' said Emily. 'What about
"Scots, wha hae wi' Wallace bled"? That sounds good
and rousing.'

'Ah,' said James. 'That's your Tam o' Shanter mate,
Burns. But we know this. Join in when you can, Emily.'

James had a good voice too, and Emily became more
and more confident, knowing her light soprano would
be drowned by the big male voices, even when they
threw her by going into harmony.

By the time she needed to go down and make tea for
the brothers, she had completely forgotten about feeling
sick.

When she emerged from the saloon, holding a plastic
box containing three mugs of tea and a few bits of cake,
she realised it was all a lot rougher than she'd realised
– a lot rougher than it had been. She lurched against
bits of puffer as she negotiated her way aft towards the
wheelhouse. She was glad she'd put the cake in a plastic
bag or it would have been very soggy by the time it got
up the ladder to the point of command.

'Would you two rather be alone?' she said when she'd
handed out the mugs, wondering if she should have left
her own mug down below.

'Not at all!' said James. 'We need in-vessel entertainment and you're it. There's just about room for three.
I'll steer now. Alasdair, shove over and let Emily have
the stool.'

'The weather's got worse,' said Emily when everyone had shuffled around a bit.

'A bit,' James agreed. 'We're still making very little headway, but we can't go any faster. I've spoken to Bob who's doing his best but we're a little ship with a big job to do. It's not going to be quick, getting back.'

'Have you heard from Becca?'

'She's fine. Twinges all gone. She's snuggled up in front of the wood-burner, watching a DVD and eating chocolate, she said.'

'That sounds fine.' But it occurred to Emily that she might say something like that herself if her husband was out at sea and couldn't get to her any faster. Why let him worry if the pains had actually got worse?

By the time they were finally approaching their home port it was eight o'clock at night. All the soup and sandwiches had been eaten and more made. Emily felt she'd been crossing an angry ocean and, although no one said much, she sensed that others felt the same.

The wind and lashing rain meant there was no one about to greet them. Then, just as Emily was wondering how on earth they would moor up without anyone there to catch a line, a man appeared. He was wearing oilskins and a sou'wester. He caught lines and helped make the puffer secure.

When James emerged from the wheelhouse, rubbing his hair, which had been flattened by his woollen hat, the man called to him: 'I think you'd better get along home p.d.q., James. Your missus needs you.'

Chapter Thirteen

By the time Emily had packed her bag – a process which took about ten seconds – and come back up on deck, James and Alasdair were waiting to help her off the puffer, which was rocking a bit.

'OK, Drew? Bob? Billie? You'll be OK here?' said James. 'You know what to do. Keep warm. I'll text if you should open a bottle to wet the baby's head. In the meantime, open other bottles.'

Then he was striding towards the waiting Land Rover, Alasdair and Emily hurrying after him.

Emily found herself in the front of the vehicle, holding on as she tried to buckle her seat belt while they sped off.

'So, what's the score, Angus?' asked James, leaning over to talk to his friend.

'Rebecca sent the boys across to us a while ago. She said she wanted a bit of rest,' said Angus. 'Then later she said she was going to phone the hospital and could I wait for you and drive you there when you arrived.'

Emily felt a wave of anticlimax and then chided herself and decided what she was feeling was relief. She wasn't going to deliver a baby in a storm. Mother and baby were going to be in hospital, as planned.

'So, she's on her way?' There was no doubt about how James felt: full of relief and excitement. 'We'll get to the hospital in time. Babies take ages.'

Emily didn't speak. It wasn't the time to say that third babies could behave quite differently from their older siblings.

'Well.' Angus's tones were measured and reassuring. 'There may be a little problem with getting there. There's been trees down.'

'Where?' asked James sharply.

'Not sure,' said Angus. 'There's been a few. Our road was clear on the way down so we should be OK for getting back. Ambulances who have to come from the main road might have more trouble.'

Emily heard Alasdair's voice and turned to see him talking into his phone. 'The ambulance might have got through to Becca,' he said when he'd finished. 'But they won't have been able to get to the hospital.' Alasdair put his hand on his brother's arm. 'But don't worry, ambulance men deliver babies all the time.'

'So do midwives,' said Emily carefully. 'And I am one.'

'Yes!' said James, sounded excited. 'You can deliver it!'

'Only if it's an emergency,' Emily went on. 'I'm not licensed up here.'

'If we can't get to hospital,' said James, 'it'll be a bloody emergency!'

'It'll be fine, whatever,' said Emily, secretly amused to

see James, who was always so serene under any circumstances, showing signs of agitation.

'Nearly there,' said Angus calmly. 'You'll all soon find out what's going on.'

There were a lot of branches on the road and there were still strong gusts but fortunately there were no trees to block their path and they were at the house fairly quickly.

The front door opened as they drove up. Rebecca stood there, outlined against the light, looking, Emily thought, like the heroine of a novel, or possibly the star of an episode of *Little House on the Prairie*.

'Hello!' she said. 'I'm so glad you're here—' Her voice turned into a groan.

Mm, thought Emily, can't really talk. Things may be quite far along.

'I'll be off then,' said Angus. 'Let us know if you need anything. We're not far. And don't forget the boys are dying to know if they're getting a baby brother or a sister. They really don't want a sister.'

James laughed. 'They've made that perfectly clear already. And thank you so much for picking us up,' he added. 'You've been a hero!'

Angus thought this highly amusing. 'There'll be better heroes than me before this night is over,' he said.

They went into the house, through the hall and into the sitting room, which, Emily noted, was good and warm.

'So?' asked James, stiff upper lip well in place, 'ambulance on its way?'

'I called it!' said Rebecca, sounding defensive.

She called it eventually, thought Emily, a bit later than she should have done.

Alasdair, who had disappeared into the kitchen, came back. 'Well, the ambulance set off but according to them, there's a big tree down so it'll take them a wee while to get here. They're working on the tree but it'll take time to move it out of the way.'

'Safer to have a home birth, then,' said Emily, 'or prepare for one anyway, than to risk waiting and then having it on the side of the road, in a storm.'

'That's what I th—' began Rebecca, her sentence stifled by another contraction.

'You didn't do this on purpose, did you, Bec?' asked James when he judged his wife was in a condition where she could speak.

'Of course not!'

It was unlike Rebecca to snap, thought Emily, and wondered if she was in transition. If so, there wasn't too much time to get ready.

'Becca knows I'm not licensed to deliver babies up here,' said Emily, 'but this would be an emergency. It would be legal and – we hope – safe.'

'Home births are not ideal,' said Alasdair.

'They *can* be ideal,' said Emily.

'What if something goes wrong?' said Alasdair. 'We're miles away from help.'

'Then we have to make sure nothing does go wrong.' Emily spoke in measured, reassuring tones. This was not the time or place to have a discussion about where the best place to have a baby was.

'I want Emily,' said Rebecca. 'I trust her. I don't want

198

to go in a bumpy ambulance to have my baby. Even if it can get past the fallen tree.'

'Do we know when this baby is likely to be born?' asked James, ignoring Rebecca. 'Then we can decide what's best.'

Emily again suppressed her irritation with these men. They seemed to think it would be better for Rebecca to wait an unspecified time for an ambulance that may well not appear than to use the services of a qualified and experienced midwife. They'd be happier if she had a navy blue uniform and a little hat, Emily thought. Or, given recent television programmes, a nun's habit.

'If Becca and I retire to the bedroom for a few minutes, I might be able to give you a rough idea.'

Just then, the lights went out. 'OK,' said Emily, 'I might need a torch.'

'I'll get one and reset the trip switch,' said James.

'I'll put the kettle on the Aga,' said Alasdair. 'My phone will guide me. Where do you keep the candles, James?'

'Are the lights likely to be out for long?' asked Emily when they were alone, expecting Rebecca to say they often went off for short periods and came back on again once the trip switch was reset.

'Depends why they've gone off,' she said. 'If a tree's come down on the lines – well, that'll be it for a little while.'

'Well, if we have to do it in the dark, we have to,' said Emily. She sounded relaxed, she realised, but actually she was a little bit anxious. 'I have delivered a baby by firelight in a yurt, where there was no electricity, so anything is possible.' But she had been prepared for that birth. It would be a trickier getting ready in the dark, but not impossible. 'While we're waiting for the torch, tell me briefly about the boys. Were their deliveries straightforward?'

'Think so. Sorry, excuse me a minute.'

Emily was aware of Rebecca leaning on something and then having a contraction. When she'd finished, she said, 'I quite fancy having the baby in front of the fire.'

'So you'd like it in the sitting room?'

'Can I? The bedroom's a bit cold.'

'You can have what you want. And warmer is better. We'll make a nest for you, make you as comfortable as possible.'

James came back. 'No luck with the electricity, I'm afraid, but here's a good torch and plenty of candles.'

'I'm going to have it in the sitting room, darling,' said Rebecca. 'By firelight. Not in an ambulance.'

Emily laughed. 'Come on you, let's see how far along you are.' As Rebecca's temper seemed back to normal she decided she wasn't in transition yet.

'OK,' said Emily a few minutes later. 'We haven't got a birthing pool but maybe a bath would help relax you. But don't if you'd worry about getting stuck.'

'No, a bath would be good. Especially if you can haul me out again.'

While Rebecca huffed her way through another contraction, Emily went into Rebecca's sitting room, a pale, usually sunny room, that she'd always loved. There were several oil lamps and a camping lantern lit and the fire was well made up. Apart from the lantern, which was too bright for now, but might come in useful later, it looked lovely. With a massive rug over the stone flags, it was a perfect place to have a baby.

Then she noticed the expressions on the faces of James and Alasdair. Even in lamplight she could see they were obviously not calmed and comforted by the pleasantness of their surroundings. She also realised that although Alasdair was a doctor he probably wasn't accustomed to home births. In this area, far away from hospital, home births wouldn't be encouraged, in case something went wrong. He had his doctor's bag that he obviously never travelled without.

James was anxious because it had been a while since his wife had last given birth and then she'd been surrounded by professional, medical people, in surgical gowns and masks.

'It's all going to be fine,' she said composedly. 'If one of you could run a bath for Becca and the other make some tea? I'm sure you'd both rather have a stiff drink but that's for later. And maybe some toast? Can we manage that without electricity?'

'Aga toast,' said James.

'Good. She'll need a bit of energy for what's coming so toast and honey might be just the thing.'

'We've got some nice honey,' said James and hurried to the kitchen.

'I'll do the bath,' said Alasdair. 'I'll put tea lights in there. There were some in with the candles. Lukewarm, do you think?'

'No, a comfortable temperature. Why don't you just get it going then Becca can decide how hot she wants it? Now, do you know where the airing cupboard is? We'll need plenty of towels and sheets.'

Home births were not just about the mother and baby, Emily knew. They were about the family, the father, the environment. Having Alasdair there was, in a way, a complication. If there was a problem, he'd be a godsend, but if there wasn't, he might get in the way dreadfully.

Alasdair had made a good job of the bathroom. There were tea lights everywhere and he'd found an oil burner, so the smell of orange and lavender filled the room.

'Ooh, very romantic,' said Rebecca as she came in, supported by James's arm. 'It's a shame we can't use it for something more exciting than childbirth.'

'There is nothing more exciting than childbirth,' said Emily. 'Now you two stay here as long as you feel comfortable. James will lift you out if necessary, Becca.'

'As long as he doesn't do his back in,' said Rebecca. 'That toast was lovely, by the way.' Then she stopped talking as she had another contraction.

Emily, who was holding her own mug of tea, downed it in one. 'Midwives run on tea,' she explained to a rather startled James. Inwardly, she smiled. For several weeks James had known everything and she nothing, but now she was completely in her comfort zone while James, always unruffled, always positive, was looking to her for reassurance. 'I'll leave you both to it. I've got things I need to do. Call me if you're worried.'

She went back to the sitting room and set about turning it into a birthing suite.

For Alasdair's sake as much as anything, she took sheets and draped them on the sofas, keeping them in place with the legs of the sofas and gaffer tape which she found in a very tidy little cupboard by the front door. She guessed this was a cupboard Rebecca had sorted out recently, when the nesting instinct that got mothers whitewashing coal cellars and other unnecessary housewifely actions had taken over.

This would mean Rebecca would be able to lean and move around in relatively hygienic conditions. She found a couple of huge floor cushions that she quickly covered, again using sheets and tape but with some very large, swift stitching as well. Then she got duvets, put clean covers on them and a made a nest on the floor.

'It looks like a play area in a posh soft-furnishing shop,' said Alasdair, bringing Emily another mug of tea. He'd been boiling scissors and, at Emily's request, heaping towels on the Aga so they'd be warm to wrap the baby in when it first arrived.

'It'll be perfect. Cosy, comfortable, as germ-free as it can be.'

'Just as well they haven't got a dog. It would never be hair-free if anyone tried to have a baby in our house. Rupert's hairs would get on everything.'

Just for a second Emily thought about having a baby in Alasdair's house. With the right midwife it would be perfect. Perhaps Sally would come up and look after her. Then she banished the thought as rapidly as it had come.

'I'm sure it would be just fine, Rupert hairs or not,' she said.

'I think I'd still prefer a nice, sterile hospital.'

Emily laughed. 'After this is over, you'll never think

about childbirth in the same way again. It'll be natural births for you all the way.'

'How is Becca going to manage without pain relief?'

Emily usually had gas and air for home births, but she'd delivered plenty of women without. 'She'll do very well. She's going to be a total star. You'll be surprised how well mothers do without all the technical equipment.'

James came in. 'Becca wants to get out of the bath.'

'Can you help her out then? And find her something to give birth in, a nightie or something. But not her best one.'

She looked at Alasdair. If he wasn't here, Rebecca might like to be naked but she might not want her brother-in-law – someone she'd be seeing at family gatherings for the rest of her life – seeing her puffing and panting on all fours. Childbirth was a beautiful, natural and life-changing thing, but it wasn't very dignified. 'I'll go and help James find a nightie.'

By now, Rebecca was in her bedroom, forehead against an arm that was leaning against the doorframe. She was wrapped in a bath towel, groaning. James was opening and shutting drawers like an indecisive burglar.

'Becca, we need to know,' said Emily, 'shall I send Alasdair away? Are you going to be embarrassed forever if he sees you do this? We don't need a doctor. We could send him to the neighbours, like the boys?'

'I'd much rather he stayed, Becca,' said James, stopping his search in shock at the thought of his brother leaving. 'We might need a doctor.'

'We really don't. And if we do, he won't be far away. He could be here in moments.'

'Think it'll be OK,' said Rebecca when she could speak. 'We can send him into the kitchen if I change my mind.'

Emily nodded. 'Fine. James, help her through when she's ready. I just want to make sure the fire is stoked to the max.'

Rebecca appeared in a cotton nightie that went down below her knees, in spite of her bump. 'Not very glam, I know, but these are great for breastfeeding. I had several of them, when I had the boys. I don't mind if it gets ruined and it'll cover my bottom.'

'Becca,' said Emily firmly. 'You're not going to be on YouTube! You can wear what you like – or nothing!'

'Oh God, I wish people would stop telling me what I can do! I just want to have a baby!'

An hour later, Rebecca was on all fours, her forehead pressed against one of the sofas. 'Why did I think this was a good idea?' she asked the universe in the tiny break between contractions. 'I have two lovely boys! Why did I want another baby!'

'It's a bit late to change your mind, hon,' said James.

'Did we find some tags?' asked Emily, on her knees next to Rebecca. 'We won't be able to clamp the cord, obviously, so we need to tie it off.' She smiled at James quickly. This term sounded faintly nautical.

'Looking where I was told to look,' said Alasdair. 'Which was in Becca's sewing basket. I found these.' He waved what seemed to be a long narrow ribbon.

'Cash's name tapes,' Rebecca gasped. 'I inherited them from your mother. Never did sew them on anything.'

'Well,' said Emily, taking the strip and reading it, 'if

you don't mind your baby's umbilical cord being tied with tape which says James Cumming Alasdair, these'll do fine.' She frowned. 'What's with the name thing?'

'You fold under one of the names,' Alasdair explained. 'Mine if it's James's, and his if it's mine. I just get called Cumming Alasdair, instead of the other way round. It's being the youngest.'

Rebecca began to groan as another contraction overtook her.

'You're doing brilliantly, darling,' said James, beginning to look tired himself.

'We all are,' said Emily. She was buoyed up on the adrenalin of childbirth. The following day, she knew, she might well be stiff and aching from spending all that time on her knees, but now she was totally in the moment.

'I really need to push now,' said Rebecca.

Emily took a quick glance under the nightie. 'OK, James or Alasdair, could I have a nice warm towel from the Aga? And make sure there's a pile of them warming? We're nearly there.'

'If we can't listen to the heartbeat, how do we know the baby is OK?' murmured Alasdair to Emily just after Rebecca had had another contraction. 'It's a shame we can't use this.' He indicated the stethoscope round his neck.

'It won't work until the baby is born but we don't have to hear the heartbeat, we'll just prepare well, and deal with what happens.'

'I'm not used to working in the dark like this,' said Alasdair. 'Literally!'

'Well, I've done it all before, including working in the dark, so we'll be fine.'

Rebecca began to bellow.

'We have a head. Your baby is so nearly here, Becca. Just keep on doing what you're doing.'

Rebecca just groaned louder.

'Pass me the towel, someone,' said Emily. 'We'll have the shoulders any minute.'

The anticipation was enormous. 'Why isn't the baby here yet?' asked James.

'Rebecca?' said Emily, ignoring James. 'We need you to move about a bit. We just need to shift those shoulders. It's quite a hefty baby we've got here.' She got her arm over Rebecca's shoulders and pulled her down on to her back.

'Do we need to do a McRoberts manoeuvre?' asked Alasdair.

Emily really hoped they wouldn't have to tip Rebecca on to her back again and bring her legs up over her head. 'Let's get up on all fours again and see what's happened. Ah! Here we are!'

The baby slid out on to the waiting towel.

'Oh! What a big girl you are!' said Emily.

'A girl? Why isn't she crying?' said Rebecca.

'Alasdair, can you bring the torch over here, and James? Another dry towel please.'

Emily deftly transferred the baby into the towel James was holding and began rubbing quite briskly, talking and moving the baby gently around. 'Come on, little girl! Say hello to your mummy and daddy! They're waiting to hear your voice!'

She and Alasdair were waiting too, just as anxiously. Alasdair listened to the baby's heartbeat. 'It's over a hundred,' he said.

'That's good,' said Emily, 'and she's blue, which is OK. Come on, honey, little cry for Emily! Ah! There we go! And look, her face is beginning to turn pink already.'

The baby began to cry lustily and Emily placed her on Rebecca's stomach. Then she piled on another couple of towels. 'It's the best way to keep her warm,' she explained, having removed the first towel, damp now.

'She's crying!' said Rebecca.

'A crying baby is a happy baby,' said Emily. 'That's what I was taught.'

'And does that apply to fathers, too?' said James, who was laughing and crying at the same time, hugging his wife's shoulders and looking down at his daughter.

As Emily was also feeling emotional she just laughed. She looked up at Alasdair and saw relief and satisfaction on his face – and something else. She was sure her expression mirrored his, apart from that something she couldn't identify. It was as if he'd found something he thought he'd lost.

'Jolly well done, everyone,' he said huskily and then pulled out his handkerchief.

'Did we have any girls' names?' asked James, still hugging his wife.

'I'd just assumed it would be a boy,' said Rebecca. 'Although I do have a couple up my sleeve.'

'Before you get too caught up in the name thing,' Emily broke in. 'I just need you to deliver the placenta for me.'

'Oh God,' said Rebecca indignantly. 'Do I have to? I've just had a baby, for goodness' sake!'

'It'll be nothing after delivering your daughter,' said Emily. 'Come on, Bec, you can do it.'

'Doesn't she need an injection for that?' asked James. 'I seem to remember when Henry was born—'

'We're not in hospital. No injections,' said Rebecca firmly.

'Come on, then,' said Emily.

'You know I was going to make her second name Emily,' said Rebecca, 'but you've made me work so hard . . .'

'There we go,' said Emily as the placenta slithered into the bowl she had ready for it.

'Is it all there?' asked Alasdair. He produced a torch. 'Shall I hold this while you look?'

'Thank you.' Then Emily inspected the placenta carefully. 'Yup. All present and correct. What do you want to do with it? Keep it for a while—'

Rebecca interrupted her quickly. 'I'll plant a tree over it, if that suits your hippy-dippy sensibilities, but don't even say what you were about to.'

Emily laughed. 'I wouldn't dream of it. No smoothies.' As the thought of what some mothers did with their placentas made her decidedly queasy Emily had no trouble holding back.

'Well,' said James. 'I think it's time to break out the ten-year-old Jura Malt. Everyone?'

'Tea for me,' said Emily.

As Emily did her best to tidy up in the flickering candlelight she felt she'd never get over the wonder of childbirth. Seeing Rebecca and James with their baby made her want to weep. She always felt a bit like this, she realised, but this time it was far more personal.

Alasdair had retreated to the kitchen to make tea.

'The boys will be so disappointed it's a girl,' said Rebecca dreamily, comfortably lying back on all the cushions and pillows available.

'I think it's wonderful!' said James. 'You wanted a girl, didn't you?'

'I don't know how to look after girls. How do you change their nappies? There are bits missing,' said Rebecca, looking at her daughter with a mixture of shock and blissful love.

'So, what girls' names did you have tucked up your sleeve? Nothing too extreme, please. We don't want a little Ismene.'

'Actually, I like Eleanor – Eleanor Emily, Nell for short,' said Rebecca.

'Oh, Becca!' said Emily. 'That's lovely! And actually, James, maybe I'll have tea *and* whisky!'

'I don't know what we'd have done without you and Alasdair,' she went on.

'Good Lord, I didn't do anything!' said Alasdair, coming in with the tea. 'It was Emily here who was the star of the show.'

'I propose a toast,' said James. 'To my beautiful, clever wife, Rebecca—'

'And Emily, who was brilliant,' put in Alasdair.

'And don't forget Alasdair!' Emily interjected.

'Yes, to brilliant Emily, and including my little brother if you must – for bringing Nell safely into the world.'

Emily drew breath to say that she was only doing her job, but a huge lump in her throat meant she couldn't say anything. Seeing her best friend with her crumpled bundle, sleeping now, she realised how much she envied her. For the first time in her life she really wanted a baby of her own.

Chapter Fourteen

Rebecca, James and Nell had finally retired to bed. Nell was in the crib the boys had used. Alasdair and Emily were in the sitting room. Emily was still overcome by the realisation that she wasn't only a career woman, but a potential mother, too. It had taken this candlelit delivery to make her understand that. Delivering your best friend's baby was a lot more emotional than she would have thought. They were such a perfect family: James and Becca, the new baby girl and their two bigger boys. It was something Emily wanted, too.

'Emily . . .' Alasdair began.

Emily's heart began to race. Was he going to say something significant? Or just suggest another cup of tea?

'Alasdair?'

Just then, the lights came on. They were standing on or near a muddle of very messy sheets.

Alasdair gave a rueful smile. 'Well, that's spoilt the mood somewhat!'

Emily gave a reluctant laugh. 'I'm so glad Becca and

James didn't see that. They would have thought it was too much blood and worried. Almost all couples do.'

'Would it put them off, do you think?' He seemed genuinely interested.

'I would hope not. After all, by the time they get to see it they have a baby in their arms.'

'If nothing goes wrong.'

'Mostly, nothing does go wrong. If I do my job and the mother is fit and well.' She paused. 'Of course there are no guarantees.'

'No,' he agreed. 'But things can go wrong in hospitals too.'

This was generous of him, she felt, and she put her hand on his arm. 'Thank you for that. I know you weren't comfortable with this whole home-birth thing.'

'Actually I thought you and Rebecca were amazing. You really worked as a team. I don't think I've ever seen a more satisfying birth.'

Emily found herself overcome once more and couldn't speak.

Alasdair gave a half-smile. 'Mind you,' he went on, 'the alternative wasn't great! But you did make me see that home births – in ideal conditions – are a viable alternative.'

'Thank you,' she said. 'I'm glad to have shown you a different way.'

'Mostly, people are too far away from medical help for home births in this area. And we do have to think of the worst-case scenario.'

'A good maternity unit can provide an experience very similar to this, though.' She sighed, suddenly very tired.

He glanced at her. 'Right, you sit down and I'll get this lot into the wash. Do you think Becca has stain-remover in her arsenal of laundry products?'

'With two boys, I'm sure of it.' She sat on the armchair watching him gather up the sheets. 'I'm not usually around for this bit. Or at least, not much. When it's a planned home birth a lot of the stuff is disposable. And I should write up my notes. Someone will be examining them with a very close eye in the morning.'

'It is the morning. Two o'clock in the morning. You must be shattered,' Alasdair said.

'It's two o'clock in the morning for you, too,' she said.

He shook his head. 'I haven't been working like you have, not really working.'

She gave him a weary smile. 'Becca did it all.'

'But she couldn't have done it without you. None of us could.'

He was looking at her with such admiration she felt obliged to brush off the praise. 'Well, it's my job.' Suddenly she yawned so hard she thought she'd never stop.

He frowned. 'Never mind your notes, you need to go to bed. But I'm not sure where.'

The thought of not being able to go to bed made Emily feel tearful. Of all the problems she had anticipated and avoided in the past hours where she was to sleep was not one of them.

'Isn't there a spare room? Of some kind?' she asked huskily.

'Under construction. There's a little barn at the end

which is going to be a holiday let or guest accommodation, depending. But currently it lacks essentials like plumbing.'

'I can do without the en-suite and the kitchenette but not the bed.' She sighed. 'So do you and Kate never stay over? I suppose you live near enough not to.'

'We do stay sometimes – Christmas, times like that. Kate has a mattress in the boys' room and I sleep on this thing.' He gave it a kick. 'The sofa bed.'

'Well, I'll sleep on one of the boys' beds.'

'They sleep on small bunks, not very comfortable for an adult.' He hesitated. 'We could go back to mine. There's no reason to stay really.'

She was tempted. She thought of Alasdair's comfortable spare bed and him in it with her. 'How would we get there?'

'We'd have to walk. It's about fifteen minutes. I've had too much whisky to be safe to drive.'

'Then I'll stay. A boy's bed will be fine.'

He shook his head. 'No. Have the sofa bed. I'll make it up for you. You go and have a bath and it'll be done by the time you're back.'

Nothing could have sounded more tempting just then. 'If you're sure . . .'

'Yes. As a family member, I'm *in loco hostus* or whatever.'

Emily found her bag with the hastily grabbed clothes in it, which included pyjamas, and headed off.

'Actually!' he called. 'Better make that a shower. Not sure there'll be hot water for a bath.'

A shower was only slightly less tempting than a

bath. Emily raised her hand to indicate she'd heard him and trusted there'd be some sort of towel. She'd used so many for Nell's entry into the world, there was a chance there were none left. When she'd had her shower she'd write her notes. If she could stay awake.

A little while later, clean but some basic notes written at the kitchen table and still very sleepy, she went back into the sitting room. Alasdair had done an amazing job clearing up. She could hear the washing machine chugging away from the little utility room. A single reading lamp supplemented the firelight. She almost fell on the bed and crawled in.

'Would you like some whisky now, or are you asleep already?'

She was asleep already – or very nearly – but she didn't want Alasdair to go away. If she had a drink he'd have one too and stay with her a bit longer. 'I'd like that.'

He handed her a glass and perched awkwardly on the arm of the sofa. 'Come and sit next to me,' she said. 'I can't relax with you up there.'

He didn't argue. He brought his drink and lay on the bed next to her, on top of the pirate duvet cover, which Emily realised must have been the only one available.

'Here's to you.' He clinked her glass with his. 'You've done brilliantly.'

Emily smiled. 'Rebecca did brilliantly; we all did brilliantly. Oh goodness! The ambulance isn't going to arrive at any moment, is it? Have they got past the tree?'

'I should imagine they'd realise it was all too late.

And if they were still needed that somehow we'd get a message through.'

'I do hope you're right. Imagine how embarrassing it would be if they burst in here and found us in bed together.'

He glanced at her. 'Are we in bed together?'

'We would be if you got under the duvet.'

He kicked off his shoes and got under it.

'How come this has pirates on it? Do James and Becca have a thing for Johnny Depp or something? Usually novelty bed linen is for children.'

'They had a family bed when the boys were very little. They all slept under it.'

Emily sipped her drink and snuggled further down. 'Maybe you should get undressed. You'll be too hot later if you don't.'

'Do you think that's wise?'

'Yup. Very wise. Old midwife lore says that she needs to be cuddled after delivering a baby.'

It was actually brand-new midwife lore, invented by Emily just at that moment, but he seemed to believe it because he pulled his clothes off down to his boxers.

'I wouldn't want to go against midwife lore,' he said and got in beside her.

'Would you mind putting the lamp out? It's in my eyes, rather.' Then she wriggled close to him so she could put her head on his chest. She could hear his heart going thrum, thrum, thrum under her ear. She was aware of his arm coming round her and then she fell asleep.

An hour or so later she was aware of being far too hot. Her winceyette pyjamas, which had been so perfect when sleeping on the puffer, were now sticking to her. She had them off almost before she realised she was not alone in the bed. She didn't care. She pulled the duvet back over her and was about to go back to sleep when she became aware of a hand round her waist. She moved slightly towards him. Whatever they'd discussed and agreed about not doing what they were about to do just seemed ridiculous now. Emily was going to follow her heart – and her body – and have this lovely man.

Fortunately he too seemed to be happy to break his vow of celibacy. He lay next to her, gently stroking her naked body with tenderness and care. Although she could feel his desire for her easily matched hers for him.

After a little while he said, 'Excuse me, I've got to get something out of my bag.'

She giggled deliciously. She did love this man who put condoms in his doctor's bag, who must have thought of having sex with her when he packed to join the puffer on its last trip.

'Now,' he breathed into her neck a few minutes later, 'where were we?'

Emily was awoken by a banging on the front door and a short expletive from Alasdair. He leapt up and pulled on a pair of trousers before leaving the room.

Slightly more slowly she found her pyjama bottoms and Alasdair's jumper, which she hoped was baggy enough to conceal the fact she wasn't wearing a bra. Then she joined Alasdair at the front door.

Two boys, one about ten, and another a bit younger, were on the doorstep, jumping up and down with excitement. Behind them was Angus, looking like a man on the wrong end of an argument.

'I'm sorry!' said Angus. 'I know it's early but they were desperate to know and with no phones working, I had to let them come over.'

'Of course,' said Alasdair. 'I'm sure it's OK for them to go and see the baby but quietly!'

All three adults watched the boys skid towards their parents' bedroom.

'I don't think they know what "quietly" is,' said Angus.

'And I'm sure Rebecca will be thrilled to see them,' said Emily. 'As long as they don't bounce on Nell or make too much noise.'

'So,' said Angus when the boys had gone. 'We knew we'd hear if there was bad news, but did everything go OK last night?'

'It went brilliantly,' said Alasdair. 'Nothing like having a midwife with you if you're a pregnant mother caught out. Emily was a star.'

'Whisht, now!' she said. 'I was only doing my job! I'll go and put the kettle on – and oh God – fill out my notes a bit. I wonder if the electricity is back on generally?'

'There's none at our house,' said Angus. 'Nor phones. Though I think I might get a mobile signal if I drove to the top of the hill. You're lucky to have it here.'

'I will have to make a call soon,' said Emily. 'Or maybe you could, Alasdair? Just to tell the ambulance crew and hospital that everything is OK?'

'We'd better check that everything is,' he said, but sounding fairly sanguine.

When she'd made tea, having added detail to her

notes while the kettle boiled, she took it into the bedroom. It was a touching scene. The boys had joined their mother and baby sister in bed. James, who had obviously dressed in a hurry, was beaming down at his family. Rebecca was supervising Henry, the younger brother, as he held his sister on his lap. Archie, who Emily remembered was the eldest, even though they had hardly met since they were tiny, was giving advice about the best way to support the baby's head.

'Morning! Who wants tea?' said Emily. Without waiting for an answer she handed a mug each to Rebecca and James.

'Hi, guys,' she said to the boys. 'I'm Emily. I helped your mum bring Nell into the world.'

They looked at her disapprovingly. 'Is it your fault she's a girl?' asked Henry.

'No, actually that's Daddy's fault. And maybe he'll take you out of the room while I have a look at Mummy, then I'll make everyone breakfast. I expect you're starving, Becca.'

Once the others had left, Emily examined Rebecca. 'So, busy night?' she asked.

'Not too bad. I know it'll get worse!'

'You're feeling OK?'

'Fine. Just very tired.'

'Well, you go and have a bath. We did well not to need stitches, so you're spared the awful itch.

Rebecca laughed, swinging her legs round and heaving herself up off the bed. 'As if you'd know what that was like, not having had a baby yourself.'

'I've heard all about it, don't worry.'

Rebecca pulled her into a hug. 'I know it wasn't planned and if it hadn't been for the storm it wouldn't have happened, but thank you for doing that for me.'

Emily returned the hug tightly. 'You're the one who did it! I was just on standby to make sure it all went well. You were great.'

'We were a team. And you and Alasdair look great together too.'

Emily smiled, hoping she didn't look as smug as she felt. One day she'd tell Rebecca what had gone on between her and Alasdair and just how a good a team they were in that department. 'I promised your boys breakfast. I'll send James in to mind you in the bath.'

'We've run out of bread,' said James. 'At least, I've taken some out of the freezer but it'll take a little while to defrost.'

Empty cereal bowls were scattered over the table. Alasdair made space on the table next to him. 'Here, Emily, come and eat something.'

'I'm OK for the moment. If there's plenty of milk I'll make Scotch pancakes if you're still hungry. And get a soda bread going if necessary. James? Becca's going to have a bath. Can you listen out for Nell and help Becca?'

Alasdair got up. 'I must go back and pick up Kate. Can I bring her over later, James? She'll be desperate to see Nell.'

'Of course,' said James.

'Why are you wearing Uncle Alasdair's jumper?' asked Henry.

'I couldn't find my own clothes in the dark,' said Emily,

and left before either he or Archie asked any more questions.

Alasdair followed her into the sitting room. 'You can keep the sweater,' he said.

'No, you'll be cold.' She swallowed. Being with him in the room, still dark and full of memories, was both erotic and embarrassing. She was very aware of her breasts, naked under the soft wool of his jumper.

He was aware of them too and his hands found them at the same time as he also found her mouth.

After a few seconds she pulled away. 'Not the time.'

'No,' he agreed huskily.

'And while it was really lovely, it shouldn't have happened.'

'No.' He gave a rueful laugh. 'Like the baby, it was unplanned. But, I have to confess, not unthought about.'

She laughed now. 'Well, you were prepared.'

'How do you know condoms aren't part of a doctor's regular equipment?'

'I didn't know, until just this second. But I'm not complaining.'

'Oh, Emily . . .' he breathed.

'You must go. Go to Kate. I'll probably see you both later.'

'Will you stay for a while? You won't go home immediately?'

'I'll stay as long as Rebecca needs me.' She laughed to disguise the fact that tears had gathered suddenly in her throat. It was the thought of leaving that had done it. 'Off you go. I promised pancakes. And I want to check my notes.'

Chapter Fifteen

The boys were playing in the sitting room and Emily was wiping syrup and chocolate spread off the kitchen table when there was more knocking at the door. She was aware that she'd have to field the visitors. It was natural that everyone would want to see Rebecca and Nell but Emily didn't want her getting too tired. She was tired enough herself and she hadn't given birth. She opened the door prepared to be polite but firm.

On the doorstep was a woman in full cycling kit, her helmet well down over her eyes. She was holding on to a bike and looked as if she'd travelled a long way and was hot. As she was also in her late fifties, Emily didn't think her 'no visitor' rules would apply to her.

'Hello,' said the woman, before Emily could speak. 'My name is Lizzie Miller-Hall. I'm a health visitor who does a bit of midwifery when they need me. I also have some old people I keep an eye on. So I have a couple of jobs. I've cycled over from Kilvallich.'

'Isn't that quite far away? Come in! You must be exhausted and in need of tea.'

'Tea. Aye, that'll sort me. The hospital rang to see if I could get here and on my wee bike, I could. Just. And who are you, dear?'

Emily hesitated, feeling caught out. Should she say she was a midwife? Or a friend who happened to be one? She cleared her throat. 'I'm Emily Bailey. I'm a friend of Rebecca.'

'And did you deliver the baby, dear?'

The 'dear' took a little sting out of this direct question. Emily nodded. 'It was an emergency. And I am trained.'

'Och, dear! I'm not questioning you! It worries a hospital and an ambulance crew when they're summoned but can't get through.' She propped her 'wee bike' against the side of the house with practised ease.

Emily relaxed, warming to the thought of a cycling midwife. 'We did get in touch with them as soon as we could, but of course, that wasn't until earlier this morning. And of course you'd want to make sure everything is OK.' She stepped back so she was no longer blocking the door. 'Come in!'

Lizzie Miller-Hall entered the house with an air of entitlement. She was obviously accustomed to going into unfamiliar houses; she was sure of her welcome and she knew what to do.

'So, Emily – do you mind if I call you that? Have you looked at Mum today?'

Emily nodded. She had never liked the habit of referring to people as Mum or Baby but as most health-care professionals did it, she ignored it. 'She's fine. The baby is fine too but I think they're both asleep. If we could leave them a bit longer that would be good.' She led the way to the kitchen. 'Have a cup of tea, get over your journey and then we'll see Rebecca.'

Emily had found a tin full of fruit cake and so got this out to serve with the tea. Rebecca had obviously had a baking day ahead of time. When her guest had tea and cake in front of her she said, 'I'll just pop and get my notes.'

'Ah! Notes! Good woman! Very useful!'

'I like that you've put plenty of detail into these notes. It's really helpful,' said Lizzie (they were on first-name terms by now). 'But it all seems to have been fairly textbook.'

'Apart from the shoulders taking a little longer to deliver, it was a lovely labour. Nell came out blue but pinked up nicely very soon. Rebecca was brilliant. She had all the right instincts and didn't panic.'

'Husband helpful?'

'Oh yes. Once he'd got over the thought that the baby would have to be delivered here he was great.' Emily hesitated for an instant. 'We had Alasdair Cumming here too.'

'Och! Alasdair! He's great, isn't he? How come he was here?'

'He's the father's brother! We were all on the puffer . . .' She shot a questioning glance. 'You know about the puffer?'

'Aye. I'd forgotten that Alasdair was the captain's brother. We've never met.'

'Anyway, we were all on it together; I was the cook for the season. I wanted a wee – little break from

225

midwifery. We were bringing the boat home. James got a call from Rebecca and we hurried.'

'With all the trees down they were very lucky you were here,' said Lizzie.

'Well, yes. I'm sure Alasdair and James would have managed just fine but they were a bit spooked by the fact the electricity went off.'

'Oh my. I hadn't realised that.'

'Fortunately, where I come from, where we're a bit nearer to hospitals, people have quite unusual ideas of what childbirth should be like. I've delivered babies by firelight where there is no electricity, so I was on familiar territory.'

Emily wanted to keep Lizzie talking so Rebecca and Nell could get as much sleep as possible. She was fairly sure James was there too, waiting to take Nell for a little walk if she woke before her mother did.

Lizzie picked up cake crumbs on the end of her finger. 'So why did you need a break? You hadn't got fed up with mothers and babies?'

'Not at all. I'd got fed up with bureaucracy and the final straw was a run-in with a local GP.' Emily made her own attack on cake crumbs as she thought back. 'But when I popped back to sort something out I found out that everything had changed for the better.'

'So you'll be looking forward to going home and getting back to it all, then?'

'In some ways, yes.' A sigh escaped her before she could stop it.

'What's the problem?'

Emily gave a rueful smile. 'I have fallen in love with

the landscape up here, rather. I've had such an amazing time. I even saw the Northern Lights!'

'Ah, the Merry Dancers. You were lucky. We see them in the winter relatively often – though not that often – but you're lucky to see them in summer.'

Just then, James came in with a sleeping Nell on his shoulder. 'Oh, hi! This one was making noises and so I thought I'd take her away so Becca could catch a few more zeds.'

'This is Lizzie Miller-Hall,' said Emily, not quite sure of her correct title – she seemed to have at least three jobs. 'She might like to take a look at Nell, to make sure all is well.'

'Oh!' said Lizzie, ecstatically. 'Let me get a look at the wee dab!'

Emily laughed. She sounded so much more like a grandmother with a long-awaited grandchild than a health professional – it was very endearing.

'You'll want to get her undressed,' she said. 'In here is warmest. Shall I warm up some towels to put on the table?' She found a towel and did this without waiting for a reply.

James gave Lizzie one of his most charming smiles, the one reserved for passengers who were unknown and potentially hostile. 'You want to look at my daughter?'

'I do indeed! It's not often we get the excitement of a baby being born in the worst storm in living memory – or thereabouts. They sent me to do some checks. Totally unnecessary, I'm sure, but the powers that be like to be reassured.' Lizzie's smile in return was also professional – reassure the new parents that their baby isn't instantly going to be taken into care.

Emily had been sure she had been the only one who'd sensed James's slight hostility but realised this was not the case. Lizzie was very good at her job. James's doubts melted away.

'Has she had a poo yet?' Lizzie addressed James.

He nodded. 'That black stuff, like Marmite. Sticks like crazy.'

'Wet nappies?'

'Think so. I find it hard to tell with disposables.'

'I'll ask Mum, she's sure to know.' Lizzie undressed Nell carefully, talking to her soothingly all the time. Nell kicked her legs and waved her arms in reply.

Emily had done a lot of these checks herself and so said, 'I'll go and tell Becca she has an important visitor.'

'Och, I'm not important, am I, little lass?' Lizzie cooed to the wriggling baby she was checking over. 'You're the important one.'

James and Emily exchanged glances. No wonder Lizzie had everyone on her side in the first five minutes.

'Can you bear to wake up? There's a lovely woman called Lizzie Miller-Hall here to see you. She came from Kilvallich on her bike.'

'She must be fit!' said Rebecca, sounding tired. 'That's miles.'

'She's also a dear, so don't worry. She's checking Nell now.'

'But you checked her too and she's fine?'

'I did and she is. How are you?' Emily thought Rebecca looked more exhausted than she was expecting. Rebecca was always so full of energy.

'Shattered. But what do you expect? I've just had a baby!'

'Will your mum come and look after you for a bit, do you think?'

Rebecca shook her head. 'I really hope not. She fusses the boys and nags James. James's parents are good but they can't cope with the boys for too long. They are rather exhausting.'

'They are exuberant, but brilliant fun.'

'They are but my mother finds them noisy and rude.'

'Do you want some tea?'

'Yes please. Oh, before you go and this Lizzie comes in to see me – tell me about Alasdair.'

'What about him?' Emily felt herself blushing but hoped her old friend wouldn't notice.

'I thought you had a thing going.'

'What? Are you telling me, while you were huffing and puffing, you were observing body language and jumping to conclusions? You are a piece of work!'

Rebecca giggled. 'Idiot! I thought it before and I wondered how it was going.'

Emily considered and then decided her friend deserved a treat. Besides, it had been hard pretending she was completely normal with her when she was in a fog of post-coital bliss. 'OK, it can't go anywhere, we both know that, but last night . . .'

'Last night? You had sex last night? After all that had gone on?' Rebecca frowned for a second. 'Hang on. Where – where were you?' Rebecca had lost her look of exhaustion and become animated. 'OMG! I know! On the floor in the firelight! How romantic!'

Emily smiled, torn between the sweetness of the memory and the need to stop Rebecca getting over-excited. 'Very romantic, just on the spot where you'd just given birth.'

'But James said there was damp bed linen draped all over the boys' bedroom. You didn't do the washing as well, did you?'

'Alasdair did it, not me. You can't help loving a man who knows his way round a washing machine.' Washing machines weren't the only thing he knew his way around but Rebecca did not need to know that.

Rebecca settled back into her pillows looking very satisfied. 'Do you know, I never thought about where you'd stay.'

'Of course you didn't – you were busy. And we had the sofa bed but as all the bedding in the house was dirty, we had to share.'

'I could hardly have planned it better! Only I didn't plan it.'

'Well, you can take the credit anyway.'

There was a knock on the door. 'Can I come in?' Lizzie didn't wait to be given permission. 'Hello! Rebecca, is it? You have a really lovely baby. The image of her father! Now, do you mind if I have a look at you? I'm sure Emily has asked you all the right questions but you know the medical profession, they'll want their form filled in.'

'I'll leave you to it,' said Emily. She went to the door. 'Oh, do we know how much Nell weighs?'

'No, we don't. I haven't got any scales with me,' said Lizzie.

'Don't tell James,' said Rebecca. 'He'll want to start a book on it.'

'He already has. He reckons eight pounds,' said Lizzie. 'I'd say eight and a half. The boys have had guesses as well and want to know what the prize is. If it's a bottle of whisky, let me know if I've won.'

'I'd say eight pounds ten ounces,' said Emily, taking Nell from James, back in the kitchen.

James wrote it down.

'So, what is the prize?' asked Emily, patting Nell's back as she lay over her shoulder.

'I think it depends on who wins it.'

'Lizzie wants a bottle of whisky and I think I'd like that too.'

'The boys will want some outing or other, I expect. Though they'd have to wait.' He looked at Emily. 'Did either of us ever say thank you for everything you did last night?'

Emily smiled. 'I was only doing my job.'

'No you didn't! As far as I'm concerned your job is as the puffer cook. We'd have been completely stuck without you.'

Emily pulled out a chair and sat down. 'That's my holiday job. Being a midwife is what I do. It's my profession.'

James sat down too. 'Do you miss it? Being a midwife?'

'Well, I've just had an amazing time with you all on the puffer, but I would miss being a midwife if I couldn't do it. Dreadfully.'

'I can see why. You're obviously great at it.'

Emily laughed. 'Well, Rebecca knew what she was doing and Nell was a healthy baby after the little hiccup with her shoulders. It was magical, though.'

'Something to embarrass her with later,' said James. 'You were born by firelight, in a storm, with . . .' He paused, searching for the right words.

'Only a trained midwife and a doctor present?' suggested Emily.

'That does take the drama out of it a bit,' James complained. 'Couldn't we build it up into something more exciting?'

'Well, the fact there was no electricity and no phone and we couldn't have got to the hospital if anything had gone wrong made it fairly exciting for Alasdair and me,' said Emily. 'But of course we didn't make too much of that at the time. No need to terrify the parents if you can avoid it.'

'You know, that hadn't occurred to me,' said James. 'You and Al were so calm, even when Nell got a bit stuck.'

Emily smiled. 'We might not have been so calm if there'd been an emergency, but I hope we would. Panicking isn't helpful, on the whole.'

'Too right! Oh, here's Lizzie. And Becca! Sit down, love. Should you be out of bed?'

'I thought I may as well totter in here and see what you're all up to. Where are the boys?'

'In the sitting room. I'll get them out later,' said James. 'Take them to look at the storm damage. Lizzie? Tea? Coffee?'

'I must be getting along. It'll take me a while to get

back,' she said. 'But it's been lovely meeting you all, especially this wee one.'

'Listen,' said James, getting to his feet. 'Let me give you a lift. We'll put the bike in the car and then I'll take you as near as I can to home – fallen trees and floods allowing – and then you can cycle the rest of the way if you have to.'

'That would be very kind,' said Lizzie, 'but I can't let you leave your family at a time like this.'

Emily could see that Lizzie had been very tempted by the offer. 'Why don't I take Lizzie? She can direct me on the way there, and on the way back, I'll just get lost.'

James put Lizzie's bike in the back of the car, which, with its back seat down, took it quite nicely. 'I know you wanted an adventure, but there's the satnav. When you get Lizzie as far as you can, just put in Home.'

'But it'll still be an adventure,' said Lizzie, 'because Ms Satnav won't be able to get home the way she wants too, and will have to keep "recalculating".' She said this with some satisfaction, obviously regarding the satnav as a bossy official who must be outwitted if possible.

'We'll see what we can do,' said Emily and they set off.

'One of the things I love about this part of the world is that, even when the weather isn't doing anything in particular, it's still stunningly beautiful,' Emily said after a few moments.

'Yes. And if it is doing something – like the sun shining, or an early-morning mist appearing, or snow – it's even more beautiful. I've lived here over thirty years now and I still feel lucky.'

Emily sighed suddenly.

'Something on your mind?' Lizzie asked.

'Not really. I'm just tired, I expect.'

'There's a definite hint of "wist" about you, even though you are tired!'

Emily had to laugh. 'Well, there may be. I'll be going home soon and I'm not ready to leave. It's so lovely here.'

'But your work is at home?'

'It is. And it's good work.' She went on to to tell Lizzie about the injection of funds the maternity unit had received and how all the reluctant GPs – well, the only reluctant one – had changed his mind and the unit was going to become bigger and she'd been offered the job of running it.

'That sounds a great opportunity. You'll not be wanting to leave that then, and stay up here,' said Lizzie.

'I couldn't anyway. The puffer only has quite a short season really. I couldn't live on the money. No, it's just been a lovely break.' She gave a small, wistful chuckle. 'I had a summer at sea but now it's over. I'll take my grand new job and do great things.' She paused briefly. So,' she went on briskly. 'Which way?'

They came up to the fallen tree that had stopped the ambulance getting through and Emily pulled in to the side of the road. It was cleared now but seeing the enormous trunk on its side was frightening.

'Suppose someone had been driving underneath when that went over?' Emily said.

'Dead as a doornail,' said Lizzie. 'Beeches. They have shallow roots. And that wasn't the only one, either.' She was silent for a few seconds out of respect for what might have happened and then went on, 'Still, there'll be plenty of firewood.'

When they reached Lizzie's house, removed her bike from the back of the car and Emily had refused offers of tea and coffee, Lizzie said, 'I'll let them know what a grand job you did.'

Emily laughed. 'As I've said before, it was Rebecca who did the grand job.'

'You wrote excellent notes,' said Lizzie firmly.

'Well, I knew you'd need them. Now, do you need a hand with your bike?'

Lizzie correctly interpreted this as Emily saying she wanted to get home and not have praise heaped on her for what she just considered normal.

'No, I'll be fine.' Lizzie propped the bike against the fence. 'I'll just give you a wee hug anyway.'

Emily was smiling as she set off. She decided not to use the satnav and give herself a little magical mystery tour. If she got lost, she would switch on the machine.

She arrived home to a row of glum faces. Everyone was in the kitchen sitting round the table. The boys were picking at baked beans on toast, James, with Nell on his shoulder, was drinking coffee.

'Hi!' said Rebecca, looking a little strained in spite of her cheery greeting. 'How was that?'

'Lovely. She's so nice. Talking to her helped me make my decision. I will take my job.'

'Lovely!' said Rebecca.

'Oh God, what's wrong?' said Emily. 'You're all looking so miserable.' What on earth could have happened to the happy family she had left a couple of hours ago? There seemed to be nothing wrong with Nell, who was sleeping calmly.

'My mum's coming to stay,' said Rebecca. 'To "help".'

'Well, that's lovely!' said Emily. 'It'll be nice to see her and have a hand with the cooking and things. You're not going to be feeling your normal self with all the broken nights and things.' She looked around. No one seemed to take in her cheery words.

'Gran's a bit strict,' said Archie. 'She doesn't let us watch telly.'

'Well, that's good thing! I expect she takes you on picnics and bike rides.' Emily's mind flashed to the picnic she'd had with Alasdair and Kate when they had seen the otters.

'She doesn't,' said Henry. 'She wants us to make models with cardboard but not make a mess. I don't like making models.'

'She's good at jigsaws,' said James, forcing some enthusiasm into his voice somehow and handing his daughter back to his wife.

'She says we have outside voices and inside voices and we're not to use the outside voice inside but I don't know the difference,' said Archie.

'I met your mum when I was your bridesmaid,' said Emily to Becca, thinking back. 'I seem to remember her as sweet. She gave us tea and biscuits.'

'On a plate with a doily,' said Rebecca. 'I was so embarrassed.'

'You shouldn't be embarrassed about your parents, Bec! They're part of you.' Emily thought of her own parents, eccentric but harmless, creating a garden in France, where they now lived.

'Don't make it worse than it already is,' said Rebecca, patting her daughter as she began to murmur.

'Cheer up, Sausage,' said James. 'Al's bringing Kate over to see the baby.'

'I don't know why you're being so damned cheerful,' said Rebecca. 'My mother runs you ragged. Nothing you do is good enough for her. She runs me ragged too, saying I don't look after you properly because I don't iron your pyjamas.'

'I don't wear pyjamas,' said James, confused.

'So, where's she going to sleep?' asked Emily. 'You can't put your mother on the sofa bed for more than a night.' She felt proprietorial about the sofa bed after what had happened in it.

'Here's the thing,' said James. 'There's the bothy, at the end of the house. It's nearly ready to go. It just needs a bed and things in it.'

'If you'd like me to help you get it ready—' Emily began.

'No! I told my mother she couldn't stay because there was only the sofa bed, which she says is terribly uncomfortable.' Rebecca had clearly taken this personally.

'And . . .?' Emily looked at James and Rebecca, hoping for enlightenment.

'She's staying up the road,' said James. 'Our friends have a B and B. She's booked in with them.'

'Oh, well, that's OK!' said Emily. 'She'll hardly be here. It'll be fine.'

James shook his head. 'She's arranged for Bed only.

She'll be on our doorstep at seven a.m., every morning, dressed and ready, and she'll expect us to be dressed and ready, too.'

'But she'll leave at seven p.m.?' said Emily, determined to find the positive in this. 'Leaving you to have the evening on your own?'

'No chance,' said Rebecca. 'She won't leave until after the *News at Ten*, which she'll insist on watching. I can't bear it, Em, I really can't!'

She did seem close to tears and Emily went over to her to pat her back, trying to think of something encouraging.

'The thing is,' said Rebecca, 'I always get a bit of baby blues – nothing major and nothing I'd usually pay any attention to – but with her here, I know it'll be worse. I'll cry all the time and she'll tell me how lucky I am.'

Emily bit her lip to hide a smile; Rebecca *was* quite lucky but it would tactless to point this out when she was feeling anything but. 'Make a calendar,' she said. 'Get the boys to do it, and cross off a day until she's gone. You could even divide the day up into sections, so you all get a chance to colour in a section. You know, breakfast to morning coffee, coffee to lunch.'

The boys regarded her with interest.

'You'll be too busy to fill it in often, so when you do, there'll be loads to do. The time will fly by!'

'I'm not convinced,' said James. 'But we'll cope.'

Just then the back door opened and Kate came running in. 'Can I see the baby?' She screeched to a halt. 'Oh,' she whispered. 'Is that her?'

'You don't have to whisper, Kate,' said Archie. 'She's asleep!'

'Yes, but we don't want her to wake up, so whispering's good,' said Rebecca. 'Hello, Kate! Come and give me a kiss and then you can see Nell.'

'Could I hold her?'

'Of course, but we're doing it sitting on the sofa at the moment, until the under-twenty-ones are better at it,' Rebecca explained. 'Oh, here's your dad.'

Emily's eyes flew to Alasdair and caught him looking at her. There was a flash of something – desire? Passion? Possibly even regret? – in his expression and she hurriedly turned her gaze to Kate, fervently wishing she hadn't told Rebecca they'd slept together. But Rebecca didn't let her down.

'Hi, Al! Lovely to see you. Come and see your niece and then we'll go to the sitting room and Kate can have a hold.'

Alasdair negotiated his way past the table and chairs until he got to Rebecca. He kissed his sister-in-law and then came round and kissed Emily.

'Have you heard the bad news?' said James.

'No, what?' said Alasdair. 'What's happened?'

'Nothing – yet,' said Rebecca gloomily. 'But my mother is coming to stay. And Emily's going.'

Emily felt like a traitor. She'd said she'd stay as long as Rebecca needed her but she hadn't realised she'd still need her now the baby was safely here.

'Well, that's easily sorted,' Alasdair said. 'Why don't you ask Emily to stay for a bit? She can help keep off the mother-in-law from hell.'

'Al!' said Rebecca. 'That is a genius idea! Em, would you? Do you have to go back immediately?'

Emily thought for a moment. She could probably ask to delay her start time – especially as she hadn't yet had a chance to tell anyone she'd decided to accept the job. She had a couple of weeks anyway. 'I could probably stay for a little bit . . . But where would I sleep? I may think the sofa bed is perfectly comfy, from what little I've slept on it, but—'

'No!' said James, pouncing on this offer. 'We'll fix up the bothy, put you in there. It'll mean sleeping on the sofa for a few days, but—'

'Mum would really not like that,' said Rebecca. 'She'd say it was slummy having a guest on the sofa.'

'Emily could stay with us,' said Kate. 'We've got a spare room.'

'That's a brilliant idea!' said Rebecca. 'Just until the bothy's finished.'

'It's too far away, really,' said Emily, embarrassed at being forced on Alasdair by his daughter. 'Unless there's a spare car going it would mean getting lifts. No, I'll manage on the sofa until the bothy's done. It's first thing in the morning you're going to need me,' she said to Rebecca, who seemed about to protest. 'Your mother will just have to cope with it being slummy.'

'Had an idea,' said James. 'Why doesn't Emily go and stay with Alasdair and Kate at least for tonight? She can have a good night's sleep and then come back before Bec's mum gets here.'

'Goodee!' said Kate. 'Emily's coming to stay at my house!' she said in a sing-song voice.

Her male cousins regarded her darkly. Had Kate stolen the star guest even before she'd really settled in? 'Not fair,' said Henry.

'Fair!' said Kate. 'I knew her before you did and she's stayed in my house before.'

'Guys!' said Emily. 'Before you start treating me like your favourite toy, how am I going to help out in the morning if I need a car to get here? Is there a bike I could borrow?' She was thinking how well Lizzie had managed with her bike.

'We haven't got a bike and you're right about the lifts, but what about this for a plan?' said James. 'After lunch, Alasdair and Kate will take Emily to their house where she can have a long sleep. Mum will take Nell to bed where she can have a long feed and a long sleep. And the boys and me will start on the bothy. How's that?'

'Perfect,' said Emily, suddenly longing for sleep.

'But lunch first,' said Rebecca. 'There's soup in the freezer—'

'I've already defrosted it in the microwave and put it on the Aga,' said Emily. 'And I found some rolls.' She saw the boys looking at her and realised they hadn't taken in an important fact. 'The electricity's back on, by the way.'

'Telly!' shouted the boys and all three children ran out of the room.

Emily went to Rebecca's bedroom for a minute and sent the email accepting the job. She was worried that if she didn't do it now, she'd keep making excuses not to, and she knew it was the right thing to do.

Chapter Sixteen

⁕

Emily fell asleep in the car although it wasn't a long journey. When she woke up, as they drew up in front of the house, she said, 'I'm so sorry. You've been through everything I went through and you're still awake.'

Alasdair laughed. 'I did fit in a quick power nap and I expect James is in front of *Scooby-Doo* or some such, with the boys.'

'*Power Rangers*,' said Kate. 'They like *Power Rangers*.'

It was soon obvious that Kate and Alasdair intended to treat Emily like an honoured guest. Kate pulled her into the house. 'We made a cake. But it's all right, there are no dog hairs.'

'That's good,' said Emily, 'although the odd dog hair can add a bit of flavour, I think. But before cake, I'll just go and wash my hands.'

'You don't have to. Dad doesn't mind!'

'I need a wee, love,' said Emily. 'It's just a polite way of saying it.'

When she came back to join them in the kitchen Kate

was saying, 'So why don't people say they're going to wash their feet?'

'Because they'd have to take their socks off,' said Alasdair, 'and people maybe don't want to do that.'

'But if they're really having a wee—'

'It's just old-fashioned manners,' said Emily. 'And they don't always make sense.' She smiled apologetically on behalf on the incomprehensible adult world.

'Let's have tea,' said Alasdair. 'It's all ready. I hope you don't mind having it in the kitchen.'

'It's the only place to eat in my little cottage,' said Emily, pulling out a chair. 'I've turned the dining room into a study.'

'Do you miss your house?' asked Kate.

'I was thinking about it,' said Emily, 'but I don't think I do. It's there and it's lovely, but I'm here and that's fine.'

'Are you happy with builder's tea? Or would you rather have Earl Grey?' said Alasdair, interrupting Emily's philosophical meanderings.

'Builder's, every time.'

After tea and cake – which was indeed very good – they went to the sitting room and Alasdair lit the fire.

'We're going to watch a DVD,' Kate announced. 'One that's suitable for me and not boring for adults.'

'Sounds lovely,' said Emily, putting a cushion into the small of her back. She managed to stay awake for half the credits and then fell asleep again.

Kate was frowning at her when she woke up. 'You missed all the film! Daddy said I wasn't to wake you but it's a waste!'

'Not really, sweetheart,' said Emily. 'If you really liked the film and I haven't seen it, it means we can watch it again, together. It's always nice to have a good film for when the weather's horrible.'

'But you're going away! You won't be here!'

'I'm not going for a little while, Kate. We'll probably have time to watch it.' Although she was trying to comfort Kate, Emily found she was just as sad at the prospect of leaving the little girl.

'Come on, you two. Beans on toast then it's bedtime.' Alasdair looked at Emily ruefully. 'I'm afraid I used up today's supply of cooking on the cake.'

'Beans on toast is my favourite – well, second to toast and Marmite, but that's not supper really, is it?'

'Not really. But you can have it for pudding if you insist.'

'Toast and Marmite isn't pudding!' said Kate indignantly, leading the way to the kitchen.

'OK, Katkin, bath and bed,' said Alasdair.

Kate's mouth turned down but before she could protest Emily said, 'Would you like me to come and talk to you while you have a bath? Maybe play with your boats – have you got boats?'

Kate nodded. 'I have. Uncle James made me one out of wood when I was little. And I've got one that's a bit like the puffer.'

'And then, maybe I could read you some stories while you're in bed? I haven't read anyone a story for ages.'

It was only when Emily saw Kate's teddy wearing his tam-o'-shanter that she remembered the Fair Isle scarf she had started for him what seemed a lifetime ago. 'Oh my goodness! I forgot all about it and I've left it at Rebecca's but I've got a surprise coming for Ted. He's going to love it. He'll be matching.'

'Is it a scarf?' said Kate, excitedly.

'How did you guess?'

'It doesn't take a genius,' said Kate, sounding about fifteen.

'You're so nice to Kate,' said Alasdair when Emily emerged from Kate's bedroom some time later.

'I like spending time with her. I hadn't read *Milly-Molly-Mandy* since I was little. My grandmother had the books and I loved them then and I still do.'

Alasdair laughed. 'I'm afraid I could never get my head round *Milly-Molly-Mandy*. Catriona's mother gave them to Kate but we don't read them often. Ever, really. I'm more of a *Katie Morag* man.'

'Each to his own. I could never get on with *Little Grey Rabbit* myself, although the pictures were wonderful.'

'Come on through to the sitting room and have a well-deserved dram.'

Emily took a breath. 'Actually, I think I'll just go to bed myself. I'm so tired and you must be too.'

He looked at her questioningly.

Emily went on, 'There's an elephant in the room, here. I really don't think we should sleep together.'

He raised an eyebrow. She persevered. 'Supposing Kate found us? It would be terribly confusing for her when we know it can't last. It's just a sort of holiday romance. Real life is going to start very soon.' She cleared the gathering tears from her throat. 'I've got a new job to go to.'

He frowned. 'What new job is that?'

Emily shrugged, not wanting to talk – or even think – about her new job. 'The maternity unit is going to be refurbished and expanded and they want me to run it. It's a really great opportunity.'

'I see. Well, if I can't take you to heaven and back, can I offer you a drink? It'll help get you off to sleep.'

'That would be very nice if I can take it to bed with me. I'll be off in no time, then.'

'I'll get it for you.' He paused. 'Of course you're right about us not sleeping together – it would be confusing and possibly upsetting for Kate – but I am disappointed.'

Tears threatened more sharply now and Emily couldn't speak. She just nodded and looked at him. He reached up and put his hand on her cheek for a few seconds before going to fetch her whisky.

Alasdair dropped her off at Rebecca and James's house at eight the following morning, on his way to take Kate to school and to go to the surgery.

Rebecca was sitting at the breakfast table feeding Nell while James harried the boys into eating their cereal.

'They don't want to go to school,' said James, 'but I'm going to be really busy getting the bothy ready—'

'And I'll have to clean for my mother,' said Rebecca. 'If they don't hurry up they'll miss their lift and then James will have to take them.'

'OK, boys, tell you what, I'll make your favourite cake

for when you come home,' said Emily, trusting that the way to hearts via stomachs rule applied to boys as well as men.

'Chocolate cake with Smarties!' they yelled in unison.

'It shall be yours!' said Emily. 'Now eat up. And off you go. Have you got your homework? Packed lunches?'

'We have hot school dinners,' said Henry. 'Although sometimes it's cold.'

'Life, eh?' said Emily. 'Isn't it just baffling sometimes?'

When at last the boys were off to school and James could be heard banging in the bothy, Emily took Nell out of Rebecca's arms. 'So how are you? Milk coming in?'

'No problem there, she's been tugging away at me all night.'

'Well, she's asleep now. Why don't you get a shower and maybe get dressed? I'll look after her.' She peered at the bundle that was Nell. 'Golly, you are sweet! Your grandmother is going to go wild with excitement!'

'She won't,' said Rebecca. 'I think deep down she thinks my children are too much for me and I shouldn't have so many of them. It's ironic. I'm not saying the kids aren't exhausting and hard work but she's much worse. At least I can be myself with the boys. And Nell now, of course.'

'OK,' said Emily briskly. 'Off for a shower and then a nap. You'll be fine if you get enough rest. I've got Nell and we'll be very happy together. And I'll do any cleaning that's required.'

Emily found that Nell liked the sound of the hoover – or at least didn't complain about it. While she couldn't do a brilliant job, Emily did get round the house giving it a lick and a promise while Rebecca had a nap. She knew it wouldn't be good enough for Rebecca's mother but deeper cleaning could go on when Emily didn't have a sleeping baby in her arms.

When Nell woke up properly and couldn't be fobbed off with jiggling and singing, Emily took her back to Rebecca, who accepted her warmly. 'When I've got her down again I'll clean.'

'I'm doing it already,' said Emily firmly. 'And cake-making. Does your mother have a favourite cake? Or will she fight the boys for Smarties?'

'She likes lemon drizzle,' said Rebecca, 'and always opens my fridge and asks me when it was last cleaned out. Which is probably when she last came.' Rebecca wrinkled her brow. 'It's funny, I'm so meticulous about hygiene on the puffer but here, I'm a bit of a slob.'

'OK, I'll make both cakes and clean out the fridge. Are we OK for ingredients? And if we're not, where do I go for them?'

'There's a lovely little shop in Tayvallich. They'll have everything you want.'

'So what would you like to eat tonight? And what about your mother? If we have a menu plan it'll make it less stressful.'

'Having you here is making it less stressful. Honestly, Em, I can't thank you enough for staying.'

'Honestly, Becca, it's an absolute pleasure. Really it is. I love spending time with you guys.'

'And Alasdair? Did you have a nice time with him last night?'

'Calm down. We did have a very nice time indeed but

I was mostly with Kate, who may be my new best friend – after you, of course.'

'You're so good with children,' said Rebecca, admiringly.

'I'm not. I have no idea how to be with children.'

'Well, we couldn't have managed without you, whatever you say.'

'Say thank you to Emily for the cake, boys,' said James, eyeing the sweetie-covered mound eagerly. He had collected his sons from school and brought them home to a kitchen scented with chocolate and lemon.

'I had so much fun doing it,' said Emily. 'I made it my challenge to get the entire tube of Smarties on it and I could only get one of those big tubes. And I didn't have to do any piping or writing or anything. Brilliant fun.'

'Thank you very much indeed,' said Henry solemnly. 'Mum? Will we be able to eat it when Grandma is here? She doesn't let us have sweets.'

Rebecca looked anxious. 'Well, it's a cake, darling. Maybe only eat it in the kitchen? Grandma can have her tea in the sitting room, with her lemon drizzle. In fact, we'll have an eating-in-the-kitchen-only rule while she's here. OK, guys?'

Her sons, seeing the sense in it, agreed to this restriction. 'I do like Grandma,' said Archie, 'but she is hard work.'

'Lots of the best people are hard work,' said Emily. 'Look at Nell! We all love her to pieces but she takes a lot of looking after.'

'She's not that fussed about table manners, though,' said James. 'And while I am too, my standards aren't quite as high as Grandma's.'

Rebecca sighed. 'She wasn't nearly as strict when she was just my mum. But she thinks we're far too lax about everything and tries to fit in all the upbringing she thinks the kids aren't getting into her infrequent visits.'

'Sort of manners-cramming?' said Emily.

Rebecca nodded. 'She thinks my life would be easier if my children were better trained and if I just put the effort in now I'd reap the rewards later.'

'That sort of makes sense, love,' said James.

'In theory, maybe, but not in practice,' said Rebecca. 'And I hate people telling me how to bring up my children. The irony is, my mother would never have put up with anyone telling her how to look after me and my brother.' She sighed, and Emily thought she sounded tired and fed up.

'I'm going to make tea,' said Emily. 'Earl Grey for Becca, builder's for me. James? Boys?'

'Earl Grey, please,' said Archie and James nodded.

'Grandma introduced it to the boys a couple of visits ago,' said James. 'We all drink it now. Even Henry.'

'You should have said! I've been giving you the wrong kind. Now, let's have a timetable. When is Grandma expected? And has she got very big eyes and ears?'

'You mean, is she a wolf!' said Henry delightedly.

'Well, I was wondering,' said Emily. 'No offence, Becca.'

'None taken,' said her friend. 'She'll get here later this afternoon. She'll want to get settled in to her B and B before she comes here. She'll bring a mattress topper and her special pillow with a silk cover.'

'Blimey!' said Emily. 'I can see the sofa bed is quite unsuitable!'

Rebecca looked rueful. 'She means well, she really does . . .'

'But she's just rather hard work,' Emily finished for her. 'We'll all get on fine.'

Once they had planned every meal – including morning coffee and teatime – Emily said, 'How does she get here?'

'She flies and I usually pick her up,' said Rebecca. 'It'll have to be James this time.'

'God, Bec! I could really do with the time that'll take,' said James. 'I mean, I know we're not desperate for her to move into the bothy, but we want it for Emily. And doing it, we would at least look as if we're able to have her to stay in the house next time she comes.'

'Don't do the bothy for me, James. I'm quite happy on the sofa bed.'

'To be honest,' said James, 'it being ready for you was a bit over-ambitious.'

Emily smiled. 'I could pick her up,' she said. 'I've always fancied standing at the airport with a bit of cardboard in my hand, waiting for someone I've never met. Or in your mum's case – not met for years.' She suddenly remembered Sally's notice and turned to the boys. 'Hey, guys, you could make me a really cool sign! What about that, Becca? Would you trust me to collect your mum from the airport?'

'Absolutely. That's a brilliant idea. Now, boys, can you make a lovely sign – quickly? But don't put Grandma on it. Put Mrs Craig-Fforbes.' She paused. 'I'll write it out for you. It wouldn't do for you to spell it wrong.'

In spite of her confident exterior, Emily was rather dreading collecting a woman described as hard work by her grandsons and making polite conversation with her.

She held up her sign, only slightly embarrassed by the neon colours and reflective stickers that surrounded the name. It was quite a big sign, too. It had a long name on it.

'Well, at least I had no trouble finding you!' said an elegant woman with a blond bob, a huge suitcase, a carry-on and several duty-free bags. Emily could hardly recognise her from their brief meeting years before. Then she'd been a bit dumpy with mousy hair. Now she looked super-fit and hyper-groomed.

'The sign worked, then! I'm Emily. Becca's friend from university? I was her bridesmaid?'

Mrs Craig-Fforbes gave a rather tight smile. Maybe she'd discovered Botox since Emily had met her or perhaps she was a bit starchy. Emily hoped for the former. 'Of course I remember the wedding and if you were wearing peach satin I would probably recognise you, but otherwise, not.' The smile was broader this time. 'Is the car a long way away?'

'Not far at all. Let me take your things.'

Once settled in the passenger seat of the hastily cleaned-out Volvo, her luggage disposed about the car, Rebecca's mother produced an eye mask from her handbag.

'Would you think I was frightfully rude if I put this on and rested my eyes on the journey home? It was a very early start and I want to be at my best to meet my granddaughter. And the boys, of course,' she added.

'Not at all rude. It's a very good idea. There's a houseful of people very eager to see you and that's always very tiring.'

'Oh, I won't sleep. I never sleep during the day, but if I just rest my eyes, I'll be fine.'

As Emily drove her passenger home she wondered what Mrs Craig-Fforbes was going to make of the chaotic but adorable family that awaited her.

As requested, she drove Rebecca's mother straight to the Bed and Breakfast. She'd stayed there before and was welcomed with offers of tea and shortbread. They were obviously accustomed to their fussy client and were unfazed by her need to bring her own pillow and mattress topper.

'Did she like the sign?' asked Henry eagerly when Emily got back to the house. He'd applied some of his favourite stickers to decorate it and needed to know if it had been worth the sacrifice.

'I think so,' said Emily. 'She said it made me easy to find. I wouldn't be surprised if she didn't want to take it home with her and frame it.' After all, behind that glamorous exterior there might be a cosy granny figure, fighting to get out. Not fighting very hard currently, though, Emily thought.

'She might do that.' Rebecca's tone implied this was a fairly remote possibility.

'She's certainly changed since I last met her,' said Emily. 'What a glamorous granny.'

'Yes, she went on a major health kick, lost loads of weight, ran a half-marathon and now divides her time between fitness and supporting the beauty industry.' Rebecca sighed. 'You'd think being on her own since Dad died would make her more child-friendly – more eager to spend time with us – but it hasn't. He'd have loved the boys clambering over him but she's never been keen.'

'Well, maybe that's all about to change!' said Emily, worrying about the boys hearing all this about their granny.

'That's true,' said James. 'And I know she can be hard work but I am looking forward to seeing the old bat.'

'The Old Bat' arrived soon after, dressed down in beige slacks with a matching jacket and chunky gold jewellery.

'Darling!' she said as she embraced Rebecca. 'Should you even be up? You've just had a baby. And where is she? How lovely to have a girl at last. You must be thrilled!'

'We'd have been thrilled with whatever sort of baby we had,' said Rebecca crisply. 'And I'm sure I'll get used to having a girl eventually.'

'We wanted a boy,' said Henry.

James nodded. 'We know where we are with boys.'

'Oh, but little girls!' said Mrs Craig-Fforbes dreamily.

'What about a glass of fizz?' said James. 'Let's go through to the sitting room. Becca, go and see if Nell's awake. I know your mum is dying to see her.'

'James, dear, you really must call me Valerie,' said his mother-in-law. 'You and Rebecca have been married for years now.'

'I do in my head,' said James. 'Now you sit down and I'll bring the champagne.'

James distributed glasses of champagne and sparkling elderflower to the boys, in the same flutes. Valerie looked anxious, assuming they would instantly break the glasses. But Emily noticed they took their responsibilities with regard to the champagne flutes very seriously. They were in no danger.

'So, how was your journey, Mum?' said Rebecca, holding the audibly hungry Nell.

'Fine, really. I had to start at silly o'clock, of course.' She sighed. 'It is a shame that you live so far away from me.'

Rebecca looked guilty. 'I know, Mum, but it's been a while now. We've lived up here for well over ten years.'

Nell's cries became louder and Emily wondered why Rebecca didn't latch her on and so stop the crying. There must be a reason.

'Would you like me to put a clean nappy on Nell, and then you can feed her?' she asked.

'Thank you!' said Rebecca, handing the screaming bundle.

As Emily whisked out of the room she overheard Valerie say, 'I'm so glad you've got the woman who was your bridesmaid to be your nanny. I never thought you'd do anything so sensible!'

'Mum!' wailed Rebecca. 'She's not a nanny, she's my best friend!'

'Well, it's good to employ someone you know and if you want to call her a mother's help, let's not worry about semantics.'

'What are semantics?' asked Archie.

His mother ignored this reasonable question.

'Not only is she my friend,' Rebecca went on, 'she's my midwife! She delivered Nell – during a storm with no electricity.'

'My God, Becca, darling,' said her mother. 'I didn't realise things were as bad as that!'

Chapter Seventeen

Nell wasn't crying any less by the time Emily brought her back to Rebecca. She took her screaming bundle and looked at her mother.

'She needs feeding, Becca,' said Emily. 'Why don't you plug her in?'

'You're surely not suggesting that Becca feeds her baby in the sitting room? In front of the boys?' Valerie seemed horrified.

'I am,' said Emily. 'Then she can carry on talking to you. She won't want to tear herself away when you've only just arrived! And the boys have seen their baby sister being fed lots of times already.' Emily wondered if hearing herself referred to as a nanny had somehow turned her into one – a bossy one at that.

'I suppose – if it's the modern way,' said Valerie, shuddering slightly.

'Didn't you breastfeed in front of the family, Mum?' asked Rebecca, much more comfortable now her baby was no longer crying and making little whimpers of satisfaction instead.

'No, darling. I couldn't breastfeed. Didn't I ever tell you? You cried and cried but however much they told me it was best I just couldn't feed you.'

Rebecca was apologetic. 'You may have done, Mummy, but I'd forgotten. You know what being pregnant does to your brain, turns it to mush. Well, in my case.'

Emily hadn't noticed Rebecca being remotely mushy but she realised she was pacifying her mother. Had Valerie actually applied her nipple to her daughter's lips when she was crying and crying? Or couldn't she bring herself to? Still, not everyone wanted to breastfeed. Emily personally encouraged it but she hoped she was never bullying.

'Supper?' she said, getting to her feet. 'Valerie, you must be tired after your journey and the boys need to eat.' Without waiting for anyone to agree with her she went into the kitchen.

Later, when James was reading to the boys, Rebecca, her mother and Emily sat in the sitting room. Soon, James would walk Valerie to the Bed and Breakfast but now, there had to be conversation. Emily had her knitting.

'If you don't mind me saying so,' said Valerie, obviously going to say it anyway, 'that scarf is very small, even for a newborn baby.'

Emily laughed. 'Oh, it's not for Nell! It's for a teddy. I'll knit one if Becca wants me to, but it'll take me ages. I'm much slower than usual doing Fair Isle. I've only just learnt it.'

'For a teddy?' said Valerie, still not sure she understood.

'Yes. Ted belongs to a little girl I know.' Emily looked at Rebecca. 'Maybe your mother's met Kate?'

'Oh, Kate!' said Valerie. 'Yes, of course I've met her. Charming little person. Such a tragedy losing her mother like that. You'd have thought Alasdair would have found a new wife by now.'

'I don't think he wants Kate to think her mother was replaceable,' said Rebecca. 'Besides, she was beautiful. A very tough act to follow.'

Emily remembered that Rebecca didn't know that the tough act was actually walking out on her family when she was killed in a car accident. That probably had more to do with Alasdair still being single. He'd have trust issues and if one woman – her own mother – could let Kate down, why would someone not her mother be any better?

'He must have women queuing up. A handsome man like that,' said Valerie. 'A doctor, too.'

'I think he finds all that a bit daunting,' said Rebecca.

'Kate might not want to share her father,' said Valerie. 'If it's just been the two of them for a while. She may have made it difficult for Alasdair.'

'So,' said Emily, desperate to change the subject, 'Kate has a teddy who has to be knitted for. I'm hoping to get this scarf done quickly, before I go home.' Suddenly Emily wanted to knit really slowly, as if she wouldn't have to go home until the scarf was done. Although an exchange of emails with her future boss had told her that time was ticking away fast.

'You're not going home just yet,' said Rebecca firmly. 'You've got plenty of time to finish the scarf. You've got, what . . .?'

'A couple of weeks. I thought I could stretch it for a bit longer but now they want me as soon as possible.'

'That soon? I know you'd told me but I somehow blanked it out of my mind.'

'I think I had too, in some ways.' The women exchanged anguished glances.

Unaware of their reaction, Valerie went on, 'Plenty of time to finish the scarf then. It's very small. Are you going to do it all in Fair Isle or just the ends?'

Just then, knitting was the very last thing that Emily wanted to talk about. 'All of it, I think. And by the time I do go, you won't need me any more.' The thought was heartbreaking.

'We'll always need you!' said Rebecca, sounding as desperate as Emily felt.

'But, darling, you said Emily wasn't a nanny,' said Valerie. She turned to her. 'So what are you? You told me you were Rebecca's bridesmaid but—'

'I'm a friend, helping out a friend,' Emily broke in to save Valerie from embarrassment, forcing herself to smile. 'But as I'm a midwife, I understand babies.'

Valerie nodded. 'So that is how you could deliver Becca's baby in a storm with no electricity.'

'Yes,' said Emily. 'And it was fun, wasn't it, Becc? A bit dramatic maybe, but we all managed brilliantly.'

Rebecca sighed. 'It wasn't what we'd planned but it was far, far better than going to hospital.'

Valerie shuddered. 'Well, I'm so glad things turned out as they did but if I'd known what was going on I'd have been beside myself with anxiety! I really wish you'd told me,' she added.

'The phone lines were down, Mum, we couldn't tell anyone. And if you'd have been anxious we wouldn't have wanted to inflict that on you.'

'Besides,' said Emily, 'it all happened rather quickly and you must have been delighted to hear it was all over—'

'And it was a little girl!' finished Valerie, still ecstatic. 'I do hope she has ballet lessons. You had ballet lessons and looked so sweet in your little tutu.'

'I think it's too early to say,' said Rebecca, smiling down at her daughter but possibly amused by her mother.

James came in. 'That's them asleep. They were tired.'

'I think, James, if you don't mind,' said Valerie, 'I'll ask you to take me along to Wee Nook now. You'll need me bright and early in the morning.'

'No need to be too early, Mum,' said Rebecca. 'We've got Emily. You take your time and come along for coffee, at about eleven? We'll be sorted by then.'

'Very well, if you're sure,' said Valerie.

'Quite sure, Mum. And it's lovely to have you here.'

Just after lunchtime the following day, Lizzie Miller-Hall came to check on Rebecca and the baby. She pronounced them both to be very fit and well. Valerie had fallen in love with Nell and was holding her, actually cooing, while Rebecca lay on the bed.

'Emily, are you busy just now? I wondered if you fancied a little run-out. I've my rounds to do and if you came with me, it would be a way for you to see a bit more of the countryside.'

'I'm needed here—'

'No you're not!' interrupted Rebecca. 'Why don't you go out for the day? You'll be leaving us soon and you haven't been out and about much. I've got Mum and James. We can get him in from his carpentry in the bothy if necessary. Lizzie's right! It would be a great way for you to see some more of the area.'

'And – no offence, dear,' said Valerie, 'it would be nice for me and my daughter to have some bonding time together. We see each other so seldom.'

Emily considered and then shrugged. 'Oh well, if I'm officially dismissed, I'd love that!'

'You're officially dismissed,' said Rebecca, making shooing gestures. 'See you at teatime. Don't haste ye back.'

'Well, this is fun!' said Emily. 'Like a mini tour.'

'Fun for me too,' said Lizzie, changing gear on her ancient Peugeot. 'Company on my rounds. After the storm I want to check up on a lot of my elderlies.'

'So what is your job-title exactly?'

Lizzie laughed. 'I have a few part-time jobs that blend well together. I'm part health visitor, part midwife – you know about that part – but I also do a bit of district nursing. I do that most.'

'And are your patients mostly elderly?'

'Clients? Yes. Although I do a few sessions at the maternity hospital if they need me. I like babies.'

'Obviously I do too, but I also like old ladies. There was a wonderful one I met when I was cooking on the puffer: Maisie. She taught me how to do Fair Isle knitting.

I finished a jumper for her. I have been to her house but I can't quite remember where it is.'

'I know Maisie! Let's call in on her when we've done the other stuff.'

Emily enjoyed her trip as much as she thought she would. Lizzie insisted that she came in with her for every visit and it seemed more like a string of social occasions than anything else.

'What we have round here is community, Emily,' Lizzie explained. 'The younger people help out the older ones – even the really difficult older ones. Well, actually there's only one – she never remembers to say thank you – and yet her neighbours across the road do everything for her, mowing her lawn, doing her shopping, taking her dog for walks. It's what makes the world go round. Fortunately, most of my Golden Oldies are delightful. But it's the community that keeps people going.

'That's brilliant, isn't it? You know Maisie has a knitting group? A bus comes once a fortnight or so – whenever they want it really – and they get together and knit. Or just chat. I heard they had a lovely party.'

'I was there!' said Emily. 'It was indeed lovely.' And Alasdair had come, right at the end.

'So, are the local doctors supportive?' Emily went on, wanting to hear Alasdair's name, even if it was only in passing.

'They're amazing,' said Lizzie. 'Especially Alasdair Cumming. He's a great favourite with the ladies, especially with the more elderly ones.'

But not exclusively, thought Emily.

'And his little girl – what a sweetheart. Of course she's

quite old for her age, it being just the two of them, but a darling.'

'I know Kate. And Maisie taught her to knit. I wonder if she remembers how to, now.'

'You'll have to give her another lesson, to make sure. It's not easy to teach a little one to knit.'

Emily fell silent. Was it right for her to be friends with Kate when she was in love with her father? If Kate found out she'd think Emily was just like all those other women, sucking up to Kate to get to Alasdair. And while Emily was in love – or lust, or whatever you called it – with Alasdair, she did really love Kate too.

They called in on Maisie after they'd done all their other visits. She was delighted to see Emily and Lizzie. When she had made tea and got out the tin of shortbread, she said, 'Now I want to hear all about Nell's birth.'

Emily laughed. 'You don't want all the gory details, do you?'

'No,' said Maisie. 'Just the ungory ones. It's like that television programme about people having babies.'

'*One Born Every Minute*?' Emily asked. 'It wasn't like that at all. This was a home birth, only we hadn't made all the preparations I usually do for a home birth.'

'This is interesting,' said Lizzie. 'We don't have home births much here. We're too far away from help if something goes wrong.'

'I do deliver babies in hospital too, but we make it as calm and home-like as we can.'

'I'd be interested to hear how you arrange that,' said Lizzie.

'I'll tell you later, but I'm very pleased to report to

Maisie that Nell is absolutely perfect. The image of her father.'

'Such a good-looking man!' said Maisie. 'And that brother of his! I'm not sure how those looks would settle on a tiny baby girl though.'

'She'll end up as pretty as a picture, I know,' said Lizzie.

'She will,' Emily agreed firmly, wondering about the Cumming family nose and then about one particular member of the Cumming family.

'And her mother is doing fine,' added Lizzie, 'although of course she's tired.'

'I've a little something to give the baby,' said Maisie. She got up and slowly crossed the room to a drawer. From it she produced a twist of tissue paper with something inside. 'It's a spoon,' she said and unwrapped it.

It was silver, with a pear-shaped bowl and a twisted handle. It was extremely pretty. 'I hope Rebecca won't feel obliged to keep it clean – she has enough on her plate – but it's a little something from an old friend.'

'I think she'll love it!' said Emily. 'Rebecca loves antiquey things and this is probably really an antique!'

'It is, it's really quite old. I like to think of it finding a good home.' Maisie looked pleased. 'Now, another piece of shortbread, anyone?'

'I couldn't eat any more,' said Emily, 'but if you've got any examples of your knitting, I'd love to see them.'

Maisie was delighted and produced a large dress box smelling of mothballs. It was full of pieces; some were finished items and some samples of different patterns.

'I can't do much now,' she explained to Lizzie. 'I'm too

265

arthritic, but I did a lot up until a couple of years ago. Emily here very kindly finished a pullover I was knitting for my youngest grandson. It's a tradition, you see; they all have Fair Isle jumpers knitted by me and I'd done half of it. Thanks to you, Emily, he now has one.'

'And it was thanks to Emily that Rebecca had her baby in the warmth and quiet and not in the back of an ambulance,' said Lizzie. 'I haven't experienced it myself but it doesn't look comfy.'

'I don't think any woman would describe childbirth as comfy,' said Maisie and they all laughed.

Emily looked at her watch. 'We've had such a fun day,' she said, 'but shouldn't we be getting back?' She was suffering a pang of guilt for leaving Rebecca so long with only James and her mother for assistance.

'So, when will I see you again, dear?' asked Maisie.

Tears rushed to Emily's throat making it difficult for her to speak. 'Actually, Maisie, I have to go home, back down south on Sunday week—'

'Oh, my dear,' said Maisie and took her into her arms to give her a hug. 'We're going to miss you.'

Emily recovered herself as soon as they'd said their final goodbyes and got back in the car.

'So,' said Lizzie, 'tell me how you make your maternity unit homely?'

Discussing something she was passionate about helped Emily pull herself together. She gave Lizzie all the details.

'Well, it would be lovely if you could come up and see our maternity unit sometime. Maybe give us some tips?'

'I'm sure that would be possible. And now there's Nell, as well as Rebecca, James and the boys, I'm sure to be up all the time.'

But would she be? Would she be able to cope with coming to a place that had such special memories? Did anyone go back to the site of their holiday romance? Probably not, for very good reasons.

'Alasdair called in,' said James at supper, a meal that Emily had cooked as soon as she'd got in.

'I didn't see him!' said Rebecca.

'No, he came into the bothy, helped for a bit. We're nearly done now.' He gave his mother-in-law his best passenger smile. 'You'll be able to stay in the house next time, Valerie.'

'Actually, I think I like the Wee Nook,' Valerie said apologetically. 'It's lovely and quiet in the mornings.'

'The bothy will be quiet,' said James. 'You won't hear the boys—' A look of pain crossed his face and he suddenly stopped.

'Mummy,' said Henry. 'Did you just kick Daddy?'

'Of course not!' said Rebecca, blushing. 'Why would I do that?'

'Anyway,' said James, hastily saving his marriage. 'He told me there's going to be a big old hooley up at the big house. It's in aid of something or other – can't remember what – but I think we should all go.'

'Will there be bagpipes?' asked Valerie.

'Oh yes. Alasdair's band is playing too. It's going to be great fun. All kilts and sporrans.'

'Will you wear your kilt, Daddy?' asked Archie.

'No. I hate wearing kilts,' said James. 'I spent a childhood with chafed knees because I was always flapping around in wet tartan. But Alasdair might wear his.'

Emily wasn't sure if he'd caught her eye on purpose. 'This is jolly delicious, Em,' he said.

'I don't think it sounds quite my thing,' said Valerie. 'I like my entertainment to be a bit more sophisticated.'

'When is it, darling?' asked Rebecca.

'Saturday week. You'll be able to come, won't you, Em? Your Highland experience won't be complete without you going to a ceilidh.'

She laughed. 'I will have to fly back to real life the following day, but I haven't booked my flight yet, so I'll go for one not too early in the morning.'

'Isn't your life here real?' asked Henry, frowning. 'It seems real to me.'

'That's not quite what I mean, Henry. It's hard to explain.'

'Henry,' said his doting granny, 'if Emily had wanted you to know she'd have told you. Now get on and eat your bits of pepper. It's very good for you.'

James and Rebecca exchanged exasperated glances. Emily didn't think he should have been fobbed off either, however hard it was to explain what she meant.

'The thing is, Henry,' said Emily, hoping Valerie wouldn't think she was appallingly rude, 'I have a job where I live in Gloucestershire.'

'You have a job here,' said Henry, still confused. 'You cook on the puffer and help Mummy with us and Nell.'

'I know but the season is over, so the puffer doesn't

need a cook. And Mummy won't need help for much longer. I'll just be cluttering up the place.'

'Never!' said Rebecca. 'You can stay as long as you like!'

'Just till after the party,' said Emily firmly. 'Now, who's for seconds?'

Afterwards, when the boys were in bed and Valerie was tucked up in Wee Nook, the grown-ups and Nell repaired to the sitting room for whisky and hot chocolate.

'Do you really have to go home, Em?' asked Rebecca, sipping from her mug and giving herself a slight moustache.

'You know I do.' Emily was drinking whisky and took a gulp; it helped get rid of the lump which formed in her throat whenever she thought of leaving Scotland. 'I have this amazing job – my dream job really – and I have to go and do it.'

Rebecca opened her mouth to protest but James frowned and shook his head. 'Don't nag her, darling. We mustn't be selfish.'

'You could live in the bothy!' said Rebecca. 'If you wanted to. Just sayin'.'

'Where did you pick up that vulgar expression?' asked James, obviously channelling Rebecca's mother.

'The boys. I like it.'

'I am going to miss you all dreadfully,' said Emily.

'What about Alasdair?' went on Rebecca, making Emily blush.

'What about him?' she replied. 'We're just friends – I'm leaving better friends than him on Sunday week.'

'Obviously! We're your best friends ever, but Alasdair?'

James cleared his throat and got up. 'I think I'll put the kettle on. I need another cup of coffee.'

When James was out of the way Rebecca said, 'So what about Alasdair?' She said it gently but firmly as if referring to a terminal disease that had to be addressed.

Emily sighed. 'Well, I do have an amazing crush on him. He is wonderful. But I have to get real, Bec.' She took another sip of whisky. 'I've realised since living with you guys that actually, I do want children, a family. And if I'm not going to be far too old I need to start looking for the man who'll give me that. Alasdair is all about Kate – and I so get that! I understand that he has to protect her from all these women who just want to be friends with her to get to him. And of course he has trust issues! He'd be mad not to! God, if Kate's own mother walked out on her, why would any other woman stick by him – by her?' She stopped as she took in Rebecca's expression: no one knew about Kate's mother, how she was walking out on her family when she had the car accident, except her, Emily.

'She was walking out on him?' Rebecca said slowly.

Emily cleared her throat, as guilty as any prisoner in the dock. 'Actually, I didn't quite mean that. I mean she was – putting her shopping trip – holiday . . .' She petered out. Guilt swamped her like a tidal wave. 'Well, she left the house and didn't have Kate with her. Which was actually brilliant! That's what I meant.'

Rebecca nodded, still stunned. 'Of course. Of course that's what you meant.'

Into the huge gaping vacuum, Emily said, 'Have I got time to learn an eightsome reel before Saturday? I'll need to do that if I'm going to a ceilidh.'

Chapter Eighteen

As Emily cleared up the kitchen, took venison out of the freezer for the following night's supper, and then unfolded the sofa bed and arranged her bedding, she berated herself and wondered what on earth she should do by turns.

She trusted that Rebecca would be too tired or too busy dealing with Nell to find a moment to tell James, but she couldn't really expect her not to tell him. He was her husband, they didn't have secrets, and this was a major secret about James's beloved brother.

By the time she finally flopped into bed, her mind still racing, she decided she'd have to talk to Rebecca more about it. She'd give her permission to tell James and then swear them both to secrecy. But if Alasdair had found out she'd told Rebecca, even by mistake, he'd never trust Emily again. And while their relationship – if you could even call it that – had been very short-term she didn't want to go back to Gloucestershire with him hating her.

Even with a decision made it took her ages to get off to sleep. There was an iron bar she had never noticed before, just in the middle of her back.

She was awoken by Rebecca holding two mugs of tea. 'Sorry,' she said, 'did I wake you?'

She had but Emily didn't mind. She was both thirsty and in need of a chat with her best friend.

'Oh, love! You shouldn't be bringing me tea, that's my job!' she said.

'Not at all. I've just put Nell down after a feed and knew I'd never get back to sleep after what you told me so I thought: tea!'

'Oh God, I feel so awful!' Emily got herself upright and sipped her tea gratefully. 'We can't pretend I didn't accidentally tell you anything?'

'No, because once I'd got over the shock I realised I wasn't that surprised.' Rebecca pulled a blanket towards her and snuggled herself into an armchair. 'You know something? I never liked her.'

'Didn't you?' Emily could sense her friend wanted a good old-fashioned bitch about her sister-in-law and say the things she'd kept bottled up for years.

'No! She was so beautiful and cold. What's to like? And she was horrid to Alasdair in a quiet, snippy way. But he adored her.'

Up till now, Emily had liked the tone of the conversation but now she sighed. 'So he's not going to love someone as warm and cuddly and utterly lovely as me, then, is he? Not that I want him to, really, given that I'm going home soon.'

Rebecca laughed reluctantly. 'Well, not if he stays true to his chosen type of woman, but why would he? Look what happened.'

'They might have worked it out, though,' said Emily,

not joking now. 'If she hadn't had that accident it might have turned out to be just a blip. She might have walked out for a little bit, got her head clear and come back. And then they would have lived happily ever after, had more children.'

'But she did have an accident,' said Rebecca. 'And as you said, you're going home soon. So it's all a bit pointless.' She sounded bleak. 'Do you want a biscuit? I'm starving!'

Emily got up. 'I'll make toast. Let's go through to the kitchen.'

'So, do you know if Alasdair ever found out who Catriona was running off with?' Rebecca wiped toast crumbs from the corner of her mouth. Then she looked up, horrified.

James was standing in the doorway, holding Nell. 'What have I just overheard?' He sounded grim, as far from his usual, gentlemanly manner as possible. Rebecca got up and took the baby.

Emily cleared her throat. 'I've done an awful thing. I let out a terrible secret by mistake.'

'About Alasdair? And Catriona?'

Emily nodded.

'She was running away from him when she had that accident,' said Rebecca. 'Al told Emily and she blurted it out, last night. It's been gnawing away at me ever since.'

'And me,' said Emily. 'I feel like crawling away into a hole and staying there.'

James's expression lost some of its sternness. 'I don't think you need to go that far, but if something's been told to you in confidence—'

'I know!' Emily wailed. 'I thought I was brilliant at keeping secrets! I mean, I have kept loads of them, but somehow this one hopped out of my mouth before I could stop it. Or rather, I forgot it was a secret.'

'I wonder why he's never told me?' James sat down and Rebecca put bread in the toaster.

'I think it's to do with Kate,' said Emily. 'He doesn't want her finding out until he's ready to tell her.'

'You're probably right. I just feel sorry for the poor chap, keeping it to himself all this time,' said James.

It was because he was so nice that he didn't blame his brother for not telling him or resent his secret, reflected Emily. She got up to make him tea.

By the time the boys had left for school and everything was squared away for Valerie's impending arrival, Emily had managed to squash her guilt into a small corner of her brain and ignore it. What had happened wasn't wonderful but it wasn't going to change anything. James and Rebecca had sworn, over a pile of toast crumbs and a jar of marmalade, that they wouldn't ever tell Alasdair that they knew. She had to be content with that.

Considering how no one had wanted her to come, everyone was sad to see Valerie go the following week. James drove her to the airport and Emily and Rebecca went into the kitchen for a consoling cup of tea.

'I know she is quite hard work,' said Rebecca, 'as my darling son so sweetly put it, but having Mum here did make us get up and get tidy. Without her – and you, Em – we could have just slobbed about all day.'

'And without her, and you needing protection from

her,' said Emily. 'I would have gone home by now. I've had several emails from work – they're desperate for me to get back. There are plans for the new building to look at. But they'll wait until next week.'

Rebecca put her hand on Emily's arm. 'Oh, God, Em! It's been so amazing having you here! Are you sure you can't stay forever? As I said you could live in the bothy.'

Emily laughed. 'Let's go and have a look. I haven't seen it for days. Is it finished?'

'All bar the shouting. You can help choose the soft fabrics. Then maybe you'd stay.'

But Emily knew she couldn't.

They carried the baby round to the little house tacked on to the main one. It was stone, with thick walls and a fairly low ceiling. It had one, reasonably sized living room with the kitchen up one end. It was furnished with a gate-legged table and chairs as well as a sofa and an armchair pulled up to the wood-burner.

'Oh, this is lovely!' said Emily.

'You think it's OK having the kitchen in the sitting room?'

'Absolutely. You could watch telly while you cook. Imagine how horrifying Valerie would find that concept?'

'She would. One of the boys said something about wanting a telly in the kitchen and she jumped down his throat. I don't want the telly on during meals unless it's something very special, when we have what James's family call "lappers". But I do quite fancy one to entertain me. When I said this, she said, "Surely when you're cooking you need to focus on what you're doing?" But frankly, I'm mostly doing other things when I'm in the kitchen, like clearing up. And of course, I can multi-task.'

'Which means chopping an onion while keeping half an eye on the box?'

'Yep.' Rebecca ran a loving hand over the sink unit. 'What do you think of this?'

'Beautiful,' said Emily. 'He's a brilliant carpenter, your James, isn't he? He's done this beautifully. Such attention to detail.'

'He is good. And it's all recycled materials so it looks in keeping. This little cupboard is my favourite.' She opened a door tucked into the curve of the ceiling. 'Not sure what you'd keep in it.'

'Little jars of jam, sauces, things like that,' said Emily instantly, moving into the little house in her head. 'Let's go and check out the bedroom.'

The bedroom was just as nice. There was even a duvet and pillows on the bed although no covers as yet.

'If you like you could sleep here instead of on that ghastly sofa bed,' said Rebecca. 'Now it's finished, you may as well be comfortable.'

The thought that Alasdair might visit her here, when they would be completely private, flashed into her head. Although why he would when they'd agreed they shouldn't, and couldn't, be more than friends, she had no idea. 'That might be nice. I could test drive it for you.'

'That would be very useful. If it's going to be a holiday let we have to make sure it's got everything anyone might need.'

Although Emily didn't say it, she felt if she was in here, for the few days that were left before she had to go home, it would give James and Rebecca more space to be with their family. And moving into the bothy would start the process of separation Emily knew was going to be hard.

'I'll put the heating on then,' said Rebecca, going back into the kitchen.

After lunch Emily said, 'Becca, would it be all right if I borrowed the car? I want to try and see Alasdair. I found out he finishes his surgery today at two. If I went now, I'd catch him.'

'You don't want to ring him? I've got his number.' Rebecca reached across the table for her phone.

'No, I'd rather say goodbye in person. He doesn't know when I'm going, I don't think, so just ringing wouldn't seem right.'

'I didn't mean you shouldn't see him,' said Rebecca, 'I meant you should check he's going to be there.'

'I'm sure he will. I rang the surgery.'

Two hours later Emily parked the car and went into the house. 'Oh, Bec! Why didn't I listen to you?' she said. 'He'd gone off early to see someone way across the other side of the area. I missed him.'

'He's not a great communicator, I'm afraid, and of course, his work does take him away sometimes.'

'I don't know why I'd expect him to get in touch. We're just friends, after all. I can't expect him to be sending me loving emails. I shouldn't have tried to see him really. It would have only made the parting more difficult.'

Rebecca sighed. 'But it seems a shame after – well you

know.' She looked questioningly. 'You could phone him, or text?'

Emily shook her head. She'd thought about these options on the way back from the surgery and had rejected them. She still felt so guilty about blurting out his secret to Rebecca she felt a phone call would be horribly awkward. And a text would seem just rude.

'No, it's OK. I'll just make a point of seeing him at the hooley at the Big Hoose.'

'The Big Hoose' was a huge old Scottish Baronial mansion, dripping with turrets, castellations and heraldic beasts, owned by a woman in her fifties. A few days before the party she knocked on Rebecca's door and Emily opened it.

'Hello! I'm Fiona McIlhose. You must be the heroine of the hour! Delivering the baby in that storm!'

Emily smiled. 'I am a midwife. It is what I do.'

'But not without electricity!'

'Sometimes. I have delivered a baby in a yurt. Did you want to see Rebecca?'

'Absolutely! And her new baby daughter. Is it convenient?'

Rebecca joined them on the doorstep. 'Fiona! How lovely to see you. Come on in.'

It wasn't long before it was evident that Fiona's visit was not just social.

'I was going to get caterers but they charge so much and they weren't that great last time,' she said. 'It's for the children's hospice.'

'OK, don't beat about the bush, what do you want us to make?'

'Frankly I oughtn't ask you to do anything when you've just had a baby and it's terribly short notice but I knew you had Emily here, so puddings?'

'How many?'

'Well, let's see . . .' Fiona appeared to do sums in her head but came up with the answer very quickly. 'Could you manage six? Anything you like but serving about eight each?'

'I do a very good trifle,' said Emily, 'as long as you don't want me to make Genoese sponges and jelly.'

'Sounds delicious. Can I just put you down for six large puds and you can decide what they are?' Fiona got up. 'Oh, nearly forgot! I've got a present for the little one. I bought it at a sale of work. I hope it's all right!'

It was a very charming little crocheted bonnet in a deep raspberry colour.

'My mother said babies should only ever wear white,' said Fiona, 'but I think this is a lovely colour. I wanted it for me only it didn't fit.'

When Fiona had left, Rebecca said, 'That woman is a living saint. She's always doing something to raise money. She told me once it was her duty. If she lived in such a large house and was comfortably off she had to do things for others.'

'I suppose she's right,' said Emily.

'I know, but think how many people don't,' said Rebecca. 'Are you all right to make all those puddings?'

'No problem,' said Emily. 'My only concern is what to wear.'

'We'll have a look in the wardrobe later,' said Rebecca. 'I hope there's something I can squash myself into. How long before I stop being the size of a house?'

Emily laughed. Rebecca didn't really look as if she'd just had a baby. 'How long will it take you to get off your baby weight? About five minutes, the rate you're going. Maybe ten?'

'That's the right answer, Em. Now shall we go and look at clothes before Nell wakes up?'

Teaching Emily a few basic ceilidh dances took a bit more time. There had been a dress in Rebecca's wardrobe, petrol blue, clingy, long enough to be decent but not so long that she couldn't dance in it. James had said 'Wow' when he saw her in it so Emily had said, 'Thank you very much, I'd love to borrow it.'

There was a pair of shoes that were a bit big, but it was decided that Emily could wear her own ballet flats to reel in.

The dancing lessons involved pushing all the furniture to the edges of the room.

Rebecca put a CD on. 'Now, you have to learn how to set to your partner. That's Archie.' She demonstrated and Nell, who, post-feed, was over her mother's shoulder, belched.

'Does that mean she likes it?' said Henry.

It was agreed that it did.

Emily eventually managed a pas de basque with Henry that was pronounced satisfactory by the others. Both boys knew the dances well having learnt them at school.

'OK,' Rebecca went on, 'now a basic gallop.'

'It's quite athletic!' said Emily, prancing up and back a few times.

'You can walk that bit if you get tired towards the end of the evening,' said Rebecca.

'But it's cheating,' said Archie, regarding Emily as if she was the sort of person who might cheat, given half a chance. 'And you have to keep your head up and not look at your feet.'

'Come on, Archie!' Emily protested. 'I'm an old lady and a beginner!'

'Looking at your feet won't help,' he said firmly.

She was certainly walking it through by the time she'd learnt how to do the Dashing White Sergeant, the Gay Gordons, Strip the Willow and Sir Roger de Coverley.

'That's very good,' said Rebecca, who'd sat with Nell operating the music. 'Tomorrow we'll teach you an eight-some and maybe Hamilton House, that's a nice one. And you'll be good to go!'

Later, in the kitchen while they got the evening meal together, Emily said to Rebecca, 'I can't help thinking that this party is quite hard work. I've had to cook up a storm and dance the equivalent of a marathon!'

'Don't be daft,' said Rebecca, pulling open a tin of beans with a practised hand. 'Nothing more than a fun run.' Then she looked at her friend. 'I really wish you didn't have to go home. We're going to miss you so much! The boys would have you reeling every night now you know the basics. Think how fit you'd get!'

They exchanged rueful smiles and Rebecca reached for the wine bottle.

Chapter Nineteen

It was Saturday evening and an autumn mist threaded its way across the sea and came up from the beach, wafting around the bottom of the big house giving it an ethereal, slightly spooky feel. James had taken the puddings up earlier so it was just the family and Emily squashed into the people carrier who had to unpack themselves into the chilly air.

'Will it be warm inside?' asked Emily, pulling her shawl closely about her, wishing she'd put her fleece on top of her evening dress.

'No, not to begin with,' said James. 'The fires will be lit and it will warm up, but until then, be prepared to shiver.'

'I know people who wear their thermals under their posh frocks,' said Rebecca, 'and take them off later. In fact, I've done it myself.'

As they walked from the car, which they'd parked in the designated field and not that near to the house, Emily realised she felt nervous and couldn't decide if it was because of the fact she wouldn't know anyone, hardly knew how to do Scottish dancing or because Alasdair would be there.

Although she knew it wasn't anyone's fault they hadn't met up after her failed attempt to see him, Emily felt anxious about seeing him, as if she was a teenager with a crush. It was so silly!

James had gone ahead with the boys, while Rebecca and Emily, with slightly less functional footwear, picked their way along behind them.

'Is Alasdair's band good?' Emily asked Rebecca when James was out of earshot.

'Yes, very, but I have to warn you that we might not see that much of him. When they're not playing, the groupies take up their time, rather.'

'Groupies?' Emily was surprised. 'I thought his band would be fairly low key, not the sort to attract crowds of teenagers!'

'Oh no, they are fairly low key but they have two bachelors, eligible ones, and there's one woman in particular who is out to get one of them. Don't think she's fussy about which one. She brings friends for moral support – or immoral in her case.'

'Oh.' This was a bit of a surprise and not really a welcome one.

'Yes. Her name is Annie and she's very tall and – though I hate to say this – rather good-looking.'

Emily felt even more despondent.

'And,' Rebecca went on, 'I don't trust her further than I can throw her – which wasn't far last time I tried.'

This made Emily laugh. 'Oh well, if he wants someone tall and beautiful I can't really compete.'

'She shouldn't really be competition. Kate can't bear her. Al told me once that when Annie was at their house having lunch, the moment they'd finished their pudding Kate said, "Isn't it time you took Mrs Stewart home?" Mrs Stewart was not impressed and said, "I'll decide when it's time for me to leave, little missie!" Kate was furious and Alasdair didn't know which of the women he should take notice of.' Rebecca paused. 'Well, he didn't actually say that, but I could tell that was his dilemma.'

'I'm not sure why you've dragged me to this do,' said Emily when they approached the house. 'I could have stayed at home with the boys and you and James could have had a lovely time with no responsibilities.'

'Rubbish! Fiona sets up a chill-out room for the kids with a couple of girls who work in the nursery part of the school. I'll leave Nell there and they'll come and get me when she needs feeding.' Rebecca gave Emily a bracing squeeze round her waist. 'Come on! You're going to enjoy this! You have to show the boys you've taken all those dancing lessons properly on board.'

The sound of pipes carried across the crisp September air. There was something mournful and plaintive about them that made the back of Emily's throat tighten. Just for a moment she thought she might cry.

'Oh look, there's Dougie, the piper,' said Rebecca. 'Do you see? Up on the balcony. This house really lends itself to pipers.'

'How romantic,' said Emily, having got herself under control. 'This is a rather marvellous house, Becca.'

'Scottish Baronial at its best. Not a turret untopped,

not a balcony uncastellated. Over the top and a bit gloomy, but fun.'

'Gloomy but fun,' repeated Emily. 'An unusual description.'

Rebecca laughed. 'So how do you feel about the bagpipes?' They were now quite near the house and the pipes were very loud.

'Love them,' said Emily, without needing to think too hard. 'I know they're noisy, but there's something primitive and exciting about them.'

'Me too,' said Rebecca, her voice sounding a little odd, too. 'And quite often they make me cry.' She paused. 'I can't believe you've got to go tomorrow. The time has gone in a flash.'

'I know.'

Rebecca cleared her throat and spoke briskly. 'James, give me Nell now. We'll go and sort ourselves out upstairs first and then come and find you.'

The huge wooden front door was open, spilling light out on to the driveway, and standing in the hall was a man in full Highland dress. Tall as a tree, he was wearing a kilt in a dark green tartan, a fitted black jacket and an impressively hairy sporran. He had scarlet flashes on his socks and black shoes. As Rebecca embraced him (he was obviously an old friend) Emily noticed he had a dagger stuck in his sock and remembered it was called a sgian-dubh.

'Emily, meet Ian. Doesn't he look magnificent? I wish I could have got James into a kilt.'

There were many more introductions to be made as people came to greet Rebecca and exclaim over Nell and how much she looked like her father before Rebecca said, 'Come on. Let's leave our coats, maybe change our shoes, and get Nell settled.'

Emily followed Rebecca up the wide oak staircase, Rebecca talking over her shoulder. 'I should imagine we leave our coats in Fiona's bedroom. That view alone is worth coming here for.'

They arrived at the top of the stairs and went along the wide corridor. 'Here we are.' Rebecca opened the door to a room, which had several women in it already, all chatting like mad.

'I'll just find where to put Nell and join you,' said Rebecca. 'You'll be all right on your own, won't you?'

'Of course,' said Emily and went in.

To her surprise she did feel a bit awkward because everyone stopped talking and then someone said, 'Oh! You're the woman who delivered Rebecca's baby!'

She smiled and frowned at the same time. 'How did you know that?'

'Everyone knows everything about everyone here,' said another woman, smiling. She seemed genuinely friendly, at least. 'I had you pointed out to me in the village shop. I'm Shona.'

'And I'm Emily,' she said, aware she shouldn't really be surprised at being recognised. 'Isn't this an amazing bedroom. Bigger than my entire cottage, I think.'

'Do look at the view,' said Shona. 'It's so lovely.'

She moved over to the window and pulled back the curtain. The view was more than lovely. There were lights dancing on the sea and on the islands; the mountains were visible against the dark sky, which had shreds of pink in it. Mist added mystery and romance to the scene, as did the faint flicker of the occasional lighted window in the distance. This beauty, combined with the pipes, which were still plainly audible, caused tears to threaten in earnest. Was it just sentimentality caused by the music, the scenery and the expectation of a wonderful evening? Or did she want to cry because she knew she had to go back home in the morning?

Most of the women had gone now and so Emily went to the dressing table to fiddle with her hair.

It was very well appointed. There was hairspray, deodorant, talcum powder, a selection of scent as well as cotton wool, loose powder and cleansing lotion. Fiona had obviously thought hard about what women might need apart from sewing kits and safety pins. There was even, Emily noted with delight, some tit tape! Scottish dancing, if done with enthusiasm, could easily cause a wardrobe malfunction, she realised.

'Becca! Darling!' said a loud, English-accented voice. 'You've got your figure back. How wonderful!'

Emily turned to see her friend being kissed by a tall dark woman in a long black dress.

'Annie,' said Rebecca. 'Thank you for the compliment. Can I introduce my friend Emily?'

Emily put on a smile, aware she was about to confront a woman who wanted Alasdair and who was annoyingly gorgeous. 'Hello.'

'This is Annie, an old friend,' said Rebecca. The way she said it told Emily that she wasn't an old friend in the way that she and Emily were old friends.

Annie took Emily's offered hand. 'So you're the midwife. The one who saved the day in an emergency.'

'It wasn't exactly an emergency,' said Emily mildly.

Annie held up a hand. 'Don't give me the details! I'm child-free and proud.'

Emily laughed. 'That's fine. No contraction-by-contraction account necessary.' She looked at Rebecca. 'Is Nell OK?'

'Oh yes. Although she might spend the entire evening being passed from kind helper to kind helper.' Rebecca glanced at Annie. 'Very keen on tiny babies in there. And the boys are in the rumpus room, getting high on ginger beer and Irn-Bru.'

Another couple of women came in. They all knew Rebecca and they'd all heard about Emily delivering the baby.

'Excuse me,' said Annie, 'if you're going to talk about vernix I'll go and get a drink. So not my bag!'

The other women laughed in a shocked way. 'She is awful,' said one of them when Annie was out of earshot. 'Did she even ask about the baby?'

'No,' said Rebecca. 'But not everyone likes babies.'

Emily nodded. If it hadn't been for the Alasdair thing, she might have liked Annie.

Then Emily was the centre of attention. 'I heard in the shop that you were amazing,' one of the women said.

'She was,' agreed Rebecca. 'I couldn't have done it without her. She's Emily, and this is Nancy, Elizabeth and Meg.'

Emily smiled and nodded hello.

'So,' said Meg. 'Was it all *One Born Every Minute* and dramatic?'

'No,' said Emily, determined to keep to keep it low key. 'There was no emergency and I was just doing my job.' She decided she didn't need to mention the slight problem with the shoulders. 'Rebecca was brilliant.'

'And Crinan's answer to Dr Finlay was there too, I gather,' said Nancy. 'I'm surprised Annie could bring herself to speak to either of you. She must have been beside herself with jealousy.'

'She could hardly be jealous of me!' said Rebecca. 'Having a baby is so not sexy.'

'Oh, I don't know,' said Emily. 'Personally I think it has a sort of primeval charm. Not that I've had one myself.'

'A midwife who's never had a baby?' said Nancy. 'I'm not sure people who haven't had babies should be midwives. They don't really understand the pain.'

Emily wasn't offended. 'People have said that to me before but I think I do understand it. And it's not that I don't want a baby. I just haven't found the right man, and if I do, and I have a baby, well, I'll understand it better!'

'Just don't leave it too long,' said Meg. 'Some of us struggle to get pregnant.'

'Well, in case any of you are planning to get pregnant tonight,' said Rebecca, 'we'd better join the party. Which means getting into shoes I can reel in. Honestly, I don't know why I bothered with my heels. I could have just come in my wellies and then put my pumps on.'

Once they were downstairs, Rebecca took Emily by the arm. 'Come on. On to the dance floor.'

'I'm not sure I can remember anything you and the boys taught me,' Emily said, suddenly nervous.

'Nonsense. People relish pushing you in the right direction if you look like going wrong. And they'll start with the easy ones. They'll save the foursome, when they swing the women off their feet, until later.'

'Fun as that sounds, I'm an entry-level dancer, I couldn't do anything like that!'

'Well, you could, but you don't have to. Now let's find a set to join.'

The band would have made the most reluctant party guest get on the floor and, although she was a bit anxious to begin with, Emily loved to dance.

The first one was the Dashing White Sergeant, one of the dances she felt most confident with. Rebecca's boys had known it well and made her practise and practise. Anxious not to let her teachers down (although they were away doing something quite else, and wouldn't ever know if she messed it up) she was concentrating really hard. Then, suddenly, she was faced with Alasdair. And he was wearing a kilt. She'd thought him good-looking in jeans and a sweater; in full Highland dress he looked sensational.

For a moment they looked at each other, and Emily realised she was smiling and smiling, every other thought pushed out of her head by the sheer pleasure of seeing him. Then they were separated again.

She was still smiling when a new partner found her and seemed to appreciate the light in her eyes and the curve of her lips.

She was enjoying herself. She liked the exercise, she

liked trying to remember the steps and the general good humour the dancing created. And it was lovely coming across Alasdair from time to time; being swung round by him, setting to him, even doing a couple of steps of the polka.

One thing that spoilt it was the presence of Annie, an experienced, efficient dancer. When Emily wasn't thinking about her feet she couldn't help regularly checking to see where they both were. And she couldn't help noticing that Annie was also checking, except she only had eyes for Alasdair.

After two long dances Rebecca found her. 'Come on, I'm gasping. Let's go to the bar.'

Emily was halfway down a pint of lime and soda when Annie and Alasdair came in. Seeing her and Rebecca, Alasdair headed towards them. Annie, trying to smile, followed him.

'So, was that your first go at Scottish country dancing, Emily?' he asked.

'Was it that obvious? I thought I did quite well!' she said.

'You did brilliantly! You must have been practising.'

'The boys have been drilling her,' said Rebecca. 'Do you want to sit down, you two?'

'No thanks,' said Annie. 'I want to dance some more.'

'I'm exhausted,' said Alasdair, finding a seat and pulling it up. 'Can I get you two another drink?'

Annie pouted. Emily realised she hadn't ever seen a grown woman pouting before. 'Well, if you can't keep up with me, Al, I'll have a gin and tonic.'

Annie fiddled with her phone while they were waiting

for Alasdair to come back with the drinks. Emily and Rebecca exchanged a quick eye-roll at her behaviour and then Rebecca saw someone else she knew and got to her feet, leaving Emily with Annie.

Annie put her phone away. 'So, how well do you know Alasdair?'

It was a tricky one. Emily wanted to pretend she hardly knew him at all but his manner with her, relaxed and friendly, indicated she knew him a bit. But she wasn't going to admit too much, not to Annie.

'Well, I was the cook on the puffer. You know? James and Rebecca's puffer?'

'Everyone round here knows the puffer; it's a local celebrity.'

'Well, that's how we met.' That would do. It wasn't too revealing but nor was it disingenuous. 'How well do you know him?'

'Oh, he and I go way back. I was friends with his first wife. Lovely woman. Really beautiful, you know? Like a model.'

Emily did not have issues with her body, she really didn't, but she instantly felt dumpy. 'Bit like you, then?'

Annie did look a bit discomforted. 'Well, we had loads in common. We used to play tennis together, all sorts of sporty things. She was very bright.'

'You must miss her,' said Emily. 'Someone as lovely as that.'

'Of course, but it's been a while. I have other friends. Ah, here comes our hero with the drinks.' She gave Alasdair a beaming smile. 'Thanks.'

Rebecca come back to join them. 'Come on, Annie. It's a drink, not the kiss of life! But thanks, Al.'

Emily took the glass he handed her. 'I feel I should say something incredibly grateful now. How about "You lifesaver, you"?'

He smiled and inclined his head. 'That'll do. So, Emily, what do you think of our Highland entertainment?'

'Brilliant! I only wish I could experience more of it.'

'There are reeling classes at the village hall if you're that keen,' said Annie.

'I would be, but I have to go home soon.' Somehow she couldn't say 'tomorrow' until she'd managed to say it to Alasdair privately. If only she'd managed to see him before now! She had a guilty conscience about him anyway and she didn't want to surprise him in public.

'Kate will be sad to hear that,' said Alasdair.

'Is she here?' said Rebecca.

'Oh yes. In fact, I ought to go and check up on her.'

'She won't want her old dad spoiling her fun. I bet she's playing with all the boys,' said Annie coyly. 'At least, that's how I'd feel.'

'I'd still like to make sure she's all right,' he said, draining his glass and getting to his feet.

'Can I come and say hello?' said Emily, abandoning her lime and soda and standing up too. 'I'd love to see her in her party dress.'

'I'd like that too!' said Annie.

'I wouldn't go now, Annie,' said Rebecca. 'Jimmy McWatt has been eyeing you. I'm sure he wants to ask you to dance.'

Annie's head shot round. 'Are you sure? Jimmy McWatt? Maybe I'll see Kate another time.'

'Who's Jimmy McWatt?' Emily asked Alasdair when they were out of earshot.

'Local millionaire.' He was striding along, the pleats of his kilt swinging as she hastened after him. She allowed herself to speculate if it was true about Scotsmen not wearing anything under their kilts. It must be scratchy, she decided.

'So where's Kate?' she said.

'Having a sleepover with a friend. I just wanted a chance to talk to you without being interrupted. Here.' He opened a door to what seemed to be an office. He held out a hand, offering her an old button-back chair to sit on. He leant back on the desk and looked down at her.

'I'm going home tomorrow,' she said in a rush. She was annoyed with herself for sounding apologetic.

His brows came together. 'Tomorrow? So soon! Why?'

'I tried to come over and see you, and tell you. I'm needed at work. You knew about my job.'

'I didn't think it was starting so soon. I thought you wouldn't be able to start until a new unit was built.'

'I thought that too but they want me to look at plans for the building. And I have to recruit staff—'

'Kate will be devastated! I told her you'd probably be here until near Christmas!'

Just for a few moments Emily had thought that maybe he would be devastated but apparently not, only Kate. Although he did look pale and tight-lipped.

'I'm really sorry you did that. I was never going to able to stay that long.'

'It was thoughtless,' he went on, ignoring her interjection. 'She's had enough people letting her down in her short life without you doing it as well.'

Now Emily was angry. 'I don't think going back home – something that everyone knew I was going to do – quite equates with letting Kate down! And it wasn't my fault that you misled her like that!'

'It will seem like that to her!'

'Well, you'll have to explain!'

'I'm a bit fed up with explaining things about women to my daughter! You of all people, Emily! I didn't think you would put your career over other people's happiness!'

There was a silence between them like a glacier. Then they both spoke at once.

'I'm sorry—' he said.

'I can't believe you just said that!' Emily said. 'What do you expect me to do? Be late starting my new job to give Kate a bit longer to get used to the idea that I'm going? I've never heard anything so bloody ridiculous!'

Any thought that he had been going to apologise vanished. There was only anger in his expression. 'Does loyalty and trustworthiness mean nothing to you?'

Emily had to fight for breath. 'That is so unreasonable! There's been no arrangement, no relationship! We both knew that from the start!'

'So it was just a bit of casual sex for you, was it?'

'How dare you!' She could hardly speak for anger and frustration.

'I'm the one who has to deal with this! I'm the one

who'll have to comfort a little girl let down by a woman – again!'

'I'm sorry about that, but it is your job! You're her father! There's no one else!'

'Please don't think I'm not aware of that!'

They glared at each other. Emily was on the verge of tears – angry ones this time – and he was a wall of anger and pride.

Then he took a breath and cleared his throat. 'Emily—'

Someone pushed open the door urgently. 'Oh, there you are, Alasdair!' It was Annie. 'They need you in the barn to do a soundcheck. You're on in five minutes.'

He hesitated, looking at Emily and then at Annie, as if he wanted to finish what he had started to say.

'Come on, Alasdair! The band needs you. You can talk to Emily later.'

A man joined Annie in the doorway. 'C'mon, man! We need you *now*. There's going to be a barn full of people wanting to hear some decent music!'

Alasdair shot Emily another glance too quickly for her to interpret and left the room. Annie stayed behind. 'Don't dash your heart against those rocks, sweetheart. Better women than you have foundered on them.'

Emily sighed and gave a rueful smile. 'I won't. I'm going back home tomorrow so feel free to put on your lifejacket and jump overboard. There'll be no competition from me.'

As Emily walked back along the corridor towards the sound of the dance music she tried to make sense of her feelings. Anger, regret, deep sadness with a good dose irritation churned inside her. She wanted to go back to James and Rebecca's and wondered if she could find someone to give her a lift. Maybe James would run her home quickly? She didn't want to drag Rebecca away from her first night out in a long time.

She bumped into Rebecca. 'Found you!' said her friend, sounding relieved. 'Come on. We must go and hear Alasdair's band. They're doing the soundcheck. If we don't hurry we won't get a seat at the front; they're terribly popular!'

There was no way out of it. She'd have to go and hear him but she was damned if she was going to sit at the front.

'You go on. I've got to go to the loo, then I'll get a drink and join you.'

'Well, don't hang about. I'll save you a seat.'

'No, don't bother. I'll take my chance. I've got to make a quick phone call first. I've had an urgent text.'

Rebecca regarded her for a couple of seconds. 'Oh, OK. I'll see you in there.'

In case Rebecca was watching her, Emily got out her phone. There was absolutely no coverage here at all. And Rebecca must have known that. Adding embarrassment to her list of unpleasant emotions she headed for the cloakroom upstairs.

Chapter Twenty

Emily took her time. She did as much to her make-up as she could with the stub of pencil and the mascara and lipstick in her tiny cross-body evening bag. Then she applied as many of the things laid out on the dressing table as she possibly could. Sadly, she didn't manage to find a use for the tit tape.

When she'd had a glass of water, used the loo and fluffed up her hair for the final time, she made her way downstairs. The sound of the crowd led her to the barn, where the band was due to play.

She was pleased to see the space was crowded. She realised there were many more people at this party than had been reeling. The huge old house had swallowed them up. But everyone seemed to be here now although there were only a couple of people and some instruments on the stage.

Because she didn't want Alasdair to see her, she ignored the front, where she knew Rebecca would be saving her a place. She stood at the back, along with many others.

'I don't know what's been holding them up,' said someone near her. 'They were supposed to start ten minutes ago.'

'Musicians! You know what they're like,' said another. 'No sense of discipline.'

'I hope you're wrong!' said the first speaker. 'One of them is my GP!'

At last, Alasdair and a girl came on. Alasdair had changed out of his kilt and was dressed in jeans, with a shirt half tucked into them. He was at the front holding a fiddle and looked so sexy Emily felt a stab of emotion that almost hurt. The girl looked young and vulnerable and extremely beautiful. She went up to the mike and started fiddling with it. Others stood around, looking at each other and then out into the audience until suddenly, they began with a love song that seemed to be aimed directly at her heart. It hurt. Music was part of Alasdair in the same way that being a doctor was, and a father.

She realised she couldn't bear to stay and let his music torture her. She left the barn and made her way to the bar.

'So, am I the only person not in the barn, then?' said Emily to the young man behind the bar.

'Not quite. It's great but obviously' – he nodded towards her – 'not everyone's cup of tea. What can I get you?'

She had been going to cry into a glass of red wine, but now the thought of tea was much more bracing. 'Now you've put the idea into my head – a cup of tea? Is that possible?'

The barman smiled. 'Of course it is. We're all set up for teas and coffees. Go and sit down by the fire and I'll bring it over.'

The armchair was comfy and there was a little table for her cup. It was perfect. Emily could sit there, sip tea, until eventually the band stopped playing and, with luck, she could find some way of getting home.

Officially it was wrong to want to leave before the stupendous buffet, all laid out in a marquee (it's all right, it's heated, Rebecca had said) but Emily just wanted to go back, finish her packing and then turn her heart and mind down south, where her real life was.

It was desperately disappointing that this evening had turned out so badly for her. She'd seen it as a sort of glorious farewell to the Highlands, and to Alasdair. It was always going to be sad, but in a beautiful, poetic way. Now it was sad because she'd quarrelled with a man she loved and was never going to be able to explain and put things right between them.

She thought about the boys, probably playing computer games somewhere with their friends, or rushing about in the huge space. She thought of James and Rebecca, out for the first time since Nell was born, enjoying Alasdair's band with their friends. And of Nell, upstairs, probably asleep or being carried about by kind women. Although all these people she loved were near her, she felt desperately lonely.

There never had been any hope for her and Alasdair as a couple, for so many reasons. There was her job, her career as a midwife, which was hundreds of miles away from his. There was the fact that she knew now for certain she wanted a baby, something she hadn't been so sure of before and which was one of the reasons she was fairly sure that Annie would eventually claim her prize, Alasdair. Or should that be scalp? Annie was very clear about not wanting children and why would Alasdair want a woman who'd have a baby and put Kate's nose out of joint forever?

For him, her going far away was the perfect solution. They'd had some great sex, some fun and some enjoyable time with Kate. But they'd always known it could never be forever. No, this wouldn't be so hard for Alasdair. He'd file her away in his memory and get on with his life.

Chapter Twenty-One

❦

The peace of the fire, the tea and Emily's melancholy thoughts were broken by the sound of a crying baby that got louder, presumably as it got nearer. A woman carrying a bundle put her head round the door.

Emily leapt up. 'Is that Nell? Shall I take her?'

The young woman holding the screaming infant nodded. 'She's hungry, poor lass.'

'You find Becca; I'll jiggle. She's in the barn, sitting up at the front.'

Emily jogged up and down, trying to convince Nell that she wasn't really hungry, she just wanted a good bounce. 'I'm going to miss you so much!' she said. She didn't bother to tell Nell that she'd really miss her mum, dad and brothers, too, not to mention her uncle and her cousin. Nell could only really think about her stomach just then. Emily understood that. But in spite of their very obvious rapport, godmother and god-daughter were both very relieved when Rebecca finally appeared.

The barman pulled the sofa nearer the fire so that

Rebecca and Nell could snuggle in together, discreetly, while both Rebecca and Emily drank tea.

'Why didn't you come and hear Alasdair's band?' Rebecca said, once Nell was firmly latched on and she could hear herself speak again. 'They were terrific. And their singer is just breathtaking! Al's got a really great voice, too.'

'I just couldn't face it.' Emily, who felt she'd been doing quite well up to that point, thought she might need yet more tea to stop herself wanting to cry. 'Besides, I don't think he'd have wanted me there.'

'Why ever not? Without you, there was no one to stop Annie claiming him as her own when they'd finished. She rushed up on to the stage and flung her arms round him.' Rebecca frowned. 'That woman is far too old to be a groupie.'

'We had a row, Bec. It was horrible. That's why I couldn't hear his band for more than a couple of bars.'

Comprehension replaced indignation. 'Oh. I'm sorry. How on earth did that happen? Bloody hell, Em! This was supposed to be a lovely last evening for you together!'

'Well, he was cross because he didn't know I was going tomorrow – he said I'd let Kate down.' That had cut deep. She loved Kate and would never do anything to hurt her. 'Then he accused me of putting my career before other people's happiness. He must have meant Kate. But it is so unreasonable.'

Rebecca nodded. 'That is outrageous! It really is. But I don't think he'd have lashed out like that if he didn't have feelings for you.'

'I don't think he has feelings, not as we understand it. He was just cross because he didn't know I was going so soon and he'd have to explain it all to Kate.'

'I think it must have been the shock about you going so soon. Unexpectedly for him.'

Emily sighed. 'Anyway, I'm sure you now understand why I didn't want to stay and hear his band. I'm not sure I could have done even if we hadn't quarrelled. I just felt so sad.'

There was silence, broken only by the sound of the fire crackling and Nell's little grunts of satisfaction. 'Do you want to go home?' said Rebecca.

'What? To my home?' This was a question she'd been asking herself for a while. She still hadn't worked out the answer.

'Well, I meant my home, now. I'll find someone to give us a lift and James can bring the boys home.'

'I don't want to drag you away from the party of the year.' She glanced at her watch. 'It's only nine o'clock. We haven't eaten yet. All those puddings we made . . .'

'I'm quite tired,' said Rebecca. 'I've only just had a baby. And I made an extra chocolate mousse. It's at home. I think we should get back.'

'Actually, that would be brilliant.'

'I can't believe I'm still doing this sort of thing now I'm supposedly a grown-up woman,' said Emily, digging her spoon into the mousse. 'Comfort eating with my mate.'

'Mmm,' Rebecca agreed. 'Comfort eating in comfort and in company. The best ever.' She topped up Emily's wine glass. 'Although it is so sad you're going. But hey! You can come back and visit! You will, won't you?'

Emily put down her glass, remembering she had to be up reasonably early in the morning. 'Of course I will. But not for a bit. Not while there's bad feeling between me and Alasdair.'

'It's so sad. Remember the night when Nell was born? We were all such a team! Surely you and Alasdair could get that back?'

'It's more complicated than that, Bec. There's my new job for one thing. And Kate. Alasdair won't want to have explained to her why I've gone away only for me to pop back up again in a month.'

Rebecca sighed. 'If you don't have him, Annie will get him.'

Emily gulped, hardly able to believe what she was about to say. 'Well – she's beautiful and she doesn't want children. She's a much better prospect for him. Because I do want children – I know that now. How would Kate feel about that?'

'Little girls love babies,' said Rebecca. 'She adores Nell.'

Emily ignored this. 'And besides, what would I do for a living? I need to work. It's part of what I am. Back home I'm a midwife, respected in the community. I need that.'

'And nanny to Nell wouldn't cut it?'

Emily shook her head sadly. 'Not really. Not forever.'

'Then there's nothing to be done. We'll just have to finish the mousse.'

*   *   *

Emily was relieved that James drove her to the airport and not Rebecca. She and Rebecca had talked it all through so many times but, inevitably, they would have gone over it all again. Now Emily just wanted to sit quietly and enjoy the scenery while she could. But every mile they travelled was a mile away from where she'd left her heart.

'We're going to really miss you, Emily,' said James, giving her a huge hug. They were at the dropping-off point so he couldn't stay long.

'And me you. I've so loved my summer. The puffer, Scotland, your family, and of course, helping Nell into the world. It's been really magical. I don't suppose anything will be quite as special again. Thank you!'

They hugged again.

'Now,' she said firmly. 'I'm going. I don't want to get emotional.'

She had plenty of time for that as she hung around, waiting for the gate to be shown. She sat there, turning the pages of a novel Rebecca had given her but although she read the words they didn't have any meaning for her.

Her friend Sally was practically jumping up and down when Emily saw her waiting at the airport.

'Oh God, Em, I've missed you so much. It's all going to be absolutely brilliant. I've been round to your tenants and they're all set to move out next weekend. Such a stroke of luck that they've found somewhere to move to in the area. And to think you'll be my boss! What were the chances of that happening when you've had a sabbatical?'

'Hi, Sally.' Emily hugged her friend. 'It's lovely to see you.' And it was.

'Everyone's been so excited to have you home. There was talk of a ticker-tape parade but then everyone said there'd be too much mess and it wasn't very green . . . Hon? That was a joke?'

'What? Yes! Sorry! I think I've got jet lag. My brain's not working.'

'It's an hour's flight with no time change. Emily, are you OK?'

'Yes. Yes, of course. You won't mind me being your boss, will you?'

'Of course not. I know just how to get round you. The car's just here. In fact we must hurry. I'm parked illegally.'

Sally's car was on a yellow line with her 'Midwife on call' badge in the front.

'I wonder where they thought you were delivering the baby?' Emily asked, getting in the front seat, having thrown her rucksack in the back.

'I don't suppose anyone noticed. Your flight was on time. So, how are you?'

This was not the time to spill her emotional beans. 'Fine. So what else is new?'

'Well, things are going really well at the unit. I've had several calls from Derek, wanting to know when you'll be back. Talk about a changed man! He's had a real Road to Damocles moment!'

'It's Damascus. The road thing.'

'Is it? Well, whatever, he's had one. He used to think we were witches brewing up poisonous plants to give to our labouring mothers. Now he thinks we're all Francis of Assisi – I know! It's a joke! That should be Francesca of Assisi.'

Emily managed something that passed for a laugh. 'Sorry, I'm being a bit slow. I think I left my sense of humour in the departure lounge in Glasgow.'

'That's because you always get there far too early. You should live close to the edge, like me, and never arrive until the very last moment.' Sally turned on to the main road. 'Live dangerously!'

'OK, but not now. Can you watch the traffic? There's so much more of it down here. I'm not used to it any more.'

Sally laughed. 'Sorry. I'm a bit over-excited about you being back. I promise I'll drive very sedately from now on.'

'So,' she said when they had reached her house and the kitchen. 'What do you want to do now? We're expected down the pub this evening, for a "Welcome Home, Emily" party, but now? Eat something? Go and visit your tenants? Have a shower? Go shopping? Tell me.'

Emily considered. Part of her really, really wanted to burst into tears and have a jolly good cry. The other part of her didn't. She decided to compromise. 'I know it's early – hardly lunchtime even – but what I'd like is a gin and tonic.'

'What a good idea. I'll join you. Gin is always the answer. Cures everything.'

'Actually, gin is never the answer,' said Emily, pulling out a chair and watching her friend look in the fridge for tonic and lemons.

'No,' Sally agreed. 'But it don't half make the question more interesting. When you've had this' – she held up a tumbler with a lot of gin in it – 'you've got to tell me why, although you're trying to look happy, you're anything but underneath.'

Emily sipped her gin and tonic. It was delicious, just as she liked it, but she knew in her heart it was a mistake. She would end up telling Sally everything, about Alasdair, the quarrel, how she felt about it and then she would cry. But, she concluded, after the second sip, it might be a good thing. She might be able to move on afterwards.

It was good to be back in the pub in town, where all her friends went if they wanted to meet up. Emily was really pleased to see Susanna: the woman who had been due to have a calm labour at home but instead was whisked off to hospital by an outraged husband.

'Emily! Hello!' She waved. 'So wonderful to have you back. I've set up the series of talks I was telling you about. You're our star speaker – you would have been before, only more so now you're in charge of this amazing expanded maternity unit this town is getting. But until you were back, we weren't quite sure where to put you in the programme.'

'Now, now, Sooz,' said a woman Emily didn't know but who was definitely from the same tribe as Susanna. 'Let the poor woman get a glass of wine first. Hi,' she said, 'I'm Annabel. You must be the amazing midwife I've heard so much about. Glass of white?'

Emily ended up really enjoying herself. There was a

great new life for her here, better by far than the one she'd left. She was going to embrace it. She even allowed herself to flirt mildly with a couple of the men who seemed drawn to a group of women all talking their heads off. Tomorrow she would sort out when she could go and see her tenants and plan her move back in. And she would go back to work.

Her new optimism lasted until she got back to Sally's, late and a little bit tipsy. She was rifling through her bag looking for clean pyjamas when she came across her knitting; the unfinished Fair Isle scarf big enough only for a teddy bear.

She started to cry all over again.

Chapter Twenty-Two

Even though she and Sally had not gone to bed until after midnight, Emily woke up before six. She knew she wouldn't get to sleep again and so got out the scarf and sat up in bed and finished it. She had to go into the office later and spend time catching up on the work she was taking over, but these couple of hours were hers. When she'd done the scarf, she crept downstairs to Sally's kitchen and made herself some tea. Then she found one of Sally's children's teddies that was roughly the size of Kate's and checked the scarf for length. And then she decided that Ted needed mittens and socks, too.

She cheated on the Fair Isle a bit but soon she had a fully kitted-out teddy and was ready to send the clothes off.

She decided to write directly to Ted. If she had hurt Kate's feelings by rushing off before she could say goodbye, Kate might not respond well to a letter. But Ted could be the conduit.

Dear Ted,

I am so sorry I had to go before we could say goodbye and before I could give you the enclosed. When winter comes on I feel you will need these warm things to wear. Please give my best love to Kate and tell her I will always remember seeing the otters, making dams and getting very muddy! And later seeing the Merry Dancers. It was magic!

Lots of love,
Emily

When she'd found an envelope she put the letter and the clothes into it and addressed it care of Rebecca. Then she had a long shower and put on far too much make-up. It was to indicate to herself that she had left her life in Scotland far behind and was again a professional woman.

She parked her car and walked towards the office where she was to work until the refurbishment of the maternity unit was finished. She felt excited, nervous and lonely. Was the loneliness because of leaving Scotland and all that had happened there? Or was it because she'd no longer be part of a team, but the head of a team? She hadn't reached a conclusion before she arrived at the door, knocked, and went in.

Derek Gardner was there. He got up from his seat and smiled as if he was really pleased to see her. After the way she had parted from Alasdair it was comforting to be greeted so warmly.

'Emily! We are so glad to have you on board at last. This is such an exciting project, it's great to have you heading it all up. Now, coffee? Tea?' He indicated a machine. 'Then we can get started.'

When she was sitting down with a cup of coffee and a couple of biscuits she looked around the room. Six people were all looking at her expectantly.

'So,' said Derek (much to her relief). 'What do you want to change about the current system?'

Emily had jotted down a few notes while she ate breakfast. 'I'd like to see more support for mothers after they've had the babies; more staff; at least two more birthing pools . . .'

Emily thought she'd known about hard work but by the time the meeting was finally declared over she felt as though she'd done a long walk for charity in high heels.

'Well, that was a marathon,' said Derek.

'Just what I was thinking! How can sitting talking be such hard work? Even my feet hurt!'

He laughed. 'I'm not sure how that happens. But I tell you what, as a reward for working so incredibly hard I'll take you out for dinner. Would you like that?'

She considered. If she was going to get back on the dating horse in order to find a proper relationship she had to start somewhere. 'I'd love to, but not tonight. I have so much sorting out to do.'

'Tomorrow then? Most decent restaurants are closed on Mondays anyway.'

'So, how did it go?' Sally asked when they caught up with each other after work a couple of days later.

'Well, he really made an effort. Picked me up in his quite nice car—'

'It is quite nice, isn't it?'

'Yes. And we went to that place over in Critchley? With the three Michelin stars?'

'Wow! And was it amazing?'

'Well, yes. They give you so much free stuff, you know, the amuse-gueules—'

'Is that the same as an amuse-bouche?'

'Think so. I couldn't tell the difference anyway.'

'Carry on then, tell me all about it.'

'Well, after you've had those little morsels which were absolutely delicious, and lovely little glasses of soup, and amazing bread, by the time you've had your starter you're pretty much full.'

'And Derek? What was he like? So far we've mostly heard about the food.'

'He was a perfect gentleman. Ordered champagne, and wine, hardly drank himself but encouraged me to. He really knows his wine. The whole evening must have cost a fortune.'

'Will it lead to anything?'

'I don't think so, no.' Emily sighed. Sally knew the bare bones of what had gone on in Scotland but Emily didn't want to burden her friend with her 'I'll never love again' line, which was how she felt. 'Derek does want children though, which is something in his favour,' she said, her thoughts drifting back to Alasdair.

'If you're just looking to have a baby, you can simply go and buy some sperm.'

'Hon! I know we're midwives and pretty robust about

such things but until I'm sure I can't find a proper father for my baby, I'd rather not do anything like that. I want a relationship, a companion, someone adult to love.'

'Oh well, internet dating is for you. I'll put you on that "find a mate for your mate" site. Simples.'

Emily smiled and tried to join in the fun. 'You have to write a short essay about how wonderful I am.'

'No problem! I'm really good at essays: I can make things up with the best of them. I've checked the site already and you're not allowed to wear sunglasses for the picture, which is a shame, but we'll do our best.'

'Honestly! Some friend you are! Now I must get on. I've got someone coming to service my boiler. And then I've got to work out how to do a spreadsheet. I know everything I need to put on it, it's getting it computer-ready that's difficult.'

'So, how are you enjoying your new job?'

'I think I'm loving it!'

Sally smiled. 'I'm so glad. I'm not sure it would be for me. I enjoy being hands-on too much.'

'I'm hoping I can go back to being hands-on, delivering babies, when we've got our plan worked out.' But would she? she asked herself as she walked to her car. Was she doomed to be an administrator now?

About a month had passed after Emily had got back home and she was now fully conversant with spread-sheets and budgets and knew how to read estimates from builders and spot the items not included. She hadn't managed to stop thinking about Alasdair, but she thought about other things too so she was doing all right. She did keep hoping to hear from Kate, with a picture of Ted in his little knitted garments, but so far had been disappointed.

She got back from teaching a breastfeeding class (very happy to be actually talking to pregnant women and mothers again) to find the post had got there before her. She picked it up and took it into the kitchen, dumping her handbag on a chair.

There was one letter with a Scottish postmark but as it came in a window envelope and had a neatly typed address she thought it couldn't be anything bad. She had dreaded getting a furious letter from Alasdair – she wasn't sure why.

The letter was from Lizzie Miller-Hall and came attached to a job application form.

My dear Emily,

I expect you're a bit surprised to hear from me but I've been thinking of you for a while.

As you will have noticed, I am a bit over retirement age but didn't want to abandon all my old ladies and young ones unless I could pass them on to a safe pair of hands. I think you are those hands!

Fill in the form and come up and talk to the team. I know they'll love you and, in fact, you've already had an interview of sorts when you came out with me that day after Nell was born.

In case you hate reading forms (I do!) I'll tell you briefly. It's for two part-time jobs, the ones I've been doing just fine for years but they might want you to do a bit of training and take some exams. You'd be a part-time

health visitor who does a few shifts as a bank midwife.
It's a lovely job with lots of variety and a great deal of
job satisfaction. Do give it a go!

From habit, Emily put the kettle on, and then she phoned Sally. She made tea and sat down at the table

'So, what else is worrying you? You're a bit agitato, I can tell.'

'For someone who abuses language like you do, you're surprisingly perceptive,' said Emily, smiling in spite of herself.

'What's that when it's at home? Now tell all.'

When Emily had finished, Sally, serious now, said, 'Well, you have to apply and go for an interview or you'll always regret it.'

'Why would I? I don't want to work up there. My work is here. I have my great new job, full of new challenges. And I'm good at it! Although I do miss the baby stuff.'

'And you'll get back to that when everything is set up – you're still part of the team.'

'Exactly. It's the perfect job.' She hoped saying it out loud would make it true.

'But if you don't go and check out this other job you will always wonder what might have been. You need to see Alasdair, too.'

'I'm not going if I have to see Alasdair,' said Emily, needle-sharp. 'I have absolutely nothing to say to him, or him to me.'

'OK, well, don't see the man who might well be the love of your life if that's how you feel, but apply for the job.' Sally paused. 'Go up there, check this out, and it's not for you, then you'll know for sure, and come back to us with a whole heart.'

'You think?'

'I really, really do. Now go and get some sleep and then fill in the damn form.'

Rebecca, of course, was delighted when Emily phoned her. 'Try and come up for a few days, stay in the bothy, which is now so beautiful you'd hardly recognise it. Everyone will be so thrilled to see you!'

Emily had been afraid of this. 'Rebecca, I'm not seeing Alasdair. I can't. Not with things how we left them.'

'You won't give him an opportunity to apologise for what he said to you at the dance?'

'He won't apologise. In my experience men don't, unless it's for something tiny like knocking your arm when you're holding a drink. You've got to promise me not to invite him for dinner or anything when I'm there.'

'What if he just drops in, spontaneously?'

'Well, he can drop, but I don't have to see him.' Emily paused; her head, which was in control of her speech, was saying one thing; her heart was feeling something quite other. 'Have you seen much of him lately?'

'Actually, no. He's been working really hard and although James has dragged him out to the pub a couple of times, he hasn't been here much.'

'Well, that's good, from my point of view. It means I can come up and see you lot and not worry.'

'You would like to see Kate, though? She was so thrilled with the knitted things.'

Emily sighed very deeply. 'I think it would be better if I didn't see Kate. Much as I would love to. I don't think it's fair on her.'

'You're probably right,' said Rebecca after a moment's pause.

Emily's interview suit was navy blue. Although this was by chance – it had been very well reduced in a sale – there was something reassuringly medical about navy blue. It represented matrons, institutions, officialdom and made Emily feel like a proper health-care professional. However, her suit had a pretty stand-up collar that framed her face and she wore it with three strands of seed pearls which made the whole look much more attractive and friendly. She sat in the waiting room in Lochgilphead, looking at her boots, wondering if she should have worn court shoes. But Scotland in October was not especially warm and even with thick tights she'd have shivered without her boots.

She distracted herself from worrying about her footwear by looking out of the window. Scotland may not have been especially warm but it was especially beautiful, she realised. It was as if the scenery was testing her resolve to just have the interview, turn down the job and then go back where she belonged.

The larch trees were golden, the water so still it was a dark mirror, reflecting the clear blue sky, the heather-covered hills and the little boats that filled the harbour. There were faint trails of mist. It was a wonderful spot for an office, she thought, really uplifting. Her new temporary office at home was perfectly nice, but it looked on to a busy street in not the most attractive part of town. She had never looked out of the window and thought how wonderful the wheely bins belonging to the takeaway pizza place were. Here it would be different.

Emily had already decided there was no point in coming up all this way for an interview if she wasn't going to try her best and once she was in the room, in front of a panel of six people, she realised she was enjoying herself.

The panel asked her numerous questions and very many of them were about how the maternity unit where she lived was run. She always loved talking about her work and was soon giving them her opinions frankly.

Then they asked her about her experience with old people.

She smiled. 'I've only recently got into old people,' she said. 'Obviously in Frometon I deal with young parents, babies, and a bit with children, but when I was up here in the summer I discovered just how interesting the elderly can be.'

'You were working as a cook on the puffer?' asked a man, having glanced down at his notes. 'Did that bring you into contact with senior citizens?'

'It certainly did. But there was one old lady in particular I really got to know and love. She taught me Fair Isle knitting and my friend and I helped her arrange a way of keeping in touch with her knitting buddies.' She paused. 'I learnt such a lot from her and now I think the elderly should be put into schools to talk to the children, tell them about "the olden days" before all their huge knowledge is lost!' She stopped suddenly. 'Oh, sorry, I've gone way off topic.'

I've probably blown it, she thought, downcast. And then she wondered why she felt like that. She really didn't want this job, after all.

There were a few more questions, which, to her relief, she could answer sensibly, giving her a chance to show she wasn't a complete idiot. Then the woman in charge smiled. 'Well, I think we've learnt enough for us to be able to make a decision, and indeed, come back to you quite quickly. How long are you staying up here?'

'Until next Monday.' She had managed to book an entire week off.

'Oh good. And we have all your contact details? Well, I think we can let you go now.'

Lizzie was outside the boardroom where the interview had been held, kettle on and lemon drizzle on a plate. 'I brought this in from home, obviously. I thought you might need it. So, what do you think?'

'Well, I think it's a wonderful job for someone,' said Emily. 'But I think I may have blown it and even if I haven't, I'm not sure . . .' She trailed off, sudden tears making it difficult for her to speak. She stared out of the window, watching some birds flap their way to the sea.

'Oh well, we'll see what we shall see. Eat your cake otherwise I'll end up eating it all myself and that would never do!'

Rebecca had to have a detailed description of the interview too, but her incentives were wine and olives.

'So, do you want the job?' she asked when Emily had finished describing it.

'If it wasn't here, I'd love it!' said Emily. 'It'll be varied, I'd be learning lots of new stuff for the health visitor aspect of it. And I think they could learn a lot from me on the maternity side. But it is here.'

'And what's wrong with "here"?'

'Oh, Bec, you know! It's Alasdair! He's in every blade of grass and bell of heather. And sorry if that sounds like a cheesy song lyric. I'm not over him and if I was up here it would take me far longer to do it. I'd be constantly worrying that I was going to see him or yearning to see him. My head would be a mess. I need to go back home and find a man who wants children, who wants me! Not hanker after a man who never will want me.'

Rebecca didn't speak for a long time and then she sighed. 'You wouldn't, just for me, see Alasdair?'

'No, not even for you. There is no point.' But in her heart she wished he'd come looking for her.

Emily threw herself into family life for the next couple of days. She cooked meals, played with the boys, carried Nell around and shooed Rebecca and James out for an evening, promising them she was perfectly capable of giving a baby a bottle even if it was one used to being breastfed. And Nell, possibly wanting to keep in with her godmother, took it beautifully and fell back to sleep almost immediately afterwards.

The next day, Emily had a phone call offering her the job. Rebecca convinced her it would be rude to reject it by email as a couple of the people who had inter-viewed her probably didn't get email. So, when Emily had written a proper letter, they set off for a day's shopping in Glasgow, something Rebecca found hard to do with Nell, leaving the letter for James to post.

'So,' said Emily when they had set off, 'when do we have to be back?'

'In theory, Molly – you know? Angus's wife – they look after the boys quite a lot during the season?'

'Of course I know Molly. Lovely woman.'

'Anyway, she'll give the boys tea with her lot and keep them until six, but honestly I don't have much stamina for shopping these days, so let's focus on what we want and get off home.'

'I don't want anything. I'll hold Nell; you focus.'

Rebecca mostly bought clothes for her children and James in Marks and Spencer's before adding some basics for her. And as she had predicted, they were setting off for home in the early afternoon, eating sand-wiches in the car. They were neither of them in the mood for lunch out.

'Although really I should be pleased I am a bit disap-pointed that Alasdair has made no attempt to get in touch with me since I've been up here,' said Emily, unable to keep her thoughts private any longer.

Rebecca didn't respond for a few moments while she overtook a lorry. 'That could be something to do with me.' Emily looked at her sharply and received an apolo-getic glance in return. 'I really hate to have to confess this but I was talking to him about you . . .'

'Yes?' Emily didn't know if she was furious or glad.

'He doesn't seem remotely happy and I thought it might be something to do with you.'

'But it wasn't?'

'Apparently not.'

'Maybe that glamorous Annie woman knocked him back?' Emily hoped flippancy might stop her wanting to cry.

At least it made Rebecca laugh. 'I don't think so! More the other way round. But anyway, let me confess and then at least I don't have to feel doubly guilty.'

'I think I can guess. You told Alasdair – or made it clear – what I'd told you about his wife being about to leave him.'

'God, Em, I am so sorry! I just blurted it out!'

Emily sighed deeply. 'Well, obviously it would have been better if you hadn't but as I did exactly the same thing to you, I can hardly blame you.'

'He was furious, as you can imagine.'

'I can imagine.'

'Oh, Em! What can I do to put it right?'

'Nothing. And it was my fault for telling you in the first place. It's awful, but, and quite honestly, it wasn't the deal-breaker, was it? He wasn't showing boundless enthusiasm before he knew I'd told you.'

'No,' Rebecca agreed quietly.

Emily cleared her throat but didn't speak.

A few miles further on, Rebecca said, 'Tomorrow is Friday. We should do something special. The weekend will be full of boys and people. But tomorrow it'll still be you, me and Nell. We must have a special treat – as special as I can make it anyway. It's the least I can do. What would you really like best?'

Emil didn't have to think too hard. 'I want to see the otters – or rather, go to where they are, even if we don't see them. Do you know where that is?'

'If I don't, I can find out. Leave it with me. Would you like to take a picnic? The weather forecast is quite good, I think. And if not, we can always eat our sangers in the car.'

'A picnic would be lovely.' Emily patted her friend's arm. 'I know it's going to make me awfully sad, but I do want to go there. Just to see it again.'

'It can be part of your memory bank. You can go there in your head whenever you want to.'

Chapter Twenty-Three

In the morning Emily made sandwiches while Rebecca
and James harried the boys into their clothes and to the
breakfast table. Later she discovered some lost PE kit
and stuffed it into Archie's hand as he ran out of the
door.

But soon after the boys had left, 'the girls', as James
described them, were ready to set off.

'Damn,' Emily said after they had driven a little way.
'We didn't bring a flask! Or are we going to build a fire
and boil a billy?' The last time she had gone looking for
otters was at the forefront of her mind. Then tea had
been made over open flames.

'Oh! Dash! I'm afraid I haven't got a billycan. We'll
just have to make do with apples. You did put in apples?'

'Yes,' said Emily bleakly. She'd been wondering if this
outing was a hideous mistake since she woke that
morning and now the prospect of eating sandwiches
without a cup of tea or coffee to have with them made
her almost tearful. Some part of her realised this over-
reaction was nothing to do with tea.

'Listen,' she said after a few more minutes, when she was certain there was no risk of her throat closing with tears, 'why don't we give this a miss? Why don't we go somewhere else? Where there'll be a café? There's something about not having tea that is making me quite gloomy.'

'It's not the tea that's making you gloomy, it's where we're going.' Rebecca drove on relentlessly, not even glancing at Emily.

'And that's why I want to go somewhere else!'

'No,' said Rebecca. 'You have to see the otters, or at least go to the island. This is your farewell to Scotland. You have to do it properly.'

'I don't know why you begrudge your old friend a cup of tea,' Emily said a little later, when she was feeling more rational about it.

'I don't. I just think we should do what we came to do and then see about tea afterwards.'

'Oh, OK,' said Emily. 'That's reasonable.'

They were very nearly at the place to park the car when Rebecca looked at the dashboard and said suddenly, 'Oh no! A warning light has just come on.' She sounded worried.

'What sort of warning light?' said Emily. 'Should we ring the AA?'

'Probably not. It may not be that serious. Besides, I'm not a member.' Rebecca swung the car a little way off the road. 'Can you be a dear and see if it's just a brake light that's gone? Just get out and I'll brake. Tell me if they're both working. If it's only that we don't need to worry.'

Emily got out and went to the back of the car. 'OK! Brake now!' she called.

But Rebecca didn't brake, she accelerated, and the car shot off leaving Emily standing there, her mouth open, in a state of shock. Had Rebecca pressed the wrong pedal? What the hell was going on?

She was still staring in the direction that Rebecca had disappeared in, waiting to see her coming back towards her, when a dog boofed her in the stomach.

She saw it was a red setter and just as she recognised it as Rupert, she saw Alasdair appearing from behind a little thicket.

She stared at him, completely confused.

'Sorry, did Rupes give you a fright?' said Alasdair, walking towards her and catching the dog as he ran back to him.

Emily didn't reply. She felt as if she was in a weird dream and if she didn't move or speak she'd wake up.

Alasdair came over and smiled ruefully. 'Actually my dog assaulting you is really the least of my sins. I have so much to apologise to you for I don't know where to start.'

Emily took a deep breath and realised it was a reality she'd have to deal with. She also had something to apologise for but wasn't going to now. 'I can't help you, I'm afraid.'

'I'll start with saying sorry about the dog. He was just pleased to see you and I wasn't holding his lead properly.'

'That's OK. I can forgive Rupert anything.'

Alasdair nodded. 'I realise I might be quite a bit harder

to forgive. Can we go to the boat? I apologise better when I'm on the move.'

Emily shrugged. 'I thought I was here to see the otters.'

'You are and I've done my best to arrange them. Rebecca did too.'

'I feel tricked and slightly stupid,' said Emily. 'Becca and I were coming here together and she abandoned me. She should have told me what was going on.'

'Would you have come if she had?'

'No.' She knew this was true but she wasn't absolutely sure she'd have been right to refuse.

'Rebecca knew that. She wanted to bring us together and thought if I just came over you'd go out or something.'

'I've been here for days. You could have got in touch in the normal way. I would have seen you.' Then she frowned. Would she have seen him? No, not if she'd had any warning.

He hooked his arm through hers. 'Come on. Let's go.'

As she walked, Emily tried to clarify her thoughts. She'd had Alasdair on her mind, almost every minute of every day, for weeks. Now she was next to him she felt slightly sick. Abandoned to him by Rebecca, she wanted to see him and she didn't want to see him. She wanted to cry and a very small part of her was happy. She felt like a lava lamp, emotions rising and falling and refusing to settle.

They reached the boat. 'Get in?' he suggested, still tentative. Rupert, hearing what he took to be a command, jumped in.

Emily laughed softly. 'Yes,' she said, and when he'd

half pushed it off, she clambered on and sat in the stern, remembering from last time.

He swung a rucksack off his back into the boat and then gave it another shove before getting in and picking up the oars. He put his feet on the stretcher and started to pull on the oars.

The calmness of the loch and the beauty of the mountains reflected in it had a calming effect. She was still muddled but relaxed enough to allow a little happiness to creep in. 'Are we having a picnic?'

'I very much hope so.'

'I'd made really good sandwiches for the picnic I thought I was having,' she said. 'But we'd forgotten a flask and Becca doesn't have a billy or anything.'

'I'm afraid Becca didn't bother with a flask because she knew I would give you tea.'

'It's really horrible being plotted about. I feel such a fool!'

'My sweet, darling girl, you are anything but a fool and I'm terribly sorry I've made you feel one. Really, it was the very last thing me or Becca intended.'

She looked at him properly. 'What did you call me?'

'"My sweet, darling girl".'

The words were enchanting but she couldn't let herself believe he really meant them. He'd been so angry with her the last time she saw him, had accused her of putting her career before people who loved her, of letting his daughter down. And he knew she'd betrayed his trust in her. 'But that's not how you feel about me.'

'I know you'll find it hard to believe but it is. And I've felt it for a long time.'

331

'If you don't mind me saying this, you have a funny way of showing it.'

He half smiled but didn't reply. He glanced quickly over his shoulder and then continued to row with long slow strokes, moving the boat swiftly across the water.

She watched him, seeing him perfectly at home with boat and oars. He was unconsciously graceful, every moment efficient. It was both joyous and heartbreaking to watch. A curlew whistled overhead, adding to the poignancy.

'I never meant to fall in love again,' he said. 'I was determined that I would give Kate the most stable life possible. I wouldn't bring a new woman into her life, who might let her down like the first one did.'

'I understand that.'

'But then I met you. Everything changed.'

'You know that I would never, ever do anything to hurt Kate. I think your reasons for staying single are absolutely right.' However much it hurt to say it, she did sincerely believe it.

'But I was thinking about my wife, about the women who pursue me because I'm a doctor with an adorable daughter . . .'

Emily suppressed a smile. It wasn't only because he was a doctor and had Kate that made women pursue him.

'I hadn't met you then. You're different. You seem to like Kate more than you do me.'

'Oh, definitely! She's very much easier to like.' As her spirits lifted Emily began to feel more positive.

'The way you played with her, properly played,

getting muddy and cold and not caring – like a real friend.'

'That's what real friends do, though I'm not sure Becca and I would make dams together.' She frowned. 'Although some friend she turned out to be.'

'You know she meant well. It may have gone a little wrong, but her intentions were good.'

Emily shrugged. 'The road to hell, paved with good intentions.'

He smiled, his teeth flashing white. 'I'm sure you've forgiven Becca, even if you haven't forgiven me.'

'I expect I have,' she agreed. Then she became serious. 'I couldn't be a mother to Kate, you know that. I can be a very loving friend, who always looks out for her, but I can't replace the woman who gave birth to her. If that's what you want, I'm not the person.'

'I don't want a replacement mother, nor does she, but I feel – she feels – that our lives would be very much happier and more joyful if you were part of them.'

'Really? You asked her?'

'Yes. I had to.' He paused. 'You know I have fought this so long. Ever since I picked you up in the car and drove you to the puffer, in almost total silence. I thought how lovely you were then and now I think you're more than just lovely. And now I've stopped fighting my feelings it's easier.'

Emily didn't speak. What he'd said was wonderful and should have filled her with joy and on one level it did. But she'd turned down her chance of working up here and she couldn't just be a homemaker; she needed more: a career, or at least a proper job. And the job she had down south was a step up, even if currently it didn't seem very rewarding. It gave her a real opportunity to make a difference.

He glanced over this shoulder. 'We're here. We don't have to talk any more. We can just have a picnic and look for otters.' He smiled again and she felt no sunshine would ever equal the warmth of that smile. Like a ray of light in a deep dark forest, it lifted her heart.

A few minutes later, he got out of the boat and lifted out his rucksack. 'You stay sitting, I'll pull the boat up a bit and then help you out.'

Soon she was sitting on a rock, facing the beach where the otters had appeared before.

'Now, I'll just get the fire going, as I get the feeling that the tea is the most important part of lunch for you,' he said. He opened his rucksack and took out newspaper and matches.

'I'll find firewood,' said Emily, not content to sit and be a guest. She was losing the awkwardness she had felt when he'd first sprung out on her but she still wasn't relaxed. There was too much to think about for one thing.

When the fire was going well he came and sat beside her and put his arm round her, hugging her to him. It felt right, as if they were two pieces of a puzzle, slotting in together. Then he kissed her cheek and she blushed, feeling incredibly girlish. And then she began to feel like a woman and realised just how deep her feelings for him were. There would be a way round their problems. There had to be.

A little later he handed her a sandwich. Brown bread,

butter and smoked salmon. 'I have to say, this is nicer than the sandwiches I made,' she said when she'd taken a bite.

He handed her a hip flask. 'Have a drop of malt with that. I won't join you so drink it all if you like.'

She accepted the flask and the peaty strength of the whisky was bracing. It stilled the lava lamp of emotions somewhat. 'I might almost accuse you of trying to get me drunk,' she suggested.

'I might be guilty of trying to soften you up a bit. I've declared my love for you . . .' He paused. 'Did I remember to tell you how much I love you? I'm not sure I did.'

'You sort of did.'

'I'm not sure "sort of" will cut it.'

'No.' The trouble was, she needed him to say more, to say something he didn't know she needed to hear. She wanted him to say he'd want more children – her children.

'There's a "but" hovering there somewhere?'

'I was just thinking it would be nice if we didn't have to say anything meaningful, if we could just pretend we're having a day out, to see the otters. Would that be cheating?' It hadn't been what she'd been thinking, of course, but now she had thought of it, it seemed an excellent idea.

'I'd like that. I've realised I'm at serious risk of messing up what could be one of the most important relation- ships of my life. It would be nice to stop worrying for a while.'

'I think that's how I think about it, too,' said Emily.

Then she worried that she'd said too much. She'd acknowledged – to him and to herself – that their relationship was important to her. But although he gave her a glance, he didn't comment.

'It's apples for pudding,' said Alasdair when they had both eaten two sandwiches, and Emily had sipped enough whisky to make her head swim a little, although actually not a lot of it.

'Perfect. I know apples aren't really good for your teeth but they do feel better after a good crunch. Your teeth, I mean.' Was she actually a bit drunk? Maybe it was a good thing.

'Well, spoil that by adding chocolate.' He threw a bar down beside her. 'I should have put much more thought into this picnic. I'm afraid I was very distracted when I made it.'

'Was it work distracting you?'

He shook his head. 'No, much more important than work.'

'Well, it's the best picnic. Simple, delicious food. I love it.' She yawned suddenly.

'I did bring something to lie on though,' he said and looked into the rucksack. 'Here we are. You can lie on this.'

'I don't know why I'm so sleepy. The whisky, probably.'

'Or maybe you haven't been sleeping well. I know I haven't.'

'You're right, I haven't.'

Having unzipped it, he spread out the sleeping bag and then produced a couple of camping pillows. 'It's a single, but should be just about big enough for two.'

Without knowing quite how it happened, Emily found herself lying on a sleeping bag, covered with a blanket, Alasdair very close beside her.

'This is so good,' he said and put his arm round her, getting her to put her head on his chest.

Emily sighed. 'It is.' It felt right. And with so much going on in her mind it was good to feel certain about one thing.

'Mm,' he said in agreement. 'And what about this?'

He started to kiss her, gently and then with intent. He was concentrating hard on what he was doing and it had exactly the right effect. Emily relaxed and let herself enjoy the moment.

She didn't complain either, when his hand found her waistband and pushed up over her skin. She just wriggled into a more comfortable position. Soon her hands were finding their way under his clothes, finding the curve of his muscles, possibly honed by rowing, as urgently as he was undoing her bra and kissing her stomach.

'Oh my goodness,' said Emily a while later.

Alasdair sat up and started gathering discarded clothes and handed them to Emily. 'I want you to know that was absolutely *not* on my agenda for today!'

Emily laughed gently. 'I'm so glad. I'd hate to think you'd written a list with "make love to Emily" on it.'

'It was absolutely on my wish list, though,' he said, looking her intently. 'But not on a Scottish beach in October.'

'It worked out OK, though.'

'It was wonderful, but next time it's going to be somewhere comfortable, not a beach, not a sofa bed with an iron bar running up the middle, but possibly a five-star hotel with a super-king-sized bed.'

Emily pulled on her sweater. There might not be a next time, although she could imagine there could come a time when she'd fly up to Scotland for the weekend. It would be like an affair where neither party was married. It could be fun but it would never be truly satisfactory. 'There's nothing wrong with spontaneity.'

He glanced at her. Had he heard misgiving in her voice? 'Maybe it's time for tea.'

As Emily watched him find sticks, break them and build a fire she felt a rush of love for this man who may or may not be hers. He was sensitive enough to know she didn't want to talk about her feelings. She wanted to be really clear about them herself before she shared them with Alasdair.

Eventually he handed her a mug, full of smoky, strong tea, with a few tea leaves floating in it. 'Shortbread. Made by a patient.'

'Do you ever have to make cakes or biscuits in your house?' said Emily, accepting a triangle of biscuit she knew to be called a petticoat tail.

'We don't ever need more of those things but Kate likes to make them sometimes.'

'Do you help her?'

'I'm the sous-chef. I wash up and put together the icing kit.'

'Technical stuff.'

'Indeed.' He looked at her. 'I don't mean to push but

Kate would really appreciate someone who knows more about cooking than I do to help her.'

Just for a second Emily wondered if she could pretend she couldn't cook but of course she wouldn't get away with it. 'If it was just about living with Kate, I'd be there like a shot.'

'So, it's me who's the problem?' He sounded so desolate she put her hand on his.

She shook her head. 'I would have thought you'd have worked out that you're not.'

'I'm flattered, but lust is one thing, love is another. I'm afraid lust on its own isn't enough.'

Emily sighed. 'It's not my feelings about you we need to worry about.'

'Then what is it?'

She could appreciate she was being difficult but although she knew she loved him she didn't feel she could tell him everything, especially about wanting a baby. He might feel trapped. She would mention it, but not just this minute. She couldn't.

'Well?' he prompted, obviously unable to wait for an answer any longer.

She fell back on her career. 'It's my job. It's great. I'm the midwife in charge of a greatly expanded midwife-led unit. I'm recruiting, looking at plans for the new building, dealing with budgets. Everything, really.'

He nodded. 'So how's it going? Are you enjoying it?'

'Yeah – well, sort of. It's certainly challenging but . . .' She sighed. 'I miss the hands-on. I may get to deliver the odd baby eventually, when it's all set up, but I might not.'

'Well, I can see the job you've been offered up here can't measure up.' Not waiting for her to reply he went on. 'You can make a difference here, but there's no prestige involved. No fancy office, no fancy salary.'

Suddenly she became aware of how she must sound, and remembered the row they'd had at the party when he'd accused her of being a career woman, more interested in work than people. 'Listen, I don't care about prestige or any of that stuff – as long as I make a living wage – I just want interesting, useful work.'

'Then take the job you were offered here,' he said. 'I know it is for very selfish reasons but I really want you to have it. Lizzie Miller-Hall and I worked hard to devise it – making sure you'd get to do some midwifery – so it was appealing for you.'

'You did that for me?'

'Yes! Although you could say I did it for me. Lizzie's job was available but she's a health visitor. You'd get to see plenty of babies after they were born, but you wouldn't bring many of them into the world. I understand that you need to do that; it's who you are, a midwife.'

'Oh God! This is getting worse and worse!'

'Why? How could it be worse?'

'Because I turned it down!'

'Why? If you don't want the fancy office or the car – was there a car with the other job?'

She shook her head, desperately wanting to burst into tears but knowing she had to really focus to find a way out of this mess. 'I don't care about the car!' She swallowed and exhaled and confessed. 'It was because I didn't think I could work up here if you . . .'

340

'If I what?'

'If you didn't want me. I couldn't have spent my life driving round roads you may have driven on, seen views, looked at scenery, when you were in every speck, every pebble, every ripple on the water.' She paused. 'Every time I heard a curlew I'd think of you.'

He took precious seconds to take this in. 'Then, my darling girl, we don't have a problem, because I feel like that about you. I adore you and would do anything to keep you near me.'

'Alasdair! You've forgotten! I turned the job down!'

'But you do want the job?'

'Yes! Of course I do! If – everything else is OK – it's a fabulous job!'

'Then you won't mind that I intercepted this.' He pulled a crumpled envelope from the pocket of his coat.

She wondered briefly how he'd got hold of it but then realised it would be to do with James and Rebecca. 'How did you know I'd turned it down? That letter – I can see you haven't opened it – could have been accepting the job? And I'm not going to even bother to ask you how you got hold of it. Rebecca!'

He nodded apologetically. 'She had the very best intentions.'

'I know.'

'Would another swig of whisky make this better?'

She nodded and accepted the flask. Actually she felt this was the best it could be, bar one tiny detail which she could sort out another time. But emboldened by the neat spirit, she said, 'I've got a confession too. I told

341

Rebecca – completely by mistake – about your wife. But I think you know this.'

'I do. Rebecca told me. I was angry at first but then I thought that maybe it's a good thing it's out in the open. It was all a long time ago now and Rebecca won't tell Kate until I've found the right moment.' He smiled. 'I think she felt so guilty she devised this entire plan to bring us together.'

Emily laughed gently. 'What would she have done if I hadn't said I wanted to see the otters?'

'She'd have thought of something. She's very resourceful, my sister-in-law.'

But Emily's attention had wavered. 'Look! Running along the shoreline! Otters!'

They watched in silence for a few minutes. 'She really did take a lot of trouble to make this work,' said Alasdair, putting his arm round her again. 'I won't ever be able to express how grateful I am.'

Chapter Twenty-Four

'Kate would really like it if you came with me to pick her up from school. Unless you'd rather I ran you back to Becca's?'

They were all packed up and Alasdair had rowed them back to where his car was parked.

'I should talk to Becca. Except I left my phone in her car, along with everything else I might need on a picnic.' She remembered her shock and sense of abandonment when her friend had driven off. Of course it had been for the best – the very best – but she still felt a bit odd about it.

He smiled, got out his phone, clicked through the numbers and then handed it to her. 'She's probably desperate to hear from you. Wants to know if you're ever going to speak to her again.'

'I expect she's worked out I'm still speaking to her or I'd have not spoken to her – very loudly – before this!'

'You mean you'd have had a long, loud – er – discussion, and then told her you never wanted to speak to her again?'

She nodded. 'Right after I'd demanded that she pick me up immediately.'

He put his hand on her shoulder for a minute. 'Right, I'll let you get on with that then. I'm going to take Rupert for a wander. You might need to say things unfit for my delicate doctor's ears.'

Emily watched him move off, glad he was so sensitive; and how pleasing it was to see dog and man walking, one behind the other. She remembered the time she'd seen them walking on the horizon, when she didn't know it was him, and Kate was dancing along behind. Then she'd felt envious of the woman waiting for them at home. Now, that woman would be her. She felt very lucky.

Rebecca must have had her phone in her hand because she answered in seconds.

'Alasdair?'

'No. It's me, Emily. I had to borrow his phone. Mine got left in your car, remember?' Emily kept her voice even. She wanted to punish Rebecca a little for setting her up.

'And?'

Rebecca had obviously been on tenterhooks since the moment she'd driven away, leaving her friend staring at the back of her car, totally confused.

'And what?'

'Oh, God, Em! Don't keep me in suspense! What happened?'

'What do you mean, what happened? Do you want to know if we had sex on the beach?'

'No! TMI!' protested Rebecca. 'Of course I don't mean that!'

344

'I'll take that as a yes, and tell you.' Emily was ruthless. 'Yes.'

It seemed to take Rebecca several moments to work out what Emily had said. 'Really? So is it all going to be OK, then?'

Emily didn't mean to sigh, and yet she did. 'I don't know.'

'What do you mean, you don't know?' Rebecca went on urgently. 'Do you love him, does he love you? Although of course he loves you or he wouldn't have gone along with all that plotting.'

Emily couldn't hold out on her friend any longer. 'Yes. I mean, it really does look like that. As far as anyone can tell. I do really love him, and he says he loves me.'

'That is such a relief! I can't tell you. I've been beside myself. So it's all going to end happily ever after.'

'It's not quite as simple as that. There's the matter of my job.'

'Is that going to be OK?'

'Don't you know? You must have helped Alasdair intercept my rejection letter. And thinking about it, it was you who said I couldn't reject it by email.'

Rebecca sighed, sounding guilty. 'I did tell James to get the letter to Alasdair the moment we left the house.'

'And he did! So all I have to do now is accept the job.'

'And you will?'

'Oh yes. To be honest, being a high-powered administrator isn't really me. At least this way I will get to deliver the occasional baby.'

'I'm so glad. I can't tell you how guilty I've been feeling about all this, hijacking you like that and making sure you didn't reject the job out of hand. If there had been another way apart from dumping you on the roadside – or one that I could think of – I'd have done it.'

Any resentment Emily was still clinging to vanished. 'I'm sure you would, and offhand, I can't think of anything else you could have done either.'

'And you think it will be all right? Between you and Alasdair?'

Emily sighed ecstatically as she remembered some of what had passed between them. Whatever their problems, lack of chemistry was not one of them. 'If it was just us, definitely. But there are other things to take into consideration. I need children, Bec. I didn't think I did for ages, but I do now, and Kate might not like that.'

'Kate would LOVE babies! I've already told you that. You've seen how she is with Nell!'

'But one that lives in the same house would be very different. I need to be sure before I can commit—' She heard a sound and looked up and saw Alasdair, Rupert by his side. Rupert looked a bit worried. 'I'd better go. Alasdair is waiting for me.'

As she disconnected she realised how very poignant and wonderful those words were.

'So, are you up for coming with me to fetch Kate?' he said. 'Or does Becca need you?'

'Becca doesn't deserve me!' Emily smiled, thinking that actually, she had a lot to be grateful to her friend for. 'And anyway, my priorities have changed. If you think Kate would like it, I'd love to come with you.'

'I wouldn't have suggested it if I didn't know she'd be thrilled to see you. Your knitted garments for Ted

346

have all been taken into school and shown off. You could probably open a small business selling Designer Fair Isle Knitted Items for Teddies.'

'Catchy title. It's a thought! But seriously? She's not cross with me for rushing off?'

'Not since I promised her I'd bring you back.'

This was significant. Emily knew Alasdair couldn't commit to a woman unless Kate could also commit to her. And he was right. He owed it to Kate to put her first, at least until she left home. She was glad that so far, and she'd have to make sure of it herself, he was doing this.

'OK, then.' She made a face. 'Damn! I forgot to ask Becca when she was expecting me back.'

'She's not. At least, she won't mind if you're not home for dinner. Or breakfast, actually. It's up to you.' His smile was diffident, in spite of what had gone on between them. He was taking nothing for granted.

'We'll have to see. We mustn't rush Kate into anything. She'll need time to get used to us being together.'

'One of the many things I love about you is the fact you put my daughter first.' He kissed the top of her head.

'I have to. She's a child and none of what's happened in her life has been her fault. She mustn't have anything else going wrong for her.'

He kissed her again. 'Let's get going. Then we can buy sweeties at the shop before we pick her up. Sweeties are not something we have all that often in our house.'

'Wouldn't it be more fun for Kate to choose her own sweeties? On the way home?'

'It would! I didn't think of that.'

'I expect it's because you're a bit older than me. I can remember that far back . . .'

They were in the playground a little early but soon saw Kate emerge from the door with a group of little girls.

Kate spotted Emily and her father immediately. 'Hey! It's Emily who knitted those clothes for Ted!' she called. 'Emily!' she said as the group reached them. 'Daddy said he'd bring you back!'

Emily had to swallow hard not to burst into tears right there. She put her arm round Kate and patted her while she got her voice under control. 'And he did. Here I am. But I haven't got any more clothes for Ted, I'm afraid.'

'Oh!' said one of Kate's friends, with that upward inflection that indicated deep unfairness.

'Well, I'd have to see what he needs,' she went on. 'No point in knitting him a onesie if he's already got one.' Too late she realised she was committed to doing this now and, more than likely, making up the pattern.

'I think a onesie would be just great!' said Kate ecstatically.

'You don't think it would make him look fat?' suggested Emily, hoping to get out of knitting one.

'Teddies are fat, Emily,' said Kate, stating the obvious. 'Whatever they wear.'

'I'll get some wool, then,' said Emily, resigned but happy.

'Come on, Katkin,' said Alasdair. 'Let's go home. Emily said we should stop and buy sweeties at the shop on the way.'

Kate gazed up at Emily with adoring eyes.

'It's a just-this-once treat!' Emily said, hoping she hadn't set a terrible precedent. 'It won't be sweets after school every day. Unless your dad says . . .' She felt she'd fallen into the role of stepmother even before it was hers, and certainly before she knew the rules.

'Come on, you two,' said Alasdair. He seemed far more relaxed than Emily. 'Let's get the sweetie-choosing over and then go home and have something sensible to eat.'

'Are baked beans sensible?' asked Kate as they walked along to where they'd parked the car.

'Well,' said Emily, 'maybe not individually, but as a group they could probably have a certain amount of common sense.' Her companions looked at her, utterly confused. 'Oh! You mean are they healthy? I think so, yes. But Alasdair here is the doctor.'

'But you're nearly a doctor,' said Kate. 'You deliver babies, don't you?'

'I do, but that doesn't mean I'm even nearly a doctor. Although of course I do know some simple stuff.'

'Daddy delivers babies sometimes. He told me,' said Kate.

'I had to tell her – and it is true – because otherwise she wouldn't believe I had any credibility at all!' Alasdair complained when Kate had run ahead.

'Really?'

He nodded. 'I'm beginning to worry about you two ganging up on me.'

'Oh, we will,' said Emily. 'Definitely.'

'I think I might like that,' he said, and unlocked the car.

* * *

Later, after Emily had cleared away supper so Alasdair and Kate could have an important private talk together, Kate joined Emily, who was sitting by the fire. She had her teddy and his Fair Isle wardrobe.

'Could you really knit him a onesie?' she asked.

'What's a onesie?' asked Alasdair. 'I'm sure I ought to know but that one's passed me by.'

'An adult Babygro,' said Emily, 'and I'm sure you know what Babygros are.'

'Oh yes. Kate wore them, at least for a little bit,' he said.

Emily looked at Kate. 'There is a danger that people will think Ted is a baby, not a very smart bear wearing the latest fashion. Are you prepared to take the risk?'

'Yup,' said Kate.

'Then be a love and find me a tape measure or a ruler or something and I'll measure him up.'

After a steel rule – the nearest thing to a tape measure in the house – had been found, and Ted's inside leg measurement taken, Kate retired to the bathroom for important teeth-brushing. Alasdair went with her, claiming he was going to brush his too.

Emily forced herself to think about the chaos her abandonment of the maternity unit would cause. It wouldn't last long. Sally might get offered her job and get over her objections to taking it. It might work well for her – easier to fit her family into an admin job. Or they might recruit someone new. Whatever; it would work out one way or another. No one was indispensable from a work point of view.

But as she couldn't do anything or tell anyone without

her phone, Emily decided to just stay in the present, and love everything about it.

'So,' said Kate when Alasdair and Emily had both read her stories, 'are you and Daddy going to get married?'

Emily blushed hotly, taken completely by surprise. And as Alasdair didn't say anything, began, 'Well, darling—'

'But, Daddy!' Kate interrupted. 'You said you were going to ask her!'

'I know, and I will, but these things are usually done in private.' Alasdair was as embarrassed as Emily had been.

'Do it now! Ask her!'

He looked at Emily helplessly. 'Darling Emily, will you please do me the very great honour of accepting my hand in marriage?' His eyes twinkled with excitement and suppressed laughter.

She inclined her head gracefully. 'The honour would be all mine and I'd be delighted to accept your very flattering offer.'

Kate looked at her father and then at Emily, confused. 'Is that what you have to say when you ask someone to marry you? All those words? And did she say yes?'

'Yes, and yes,' said Alasdair, looking very pleased. 'We are so lucky, Kate!'

Kate sighed in relief. 'So does this mean you'll share a bed like Uncle James and Auntie Becca?'

This was quite a quick step – becoming engaged to sharing a bed – even if that was how it usually worked. 'Perhaps—' Emily began.

'Yes,' said Alasdair firmly. 'Definitely.'

Kate nodded and then frowned. 'But does that mean if I have a nightmare I can't get into bed with you, Daddy?'

'It certainly doesn't,' said Emily. 'You must always come in if you have a nightmare.'

'Even if you have a baby?'

Alasdair coughed and cleared his throat. 'Darling,' you really can't ask people things like that.'

'It's OK,' said Emily. 'You can ask me anything. And yes, even if we have a baby, there'll always be room for you.'

'What if it's twins?' demanded Kate, wanting to make sure about everything.

Emily nodded. 'Even if we have to get a bigger bed, there will always be room for you in it. You might all have to take turns sometimes. But you will always be our eldest, our first lovely girl.'

'Really?' asked Kate.

Emily nodded. 'But the question of babies is also up to your dad, here.'

'You can't just have babies to order, you know, Katkin. It's not like ordering a puppy from a breeder. But I promise that Emily and I will talk about it.'

'What? Getting a puppy?' Kate's eyes were huge with excitement at the prospect.

'Sorry, darling!' Her father apologised. 'It was just an analogy – you know, an example of what something might be like.'

'I'll tell you what,' said Emily, taking a chance, 'if it's all right with Rupert, who was here first and has to be consulted, we can have a puppy. But we will ask Daddy, too.'

'Why bother!' said Alasdair, although he did not sound displeased. 'You two seem to have the whole thing sewn up. A bigger bed, twins and a puppy, even before we're married!'

'Us girls like to get things organised. Now, I'm going to say goodnight.' She kissed Kate. 'And leave you two to talk things over. I'm going to make sure the fire hasn't gone out.'

'I think you'll find that the fire is anything but out,' said Alasdair when he joined Emily in the sitting room a little while later. He kissed her neck. She was sitting on the sofa with her feet curled up under her.

'You seem to have only one thing on your mind,' she said, kissing his hand, which was the only thing she could reach at that moment. 'Have you sorted everything out with your daughter?'

'Very much to her satisfaction. Now, a drink?'

'Mm, yes please.'

'So, this baby thing,' he said, putting a glass of malt whisky in her hand. 'What do you think?'

'What do you think? What does Kate think?'

'Kate is keen. I have explained about the broken nights, the constant howling, nappies, puke, the general disgustingness of babies and she doesn't seem to mind.'

'In which case, I think having a baby would be brilliant! I would prefer to have at least started my job – and possibly even got married first – but—'

'As we may have started one already things might not happen in the accepted order?'

'You know? I wouldn't care a bit. Not really.'

'Nor would I.'

'I need to do something about accepting that job. And telling my colleagues at home about leaving the other one.'

'Will that cause a lot of upset?'

'Yes, but I don't care. And my best friend down there, Sally, will be delighted for me.'

'We should invite her to stay when we're organised,' said Alasdair. 'But not just now. Right now we should celebrate being together, having a future, making a life.' He got up and clicked buttons and seconds later the room was filled with the sound of a fiddle. Then Emily realised what she was listening to.

'It's your band! The one I never got to hear at the party.'

'That's it. I'm not great at saying how I feel. You'll get the message more clearly if you listen to the song.'

She smiled at him. 'I think I've got the message. I think you quite like me.'

'So, so much more than like.' He came and sat next to her on the sofa and took her face in his hands. 'I'm not sure proposals under duress really count so I'm going to do it again. Will you marry me, Emily?'

'I will.'

'And can you face living with a grumpy GP and a sometimes difficult daughter, not to mention an old, smelly dog?'

'I can.'

'And will you mind if I've already made you pregnant, although we didn't talk about it and plan it?'

She shook her head. 'You know? I think whatever happens, about the job, having a baby, or a puppy, or all three, it will all work out for the best. You, me and Kate, we're a team, and we'll win, whatever happens.'

Then she pulled his head down to hers and kissed him.

Author's Note

I once heard someone describe Crinan as the floor of heaven. It is indeed so. But for the purposes of fiction I have had to alter the floor of heaven, which is the height of insolence, so I apologise profoundly.

I could have called the place in my novel something fictional but nothing seemed right.

If you haven't been there and meet it through the pages of this novel, do go – it is even better in real life.

I have also been a bit cavalier with how the National Health Service operates with regard to maternity units, social services, health visitors, etc. Please forgive me. I was going for emotional truth rather than strict accuracy.

Loved the book?

Join thousands of other
readers online at

AUSTRALIAN READERS:

randomhouse.com.au/talk

NEW ZEALAND READERS:

randomhouse.co.nz/talk